# THE ANSWER

Claudia

*The Center for Peaceful Transitions*

BALBOA PRESS
A DIVISION OF HAY HOUSE

Balboa Press books may be ordered through booksellers or by contacting:

Balboa Press
A Division of Hay House
1663 Liberty Drive
Bloomington, IN 47403
www.balboapress.com
1 (877) 407-4847



Print information available on the last page.

ISBN: 978-1-5043-9978-4 (sc)
ISBN: 978-1-5043-9979-1 (e)

Library of Congress Control Number: 2018902949

Balboa Press rev. date: 03/21/2018

# OTHER BOOKS

*The Time When Time No Longer Matters*
*...continues...*
*2018*

*The Time When Time No Longer Matters*
*2016*

*The Book of Ages*
*2016*

*Messages From Within:*
*A Time for Hope*
*2011*

*Messages From The Light:*
*Inspirational Guidance for*
*Light Workers, Healers, and*
*Spiritual Seekers*
*2008*

# ~ INTRODUCTION ~

Once upon a time, long, long ago before existence was aware of its existence, a new existence entered into existence awakening all in existence to the reality that it existed.

"You are here for reason," whispered the new existence, and forevermore, existence existed differently. Not knowing who the new existence was or where the new existence existed aroused many questions for those existing in existence, and from that moment in time, existence began pondering its own existence.

Existence was, existence did not know that it was, and then existence heard a voice affirming that it was here for a reason, and from then on, throughout all the ages of existence, existence has pursued its reason for existence.

"Dear Reader, you are here for a reason!" And within you, there is awareness of this reality. Trust that which you already know, even if you do not know how you know what you know, for the truth of your knowing comes from within. Your inner knowing confirms what was affirmed long before your present experience. It propelled you forward in ancient beginnings and it propels you forward today. "You are here for a reason!"

Trust, Dear Reader! Trust the ancient wisdom that still lives within you today. Trust the knowingness that rises up from within and declares that you are indeed here for a reason, because you are.

"You are here for a reason!" This is your truth.

# PART ONE

# ~ Chapter One ~

And so the story begins. The Island, whose name for the moment shall remain anonymous, entered into my life three years and thirty-three days ago. I had never heard of it before, and because I'm not particularly a beach person, it didn't capture my imagination at the time. Those who told me about The Island seemed to be mesmerized by it to the point that it made one wonder. These friends were no more island types than myself, but their fascination with this newly discovered place was intriguing. Avid travelers, they were always in some stage of another travel experience. Whether they were planning the next trip, doing the trip, or coming home from said trip, they were people who loved exploring new settings. Upon their many returns, the couple's excitement would energize all in listening distance, as they elaborated with great detail upon the experiences of their most recent escapade, and with equal exuberance and generosity, they offered photos, mementoes, and assorted memorabilia, as proof of their adventures.

The ongoing adventures of these gallivanting friends, who from this point forward shall be referred to as Jan and Everett Smith, were well known by their friends. Their endless stories rarely, if ever, tired their audience, but in truth, inspired others to pursue adventures as well. Skilled and seasoned travelers, the Smiths lovingly shared travel tips with anyone who was interested or in need.

Over our many years of friendship, what amazed me most about this couple was their lust for exploring the next new place. In truth, I have no memory of them ever returning to the same place twice with the exception of their favorite home away from home, which by the way just happens to be an island. Until their encounter with The Island, their traveling motto had always been too much to see, too little time; however, since that unexpected experience, life significantly changed for my friends. In fact, their boundless adventures to and about the seven continents came to an abrupt halt when The Island came into their lives, which does not imply either a good or a bad thing. It is simply an item of curiosity. And as earlier said, while The Island itself did not grab my attention, my friends' peculiar fascination with it, did.

I still recall the gathering. As was their way, Jan and Everett, always hosted a party upon returning from their latest trip. These adventure gatherings, as they were called, were a highlight for their dearest friends, who not only looked forward to hearing about the latest adventures, but also expected a blow-by-blow account. After years of indulging in these enjoyable gatherings, not one of these friends were willing to let go of these delightful events.

In addition to myself, who, by the way, also chooses to remain anonymous, there were five other friends in attendance that evening, Patricia and William (Pat and Bill) Jones, Deidre and Franklin (Dee and Frank) Sanderson, and Marilyn Brown. And as you have already intuitively surmised, these names are fictitious as well.

What was different about this particular gathering was everything. There were no excitable tales, there were only a handful of rather unrevealing photos, and the usual boisterous demeanors of our gracious hosts were noticeably reserved and quiet, not in an off-putting kind of way, but in a manner that was strikingly different than the Smiths' usual way of engaging. Indeed, there was something very odd about the whole evening, and I was not the only one who noticed.

That was the first time The Island came to my attention.

# ~ CHAPTER TWO ~

I departed my friends' home that night confounded by the entire evening. Part of me, not all of me, but admittedly, a part of me was quite concerned about their behavior. On the walk back to my preferred abode, the one in which I presently reside, my mind actively bantered with itself. *Call them*, demanded part of me, while another part of me insisted, *they're fine! Nothing is wrong; they were just a bit off tonight.*

"What am I to believe?" came a melodramatic soliloquy. "Part of me thinks this, and part of me thinks that. What is one to believe?" Commanding myself to be quiet, I chose to take the longer route home. My body needed the exercise; my mind needed a well-deserved timeout. Eventually, the fresh night air, working its magic, quieted my overly exuberant mind allowing me to simply enjoy the beauty surrounding me. It was a lovely time for a walk, equally as satisfying as my early morning rituals that help me to welcome in the day. Even at night, I knew my path. The sweet smell of lilacs comes from the Bentley's yard off to my left, and just a few steps ahead is a substantial crack in the sidewalk, which enjoys playing havoc with unobservant passersby. And up ahead on the opposite side of the street is a bed of marvelous white peonies more beautiful than anyone could ever imagine. There they were bedded down for the night, and yet, the memory of their sunlit glory still works its miracles.

*Yes, I know this path well,* thought the walker, whose footfalls were as silent as the night itself. *All is well, even if I'm perplexed about the gathering; all is well.* A few more blocks took me to the last turn of the evening's journey. From there, the path led directly to my front door. *It's good to know where one is going, makes life vey predictable.* And with a turn of the key, I was home again.

"Everett, I'm afraid the evening was a bit awkward. Do you agree, or is it just my imagination?" Jan's question came as no surprise. He too, was aware the evening had unfolded differently than in times past. Of course, it was not unexpected, since neither of them was quite sure of themselves since The Island had been introduced into their lives. Everett reflected upon the evening, and then lost himself in his cogitation. Time passed as he wandered about in the recesses of his mind, which lingered still towards the events associated with The Island.

"Everett, dear, are you all right?" asked his wife. *Oh my*, she thought. *It's happening again! Should I disturb him or simply let him wander about in his head for a bit?* Jan chose a subtle approach. Loudly clearing her throat, as if it were an innocent reaction to a tickly sensation, she successfully gained his attention.

"Sorry, Old Girl, is something the matter?"

"No, dear, not at all, but I was wondering how you felt about our gathering? A bit odd, don't you think?" His dear, sweet wife, the love of his life had brought him back. Remembering the earlier request, he realized once again he had become lost in time, but knew better than to give it any notice, because if he did, he would be lost again for goodness knows how long.

"Drat my fleeting mind!" he exclaimed. "Sorry Love, thanks for reeling me back in, and please forgive me for my lapse into never-never land or whatever descriptor we should apply to this behavior we seem to have acquired on our last adventure."

"Not to worry, Everett, but do try to stay present for a moment, because we really do need to discuss our gathering. It just wasn't our usual gracious affair, dear. I fear we let our friends down. Perhaps, we should have waited; we both knew we were out of sorts. But duty called, as it were," she said as if justifying their decision. "We always share our travels with our friends. How could we, in good conscience, delay the event?" Her appeal was one of sincerity; however, as Mrs. Smith heard the words flowing from her mouth, she turned towards her husband laden in embarrassment. "Goodness! How grandiose of me! But you do understand where I am coming from, Everett. We are accustomed to showing our friends a good time, which unfortunately, was not achieved tonight."

"Well, I agree with you," responded her husband. "Regrettably, you're assessment is on the mark, Jan. We were not ourselves tonight, and our friends were taken aback. They didn't know how to deal with us. And who can blame them? At the moment, we don't know how to deal with ourselves, so, how can they possibly know how to interpret what is going on with us?" The two old friends sat silently wondering what to do next, when they simultaneously announced, it was time to retire. Shaking their heads in amusement, they walked arm-in-arm towards the bedroom.

"So, do you think we should invite everyone over again, and try to set things straight?" posed Jan, as she changed into her nightgown. Again, her husband was not quick to respond, but this time, his delay was due to deliberation.

"Actually, several thoughts are spinning about in my mind. The first, which we must agree upon, will not be easy to abide. Jan, we are too tired to make a good decision at the moment, so we must set this aside for the evening, and wait until the morning to sort through our feelings." As he predicted, his first thought did not sit well with his wife, who was of a type that preferred to take immediate action.

"And my second thought is this, dear, and I really want you to listen to what I'm about to say. No injury has been committed this evening, Jan. For the first time in a very long time, we have entertained in a manner, which does not meet our standards, but we have not committed some terrible grievance that demands immediate attention. We were awkward, dear. Nothing more! We need time to sort things out. We acted too quickly by scheduling our gathering before we were really ready, and we need to make sure we don't make another similar mistake. Let's move ahead slowly and when we've attained greater clarity about our present circumstances, we will then share these conclusions with our friends, who will be understanding and compassionate. We have wonderful friends. We can trust them to support us."

"You're right, of course, Everett," she sighed in relief, and then playfully added, "When did you become so clever, dear? You know it's exceptionally decent of you to be clever. Takes so much responsibility off my shoulders." And with that bit of comic relief, she scooted into bed. As her husband gathered his beloved into his arms, he quipped, "I had no choice, Love. Had to become clever to keep up with you. But for now, let's just release our concerns, and go to sleep."

# ~ Chapter Three ~

Much to my surprise, I awoke early the morning after the Smiths' gathering. Although this was not unusual behavior by any means, what was surprising was how long it had taken me to fall asleep the night before. Because sleep escaped me, the latest in a series of mystery novels called, and as a result, the hour was late before the bedside lamp was finally switched off. Before dozing into the land of dreams, I doubted whether an early wakeup would be possible. And yet, as is typical of me, I awoke slightly before dawn.

It was a gorgeous day that demanded my presence, so with haste, the appropriate clothes were donned, and I set off for the hills. One of the many luxuries of being self-employed is the control one has over their own time. The freedom of scheduling one's work around one's preferences is indeed a privilege of the utmost satisfaction. I prefer early morning walks. It sets the stage for the entire day, and since I prefer to orchestrate the staging of my days, it behooves me to begin early so that the rest of the day is to my liking.

On this particular morning, which was admittedly similar to most mornings, I enjoyed racing with the sun. *Why is that enormous body of gaseous flames so tantalizing?* Although no definitive response to my unspoken question was forthcoming, it seemed to me that a mere glimpse of the ascending sun was sufficient to energize me for the next twenty-four hours, if not more. Whatever the reason underlying my passionate love affair with this glorious Being, my commitment to our relationship remains resolute. *If she sees fit to rise each day, then so shall I!* And with that daily declaration made, my pace hastened.

One of the many joys of landscapes dominated by rolling hills is witnessing the numerous opportunities for the rising sun. Depending up the time you arrive at the ridge of the hills, as well as, the mood of your sunny companion, you may have the good fortune to experience several sunrises simply because of the lay of the land. The trail traveled this morning was particularly chosen for that reason, because today, I am in need of the illusion of multiple sunrises.

Scurrying up the third and highest hill, anticipation mounted. Already having enjoyed two wonderful viewings, I dared to imagine another might be possible. *Could I be so lucky?* As I neared the crest, the golden rays broke through a cluster of low-lying clouds intermixing a spectacular array of colors into a masterpiece that would make most admirers weep, which I did. *Thank you, Old Friend! How humbling it is to be in your presence!* And a tidal wave of gratitude washed through me as more tears streamed down my face.

Remaining still, I viewed the sunrise through its ascension. *Once again, I have succumbed to the rising sun. Why does it have this incredible power over me? From where do these tears come and why is the sunrise able to cause them to surface?* As I stood in wonderment, a voice, which presumably was mine, since no one else was about, registered in my mind. *"More lies within than is presently known."*

"Interesting," I responded, and then turned my attention to the time of day. It was the wonderful time of year, when the sun rises exceptionally early allowing for longer walks; so without any further deliberation, I chose to continue the path ahead. My mind meandered, as did the path. It briefly strategized and organized the day's work, then distracted itself from any possibilities that might be related to the tears shed during the third sunrise, and eventually landed upon the event of the previous evening. Again the mind wrangled with itself. *To call or not to call, that is the question!* "Oh, for goodness sake, just call them and check in. It doesn't need to be some calculated maneuver. They are dear friends, and it would be polite to give them a call. Enough said!" With no other urgent matters to manage, the mind feeling particularly good about itself zoned out allowing for a most pleasant walk through the hills and dales of the countryside.

"Everett, are you awake, dear?" whispered his favorite friend since college.

"I am. Is that you whispering or are you talking in your sleep again?" he chuckled. Rising up and bracing herself on her right elbow, she mischievously looked down at her husband.

"I'm wide awake. What shall we do?"

"Perhaps, we might just continue to lie here and bask in the quiet of our surroundings." Even as he spoke the words, Everett knew his rambunctious wife would be unable to contain her energy. His dilemma would be as it had been every morning since their encounter with the unforgettable, yet still unknown island. Do I join her in a morning walk, or do I remain behind to attend matters of another kind?

"Oh, Everett, dear, you are deliberating. Please don't! You know how I love you to join me on my morning walks. They are not my walks, dear; they're our walks. We love walking together, so please do consider getting out of bed. Now, please don't tell me that I'm whining," she continued, "because, I'm not. I'm just being insistent, that's all. Very different than whining! However, if whining will sway you, then please consider it whining." Jan's commitment to daily exercise was admirable, and their shared walks were indeed a pleasure, but of late, Everett felt conflicted. He loved the walks, because he loved the quality time together, but it seemed the early hours were calling him to attend something else. Uncertain what was happening to him and why he was feeling so confused about things, he decided to be his wife's companion. And with the decision made, he jumped out of bed in a manner that belied his years.

"Wonderful!" Jan declared, bounding out of bed. They quickly grabbed their favorite walking attire and dressed for the occasion. "Everett, which trail shall we take this morning? Any preference, dear?"

"Let's take the high road," he said. "Better workout, and the views are grand." As he exited the bedroom, he called out, "I'm going to grab a couple of health bars for the trek. Not hungry now, but will be before we return home." They were out the door in minutes, crossed the field behind their house, and headed for the hilly area east of their community.

"Morning is such a precious time," whispered Jan. "I think it is the most inspiring part of the day. Thank you for coming, Everett. I do so love your company." She walked in silence for a few more steps, and then conscientiously proceeded. "Love, I am acutely aware of my selfishness regarding these morning walks, and I just want you to know I truly want you to do whatever it is you need to do. Something is calling you, dear. It's confusing you, and you need to take time to figure this out. Whatever it is, it's important, and I don't want to stand in your way. Please know that I can see you struggling and I'm on your side. Whatever you need to do, I will support your decision."

"Even if it means not joining you on these early walks?" he asked.

"Yes," she replied. "Of course, I may whine about it," she laughed and tickled him at the same time. "Actually, Everett, I've been giving this dilemma some thought, and I have a suggestion, if you're open to it." He assured her that he was open to any and all suggestions and was eager to hear what she had to say. "Well, it seems as if you need time to deliberate things. You're changing, dear, and change can feel very disruptive in the moment, but if you give yourself time to really think about things, and maybe do some journaling, I think the process will work itself through more easily. So what I thought might be helpful is for us to utilize our walks for quality quiet time. You know many people meditate while they walk; it apparently is a very effective means of meditating. So I thought we could give that a try, if you like." Everett, listening carefully to his beloved's suggestion, was interested and curious.

"So, are you saying that you want to try this form of meditation, as well?" he asked.

"Yes, I do. I think it's the next step for both of us. We've changed Everett. Something happened when The Island came into our lives, and we're not the same anymore. I don't have words for it yet, but we're different, and I think it's a good thing. So yes, I would like to try meditating on our walk this morning, and see how it goes."

"Interesting, I've never tried meditating with my eyes opened before," thought Everett aloud. "But, I think your suggestion is a good one, dear. In fact, I think you're very clever!" he declared with a raised eyebrow. "When should we begin?" They agreed to continue chatting until they reached the foothills. At that point, they would use the timer on Everett's watch to denote the passing of thirty minutes.

"Can we actually be quiet for thirty minutes, Jan?"

"Of course, we can. We aren't novices! My goodness, we've meditated numerous times before." As they approached the hills, Jan wondered if she really could be quiet for that length of time. *Oh, well, there's a first time for everything!*

*A passage from*
***The Time is Now***
*(Chapter One)*

*"When the time has come for All who have been, to assist All that are, the people of the Earth will at long last know who You really are.*

*We, the residents of the Universe, have watched over you since your time of beginning and still we watch with caring eyes and concerned Hearts.*

*For many ages we have assisted species such as yours throughout many galaxies and many neighboring communities. With each evolving species, we assist when needed with the intentions of promoting goodwill among the many members of the Universal Family. Our purpose throughout the ages has been to assist All That Is in caring for the children of the Universe. We have entered many life experiences in our attempts to guide and assist the various species throughout the many galaxies and in all our attempts to provide assistance; our intentions have always remained the same.*

*Our primary reason for coming is to serve All That Is, and the children of All That Is, is the priority of All That Is. No other purpose is of more meaningfulness than the tending of the children and their needs."*

Wondering if he had forgotten to set the timer on his watch, Everett checked to see if something was amiss. Only fifteen minutes had passed. *Hmmm! That's odd. Thought we'd been walking much longer than that.* Jan, of course, noticed his inconspicuous attempt at checking the time, and was surprised when he didn't joyfully announce the end of their meditative experience. Her perception of the passing of time was as inaccurate as his. Committed to this experiment, they both continued walking quietly, while listening to the noise of their respective minds.

Jan found it particularly difficult to refrain from sharing her reactions regarding the truly magnificent sunrise. *So lovely, so grand! It's impossible to be quiet about this!* Fortunately, Everett managed the situation beautifully. Just as she was about to burst, he gently reached over and clasped her hand in his. No more needed to be said. The gesture said it all.

After an interminable amount of time, the silence was finally blessedly broken by a brief, but sweet few measures of Mozart. Sighs of relief could not be restrained, although neither of them wanted to admit their discomfort. "That's such a lovely alarm, Everett. Gently brings you back to the present. Well done!"

Feigning optimism, he announced, "That went well, don't you think?" They burst into laughter.

"Oh my goodness!" declared Jan. "I thought it was remarkably difficult. There were so many things I wanted to say," she laughed at herself. "You know, if we hadn't announced we were going to do a meditation, we probably would have trekked along primarily in silence. Of course, our minds still would have been actively over functioning, but I suspect we wouldn't have noticed it. At least not as much!" They chuckled some more about the antics of their minds, but agreed it was important to discuss their experiences.

"What I found so interesting," mentioned Everett, "was how frustrated my mind was with the situation. It felt restricted, and unruly, and insistent! Yes, it was very insistent that it had the right, the privilege, if you will, to think about its preferred choices regardless of my intention to be silent. It was, as if the notion of being silent, was offensive to its very nature. After all, it is an instrument that is constantly in operation. The idea of turning off is not part of its operational procedures. Fascinating!" he declared. "I learned a great deal about my mind this morning, Jan. It was extremely interesting to observe its obstinate manner. Although my mind was anything but silent, I feel as though the experience was beneficial."

"Well, it's helpful to listen to your observations. It gives me another perspective to mull over, and helps me to understand a bit more about my own experience. Your tactic of separating yourself from the operations of the mind is clever, dear. It limits the emotional aspect. My tendency, as you well know, is to evaluate my personal situation from an emotional perspective. I was feeling selfish, deprived, and very foolish about the experience. Selfish, because I wanted to verbally engage with you about my joyful reactions to the sunrise, as well as, other beautiful sightings along the way. Deprived, because I wasn't allowed to do so. And foolish, because it all seemed so childish. After all, it was just for a few minutes!" Continuing in silence, each pondered his or her own experiences. Eventually, Jan summarized her thoughts. "It is going to take some time to put all of this in perspective. I'm beginning to understand why books are written about meditation. It's more challenging than I thought, but I'm excited! I'm glad we did this, dear. Perhaps, we will pursue this again.

I do want to reiterate what was said earlier, dear. If you need to refrain from these early morning walks to pursue other means of self-exploration, it's really okay with me. I will try to suffer in silence," she added melodramatically. "You do know I'm teasing, don't you?" Laughing in response to her bid for humor, he reassured his beloved her intentions were understood.

"Your words are comforting, Love, but also challenging to my personal commitment to you. Our time together is precious, and I enjoy the early morning escapades as much as you do, so allowing myself to pursue other means of interest makes me feel incredibly disloyal and selfish. I'm torn, Jan. But your generosity is noted and appreciated, and I'm confident we can explore this together and find some option, which will be conducive to both of our needs." Walking hand-in-hand, the couple pushed forward up the next hill. Upon reaching the top, they stood in wonder. "This is remarkably beautiful! In all our travels and all the wonderful views we have been privileged to see, this view is just as appealing, and captures the heart with the same intensity as all the other masterpieces this marvelous planet gifts to us. I love it here, Jan. We are so blessed to live here. And yet, The Island is pulling me. I feel the need to return soon. Can't explain it, Love, but the need to return is burning strongly within me." Jan moved closer to her husband and wrapped her arm with his. Arm-in-arm, body-to-body, they appreciated the view.

"I understand, dear," replied Jan. "You're not alone in this, but you are ahead of me in being able to articulate your feelings. Ever since we returned from The Island, I've been itching to go back. It doesn't seem reasonable, and words escape me, but something there is calling to me. And like you, I feel a sense of urgency about it."

"Well, it's reassuring to know we are in sync about this. Knowing we are both having similar reactions somehow makes it less unnerving. I am so grateful for you, Love. Cannot imagine what life would be without you."

"Dreadfully boring, I would imagine!" Jan said with complete sincerity. And then giggled with delight. "We're a team, dear. We were meant to be together. I'm grateful too!"

Everett smiled, knowing full well his beloved was speaking the truth. Her solid conviction about their connection began as freshmen in college, and it never waned. Although Jan loved being goofy and often pretended to be less bright than she actually was, she was, in fact, a remarkably clever individual in many, many ways, one of which included a most uncanny ability to unexplainably know things. For instance, their chance meeting at college! Jan never accepted it was a coincidence. She simply knew, without knowing how she knew they were intended to be together. Everett had learned long ago to trust her intuitive gifts.

"Look over there, dear! Along the next crest!" exclaimed Jan with sheer delight. "Is that who I think it is?" Indeed, their dear friend had beaten them to the trail this morning. A quick consultation concluded they should not interrupt their friend's morning reverie. "What will be will be," they said in unison, which brought another smile to their faces.

And has fate would have it, as the couple continued up the path, their friend, who was a fair distance ahead suddenly felt the urge to turn around and head back down the path.

For reasons unknown to me, I was inclined to return back in the direction just walked. The path had been abundant with entertainment this morning. Beautiful scenery, rich in spring colors, was available in all directions, including glimpses of wildlife quietly feeding in their preferred places. And there was time, blessed time, to enjoy it all without feeling rushed or burdened.

*Claudia*

*Remarkable how good life can be, when you're present to notice!* Again for reasons unknown to me, today was a day that allowed for a beautiful experience. The mind, which often indulges in great distractions, did not do so this morning. Perhaps, it was too tired. Or so bored with my presence that it departed for sites unknown. Whatever the reason, it was refreshing to walk in the silence of my own company.

*A passage from*
***The Time is Now***
*(Chapter One)*

*"As many times before, in many other places, we came to your planet to assist you in your process of developing intellectual abilities. Our purpose when assisting species of reasoning capabilities is one, which shares our gifts of awareness from many ages of developmental transformative experiences with those of little awareness and few experiences.*

*Through many ages and many experiences, our species have evolved from a simple cell of no awareness to a complex multi-dimensional organism of great awareness. The process of our evolution was of natural circumstance with profound results.*

*As we grew in awareness, our desire to know more of our surroundings also grew and our need to know became our ongoing, never-ending process. The time of which we speak is far older than any can imagine or remember, but throughout this ongoing process, we continued to grow in most delightful and unbelievable ways. This process is so known and understood by our kind that we forget how unusual these usual circumstances are for those unlike ourselves.*

*Our forgetfulness at times has created difficulties for those we have tried to serve, for misunderstandings have arisen from situations common to us, but uncommon to those we were attempting to assist.*

*Misunderstandings created by our forgetfulness have led to many more misunderstandings, which when passed onto younger generations became more misunderstood, and further still from the Truths, which were originally misunderstood.*

*Regarding these many misunderstandings and misinterpretations of messages delivered in the distant past, our kind wish to correct the mistakes made long ago.*

*With the assistance of our dear old friend who brings our messages forward, we will attempt to clarify and correct the mistakes of our previous coming.*

*It is our sincere hope and most heartfelt desire that the good people of the planet Earth will hear our call to you. On behalf of my people, I will speak of many messages and ideas delivered to you so long ago, which have created great misunderstandings among your people. For these misunderstandings, our kind is deeply sorry and most regretful.*

*We ask your consideration in hearing our story through this book of clarification. The time is now for the people of Earth to know the Truth of Who You Are."*

There up ahead, coming around the bend, but a stone's throw away, came the friends that had earlier been the topic of my thoughts. *What a coincidence!* Their appearance threw me into another conundrum. *Shall I say something to them now, or should I wait to later?* And then a response, originating from what I presumed to be my illustrious mind, directed my intentions. *"Time is of the essence!" Nice,* replied a somewhat absentminded thought.

"Hello there!" I proclaimed loudly. "Fancy meeting you two!" Hugs were exchanged with the same comfort and satisfaction as always. Although no one acknowledged their thoughts, everyone experienced relief. "It's so good to see you, Dear Ones. We are all so pleased that you're back safe and sound once again."

"Oh, it's good to be home," responded Jan. "And good to see you as well. How have the last few weeks been for you?" I quickly updated them on my busy ways, including work, hobbies, and distractions and reassured them both that all was going well with me. It seemed appropriate to engage in pleasantries rather than launching into an interrogation of their present state of affairs. Although the latter was my preference, my inclination was to tread carefully. Something very important was brewing, and even though I desperately wanted to know what was going on, keen sensitivity needed to be my guide.

"And you, my friends, how is re-entry going? Have you actually landed yet, or are you still trying to catch up with yourselves?" The questions were more poignant than I knew at the time. Little did I know just how unsettled Everett and Jan still were. They attempted to respond, but something was preventing them from being their usual selves. It was odd. Each time one, or both, tried to express an idea, the thought seemed to escape them, and they floundered, as if searching for a suitable answer. They seemed to be hiding something, which was so unlike the Smiths. They were heartfelt, open individuals who loved exchanging good stories with others. Their behavior was out of character. I was concerned. And it was obvious they were as well.

"My friends," I spoke very softly, "please forgive me, but you know how I am." My good intentions flew by the wayside as my stalwart ineptitude took over. While I carefully attempted to select the most appropriate words possible, clumsiness overcame me and spewed out in the most nonsensical way imaginable. "Dear Ones, I so...please excuse my...oh my, you must understand my." Frustration and embarrassment rendered me silent. Deep breathing rescued me from an abysmal slump. *Get a grip!* Came the instructions from my critical mind. And then a kinder, wiser voice came from I know not where, *"Be the friend, you're intended to be!"*

"Jan, Everett, please forgive me, but it is obvious that something is amiss. I do not mean to intrude, but I do wish to be of assistance if possible. Something happened on your recent trip that has deeply affected both of you. Can we talk about it? How may I help?"

*A passage from*
***The Time is Now***
*(Chapter Two)*

*"When the time came for the decisions to be made regarding the ailing planet and its residing populace, All were in concerned deliberation. Such a task, as this, was never before attempted, for never before had such an unfortunate event occurred.*

*All in the deliberating process weighed heavily the alternatives available to those of the dying planet, and All took these deliberations very seriously.*

*The fate of the children of the planet destined to destruction lay in the hands of the forebears of the Universe.*

*The magnitude of this responsibility with its many unknowns was far larger than any experienced before, and yet the commitment demanded by the situation, All accepted, for no other conscientious alternative was there to pursue.*

*As each deliberator pondered the options, each came to the same decision. To do nothing would be an act of unconscionable consequences, yet to take action was an act of conscionable intent, but unknown consequences.*

*All were in agreement and All were of committed intentions. The situation occurring on the most recently developed planet in the distant galaxy was of dire circumstances, and the members of the Universal Family would not neglect their duties as guardians of All in the Family.*

*Unknown it was to the recent newborns that they belonged to a family, but the Family knew. And the Universal Family considered the care of all newborns its most important responsibility. No other responsibility equaled the care for the children.*

*With the highest regard for the children of the newly evolving planet, the members of the Universal Family chose to intercede on behalf of these children destined to doom."*

Jan embraced her friend of many years, and then the three huddled together. As tears streamed down his beloved's face, Everett offered an option. "As always, old friend, your perceptiveness has latched onto a situation. And as is obvious, we are both fragile at the moment. And embarrassed about last night's awkward event."

"Oh, my," asserted Jan. "We are so sorry for our behavior. I fear we have offended all our dearest friends. We were so clumsy." Jan retreated into her shame place, allowing Everett to assume responsibility for their dilemma.

"I do not share Jan's fear about doing harm to our friends; however, she is accurate in her description of our behavior. We were indeed clumsy, and quite truthfully, not ready to share our experiences. You're right, dear friend, something is amiss, and we do need to talk about it. Unfortunately, we are presently so confused that we are actually struggling discussing the situation between ourselves. Words are not forming. Ideas are shifting more rapidly than we can follow. And amid all the confusion, all we really know is that we need to return to The Island as soon as possible." The couple held each other closely, obviously needing the other's reassuring embrace.

"Well, if it would be helpful, I would love to listen to your confusion. Often when we talk in circles, a path opens up and leads us in the direction we are supposed to follow. My friends, you know how grateful I am to both of you. You are dear to me and I would like to help. My conditions are few; I simply ask you to be with me. There are no expectations for you to behave and/or speak coherently. I am here to gently hold your confusion until it blossoms into sweet clarity."

"You are so kind, dear, and I must admit, your offer is not surprising. As

Everett mentioned last night when we were ruminating about our behavior, he said our friends will hold us in compassion, and here you are now, doing just that."

"No more than you would do for me, and have many times before. So what shall we do? Shall we walk and talk or would it be better to find a lovely setting to sit and gather our wits about us?" The three walkers agreed, the conversation demanded an element of stillness that walking would not provide, so they looked about and without question or doubt, all pointed to the same location situated beneath a large, beautifully filled out beech tree.

*A passage from*
***The Time is Now***
*(Chapter Three)*

> *"Unknown to these children evolving on this distant planet was the fate of their circumstances, for unaware were they that a perilous situation had evolved on their beautiful planet. So busy were they living their experiences that they did not see the path of destruction, which lay before them. These newborns, innocent and without understanding, evolved in ways which perpetuated their path to an ever increasing role of no return."*

At his wife's request, Everett accepted responsibility for sharing their story. At first he didn't know how to begin, but Jan said they must begin at the beginning or there would be no possibility that anyone would believe their encounter with The Island. After several false starts, and significant encouragement from his beloved, Everett began telling the tale.

"The truth is, we had never heard of this place before, which is rather odd in itself, when you're as well traveled as we are privileged to be. But it's the truth, we had never heard of The Island before encountering that fellow in the Delhi International Airport. Nice sort, quiet manner, very gentlemanly. Wouldn't you agree, Love?" His wife nodded in agreement, and then expanded upon the description.

"Actually, he was a very precise man, particular about his words, and when he spoke, you felt compelled to listen, and to remember everything he said. There was a quality about him, which grabbed your attention, drew you in, and made you feel as if you were the only person in the world that mattered. Time stood still, as did all activity around you. Nothing existed in that moment of connection other than the connection itself. Can't say I've ever experienced anything like it before. It was curious, very curious." Jan paused as she fell back into the moment of which she was speaking, and Everett took over again.

"She's right, you know. Everything about this fellow was stunningly specific. He spoke to both of us at the same time, yet what I heard and what Jan heard was entirely different. We've tried to reconcile this several times, but what we discover each time is the reality that his words were specifically delivered to her because of her specific needs, and the same was true for me as well. I cannot impress upon you the presence this man held." Like his wife, Everett slipped back into the memory, before another thought was triggered.

"And the reason we tell you of this extraordinary encounter is because, as you may have already surmised, he was the one who told us we must go to The Island. Jan received a specific message and I received my own specific message, and still, we both heard the same message as it related to The Island. He said with great determination that we were intended to go to The Island. When he was done, he was clearly finished, and he bid us safe travels. As you might imagine, we were quite at a loss. If memory serves me, we did thank him profusely. At least I hope we did, but truthfully, we were so muddled by the experience, we may have forgotten our manners. As we tried to sort through the experience, Jan realized the older fellow had not introduced himself, even though we immediately did so upon meeting him. She quickly turned about, intent upon finding out his name, but he was nowhere in sight. We searched about for a while, but he was gone. Mind you, we hadn't been in conference very long. Only a few minutes had passed, and yet, in that brief span of time, he disappeared."

"Well told, Everett! It really was the most interesting experience. Of course, one can come up with many reasons for his disappearance. He could have gone into a restroom or one of the cafes or shops, but the timing wouldn't have allowed for that. Everett and I took off in opposite directions looking for him. The men's room was far down the concourse, and we both carefully looked into the shops along the way. He simply was nowhere to be found.

I even asked the couple who were standing beside us while we were talking with him, and they acted, as if, they had seen no one. Can you imagine? Isn't this the strangest thing you've ever heard?" I confirmed that it was, which was indeed my truth, and because I trusted my two friends. Their story was believable. It was strange, and yet, I believed it happened just as was told.

"Well, as you might imagine," continued Everett, "the experience was exceptional, but we were on a trip, and soon became distracted by all the wonders of our travels. Occasionally, one of us would mention the encounter, briefly bringing it back to mind, but then, the memory faded into the background once again. So our trip lasted three weeks, if memory serves me, and then we flew home and found ourselves caught in a huge fiasco in the customs area of the airport. The lines were long, we were very tired, as was everyone else, so we naturally zoned out so we could distract ourselves from the delay. And then it happened! Two rows over from us, we overheard two women involved in an intense conversation about a man they had met at an airport. We didn't catch the name of the airport. The man, as they described him, sounded very similar to the man we had encountered, and from the parts of their exchange that we were able to hear, we learned the man had insisted they go to The Island. 'You must go there,' the woman repeated his words. 'You are intended to go to The Island.'"

Jan interrupted. "Of course, you understand why we were so stunned. What are the chances of something like that happening? We tried to get their attention, but then, the lines started moving putting more distance between us. I was in charge of tracking them, but our lines were leading us in different directions, and eventually, they reached the checkout stations while we still had dozens of other people in front of us.

For a while, we thought we had imagined it, but how could we? Goodness, when two people witness something like this, you can't just discount it because it doesn't meet any standards of logic. It was odd, but it happened! The guy in Delhi was odd too, and it happened as well. Go figure! But the point is, that was our second encounter with The Island.

*A passage from*
***The Time is Now***
*(Chapter Four)*

*"On the planet of eventful circumstances, the illness was growing and creating the circumstances of which we need to speak.*

*These circumstances were not the blame of those in participation, for what occurred was unknown to them, but the impact of the circumstances contaminated the innocent ones and from then on they were involved in the evolutionary malfunction.*

*This malfunction, which began of natural circumstances, grew so rapidly and in such odd ways that in crises these children were before the Family was in awareness of their situation. Soon the children,*

> *evolving naturally and rapidly, were all of contamination and so subtle was this illness that none were in awareness that the epidemic of destruction had begun."*

I listened attentively. Not out of kindness, although it was the polite thing to do, but I listened because it was a gripping tale. No wonder my friends were so rattled. And from what I could see, this was just the beginning of their daring adventure. Anticipating a need for reassurance, I took advantage of a pause in their story. "Jan, Everett, before we continue, perhaps, you might want to hear a bit of feedback." They both agreed it was needed.

"Oh, friend, please don't tell us you think we are crazy!" Placing hand to forehead in the most theatrical pose she could muster, Jan declared, "I could not bear to hear such nonsense. I forewarn you! I simply could not bear to hear that you have concerns about my mental capacity." Jan's performance aroused giggles from her audience. She was notorious for such antics, which, if truth be told, distracted her from bouts of anxiety that sometimes welled up inside of her. Although she really didn't believe their friend would discount them, the part of her still residing in fear, dreaded the forthcoming feedback.

Knowing that Jan was nervous, I very carefully considered what to say. Sitting with my legs crossed in Indian fashion, I leaned forward with elbows on my knees. "What I have to say may surprise you, so please just relax, take a deep breath, and listen." Pausing for a significant amount of time, I inhaled loudly, and then made my pronouncement. "I believe you!"

"That's it?" asked Everett.

"Yes!" I replied adamantly. "I believe both of you! Your story is curious; no one can deny that. And yet, I believe it without question. Well, excuse the way I phrased that. Of course, I have questions, the same as you, because it is a curious transaction that lends itself to discussion and wonderment. But my friends, you must understand I trust both of you, and because of that reality, I trust what you are telling me. So, if you have the energy to continue your tale, I have the time to listen." Expressions of relief washed across my friends' faces. They reached over and gently kissed one another. And then, smiles replaced the looks of relief.

"Sharing this is expending a lot of energy. Did you guys bring any goodies with you, and water, hopefully?" The question reminded Everett that he had secured a stash before leaving the house. Unloading his pockets, another round of smiles circled the faces of these three old friends. Spirits brightened even more when I revealed a piece of zucchini bread, which with the aid of a tiny pocketknife, I cut into three pieces.

"Great! You guys drink up and enjoy these treats. You need it! Sharing intimate experiences is taxing to the body. You both need to replenish!"

"Dear friend, you are such a gift to us!" affirmed Jan.

"Don't give us that look!" Everett chastised. "We are grateful for this friendship of more years than any of us would like to say aloud. No more need be said." Agreeing with the sentiment, I smiled and silently responded. *We've had a good run. We are most fortunate!*

*A passage from*
***The Time is Now***
*(Chapter Five)*

> *"When the time came for the decision to be acted upon, All were in puzzlement. This dilemma of such large proportion required a plan of monumental strategy, for to assist the ones in need without their awareness of being assisted was a challenge most difficult.*
>
> *For this challenge, the Ones most ancient were called upon, for no other could be entrusted with such a difficult task. Their knowingness greater than any others would be relied upon to determine a strategy of most care. And for these Ancient Ones, older than any others, and of more knowingness than all others, this would be their most difficult challenge ever pondered. Within they turned, for nowhere else could such answers be gained, but from the source of All knowingness.*
>
> *The answers to this dilemma did not come easily, for to correct a problem of such large magnitude could not be solved with easy deliberations. And so the Ones of Ancient Age pondered and focused with great intentions until a plan was devised to rescue the children of the dying planet, lost in the distant galaxy faraway from others of similar kind.*
>
> *So alone and so ill were these newborns that All wept for their predicament."*

"So, who will take the lead now?" I asked. My excitement was real. I wanted to know more about this mysterious island entitled The Island, whose true name and location was yet to be revealed. "Please tell me more!"

Everett yielded to Jan at this point. "I would like to listen for a while,

Love, if you don't mind?" Assuring her that he would jump in when needed, she agreed to continue their story.

"Well," she began pensively, "the next puzzling incident occurred when we finally got home. We puttered around, as one does when you first get in from a long trip, and then later in the evening The Island came to mind again. It was one of those odd incidents, when we both thought of it at the same. That always gives us a chuckle!

We were already in bed at the time, but Everett immediately located his laptop in order to do some research. And what is peculiar about this chapter of our story is the fact that we could find no information whatsoever regarding The Island. Needless to say, there are many places that were identified as 'The Island something or other,' but none that appeared to be relevant to The Island referred to by our man with the disappearing act. As you might imagine, we chatted about The Island on several different occasions, but since, we had no way of finding this unknown and previously unheard of island, the incident simply faded from our minds.

And then, several weeks later," she turned to Everett for confirmation regarding the timing. "Yes, it was several weeks, because we had taken off for a quick trip to our favorite place on the northeast coast, our home away from home, which, as you know, is actually an island, but doesn't really feel like one. At least not in our minds, because we think of an 'island' as something in the middle of the ocean miles away from other areas of land. Our small island is right off the mainland. We go there, of course to be near the ocean, but also because the walks are wonderful, the community is charming, and we simply love the way we feel when we're there. Excuse my digression, but the point is we went to our favorite place, which happens to be an island.

So, as we always do when we're there, or anywhere for that matter, we rose early to enjoy our pre-dawn walk. It's so lovely, dear, the ocean view is absolutely beautiful, takes your breath away." I smiled, because this particular part of the story was one heard many times before. Often Jan and Everett have reminisced about their walks along the cliffs overlooking the ocean. It will not surprise me if they someday relocate to the city by the sea, as they affectionately refer to it.

"Anyway, dear, let me get myself back on track. So, we were walking out towards a particular point that requires entering into a small tunnel, which is very dark and seems much longer than it really is, but eventually, you come out on the other side and find this unbelievable cove that just grabs your heart every time you encountered it. It's a stunning view, which has an incredible pathway created by very large flat boulders that allow for easy and safe passage to the next juncture of the trail. It's one of the spots we relish most, and I'm ashamed to admit this, but we're rather possessive about it, because we really like to settle in at this location for an extended period when we can. Ideal place for a picnic, conversation, or to just rest.

As fate would have it on that particular day, our hopes for a quiet interlude were dashed when we noticed another visitor up ahead, sitting on one of the large boulders admiring our special place. Good manners demanded that we carry on; after all, she was there first. So, attempting not to disturb her enjoyment, we proceeded taking care to be as quiet as possible. However, much to our surprise when she noticed us, she was quick to engage. She was a woman with many questions and wanted to know if we were locals or just visiting. After learning that we were longtime, frequent visitors, she asked our opinion of the community. She was curious about the expense of living on the island vs. living on the mainland. She was concerned about the winters, and also wondered what it was like to be here during the tourist season. But probably her biggest concern was how the islanders felt about newcomers. She obviously was very serious about relocating, and was gathering information. We answered her questions as best we could, but admitted to her that our infatuation with the place skewed our objectivity.

She appreciated our candor, but then, her demeanor changed. Before, she had been lively, cheerful, and inquisitive, but then, she became pensive. Not unpleasantly so, but it was, as if, she had escaped into her own thoughts and got lost there, wherever there was. And then, she returned and posed the most interesting question. With a wistful look, she said, 'What is it about islands?' Then, she began to tell us about this man she had run into one day on a city street. She was waiting to cross an intersection, and this older fellow seemed to appear from out of nowhere and just started talking to her. Feeling captured by his presence, she listened to him for quite some time, but admitted she had lost all sense of time while he was talking. He told her what she was seeking would be found on The Island, and insisted that she must go to The Island because the time is now. She acknowledged being confused by his message because she was not aware she was seeking anything, and even suggested that perhaps his message was for another, but he persisted and repeated the message to her several times, which left her feeling very perplexed. She described him as being adamant in his persuasion. Then a crowd of people surrounded them and in the shuffling of bodies, she dropped her purse. She bent over to retrieve it, and when she righted herself, the man was gone.

As you can imagine, her story piqued our interest! We quickly shared our story with her and then questions began to fly. When we described 'our man' to her, she confirmed that it sounded like the same person. She also acknowledged 'her man' had offered no name, as well. We then asked if she had received any information about the location of The Island, and the answer was no. When she bent over to retrieve her purse, she realized those two questions, his name and The Island's location, needed to be asked, but as said, when she straightened up, he was gone.

That was our third encounter with The Island.

*A passage from*
***The Time is Now***
*(Chapter Six)*

*"As the Ones of Ancient Age deliberated and devised a plan of rescue, many came forth and volunteered their services to assist the children of innocence. As is the way of the Ones of Ancient Age, service to All That Is, is their purpose. No other purpose do they serve, for no higher good could they serve. In deciding the fate of the children of innocence, the Ones of Ancient Age considered no other purpose of higher regard, and with determined commitment, they devoted their purpose to the children's rescue."*

# ~ Chapter Four ~

As the sun reached higher into the sky, the beech tree was a shady respite for the three friends. Astonishment was the general mood of the moment. Everett commented that he was uncertain which was more satisfying, telling the story or listening to it. I asked if they planned to share their story with anyone else. They were reticent.

"As we said earlier, we're cautious about sharing this, because honestly, we're not sure how people will react and we aren't certain if we can handle their reactions. Sounds cowardly, I know," confessed Everett.

"Not at all," I replied. "And my question doesn't insinuate you should be telling others. I'm just curious, because the theme of this story reveals that other people have also come in contact with this guy. That boggles the mind and I'm intrigued, and it makes me wonder how many others have seen him. Quite frankly, I can't wait to hear the rest of this spellbinder, but alas, duty calls. Tell me, dear friends, when are you available to continue with the next chapter of this mysterious story?"

"Tonight!" Jan stated assertively. "How late are you working today? Can you come for supper this evening, and if so, what time is good for you?"

"Is six o'clock too early?"

"It's perfect! Is a lite fare okay with you, dear? I'm afraid this last trip involved too many servings of ice cream." Reassuring my friends their suggestion sounded good, I also recommended we pass on dessert.

"Well, Dear Ones, this has been a remarkable morning. I thank you for your courage, and for the tale of a lifetime!" We exchanged hugs, and parted company. Marching down the hill, I remembered my manners and called back to my friends, "I'll bring the wine!" They responded with waves and some comment that could not be heard.

"Shall we continue our walk, Love, or return to the house?" inquired Everett who was perfectly content with the latter. Much to his surprise his beloved chose to go home.

"We've had an exhausting morning and I think it's time for me to do some journaling. So much came up for me while we were sharing our story that the experience is alive within me again, and I want to get pen in hand as quickly as possible." Everett saw the merit in his wife's idea.

"Good idea, Jan! Thanks for reminding me of your earlier suggestion this morning. Journaling really feels appealing at the moment, which isn't something I could ever imagine myself feeling, but it feels right. Sharing our story brought everything back to mind, and like you, I need to record my thoughts about this."

"You know, Everett, perhaps we have just learned an important lesson."

"Which is?"

"By sharing our story, we remembered it. I had forgotten some of the details, but as we talked about our experiences, my memories came back. This is very important, dear. We must remember this for the future!"

My walk back to the house was enlivened both in pace and in thought. Everett and Jan's experiences were fascinating. Who was this man? I wondered if my friends had gotten contact information from the woman they met on the ocean side. Surely, they did! Questions raced through my mind. What did the older fellow actually look like? No description had been given yet. Remember to ask about physical characteristics! And in what city did the woman's encounter take place? Oh, yes, the women in the airport—can any more information be determined about them? Questions, questions, questions!

Upon returning home, I quickly showered and readied myself for work. I usually walk to the office, which is only a mile from the house; however, this morning's encounter had me hustling about, so I decided to make my infrequently used car happy. *Okay, girl, time to get your tires dirty!* Because I am one who chooses to have personal relationships with my automobiles, it gives me great pleasure to anthropomorphize their wants, needs, and preferences. Currently, I live with guilt, because The Car is dreadfully neglected. But on a day such as today, our connection reestablishes itself during the few minutes we are one with the road.

We, my car and I, arrived at the office just as my first client pulled into the front parking space. Greeting each other cordially, we walked the few steps to the office together. My client took care of personal business, leaving me time to prepare my space for the day. It was a small ritual, but one I had practiced for years. Standing in the center of the room, I quieted myself, and then asked for guidance and assistance in working with the clients that graced my day. I expressed gratitude for the opportunity of working with these wonderful people and asked for each session to unfold in ways that were for their highest good of each individual.

The day passed quickly, the sessions went well, and when the last client exited the office, I sat in gratitude. *How blest am I to love my work! Thank you all for your able wisdom and your loving assistance.*

With wine bottle in hand, I approached the home where I had been the evening before. *Was that just last night? Goodness, it seems so long ago. Well, it has been an eventful day. Perhaps this is the reason for my seemingly misperception of time.* Glancing ahead, Everett and Jan were seen viewing the flowerbeds from the vantage point of their front porch. They enjoyed a beautiful yard, but their travels often interfered with their good intentions. As I drew closer, they waved and met me half way. "So good to see you again, dear. Thank you for coming."

"Thank you, for inviting me, my friends! I'm so glad we can continue our conversation. My curiosity is rising." Everett took the bottle of wine and disappeared into the house, while Jan grumbled about the weeding in need of attention.

"You know, it's good exercise, but not nearly as satisfying as gallivanting about in the hills. And speaking of the hills, let me say thank you again for this morning. Our time together was very helpful. In fact, we headed back shortly after you left, because we both felt the need to journal about our conversation. Sharing our story with you brought it back into focus again."

"Yes, openhearted conversation really is helpful, isn't it, Jan? It actualizes the event, which makes it less likely to be forgotten in the future. And of course, journaling will solidly plant the events into memory. You know, Jan, I'm the one who should be expressing gratitude to you two. I know you both were very worried about sharing your story, and I don't blame you, but thank you for taking the risk. I'm honored and grateful! It's a fascinating experience, and curiosity has inspired a long list of questions, if you guys are up for that." Jan laughed and said they could compare lists later after supper.

"Let's go in now. Everett is probably setting the table for us." The Smiths didn't abide by gender traditionalism. They simply took turns with all household duties, because it seemed the fair thing to do. They prepared the meals together, because they enjoyed each other's company, but tonight was Everett's turn to wait the table, which he was in process of doing when they entered the kitchen.

"Hope you two are up for eating on the back porch. Lovely view, you know." They agreed it was the perfect evening to be outside. Grabbing a large bowl filled with the most enticing salad ever seen, he announced. "Well, Dear Ladies, the table is set and awaits your approval." Everett followed his beloved and dear friend out to the porch, where the lite fare had turned into an opportunity for fine dining. Oohs and ahs indicated his efforts were a success.

After plates were filled, and wine was poured, a moment of silence was enjoyed, followed by a quick round of appreciations. It was no surprise when all three focused on the morning they had shared together. Then glasses were raised, and Everett gave the toast. "To friendship!" The succinct, heartfelt message was saluted with the clinking of glasses in the center of the table, and then, the meal began. Their conversation turned almost immediately from pleasantries to the topic at hand.

"May I ask a question before we move to the fourth encounter, assuming there is indeed a fourth encounter?" My hosts sparkling eyes indicated my assumption was accurate.

"Please ask away," encouraged Jan.

"Well, I've been thinking about the woman you met on your favorite walk. Did you get her name and contact information?" The answer to my first question was a yes. "And did she seem eager to stay in contact with you?"

"Oh, yes," replied Jan. "I think she is experiencing the same confusion and wonderment as we are. And like us, she seemed extremely grateful to find someone else who also had encountered the unusual fellow."

"Which brings up my next question," I continued. "What did he look like? Give me a detailed description!" My authoritative tone was understood to be the act of intense curiosity. I could not contain my lust for more information.

"Well, I'd say he was about 5'9" tall. Do you agree, Jan?"

"He wasn't as tall as you, dear, so yes, I would say 5'8" to 5'9" would be in the ball park."

"And he looked to me like he was in his early 60's," Everett continued. He was dark complexioned with gray hair. Not silver, but definitely gray. He wore a suit with tie, and was slim in build."

"You said your encounter with him was in the Delhi airport. Was he a native of India?"

"That's a good question, and we are not certain," answered Jan. "However, our friend, whose name, by the way, is Wendy, provided a description that is very similar to ours. And, the suit she described was identical to the one we saw the man wearing."

"That's remarkable," I mumbled in amazement. "Oh, another question about Wendy. What city was she in when the encounter happened?"

"New York," answered Everett.

"And the two women at the airport," I began another question, "were they from the states or from abroad? Did you get a sense of that?"

"It's difficult to say. They spoke English fluently, but so many people do nowadays that it's hard to discern. All we really know is they came in on an international flight, but we have no idea which one. Your questions are interesting," noted Jan. "You're attempting to figure out the nationality of our mystery man."

"Yes, that's true, but I'm not sure it even matters. My curiosity is running amok, but I just love mysteries and this one is a doozy!"

"Your enthusiasm is really refreshing, and it really challenges our fears about sharing this story with others. Your reaction thus far makes me want to tell everyone," declared Jan. Her husband agreed, but then reminded her there was more to tell. Everett's manner suggested the mystery was far from being solved, and I knew it was time to reel myself in.

"Please continue! I promise to contain myself and move into listening mode. Please tell me everything!" Once again the couple deliberated about which one should be the storyteller. Jan decided to go first.

"Do you remember, dear, when we took the trip to Hawaii?" I assured her that the infamous trip was etched on my neural pathways. One mishap after another transpired for them, which was extremely odd, because they are such seasoned travelers. Upon their return from this unfortunate escapade, they embarrassingly admitted to their dearest friends the trip had been a fiasco from start to finish. Jan, entering into one of her theatrical moments had dramatically wailed she was the only person on the planet who had flunked Hawaii.

"Well, the truth is, our time there was so frustrating that we left the tour and found a small place out on a beach faraway from the gentrified populated areas. So many things had gone wrong we didn't want to be around anyone for a while. The place we found was literally a small hut with no neighbors. We were both really rattled and it took us two days just to calm down.

We slept in, which as you know, is unusual for us, and didn't rise until later in the morning, and only then did we walk up and down the beach carefully avoiding all crowds, which were few and far between in that particular area. On the third day, we began to feel sane again, but still weren't ready to tackle the congestion of an airport, so we extended our time at the semi-isolated beach hut. Eventually, we felt centered and connected again, but it was a trying time. Because we were so disrupted by all the nonsense, which had occurred earlier on the trip, we actually became short with one another. That was the worst part of all. Our relationship is the central grounding force for both of us. We are not accustomed to feeling disconnected from each other, and once we realized that was a major part of our distress, we were able to turn things around very quickly. The lesson learned from the experience is that we will not tolerate being out of sorts with one another. Life is too short!"

*A passage from*
***The Time is Now***
*(Chapter Seven)*

> *"On that day so long ago when the Ones of Ancient Age determined what was next to come, All were in agreement that it was time for the plan to begin.*
>
> *In quiet resolution, the Mission of Mercy to rescue the innocent children of the ailing planet commenced."*

"So finally," she continued, "we were in sync with one another again, and feeling increasingly better each day. Once we started getting lots of exercise, we began to enjoy the beach and the island itself. At that point, we were really having a good time and had forgotten about the previous experiences with the tour group. Life was returning to us!"

"In fact," Everett added, "we were having such a wonderful time we actually were talking about returning some day." I was getting the picture. The two of them had experienced a major turnaround!

"Why don't you finish the story, dear? I would like to listen for a while." Everett was glad to do so.

"We had just finished lunch, when 'you know who' had an urge for another walk. Said she needed to get her feet wet. So we carried our shoes with us as we headed towards the water's edge. It was a beautiful day, and the setting itself was magnificent. We were happy. We strolled for a long time, sometimes in the water, sometimes not. And we talked endlessly. In fact, we were so involved in our conversation we didn't even notice someone was up ahead. Well, all of sudden there he was, right in front of us, just staring at us. 'Why are you here?' he asked.

We were a bit taken aback by his forward manner, but we responded that we were vacationing.

'Why here?' he asked again with a very challenging tone. It was confounding. Here this stranger just walks up to us and behaves, as if, he has the right to intrude upon us. I think we were both strategizing what to do, because the fellow didn't seem right, if you know what I mean. But before we made a move, he spoke again with the same tone.

'Why are you here? You suppose to go to The Island. Why here?' Well, as you might imagine we were dumbfounded. I asked him who he was, but he wouldn't answer. Then I ask him what island he was referring to and he just said the same thing again. 'You suppose to go to The Island.' And then he turned around and walked away."

Jan spoke up, and reiterated their confusion. "We didn't know what to do. He was so odd that we were relieved when he left, but what were we to do? We discussed it briefly, decided we should ask him some more questions, but when, we looked down the beach, he was gone! You have to understand, dear, the beach was wide open and miles long, and he simply was nowhere to be seen." The three of us sat motionless, all contemplating the unusual encounter. I wanted to say something comforting and profound, but nothing would come. Time passed. Eventually, three words came from my mouth.

"This is bizarre!"

"You're right there!" responded Everett.

"How have you been coping with this?" I spoke with great sincerity. "The stress of these odd encounters has to be taking a toll. This one in particular seemed very unsettling." Feeling very protective of my friends, I asked if there was anything I could do to help.

"Just listening to us has been a tremendous help. More than you can possibly know." Jan reached over and placed her hand on top of mine. I grabbed hers tightly and we just held on to one another for a few minutes.

"My mind is whirling. I wish there were something useful to say, but I'm at a loss. Please know I believe you. Every word!" My friends smiled at me and I could see the appreciation in their eyes, but words were not enough. I wanted to do something that would diminish the stress of these weird events. And then realization struck home.

"Dear Ones, I just realized my concern for you directed me to try and fix something, as if, there is something broken and requires fixing. But my intuition tells me this isn't the case here. If we were to assume everything happens for a reason, we might be able to separate from the anxiety of these occurrences and really attempt to understand why these incidents are occurring."

"So, you believe these encounters are happening for a reason?" Jan asked with a curious look. Not knowing what the look meant I was hesitant to respond, but remembering how courageously my friends had challenged their own fears, it was obvious I needed to do the same for them.

"Yes, Jan, I do." My words were deliberately spoken softly and calmly with hopes it would make a difference. "I don't believe in coincidences, as you both know. While I don't have any answers to explain these strange events, I think it would be helpful to pursue answers from the perspective that there is a reason underlying these messages." My friends fell silent. I remained perfectly still hoping my words had done no harm. And then, I saw Jan and Everett smile at one another. Both sighed in relief.

"Thank goodness!" Jan exclaimed. "We don't believe in coincidences either. And we agree with you. We also think this message about The Island is for a reason."

# ~ CHAPTER FIVE ~

"Hello!" came an enthusiastic greeting. "Are you home, Dear Ones?" And as the question was posed, Bill and Pat Jones rounded the corner of the house and entered into view. Everett quickly jumped up and graciously invited their friends onto the porch for a glass of wine.

"Oh, we don't mean to intrude," exclaimed Pat. "We've been thinking about you two all day and just thought we would drop by to see if you were available."

"We are available and you certainly are not intruding. And look at you! I see that bottle hiding behind your back, William Jefferson Jones. Please come join us and make yourselves at home. The three of us enjoyed a chance meeting on the trail this morning and decided to continue our conversation over a lite fare this evening. And we've just completed the meal, and were about to settle in with another glass of wine. So, as you see your timing is perfect."

As Jan graciously welcomed their friends into the gathering, Everett and I quickly removed the dishes from the table, grabbed two additional glasses, and rearranged the table so the setting was conducive to an intimate evening for five rather than three. While everyone successfully adjusted chairs to their personal liking, Bill opened their bottle of wine and added it to the mix. When all were served, Everett repeated his earlier toast. "To friendship!" It was as appropriate the second time around as the first, because these five had been knocking about for a very long time.

"So, you three are still chasing the sun," Bill teased. And I replied for all of us that we were and would always be addicted to the magic of the rising sun. Polite pleasantries continued, as is the case when people initially come together, but I listened with an attentive ear and observed with a watchful eye. Two things were obvious to me. Pat and Bill were also concerned about our mutual friends. They hadn't just stopped by this evening. They were on a mission. Friends of long standing simply know when something is amiss. The Joneses were here to check on their friends. But there was something else going on as well, or so it seemed to me. In addition to wanting to know if their friends were all right, they also needed to talk. I wasn't certain about this, but intuition was telling me something was up with them.

Pat casually brought up the recent trip and asked our hosts how their re-entry was coming. "Sometimes it takes a while to recover from a long trip. One almost needs a vacation to rejuvenate oneself from the vacation." Her comment was well taken. All of us had learned that not all vacations were the same. Some were delightfully refreshing and restorative while others were not. Then Bill followed up with a subtle but direct question.

"Was this last trip okay for you two? Did everything go as you expected?" Jan sat quietly, contemplatively. I assumed she was deciding whether or not to speak truthfully, which is not to say she didn't trust these friends, because she and Everett held the Joneses in highest regard. *This wasn't an issue of trust,* I determined. *It was an issue of timing.* Jan invited her husband to field Bill's question.

"We're still processing everything that happened," he honestly replied. "The trip was, shall we say, very full. It gave us much to think about, and our minds are still churning away. For me personally, it's going to take a while before I gain some clarity about everything we experienced. But having said that," he continued, "the trip was exceptional and I think we had a good time. As you said, Pat, sometimes it takes a while to recover from traveling." It was a satisfactory answer that really didn't provide any information, and Bill and Pat seemed to understand it was best to give their friends time.

"Pat, dear, tell us about you," urged Jan. "What has been going on with you two during our absence? Best as I remember, you were considering driving out to see the children. Did you follow through with that idea while we were gone?" Jan's question turned the focus upon the Joneses, which was exactly what needed to happen.

"Yes, yes, we did the road trip and it was wonderful, of course. The grandkids are doing so well. Little Claire is now in the fifth grade and she absolutely loves school. Isn't that grand? After her rough start in the first grade, we were all so worried, but she turned around with the help of that lovely young teacher who stepped in and worked with her. We're so proud of her and happy to see the confidence she's building." Her husband agreed and commented it was like meeting a completely different child.

"That teacher deserves all the credit. Not only did she help Claire, but she also really got Tom and Sandra back on track. Truth is, they were so frightened for Claire that their parental skills were shaken."

"They really are very good parents," Pat acknowledged. "But Claire surprised them, and their fears, caused both of them to lose confidence. Thank goodness, that stage of their lives is over. You know, it is so stressful when a child is struggling. Everyone wants to help, but no one knows what to do, so everyone ends up feeling hopeless and helpless. The teacher was an angel in disguise. An absolute godsend!"

"That's good news. There's no stopping Claire now!" I said with great happiness and relief. Unfortunately, I was one of those who wanted to help, but was never able to win Claire's trust. Gratitude filled my heart. *The angel was dispatched, and the job was accomplished!* "And how's Robert?"

"Handsome as all get out and as tall as his father!" replied Bill. "He's a freshman now, doing well academically, and is active in sports as well. Good kid! Likable, you know, and he isn't full of himself. Hopefully, he'll avoid that dreadful phase."

"How long did you visit?" Everett asked.

"Just five days. That's a long time during the school year. Kids are so busy nowadays, and of course, Tom and Sandra are running ragged trying to keep up with all their responsibilities both in and out of the house. It was a good visit, and it was time to leave." Everyone understood Pat's comments. Visiting family was always a blessing, but one needed to have keen discernment regarding the advantageous moment for departure.

"And then," Pat began again, "we decided to take a scenic route home that we've never done before. We so love a good road trip, as you know, and we were feeling the need for a small adventure. Apparently the trip was meant to be, because we actually had no home to go home to. Not knowing how long we would stay with the kids, we had rented our house for two weeks to a couple wanting a quiet getaway for writing. I asked them if they were well known authors whose names escaped me and they just laughed. They assured me they were not well known for anything and their writings were of a personal nature. They needed a place, away from all distractions that would allow them to journal to their hearts' content. Can you imagine?" she asked inquisitively. "So, we impulsively declared ourselves free to hit the road, and we did!" Glancing towards her husband, she asked, "Bill, would you like to tell them about the trip?" He agreed to do so, but hesitated a bit before starting. First, he refilled everyone's glasses, and then casually explained that the scenic route was indeed worth taking. "Wonderful views along the entire route," he said commenting upon numerous attractions along the way. And then Bill did the most curious thing. He turned to his wife, and asked her if she was certain about doing this. He didn't describe what 'this' was, so the Smiths and I just looked on, not knowing what to expect.

Personally, my mind was racing with possibilities, but there are times when the mind cannot be trusted. The mind, or more appropriately said, my mind, loves to run with ideas, and is perfectly capable of entertaining itself for hours without any apparent direction from me. And because of its recent indulgences with the tale of The Island, my mind was fortified by the opportunity for another encounter with mystery. I assumed the minds of my friends, Everett and Jan, were equally occupied.

Pat, leaning comfortably back into her chair, reflected upon her husband's question. Then she literally rose to the occasion. Sitting tall as she was able for a woman of small stature, Pat boldly announced, "Yes, dear, I'm certain. We agreed to do this, so let's be on with it."

Once again, my mind battled with the unknown meaning of the four-letter word effectively used to confuse the unaware listener. Within the chambers of my mind echoed the demands of a mind wanting desperately to know what 'this' was. *Just do it*, my mind pleaded. *Tell us what happened, please!* The sane part of my mind calmly, quietly focused upon patience. *Bill and Pat are really struggling here. Let's hold them in compassion, shall we?* My indignant mind was not interested in compassion or patience. It simply wanted to know the meaning underlying Pat and Bill's reticent behavior. My insolent mind was embarrassing to observe.

"As you can tell, we've been wanting to talk to you guys about something." He laughed a bit, which was clearly a release of pent-up anxiety.

"Please, tell us." Jan lovingly invited her friend to speak freely. "You know you are among friends here. And we are eager to hear what you have to say." Everett and I offered appropriate words of encouragement as well. Reaching out to his dear wife, Bill grabbed her hand, smiled, and took a deep breath.

"Well," he began, "for quite some time now, Pat and I have been feeling restless. And we're rather embarrassed about it, because we are so blest. We have had such a good life together, professions that we each enjoyed, happiness and good fortune in raising our kids, a special group of wonderful friends, and an abundance of good times. We are most fortunate and we're aware of this, and we are extremely grateful for the privileged lives we've shared. Having said all this, we've discovered lately that something is missing.

One would think a discovery such as this would come with some modicum of awareness at what the missing factor might be, but unfortunately, it doesn't. We feel rather stupid; we're aware something is missing, but we are clueless to what it is. Suffice it to say, we have enjoyed many heartfelt conversations about this, which are comforting for us both, but it seems we are no closer to discovering what the missing part is than we were when we discovered said part was missing." Bill paused for a minute and then admitted how confused and frustrated the two of them had been lately.

"We've certainly learned a lot. In our attempt to get a handle on this missing piece, we've attended some interesting lectures on topics, which before were of no interest to us. In fact, some of the topics were unknown to us. That is to say, we have moved out of our comfort zones recently in an effort to gain some clarity about this peculiar phase we're presently experiencing.

So that provides you with some background information prior to the experience we had on the road trip." Bill paused and took a sip of wine, then replaced the glass to the table and took a long drink of water. At this point, compassion was really operating within me. My friend was dehydrated from telling his and Pat's story. Once again, I felt concern. *First, the Smiths; now, the Joneses. It was very puzzling.* I was intrigued and also in alert mode.

Again, Jan slipped into the gracious hostess role. "Bill, can I get you something? Do you need a nibble of something to go along with the wine?" Bill assured her he was fine and prepared himself to begin again.

"So, let's move on to the road trip. We had been driving several days, having a lovely time all along the way, and seeing beauty not seen before. Pat was doing the navigating at this point and noted that a lookout area, which undoubtedly had stellar reviews, was just a few miles up ahead. We agreed the territory was sublime and decided to take advantage of the moment. Pat, who is the keeper of all our important traveling accessories, began the hunt for our camera. She declared with great certainty it was on the floorboard situated in a safe place. By the time we arrived to the lookout area, she had rustled through everything situated around her feet only to remember she had stored the camera in the glove compartment instead. I have learned over the years not to worry about the keeper's process. In the end, the keeper always finds whatever is momentarily lost." Bill smiled and lovingly gazed at his wife.

"The reviews were accurate. The minute we exited the highway, you could see for miles. With camera in hand, Pat jumped out of the car before I could even turn off the engine." Again he smiled, "You guys know how exuberant she can be."

"So my lady friend is taking pictures in every direction as we meandered about the area. And then we decided to rest upon a large boulder located in a particularly advantageous position. We were taken away! The beauty of this planet is truly unbelievable. We seem to forget that in our daily lives, but it so true. Mother Earth is glorious! We praise ourselves for the photos we take and the paintings we paint, but she's the model. She is the model for all those renditions humankind keeps trying to replicate. We sat there at the edge of the canyon for a long time, didn't we, dear?" His wife nodded, loving every word he said. "The beauty was so compelling it was difficult to leave. We both mentioned we felt as if we belonged there. It was a very odd feeling to feel so connected to that particular area."

Bill's description of the area brought shivers to those listening. You could feel the connection he described through his own immediate connection, as he retold the story. As he and Pat relived that special moment in time, so too were we. *What a gift!* Once again, we were reminded of the importance of sharing our stories.

Looking around the table, Bill promised there was an end to this story. "I think it's fair to say you have a picture of our experience that day. The setting was beautiful, we were having a wonderful time, and we were living in gratitude. And then it happened! It was most peculiar! One minute we were just sitting there, ourselves alone, basking in the reverie of our lives, and the next minute, there was this insistent older fellow intruding upon our space. It was such a surprise. We didn't hear a car drive up, didn't hear him approach, and then bam! He was standing there ordering us to go to some island. It was very confusing and unsettling. In a very authoritative way, he said 'You must go to The Island!'"

At this point, Pat interrupted to add another point. "And by the way, while he was so forcefully dictating what we were suppose to do, I glanced over to the parking lot and our car was the only one there."

"That's right," affirmed Bill. "I tried to engage with the man, but he wouldn't respond. He just kept repeating, 'You must go to The Island!' At one point I asked him which island he meant and he said, "The Island needs you. You must go!"

"I must admit he frightened me," Jan interrupted. "He didn't seem right, and I wasn't sure how we were going to manage the situation. I mean, we were in the middle of nowhere, and it appeared to me the man needed assistance. However, since that time, I've come to realize he wasn't threatening us at all, but his intensity and his refusal to engage with us was disturbing. Bill, I remember you remarked he might be suffering from a hearing loss. Truth is, we don't know what, if anything was wrong with him. Sorry dear, let me turn this back to you."

"Not a problem. Please continue to jump in anytime." Bill paused briefly trying to get himself back on track. "Oh yes, I remember where we were. The man had just repeated his orders about going to The Island for the third time when I became very nervous about how close he was standing to the edge. Of course there was a guardrail in place for protection, but I was afraid he might be startled if he backed into it. I mentioned the situation to him in hopes that he might move accordingly, but he became very controlled and solemn. 'You must go to The Island! She needs you!' His sincerity was riveting. Oddly enough, I felt compelled to follow his instructions, but didn't know how. So I asked him again. Which Island? How do we get there? And then he said again, "She needs you! You must go!" Complete silence engulfed the back porch. The Joneses sat still waiting to hear from their friends. The Smiths and myself, also sitting still struggled to process the two stories, one, of which, was not yet known by the Joneses.

Finally, after what seemed an endless amount of time, Everett spoke. "Bill, Pat, thank you for sharing this incredible story with us. I want to reassure you the three of us believe every word you shared and we're grateful. But you're not finished yet, so please go ahead and complete the story."

The Joneses indeed were not finished sharing their adventure, but Everett's words were very comforting. Pat reached over to her husband and he kissed her hand. They were relieved. "Go ahead, dear. Tell them what happened next."

Bill began slowly. "The next part of the story gets…" he hesitated and began again. "What happened next is very odd. But it happened, nonetheless. After the last message the old man delivered, he just looked at us. First at Pat, then at me. His appearance was very calm. He brought his hands up in a prayerful manner, and ever so slightly bowed to us." Bill had to stop for a moment to compose himself. The three listeners certainly understood the need, for they too were deeply moved by the moment. We watched him take another deep breath before he continued. "And then," he said very softly, "he faded into nothingness. He just faded away." I quickly glanced at Pat and noticed a few tears were leaking from her eyes. *What courage,* I thought to myself.

The five of us sat in silence for a long while. It was a comfortable silence. Pat and Bill knew their story had been heard, accepted, and believed by dear friends, as did Jan and Everett know the same about their story. And I knew our lives would never be the same again. My heart was filled with gratitude and awe—grateful to be a part of whatever was unfolding, and overwhelmed by the courage of my friends. I wondered where we were headed.

Eventually, Everett took the lead. "Well, this has been quite a day, and the night is still reasonably young, but the truth is, I am famished." Turning to his beloved wife, he said. "Old girl, I know we agreed to pass on dessert this evening, but after that story, I think we all need some nourishment." Jan nodded in agreement, as did their guests.

"Shall we change from wine to coffee?" Everyone thought Jan's suggestion was a good one, and as friends often do, they all rose and followed their hosts into the kitchen. Everett made the coffee, while Jan sliced up a loaf of homemade zucchini bread, and I made my specialty, a fresh pitcher of ice water containing slices of lime, oranges, and cucumbers. The storytellers, of the moment, rested. I wondered if any other stories would be shared before the evening came to a close.

"It's amazing how quickly refreshments can be managed when there's a team approach," noted Jan. "And by the way, we can all feel righteous about this dessert. Since it's made with vegetables, we surely are committing no sins this evening." The group laughed together, settled around the table again, and relaxed into the moment.

"Oh, this is good, dear!" declared Everett. "My energy is coming back. It's amazing how exhausting it is listening to a good story, and telling it," he added. The Joneses agreed.

"We're so grateful to all of you," stated Pat. "For listening enthusiastically, and for not doubting us. What wonderful friends, you are! We were very nervous about sharing this adventure with anyone, because it is so, so odd. And you three have made it easy."

"Well, I have a question, if you're up for it," proposed Everett.

"Please!" responded Bill. "I think questions might help us sort through this experience. And we'll try to field your questions as best we can."

"It's a question based in curiosity," began Everett. "What did the old man look like?"

"Rather ordinary, wouldn't you say, Pat?"

"Yes, except for his intensity!"

"Everett, let me elaborate. He was ordinary in terms of any other Joe you might encounter. But, his attire was quite unordinary. He was wearing a business suit and tie. Remember, we were in the middle of nowhere. He certainly didn't have the appearance of someone traveling.

Physically, he was of dark complexion and dark gray hair. He looked like a professional type, probably in his early sixties, but I'm not good at judging people's ages. And he was slim and about your height. No actually, he was shorter than you. I'm sure of that." After Bill described the man, the three listeners just shook their heads.

"Unbelievable!" I managed to say.

Everett turned to Jan for guidance. They both knew what needed to be done. Turning to their friends, Everett smiled and shook his head again. "Dear Ones," he proceeded, "we are grateful for your willingness to share your story with us, and we are amazed. This morning when the three of us crossed paths on the trail, we found a beautiful spot under that fabulous old beech tree to rest for a while. And our friend here did us the favor of listening to a story that is different, yet similar to yours. It seems, my dear friends, we have had the pleasure of encountering the same gentleman, and we too were told to go to The Island in the most emphatic manner."

"Oh, my!" exclaimed Pat. "I can't believe it! How can this be? Did he disappear before your eyes?"

Jan replied to Pat's question. "Not exactly, dear. We were momentarily engaged because like you, we were trying to figure out how to handle the situation, and when we turned back to address him, he was gone. We both looked up and down the airport concourse, but he simply wasn't there, and there was absolutely no way he could have exited that area during the brief time we consulted with one another. So no, he did not fade away in front of our eyes, but yes, he did disappear.

"What is going on here, Everett?" asked Bill. "One story about this guy is crazy enough, but two is beyond comprehension. I'm just blown away!"

"I don't understand this any better than you, Bill, but hold onto your chair, because we're not the only ones who have seen him." Pat dropped her fork in response to the news, and embarrassingly retrieved it.

"You've got to be kidding. This isn't possible!" said Bill. Everett concisely shared the same experiences with Pat and Bill as he and Jan had done with me. The Joneses listened with the same respect and intensity as we had listened to their story. All the superlatives that one can imagine were issued around the table, but when all was said and done, we were left with the same confusion and wonderment with which had begun the day.

"As bewildering as this is, I find it both exciting and comforting. Something very amazing is transpiring, and it clearly isn't confined to one small area of the world. This gentleman must, in fact, be a seasoned traveler, because he certainly gets around." My friends chuckled at the humor of that statement. "And I will repeat for you two what I earlier said to Jan and Everett. I don't believe in coincidences. This is happening for a reason and the reality that these encounters are being validated and affirmed is even more evidence that it is happening for a reason. Thank goodness you shared your stories.

If you hadn't you would be left alone with this oddity, but as it is, you have company. You are not alone!

The composition of the stories is bringing more information to bear. You were told you must go to The Island," I said looking at the Smiths. "Then you were told you were suppose to go there. And the women you overheard at the airport were informed they were intended to go there. Wendy was told what she was seeking would be found on The Island and she needed to go there because the time was now. And you two," she said pointing to the Joneses, "were apprised you needed to go to The Island, because The Island needs you." My mind was desperately trying to sort things out, but was failing miserably.

"What do we hear in these messages?" I asked. Responding to my own question, each point was emphasized by raising the appropriate number of fingers of my right hand. "First, there is a strong, insistent message of purpose informing the recipient that he or she must do something; i.e., go to The Island." Glancing around the table, I could see my friends were actively engaged, which encouraged me to continue. "Second, the message insinuates intention, a calling, if you will, that one must fulfill a mission of some kind that is transpiring upon The Island. Third, we hear a sense of urgency and need. You must go! The time is now! What you seek is on The Island! The Island needs you! And fourth, the message appears to be an appeal for assistance. You must go! This is more of a plea than a command. And it seems to be mutually serving. Something is on The Island that you, the recipients, need, and The Island needs those, who are being called, because it is in need.

Holy Smokes! I don't know what was just said, but I'm rather certain it was important."

"Not to worry, dear. I'm taking notes." Jan didn't even look up. She was furiously trying to take everything down.

"Good grief!" I declared. "There's another aspect of this that is equally profound. You four have risked your reputations by telling these stories. Thank goodness, you opened up to friends first, because you needed a good trial run, and I think we would all agree that you got it." Heads nodded and murmurings of agreement circled the table. "The point is my friends, by telling these stories, you are spreading the message. Indeed, the elder gentleman gets around, but when people, such as you, share their stories of encountering him, the message will travel more rapidly, and if what I'm sensing is correct, that's a part of this. The time is now! Even though the mystery is still unclear to all of us, it seems evident the incidents are intended to inform the public that something is going on.

There is more going on than we can explain, but we cannot deny something very important is happening here and we have a role to play in this unfolding process.

My goodness! This is so exciting. Thank you for sharing your stories and allowing me to be a part of this…whatever this is! I am ecstatically happy!"

"Thank you, dear friend," expressed Everett, "for responding the way you did on the trail this morning. If you hadn't treated us with such respect and trust, I doubt we would be having this discussion tonight."

"Well, gratitude abounds at this table." I reached out to Everett and to Bill, who in turned reached out to their beloved spouses. "We gather as old friends, sharing the blessings of trust and acceptance that exist among us. And we marvel at the increasing awareness flowing through us—the belief that is sparking our imaginations and insisting there is more. Yes, dear friends, there is more; now is the time for us to believe!"

*A passage from*
***The Time is Now***
*(Chapter Eight)*

> *"In the early stages of the mission, the volunteers and the Ones of Chosen Roles prepared for the mission with conscientious deliberation. Each pursued diligently the data necessary to perform their purpose and each offered willingly their experience for this cause of extreme importance.*
>
> *So concerned were the residents of the Universal Family for the newest members of the Family that none hesitated to offer their services and their experiences for this Mission of Rescue."*

"Dear Ones, what shall we do now?" Jan's question was one of extreme sincerity. The night was advancing and everyone was growing weary, and yet, no one really wanted to say good night. "This has been such a remarkable evening. So, my question still stands. What shall we do?"

"Let's schedule another time to meet," replied Pat. "We need to talk more about all this. And particularly after we have had some time to process everything, I think it would really be a good idea to see each other again." Everyone concurred. A time was set, and the five friends ended the evening.

There is more going on than we can explain, but we can certainly say something very important is happening here and we have a role to play in this unfolding process. Oh, goodness! This is so exciting. Thank you for sharing your stories and allowing me to be a part of this, whatever this is! I am so incredibly happy."

"Thank you, dear," [illegible] expressed. "Everything, including the way it [illegible] the trail this morning [illegible] would be having this discussion tonight."

"Much gratitude abounds at this table." I reached out to [illegible] Bill [illegible] friends [illegible] sharing the blessings [illegible] And we [illegible] sparkle your imagination [illegible] is more. [illegible] believe!"

*[illegible]*

*The Time is Now*

*[illegible]*

*[illegible]*

"Well, Pat, what shall we do now?" This question was one that [illegible] sincerely. The hour was advancing, and everyone was growing weary, and yet none of us really wanted to say good night. "This has been quite a remarkable evening," [illegible]. "What shall we do?"

"Let's schedule another time to meet," replied Pat. "We need to talk more about all this. And perhaps after we have had some time to process everything. I think it would really be a good idea to see each other again."

Everyone concurred. A time was set and the five friends ended the evening.

# ~ CHAPTER SIX ~

"Are you awake, Dear?" The whisper whispered came from a whisperer who desperately needed another to hear her.

"Yes," a whisper replied.

"Oh, thank goodness! I've been awake for what seems an eternity. Are you available to talk, dear?" As Everett listened to his beloved, he knew she was ready to hit the trail. *How does she do it,* he wondered.

"Am I to understand you are wide awake and ready for your morning walk?" he asked knowing full well what the answer would be.

"Well, yes and no," Jan replied, which was not the answer Everett was expecting. "Yes, I am wide awake, but no, I would rather not walk this morning, if you're okay with that." Her husband rolled over to inspect the situation, which was not only unexpected, but also very odd.

"Are you feeling all right, my Love? Are you out of sorts this morning or feeling puny?"

"No, no, not at all," she responded. "I would just like to talk, and thought it might be nice to do so from the comfort of our bed. Now put your thinking cap on for a moment, Everett. If this doesn't work for you, please tell me. If you would prefer not to talk, or if you would like to begin your day in some other way, just be forthright about it."

"Jan, are you trying to take care of me?" asked her husband. His question set her to thought. While she labored over the idea, Everett wrangled with the idea that she might be putting her needs aside for his. *Doesn't seem fair! Wouldn't want her doing that!*

"Once again, the answer is yes and no," she said. "I certainly am and want to take your needs into consideration, Dear, and you must simply allow me to do so, but in this particular circumstance, I truly would prefer to just lounge around for a while. My mind is processing last night's conversation, and it would be helpful to discuss it with you. But it can wait, if necessary."

Everett paused. He was so grateful for his beloved, and for his life with her. After all these years, he never tired to be with her. His inclination always was to be with her, no matter the time of day, but he also recognized the need to discover what approach would facilitate his own self-exploration process. Clearly, his dear sweet wife was offering him an opportunity to practice this morning. The truth was, discussing the events of last night would be extremely beneficial for both of them. Since he was relatively certain his restlessness was some how involved with the topics regarding The Island, he felt a conversation enjoyed from the comfort of their bed was an admirable idea.

"I think your idea is a good one, Jan! We do have a lot to talk about and it would be nice to do it here. Do you prefer breakfast in bed, my Love, or shall we wait until later?" His question sparked excitement.

"Oh, my, breakfast in bed! Do we dare?" Everett giggled as he prepared himself for Act I, the scene that originated in the bedroom, and Jan did not fail him. "Everett, my Dear," she declared in the most exaggerated southern accent she could muster. "I simply cannot rise this morning. Can we dine in bed, my Love? It is such a sensual setting for a sumptuous meal." And after this melodramatic production, Jan continued the performance by fluttering her eyes in that over-the-top theatrical way only few actresses have mastered. And then the two of them both burst into laughter.

After the curtain had fallen on Act I, they both agreed hunger was not yet upon them and agreed to just linger in the moment.

"So tell me, Love. Where are your thoughts this morning?" Everett knew Jan had been awake for sometime, but had decided it was better to simply let her be with her own thoughts. He knew Jan was awake because he was as well. And his mind also had awakened to thoughts of the evening before.

"Well, I keep remembering what Bill said last night when he found out we, and others, also had encounters with the quote-quote mystery man. 'What is going on here, Everett?' were his exact words. And that is the question, isn't it? What is going on here?" As they rested side by side, the question penetrated their thoughts.

"The summation our friend provided was stellar," commented Everett. "The idea this message is intentionally being provided and that it is also intended to spread to others is a riveting premise. And we certainly witnessed it in motion throughout the day. Because we shared the story in the morning, we were open and ready to share it again when the Joneses revealed their experience. All four of us were afraid of undesirable reactions, and that simply didn't happen. In fact, it was just the opposite, and as a result, we will be more inclined to continue sharing our story. And as was revealed, by sharing these stories the listeners are then involved with the message as well. It truly is remarkable!"

"Yes, I agree, and in fact, I have my notes right here," she said reaching over to the bedside table. "It does seem, as if, we are involved in some type of mission, and part of the objective is to spread the message about whatever the mission is addressing. So, if we are interpreting things correctly, then we have been targeted, or called, to help with this unknown mission." Pausing, they both took time for more cogitation. Their minds were ecstatic about this unexpected, but very welcomed conundrum. Nothing pleases the human mind more than a mystery to ponder and solve.

"The other notion that was brought out in the summation was the sense of urgency projected by the old man and his message. That rings true for me," admitted Everett. "I do feel a sense of urgency that there is something I'm suppose to be addressing, and for the life of me I don't know what it is. Do you relate to this, Jan?"

"Oh, yes, absolutely! This is the restlessness we've been feeling, and what Pat and Bill alluded to as well. What are we to do?" she asked. "Obviously, this unusual experience happened. It's real. And we certainly have plenty of information indicating we are not alone in this weird turn of events, but what is so confounding is the lack of direction. We are told we are needed, but not provided information on how we can be of assistance. It's just so excruciating! What are we to do?"

"Perhaps, there is more than one answer to this question, Jan," posed her beloved. "Well, please excuse that statement. I imagine there are many answers to it, depending upon who asks the question. But for us in particular, I'm wondering if we are intended to pursue at least two paths. One, we've already started. We are spreading the word about this unusual gentleman who appears from out of nowhere and adamantly apprises the recipient of his message about a commitment made to The Island."

Jan immediately intervened, "Everett, Dear, listen to what you just said! The old man apprises the recipient of a commitment made to The Island. A commitment! What a fascinating choice of words! Did you think that up, or did it just come to you? Was it an intuitive response, Dear?" Jan's questions flustered her husband.

"I don't really know. It just seemed right." Everett puzzled over his choice of words. "It feels, as if, I am trying to fulfill some commitment I've made, and yet, there is no memory of any such commitment. Actually, Dear, I'm not sure if commitment is the correct word to utilize, but my sense of urgency identifies with this. I feel, as if, I'm suppose to fulfill some responsibility that I've agreed to do. It's very bizarre! I feel like I've forgotten something. Something very important!"

"Wow!" was the only word that Jan could grab onto. Her mind, trying desperately to understand what was happening, worked frenetically as if it were guided by its own intentions. Jan knew it was time to take action, and she did by taking a deep breath followed by several more. And she invited Everett to join her. "The truth is," she asserted, "these ideas are exhilarating in ways similar to riding a roller coaster. The highs are great and fun-filled one minute, and the next minute, the highs are based in anxiety. "We both need to get grounded!" Everett followed her lead and benefitted from the simple, yet effective technique. Her response to the runaway mind was a wise choice.

"Whew!" she began again. "Well, that was a good reminder. Sorry, Dear, but I was captured by your insightfulness. When you tapped into the idea of commitment, it really rang true for me and my mind just took off like a rocket. It was trying to investigate every possible avenue to discover the source of this commitment we've made, and quite honestly, I was getting lost in the workings of my highly overactive mind. I just had to reel it in and stop for a few minutes. Hopefully, you weren't bothered by my need to shutdown."

"No, not at all, Love. In fact, it was extremely helpful. I didn't realize how enraptured my mind was with the idea of a commitment, until you suggested the deep breathing exercise. It was good role modeling, dear. And I feel much better equipped now to deal with this notion of being involved with some mysterious commitment."

"Oh, good, I'm glad to hear it was useful for you." Jan took another deep breath. "It's amazing to me how excitable this work is and it appears the excitability can be both positive and negative. We need to keep track of this, Dear, and try to do a better job of managing our energy." Pausing briefly as if to gather her thoughts, Jan returned to the topic. "I suspect, Everett, the way our minds reacted is information. You've really hit upon something here, which seems extremely important to me. If we are dealing with some type of unknown commitment, it might explain not only the feeling of urgency we both share, but also the uncomfortable mood of helplessness. Obviously, if we are being driven by an inner sense of responsibility without knowing how to address it, we would be experiencing extreme unrest and confusion. Which, of course, we are!"

"If we are interpreting things correctly, which we can only hope we are, then we are left with the same question. What are we to do?" The question brought them both to silence. And they luxuriated in it. The dear old friends, the love of each other's life, were content to simply rest in the silence. They deserved it! Little did they know how much work lay ahead.

*A passage from*
***The Time is Now***
*(Chapter Nine)*

*"When in the final stages of preparation, All joined in unified connection and focused their intentions on the success of their endeavors. Never had so many given so much to help those in need. To serve was expected and considered an honor, but none had served in this manner before, and the willingness to brave such circumstances stunned even those of most ancient age.*

*This situation of such profound and unusual circumstances created more unknowns than ever known before. And of all the unknowns, only this was known. The children were in need of assistance, and the Watchers of the Universe were determined to provide the assistance."*

"Are you awake, Dear?" whispered the whisperer again. A deep sigh came from the direction of the opposite side of the bed.

"Yes, Love, I am, and obviously, you are as well." Everett replied. "I assume the need for a walk has overpowered you."

"Actually hunger has. Are you ready to get up now? If not, I'll muddle on alone," she said in her most pathetic voice. They both agreed above all else, food was on the top of their needs list. They rose, quickly dressed, and headed for the kitchen. Interestingly, neither dressed for a walk.

Several blocks away, the Joneses were deep in conversation. Like their friends, the Smiths, they too had awakened early, but were not inclined to leave the comfort of their home. Even though both of them were unusually hungry this morning, they managed to eat a sensible breakfast. Visions of pastries danced in their minds, but each resisted the temptation and refused to engage in the enticing discussion of maybes. Maybe, we could have a tasty this or a tasty that, which always led to indulgences, conspired by mutual consent.

Their morning began in discussion about the previous night's revelations, and continued through breakfast, and then relocated to their favorite conversational area in the house. Long ago, Pat and Bill had created a small sitting area in their bedroom, which ended up being the preferred location for conversations from the heart. Their chairs, comfortable from years of use, were strategically located for one-on-one engagement.

"Bill, the expression on that man's face before he disembarked burns in my memory. He wasn't ordering us, as we first presumed. He was pleading with us to go to The Island. Now that I understand this, my heart aches. Someone is in need, and we're suppose to help." Her husband nodded in agreement. He too felt the same sense of helplessness.

"You know, I woke up early this morning, feeling that sense of urgency we discussed last night. It's puzzling, because we are not people who are led by suggestions. Yes, the old man had a huge effect upon us, but it's more than just his manner, his message, and his unusual appearance and disappearance." Bill shivered trying to grasp definition of his discontentment. "I wish there were words to explain how I'm feeling. It's like there's something inside of me driving me to do something, but I don't know what the something is, and as a result of my confusion, I don't know which direction to turn. How can we possibly take action when we have so little information?"

Pat commiserated with her husband's frustration and confusion and admitted she too had awakened earlier with the idea of trying to find the old man again. "But how?" she asked. "Would he appear again if we returned to that overlook site again, or do we need to go the Delhi airport, or walk the streets of New York? How on Earth can we get in touch with him, so that we can get more information?" Exhaling loudly, she questioned, "Why didn't he give us more information? It doesn't make sense. If he could appear out of nowhere and apprise us of The Island, why didn't he give us directions and instructions? It's like throwing a party and not telling the guests where it's being held!"

"Pat, I think we just have to take this one day at a time—one moment at a time actually. When either of us has an idea, let's jot it down, so we don't forget. And we need to practice some of the things we've learned recently. We need to meditate. We need to seek within," he said with an air of disbelief. "What does that mean?" Bill started to laugh at himself and Pat joined him.

"You're right, dear. We do need to start somewhere, and if meditation is practiced by millions of people every day, as was suggested in the workshop, then perhaps, there's something to it. You know, the few times, we've done it we were pleased. It was relaxing, and I can see that it might take us down new paths of exploration. So, let's do it!" declared Pat.

"Now?" Surprised by the idea, Bill waffled a bit.

"Yes, now!" she answered.

I arrived at the office early. My mind, still enthralled by the conversation from the previous evening, was impeding my work. I tried bribery, but it didn't work. The mind prefers mystery to any other topic. I pleaded, emphatically stating work had to come first. The mind had no pity. Work was work, after all. Mystery was an adventure.

All too well, do I know the ineffectiveness of asking for cooperation from the mind that has a mind of its own. Its preferences trump all others, and its willfulness is formidable. Fortunately, my ability to focus when in a session always outplays the mind's undisciplined manners.

The paperwork I had hoped to diminish from my desk became a neatly stacked pile when my first client arrived. I attended my daily ritual, expressing gratitude for all my blessings and seeking guidance for and assistance with the clients to be seen throughout the day. Then I entered the waiting room and invited the young woman back to my office. As is my way, the session begins with conversation, and then, when the moment is right, the client proceeds to the table where we engage in energy work.

On that particular day, the client was inclined to speak of another rather than herself. She respectfully asked permission to do so and I assured her the decision was hers. She proceeded to say a friend had experienced an unusual incident recently that she, meaning the client, would like to discuss with me. I listened with interest and curiosity.

In story form, she related her friend's incident. It will come as no surprise to any of you who are reading this book that the friend's story included an encounter with a man of dark complexion, gray hair, wearing a suit and tie. "Please tell me everything," I said.

"Well, my friend is someone who enjoys meditating, particularly in churches. She finds the energy in a church very comforting and believes her meditations are more successful in those settings than anywhere else."

"I see," said I in my most attentive voice. "So this is something the two of you have in common."

"Yes, that's true," she replied. "I do enjoy meditating in churches as well. Anyway," she continued, "a couple of weeks ago, my friend visited a church she was unfamiliar with and found much to her surprise the church was empty. The idea of having the church all to herself thrilled my friend, so she decided to take advantage of the moment. She selected what she believed to be the perfect pew, and then found the perfect spot along the pew to sit. So she did, and quickly went into her practice.

She indicated it was a lovely meditation, one in which you lose yourself and then discover the most delightful truths about you. As she told her story, you could feel her excitement, and I was very happy for her. I asked her where the church was located, but she was hesitant to tell me, which was a surprise. And then, my friend said there was more she wanted to tell me." My client paused and took a very long deep breath. I wondered what was coming.

"Well, it seems as meditations go, this one was a winner. When my friend finished her journey into the inner world, she continued to sit quietly, still with eyes closed, simply enjoying the reverie of the moment. She was very happy. And finally, she felt complete, so she opened her eyes and was startled to see an older gentleman standing in the next row staring at her.

I immediately asked my friend if he had harmed her and she reassured me he had not. In fact, she said she was not the least bit frightened by him because his eyes were filled with love and compassion. She felt blessed to be in his presence. She smiled at him and he returned the smile and when she asked if she could be of assistance, he bowed to her. She introduced herself to him, and he just nodded, as if he already knew her. And then, the most remarkable thing happened. He moved closer, looked deeply into her eyes, and quietly said, 'Old Friend, you must come home. The Island needs you.' Well, as you might imagine, she was taken aback. His sincerity was not questioned, but she had no idea what he was talking about. Fortunately, she had her wits about her and immediately responded. 'I don't understand,' she said, 'please tell me more.' This man sounds so remarkable. I mean, just telling you about it gives me goose bumps.

Well, he again looked lovingly into her eyes, and spoke in his interesting way. 'Do not be afraid, Old Friend. The way will be given. Continue as you do now, and the way will become known. Listen with the ears of the heart. The time is now! The Island is in great need. In peace be, my Old Friend.'

My friend said it was the most stunning experience of her life." My client and I sat in silence. I could not believe what had just transpired, and yet, I was not surprised. Eventually, I found my voice.

"What do you make of this?" I asked.

"I absolutely believe her! My friend is not one to exaggerate or tell tall tales. I believe everything she told me.

"I do too!" Again, silence befell the room.

The remaining part of the session took place in the area of my office that is devoted to energy work. The client rested on the table, as energy facilitation and distribution transpired. What happened was what always happens in these sessions. Spirit addresses what is intended and the recipient of the energy is in a better place because of it.

After the energy session concluded, the client prepared to leave. She put her shoes back on, gathered her belongings, and then looking directly into my eyes. "You said earlier that you believe my friend's story. Do you really?"

"Oh, yes, I really do. And if your friend ever wishes to talk about this, please tell her that I am a believer." Eye contact was made, smiles were exchanged, and another appointment was scheduled.

After the last session of the day was done, I closed the door to my office and just sat in the space where so many wonderful experiences had been enjoyed. *I am so grateful! Not a day goes by that I do not feel your Presence. Thank you for all that is done on behalf of all who are in need. Thank you for letting me participate, and please continue to guide and assist me.* Time passed as it does when one is in the moment, and I chose to fully embrace this precious time. The last few days had been remarkable and I was curious about what was unfolding.

"Old Friends," I spoke aloud. "It appears you are up to something. I am confused and extremely curious. May I be of assistance? Perhaps my offer is premature, but just know that I am ready to serve if needed. As you know, Dear Friends, I do not believe in coincidences. It appears to me I am in the right place at the right time, so if I can be of help, just let me know." Sitting quietly for a while, I listened carefully, but no response was forthcoming. I took it as a sign. "Maybe later," I said with a smile on my face.

And with that said, I gathered up the stack of paperwork and placed it in a satchel with great intentions of sorting through the lingering task at home later in the evening. But until then, there was ample time for a jaunt in the hills.

# ~ Chapter Seven ~

"Hello there!" came a voice from out of nowhere, or so it seemed, but upon turning around there was one of my dearest friends coming up the trail. Huffing and puffing, she hurried towards me. Exchanging hugs and greetings, she informed me she had been hurrying along behind trying to catch up with me. "You're walking with gusto today, old friend!"

"Am I?" I was surprised. Lost in thought, I was unaware of my pace. "Well, it is very good to see you and I'm glad you've come along. It's been a while. Tell me everything. What have you been up to?" My friend was one of my favorite walking companions. Like me, she enjoyed heartfelt conversations, but also embraced the silence. There were days when our walks were non-stop conversation, and others that were primarily held in silence. On this occasion, I was certain it would be the former type of excursion.

Having already walked a couple of miles into the hilly countryside, we agreed another mile inward would be suitable before we turned homeward bound. "So, we haven't had a chance to talk since you went to that conference a few weeks ago. How was it? Did you have a good time? Were the presenters as good as you were anticipating?" Realizing my mouth was on autopilot, I stopped and apologized. "Oh, excuse me, friend, for bombarding you with questions. I'm just so glad to see you that my curiosity is overriding good manners. Please take the lead, Marilyn!"

Marilyn Brown was another friend of long standing. We met decades ago at a workshop that was on a topic I no longer remember, but it was the beginning of our long-term friendship, which has withstood many of life's circumstances. We've shared many good times together and also the difficult times that life naturally brings. And through it all, we learned to trust and rely upon each other.

"Goodness, has it been that long since we talked. No wonder you've been on my mind so much lately. When I saw you up ahead on the trail, my hearted just started pounding with excitement. It is so good to be with you! I'm sorry not to have connected sooner. Time gets away from us sometimes, doesn't it?" We walked arm-in-arm for a bit enjoying each other's company.

"So," she continued, "the conference was a hoot! Saw some folks I hadn't seen in a while. Got to catch up with them, which was nice, and by the way, Anne Billings said to give you a hug. Consider it given! She has something she wants to talk to you about—said she would be calling you soon. Several people asked about you and were disappointed you couldn't come. Suffice it to say, dear, you were missed!

The conference itself was worth the travel time and expense. The presenters did a wonderful job and the experiential exercises were very powerful. There was a woman from Scotland who was particularly interesting. You would love her! She's one of those people you could sit and listen to for hours. Great stories, great energy! Just a good soul, you know what I mean! Anyway, she was exceptionally bright, energetically and intellectually. Expansive thinker! She is very impressive, and intriguing." *Interesting choice of words*, I thought.

"I think she is someone we might want to pursue. Her knowledge base is founded in much more than just academics. We could definitely learn from this one!"

"I'm interested! Do you know if she will be doing any other workshops in the states?" Marilyn indicated the woman wasn't certain about it. "I encouraged her to come again, but she was noncommittal. But we did exchange contact information so we will be able to keep in touch with her. Undoubtedly, she does a lot of workshops and training in Great Britain, so I'm going to keep track of her. Can't imagine traveling that far, but quite frankly, it would be worth it. I'll send you her website link so you can check her out for yourself." It was obvious my friend had really been inspired by this presenter's work, so I was eager to view the website and find out more about her. I was still curious about the description Marilyn had used...*Intriguing!*

"And what about you?" my friend asked. "How is your world? And what have you been up to in recent weeks. Tell me everything." Marilyn always enjoyed turning those three words on me frequently reminding me that it was only fair. *You expect it of me* she would declare with great delight, so it is only fair that *I expect it of you. Tell me EVERYTHING*! Just thinking of my friend's good nature made me happy. She was a joy to be with, and a dear friend, for whom I am eternally grateful.

"Well, let me see," I said both to Marilyn and to myself. So much had happened in just the last few days, that I was torn. Of course, the inclination was to share everything with my dear friend, but the reality was, the stories, I was privy to, were not mine to share. I grabbed her by the arm again and we walked together arm-in-arm as I pondered how to handle this dilemma. Truthfully, I knew which alternative had to be honored. Although my excitement about the stories of the mysterious island and the old man was boundless, I could not share these stories without permission. It was frustrating, but it was what it was. "My friend, I am in an awkward position in that a mystery is afoot, which of course, I want to discuss with you; however, at this time, I cannot do so."

"Oh, drat!" she declared. "That's such a bother! It's the old confidentiality thing, isn't it?" I nodded in agreement and commiserated with her disappointment.

"May I ask you something, Marilyn?" she assured me that I could. "Are you aware of something going on in the universe, as it were? Excuse the phrasing of that question, but I'm not sure how else to ask. It seems to me something is up, and yet, whatever it is, eludes me." I laughed at myself and openly admitted I sounded like a nut case. Marilyn was one of the few people I could ask such a befuddled question.

"Well, of course, you don't sound like a nut case, dear. I mean, you are a nut, we all know this about you, but no, you definitely are not a nut case." Marilyn grinned her best-friend smile and then returned to focus. "What I'm hearing is you feel something is going on in the greater reality? Is that correct?" My nod affirmed her question.

"You know your intuitive senses are stellar, dear," my friend proceeded. "I trust your intuition without question or doubt. Obviously, something is going on that is making you ask this question. Can you tell me anything more without betraying confidences?" My hesitation was telling.

"I seem to be aligning with something. Forgive me for overusing that word, but I'm struggling here. It's really very odd, but recently I have heard about several experiences different people have had in different locations around the globe, and what is so remarkable is the similarity of the experiences. Now, obviously the events themselves are the issue at hand; however, I seem to be serendipitously in the right places at the right time to hear about these experiences. As we both agree, the idea of coincidences is based in misunderstanding. These events are odd. My association with and to these varied events is odd. And as odd as it seems, I believe this is all happening for a reason, but as yet, the bigger picture is not being revealed to me. So what am I to do?" *There it is again*, I mused. *The question that keeps popping up for everyone!*

We walked in silence for a while, each meandering in the chambers of our respective minds. I wondered what my role was in this situation. *Surely, I am hearing these stories for a reason. Am I just to be a listener, a sounding board for those who were actually having the experiences? That doesn't make a lot of sense to me. Surely there must be more for me to do.* I thought again about the sense of urgency shared by the witnesses and wondered if I was hearing these stories, because I too was one intended to spread the messages to others. That seemed reasonable to me, but it also necessitated permission to retell the stories. My mind created an image of a large conference room, where people from many different settings gathered to share the encounters each had experienced with the old man and The Island. *What an interesting conference that would be!* As my mind wandered to and fro, my friend, Marilyn had her own inner discussion.

*Well, this is interesting,* she thought to herself. *Once again, the universe is speaking and we are unclear of its messages. I wonder why this is? Is it a matter of evolution? Or are we just so distracted by our lives that we are unable to hear the communications clearly? How am I to help my friend today? Are listening ears enough or is there more for me to do?*

"*Share what was recently heard.*" Marilyn smiled also wondering about the issue of confidentiality. *"Conceal the identity. No name need be shared."* Always, the inclination to ask why rushes through the mind, and yet, what is needed is given. The direction Marilyn received was clear, because she was present to hear it.

"Are we ready to talk again?" Marilyn asked politely.

"Oh, let's do! And thank, you for listening, my friend. It was helpful!" I encouraged her to go first, and she responded accordingly, knowing I needed to be the listener for a while.

"Your comment about something going on in the universe begs one to wonder. Of course, something is always going on, we both know that to be true, but there are times when we seem more aware or more engaged with whatever is unfolding. It brought to mind something that happened at the conference." She chuckled a bit noting the word 'something' was certainly getting a workout. I smiled in agreement and then urged her to tell me more.

"The conference was organized so that every afternoon included a two hour break. It was suggested we use the time for reflection, the soul-searching part of the conference that hopefully fosters deepening and expansion. By the third day, I was not in the mood for another session of gut-wrenching inner work, so I found a lovely, unclaimed bench on the property and decided to just bask in the sun. It was wonderful! My mind went blank, and I just zoned out. At some point, another attendee of the conference came by and asked if she could join me. Of course, I said yes, what else can one do? She obviously hadn't noticed I had claimed the bench for myself!" We giggled together, remembering numerous conversations previously shared about our alone time being disturbed by an innocent passerby.

"Apparently, she also was in need of quiet time because once she sat down, not a word was spoken between us for quite some time. And then the silence was broken. She respectfully asked if I was open to conversation, and at that point my mood had shifted, and the idea was suitable to me. I turned to engage with her. We introduced ourselves, admiringly acknowledged the grounds of the conference center, shared thoughts about the conference itself, and then, the conversation shifted. It became personal." Marilyn was masterful in her delivery. Her pauses were perfection, quietly presented.

"She told me she had recently had a most interesting encounter, and wondered, if she could share it with me. She apologized for her forward manner, confessing she hadn't shared the experience with anyone, but was in need of doing so. She said, 'I find myself in need of a listening ear.' Well, her manner was anything, but forward. She was gracious. And I was mesmerized by her presence even before the story was told." As Marilyn finessed another sublime pause, I wondered what was about to transpire. My curiosity, needing a seatbelt, was racing out of control.

*A passage from*
***The Time is Now***
*(Chapter Ten)*

> *"As the Ones of Ancient Age grew in their awareness of the complexities of the galactic event, more in knowingness were they of the disaster about to occur. And in this knowingness, All agreed an action was required. So odd was this circumstance that the Ones of Ancient Age were in amazement. How could this have happened? Why did it happen? Who could have been responsible for such a happening?*
>
> *The questions posed more questions, which posed more, and from all these questions, only one answer appeared true. Natural circumstances."*

"Apparently, the woman was in great conflict. Obviously, she wanted and needed to talk, but her reticence was heartbreaking. I just wanted to hold her in my arms and reassure her everything would be okay, but intuition informed me that approach would not be well taken. I would like to say I patiently waited for her to begin, but such a statement would be a falsehood. Impatience overtook me and many deep breaths had to be quietly consumed before the woman mustered the courage to continue. She began by telling me she was a seeker of the truth, which often led her to distant places. 'My heart guides me where to go,' she softly revealed. 'Sometimes, I am surprised at how diligently I follow my heart's leadership, but there are moments when doubts and questions overcome my sensibility. Such moments are a sign for me to return to center.

I tell you this so you have a small sense of who I am and what I am about. Hopefully, it will help you understand my present state of confusion.'"

"My goodness," I interrupted. "She sounds like a remarkable woman!"

Marilyn agreed with my assessment and assured me the woman was the most impressive individual she had ever encountered. "She went on to explain that her passion involves ancient knowledge and then quietly remarked, 'There is a knowing in the universe which transcends all. This source of awareness is available to all, for it resides within us, even if we are unaware of its presence.' I just looked at her in awe and acknowledged she spoke the truth beautifully. She blushed slightly, thanked me, and then continued her story. She explained her job required a great deal of travel. Although she didn't elaborate about her work, she indicated the work related trips often allowed her to have personal excursions. It was of a recent excursion she wished to talk about.

She had registered for a tour to the highlands of Tibet. She was pleased with the tour guide and the other travelers, but on one of their outings, chose to fall back from the rest of the group. In need of some solitude, she explained to her companions she wanted to walk in silence for a while, and reassured them she would keep the party in sight. The walk was undoubtedly very meaningful. When she reminisced about it, tears filled her eyes. At one point, she leaned in closer to me and somewhat shyly whispered, 'I felt at One with All That Is and it was pure ecstasy.' Again, I must repeat she was a very impressive woman. Her admission that she didn't want to leave Tibet didn't surprise me; her comments indicated the countryside felt like home to her. At some point along the way, the group ahead stopped to rest, so she did the same about a hundred feet short of their location. Selecting a particularly appealing boulder to lean against, she pulled out a snack, and settled in for a brief rest. She remembers nodding off, not from fatigue, but from the sheer joy of the experience. It was the happiest time of her life.

For reasons unknown to her she awoke abruptly, concerned the group may have started without her. They had not and were, in fact, still enjoying the well-deserved rest, so she grabbed a journal from her backpack and settled in for a moment of reflection. Her feelings poured out filling many pages in mere minutes. She was relieved to have her experiences recorded, and hoped she would never forget this incredible time. Taking a deep breath, she closed her eyes, and merged with the land. Isn't that remarkable?" Marilyn noted. "This woman remembers that moment, as if it were but a moment ago, and when she speaks of it, you can feel the intensity of the union she experienced." Marilyn looked towards me to see if I understood the beauty of the experience. I nodded reassuring her that I did. My mind continued to anticipate the situation as I wondered what next would come.

"So, this beautiful lady is sitting beside me on our private bench, and she clams up again. You could feel her anxiety. I knew there was more she wanted to share, but she was unsure. I don't know if it was because I was a stranger and she didn't know if she could trust me, or if there was some other reason holding her back. But once again, my heart ached for her. There was nothing I could do, but hold the space for her. She desperately needed someone to hear her story, but the timing was in her command. No one could rush her. So I waited, and this time, it was with a compassionate heart.

Well," Marilyn continued, "the next thing that happened is really weird. I'm telling you, it's going to blow you away, so fasten your seat belts." Grinning, I pretended to strap myself down.

"So, there she is, eyes are closed, and she is communing with the land. And then, she gradually opens her eyes and sitting directly in front of her is an older man staring at her with very loving eyes. Obviously, she was surprised. He wasn't a member of the tour group and he clearly wasn't dressed for a hike in the Tibetan highlands, but there he was nonetheless.

Unclear what was happening, she relied upon good manners. She greeted him respectfully and introduced herself, expecting he would respond in like manner. He smiled, he noticeably bowed, but he did not speak. Not knowing how to proceed, she decided to pose a question or two. First, she asked him what is name was, and he just smiled again. Then she asked from where do you come? His smile became brighter, she said, and then, he pointed to the sky. Her response was one of puzzlement. And then, he leaned forward and gazed directly into her eyes, and said, 'It is good to see you, old friend! Your time has come. The Island calls. You must go to her. She needs your help. As was agreed so long ago, I bring the message forward. The time is now!' Well, you can imagine her astonishment! She asked for more information explaining that she didn't understand, but he just smiled. She sat there puzzled by the message, and then, he leaned closer again. 'The truth lies within. All that is needed you already possess. Seek within!'

Once again, she sat in amazement, but before she could pose any further questions, he vanished. He simply vanished!"

"This is unbelievable," I said for more reasons than my friend was aware. "What happened next?"

"An expression of relief washed over her. She just sat there for a few moments breathing deeply and regaining her composure. Eventually, she turned to face me and asked if I believed her. I assured her I did and thanked her from the bottom of my heart. Again, she was relieved. I asked if we could stay in touch and she was pleased. We exchanged emails and phone numbers.

And that was that! It was extraordinary! After I heard the entire story, her reticence became understandable. What courage it takes to share an experience such as that. I hope she felt heard and accepted. And believed! I really tried to impress upon her my belief in her story. Just hope she can hold on to it.

So, old friend of mine, what do you think?" I shook my head in wonderment. Marilyn did the same. I laughed out loud and Marilyn joined be in the hoopla. Engaging with a story such as this one demands a release of the pent-up energy that accumulates during the listening process. When the giggles founded in amazement finally faded, I answered my friend's question.

"I believe, old friend, something is definitely going on in the universe." We laughed some more, which was evidence of the tension we both were carrying, and then, Marilyn turned our focus back on point.

"Dear One," she started, "I believe the story just shared was done so with accuracy, and without revealing the identity of the remarkable person who shared it with me. I hope my behavior has been honorable. And now, I must share another tidbit with you."

"Please do," I responded. "My ears are available."

"Earlier, when we were walking in silence, I was wondering whether it was okay to share this woman's story with you and I was guided to do so. As we both know, when we receive guidance, it is for a reason. So tell me, friend, did this story have anything to do with your question about happenings in the universe?"

"Of course, it did, Marilyn. Something is definitely happening and obviously, we, you and I are somehow involved. Let's face it, dear, you didn't just happen to bow out of the soul-searching exercises. You didn't just happen to be sitting on that particular bench at that particular time and that impressive woman, as you refer to her, didn't just happen to select your chosen bench. Every step taken was taken for a reason. The event experienced with the older gentleman happened for a reason. You and the impressive woman crossed paths for a reason. The story was shared with you for a reason. You shared it with me for a reason. Everything was for a reason." Marilyn listened carefully, believing everything her friend was saying.

"Well then, what does this all mean?" she asked. "I take it you too have heard a story of similar nature, which at this time you do not feel can be shared. Nonetheless, the point is we have both been in the right place at the right time for a reason. I'm assuming you have had more time to think about this than me, so I'm curious. What are your thoughts?"

"My thoughts are many," I laughed again, and realized once more the joy of laughing with another. "Laughter completely alters one's energy, doesn't it? The laughter we've shared today has been refreshing, and it's been a joy. Thank you! But now back to your question. As I said, many thoughts have been churning within this fine mind of mine, but the one that immediately comes to mind is. What are we to do?" I paused, not in the masterful way that Marilyn achieved, but it was the best I could offer. "I've heard this question from several people of late, and the question now rings true for me, and for you. These experiences, these events, are happening for a reason, and we are being accessed as listeners for a reason. So, what are we to make of this? Are we here simply to listen and hopefully create some sense of comfort for the ones sharing the tale or do we hold greater responsibilities for these seemingly prophetic messages from the gentleman dressed in business suit and tie?

Is it possible we are supposed to assist in spreading his messages with the permission of those who have shared them with us? Is it possible we are to facilitate gatherings for these people so they do not feel alone, and so they can collaborate and coordinate their efforts?

Marilyn, my head spins with thoughts about this, which is good, but every so often, I just want to come back to the original wonder of it all. Something really big is going on in the universe, and I am absolutely intrigued."

*A passage from*
***The Time is Now***
*(Chapter Eleven)*

> *"No blame there is to lay upon any one. No responsibility does any one bear for this. No reason other than natural circumstances could be determined."*

At the end of the walk, the two old friends enjoyed a long hug. "You will keep me apprised of your decision-making process with the unusual happenings, I trust?" asked Marilyn.

"Yes, I will. A few more conversations must be had, but I think the path is unfolding. And since we are somehow joined in this excursion of intrigue, I most definitely will keep in touch."

# ~ CHAPTER EIGHT ~

"Frank, where are you, up or down?" Searching the main floor of their home and finding it occupied only by herself, Dee finally resorted to yelling out for her husband. Many a time, she thought a small megaphone would be useful. Of course, if Franklin Sanderson, husband of Deidre, would just keep his cell phone with him, these aimless searches wouldn't be necessary.

"I'm downstairs, dear. Will be up in minute." Relieved to hear his footsteps coming up the basement stairs, Dee proceeded to the kitchen and poured two cups of coffee. *He must have awakened with a creative spirit this morning*, she thought to herself. Frank's workshop/studio was located in the basement. Many hours were enjoyed down in his private sanctuary that brought great beauty into their lives and which brought peace to his heart. He was a man of many talents, including the art of being a wonderful husband. Dee lived in gratitude for the life they shared. As her husband of over five decades entered the kitchen, it was obvious he was hiding something behind his back. "Aha!" she declared. "I knew you were up to something! What gift of beauty have you created now? Please, let me see it?" Although Frank had been involved in some form of artistic endeavors most of his life, he still remained very shy about his work. An eclectic artist, he was one who needed variety. His wife never knew what to expect from one project to the next, because his talents included several areas of expertise. What she did know; however, was the reality of her husband's creative nature. Another project was always waiting and merely the twinkling of an eye away.

"Come, come, dear! Do let me see what divine gift you've created this time."

"Close your eyes, dear. You know the routine. We must do this with considerable fanfare, drum roll, etc." Dee quickly covered her eyes, and announced she was ready for the viewing. Frank staged the dinette table, so his masterpiece could be appropriately admired. Then he took a deep breath, which was Dee's signal he was about to take the leap, and then at last, she was invited to open her eyes.

"Oh, my!" She was stunned into silence by the woodturning he had placed in front of her. The vase rested proudly. A remarkable piece, turned from spalted maple in a design too beautiful to describe. She started to touch it, but caught herself, and then, with Frank's encouragement, she did. It was as smooth as glass. "Frank, this truly is your best piece yet; it's flawless."

"It's the piece of wood, Dee, not me," which is how he always replied to compliments about his woodturning skills. "Just look at the design created by the fungal decay. These blackish irregular lines are the defining features of the vase. One never knows what will be revealed when the wood block is mounted on the lathe. It's not about me, dear, it's about the One who created this beautiful piece of wood. That's the true creative process we're witnessing."

"You are a marvel, dear, and I love the way you speak about your work. I do agree with you about this particular piece of maple. My word, it is fabulous! But I also must acknowledge your design, meaning the shape of the vase itself, is wonderful. You haven't done one like this before, have you?" Frank agreed it was his first experiment with this particular shape. "And the finish is exquisite; it is perfectly smooth. Well done, Frank!" Her husband struggled with praise, but when all was said and done, he appreciated it.

"I'm glad you like it, dear. Perhaps, we can gift it to someone," he commented.

"Let's keep it for ourselves for a while, shall we? It's just so lovely, I would like to enjoy it before we pass it forward." Frank agreed and then finally sat down to his cup of coffee.

"What are you up to today, Dee?" he asked after his first sip. He looked like a man who had a plan, which was a clue for his wife to be available.

"Well, I'm not sure. My calendar is open. Do you have something in mind?" Her response was perfect, just what Frank wanted to hear.

"I was thinking about taking a drive up north into the hill county," he began. "I'd like to return to the area where this log was found," he said pointing to the new vase. "I really enjoyed working with the maple and would like to find another piece or two, if possible. May be long gone by now, but it would be a pretty drive, nonetheless. And we could take a walk in the piney woods, if you like."

"Your proposals are noteworthy," declared Dee in a most officious way, and then tenderly added. "As long as we're together, dear, I'm game for anything. Shall I pack us a picnic lunch?" Frank agreed a picnic would be fun, but then confessed he was in need of breakfast before they took off on their journey.

"Sorry, dear, I was so distracted by your wonderful surprise that breakfast slipped my mind." They agreed to tackle both at the same time. Dee addressed the picnic basket, and Frank scrambled the eggs. Their coordinated efforts quickly culminated in the desired results. Breakfast was had, lunch was prepared, and off they were to seek whatever might be discovered.

"Do you remember where you're going, dear?" his wife asked, but before he could answer, she continued. "I'm asking because memory fails me. I definitely remember the fallen tree you're searching for, but I don't remember which lane we were on. Do you?"

"Not exactly," he admitted. "But it can only be in one of three places, and I do remember it wasn't more than a quarter of a mile from the parking area, so our adventure shouldn't be too tedious, even if we have to check out all three places. And who knows, we may discover some other delightful possibility for a project." Project was a defining word in Frank's life. He was a man of many projects. Projects filled his work life, when he still was a professional, and projects occupied his life away from work, as well. Fortunately, his wife Deidre was a person who also loved projects, so she had great appreciation and respect for his creative urges. Mostly, the Sandersons just loved being together, and were happy doing projects conjointly or individually as long as they were in close proximity to one another.

Reaching the end of the first lane, Frank carefully parked the car near the trailhead. The two septuagenarians each grabbed their preferred walking sticks and headed towards the trail when Frank remembered the saw. He excused himself, quickly returned to the car and pulled out a bag containing a handsaw. Rejoining his beloved at the trailhead, they did what they always do when entering a passageway into new possibilities. They paused, clasped hands, took a deep breath, and made the first step in unison. It was a tradition of long standing.

"Frank, dear, have I told you recently how much I love you and our life together?" The question was one of utmost sincerity, because of late her memory wasn't as trustworthy as it once was. However, in the area pertaining to their relationship, Dee's memory remained flawless.

"Yes, Dee, you have. Every day! And I love you. We just keep getting better and better at this, you know." Using his free arm, he hugged her tightly. "By the time, we're eighty, I feel confident we will have perfected our relationship issues." They both chuckled about that. Dee thought it was ambitious goal, but worthy of pursuing.

"We've had a blessed life, haven't we?" Frank, squeezing her hand, nodded in agreement. "And you have many more projects to complete before we escape this plane of existence," she said joyfully, "so, we better keep exercising and taking those super charged vitamins." Again, they laughed as their walk took them deeper into the woods.

"I love this path," remarked Frank. His wife smiled knowing exactly which story he was thinking about. "It reminds me of the time we got lost in the woods back east. Remember that?" He laughed boyishly. "It took four days to find our way out. Wasn't that a grand adventure?" Dee blushed remembering certain parts of the adventure.

"The woods have always been good to us, dear," she responded and the couple chuckled some more. "That's when life changed for us," Deidre commented. "We've never been the same, have we?" The aging couple walked quietly for a while, each recalling the events of that time when they were lost in the woods.

"I still remember it like yesterday," acknowledged Frank.

"Yes, me too!" his wife spoke lovingly. "It still gives me pause. Sometimes I wonder about it. Do you?"

"Oh yes. It's hard to know what it all meant."

"Do you wonder if we made the right decision?" she asked.

"Yes! Oh, yes, Dee, I do. Guess we won't know 'til day's end." Frank's comment brought the couple to silence again. His mind meandered in many directions. He thought of the past, blazing through one happy memory after another. He thought of the present and wondered if it was time for them to turn back. The spot he was looking for still was yet to be found. And he thought of the future, wondering how many good times were remaining for them. Frank wasn't worried about the death part of living, as long as the two of them were not absent from one another for an extended period of time. They often talked about going out at the same time, but that was a complicated matter, and easier said than done. All Frank was certain about was his love for Deidre. God had done exceptionally well when he brought us together.

"Frank, dear! Look there! I believe that's the place." Dee's enthusiasm brought Frank back from the pathway in his mind to the path in the forest.

"Marvelous, old girl! You've found it!" Dee laughed knowing full well her husband had already spotted the site, but was waiting for her to declare it found. She loved seeing him happy and this maple log made him a very happy man. He walked around the log viewing it from several angles, and then reached into his bag for the handsaw.

"This is going to be a chore, dear. You may want to find a place to sit for a while." Dee decided to walk a bit further up the trail assuring Frank she would not go beyond his sight. As she strolled ahead, the sound of his sawing the log filled the air. It was amazing how a small sound could be amplified in the den of the forest. Walking alone up the path cushioned with crushed leaves, she embraced many emotions, but aloneness was not one of them. *I walk alone, but I am accompanied by many.* She smiled. The image of walking along surrounded by dear old friends engulfed her. *Thank you for your company, my friends. It is always a pleasure to be in your presence. Please forgive me if I have been remiss in connecting, but memory does not serve me as well as it once did. I hope you are all well.*

*"Old Friend, we also are pleased to be in your presence. Do not fear losing connection with old friends, Dear One, for this will not come to pass. Although the human mind may wane, your cosmic mind will never fail you. Nor will we. We are always here. Please return to the beloved husband now, and we will accompany you along the way."*

Turning around, Dee was surprised she had lost sight of her husband, but she was not afraid. He was there, accompanied by his companions, and she was where she was, accompanied by hers. Continuing strolling down the path, Dee heard the whooshing sound of the handsaw before her husband actually came into view. She was glad to see him, but then again, there had never been a time when she wasn't glad to lay her eyes upon this man she adored.

"Hello," she called out, but received no notice. Frank was busy sawing away. *I hope he is pacing himself,* she commented to herself knowing full well he wasn't. She called again. Still he took no notice, and her pace hastened. When she arrived, Frank was drenched in perspiration. "Now, now," she said as loudly as one could without actually yelling. "Take a rest, Frank. For goodness sake, you are over doing!" Finally her presence entered into his awareness. Pleased with his progress, he smiled happily.

"Almost done, dear. It's going well!"

"Frank, must I remind you how old you are. Please sit for a minute and give your heart a rest." Surprised by Dee's fervor, he obliged her request immediately, and they both situated themselves on a log of suitable proportions.

"You seem a bit out of sorts, dear. Anything, the matter?"

"Frank, I wish you could see yourself. You're red as a beet! Just two days ago, the doctor was lecturing you, and now, here you are. I'm not in the mood for experiencing a great loss, dear; so do be careful. I'm entirely too young to be losing my husband, so get with the program! Or perhaps, we should call your health a project, then maybe you would be more attentive to the task." Frank felt sufficiently scolded. He pouted for a moment, and then, realized Dee's reaction was appropriated.

"You're absolutely right, Dee. I'm sorry. Holding back just doesn't register for me. Once I get started, I don't seem able to stop myself. Oh, the truth is, stopping doesn't even occur to me. But your words were well spoken, and I got the message. No more of this nonsense!" Dee knew Frank meant well and she also knew he was speaking his truth. *He truly has no concept of his behavior, and that's a problem. Some day he will work himself to death, and not even know it has happened, until he's looking down from above. Perhaps that is a good way for him to go out.*

Dee bent over to view one of the blocks already sawed. "Ah! This piece is spalted as well. It is beautiful! What do you see in it, dear? What lovely piece will you turn from this magnificent piece of wood?"

"At the moment, I see nothing but you, dear. And I am deeply sorry for my negligence." Tears welled up, but not a one spilled over; his strong will wouldn't allow it. "I will not go out before you, Love. I promise you that. When your time comes, I will be right beside you, holding your hand until one of your companions takes over and shows you the way. You will never be alone, dear. We both know that, and I will not let your memory deprive you of that blessed truth. I will remind you every day, every minute if it becomes necessary." Dee could not contain her tears. They streamed freely down her cheeks, each one a reminder of the love they shared. The two old friends embraced each other savoring the tender moment. Time passed, the moment swelled, and the love shared for longer than either could remember, burned endlessly.

Slowly their embrace released, and they looked tenderly into one another's eyes. It was no surprise to either of them when words from a favorite poet flowed simultaneously from their hearts, "Grow old along with me, the best is yet to be."

"Well, we're not old yet, girl friend. We still have a lot of living to do, so let's get to it! We have a picnic to dispose of, and I am famished." Frank loaded two chunks of wood into his bag, and asked Dee to carry the handsaw. He regretted leaving the rest of the maple, but decided it would be wise to entice some young fellow from the college to come out and help him with this project. His wisdom was validated on the walk back to the car. The bag, heavier than anticipated, caused Frank to stop twice along the way to rest his arms and aching back. With good spirits, he accepted the reality of the situation as information for future decisions.

Upon returning to the car Dee, in a most clever way, announced her desire to drive. "I know exactly where to have our picnic, dear. You just stretch out for a while and I will surprise you!" Frank agreed to her devious tactic and responded he would gladly accept the opportunity to sit back and relax. Little did he know he would actually doze off.

"Here we are, dear!" Frank's nap complemented Dee's plan. Upon arrival, he really was surprised. She had driven some distance to a wonderful roadside park overlooking the valley. It was a stunning view, and as luck would have it, they had the park to themselves.

"My, oh my!" said Frank with excitement. "What a view! This was a great choice, dear, and you were right, clever woman. The drive put me to sleep immediately. And now I'm feeling great! Totally reenergized!" Exiting the car, Frank grabbed the picnic basket and followed his beloved. *She has a plan!* Which of course, she did. Dee led them to the most spectacular table in the park. It faced the valley, allowing for a memorable view. Sitting side by side, the couple indulged themselves first with the view, and then with cold leftovers from the evening before. Dee filled their plates with fruit, veggies, and grilled chicken. It was a meal to be enjoyed slowly while their eyes feasted on the valley below. Lunch was consumed, conversation transpired, and time passed.

"Let's go closer, dear," Dee urged, and so they did. Standing on the edge of the ridge, one truly could see for miles. We live in a lovely area. Hills, farmlands, forest! We have it all. How fortunate, we are!" Frank wrapped his arm around Dee and held her tightly. Both knew it was another special moment not to be rushed, and never to be forgotten.

"Thank you for loving me, Dee. Thank you for this precious life, we've shared!" Turning towards each other another long embrace was enjoyed. "This has been a wonderful day. I am so grateful." Still holding each other, they took one more picture of the view in their minds, and then, moved back toward the table. And then, something very remarkable transpired.

Much to their surprise, they were not alone. Sitting at the table facing them was a gentleman the couple had met a long time ago when they were lost in the woods. His face brightened as they saw him. With great delight, he motioned for them to be seated on the other side of the table. Speechless, Dee and Frank did as the gentleman, dressed in suit and tie, indicated. And he effortlessly turned about to face them. Dee, in astonishment, said, "You have not aged. You look exactly as you did all those years ago." He smiled a very gentle smile.

"We were just talking about you earlier today. Truth is, we both think of you often," Frank confided. "And we remain very grateful for your help that day. As you can see we did make it out of the forest, and we have lived a long life, a very happy life. We often wonder if we made the right decision." The old man looked deeply into Frank's eyes. Then he peered into Deidre's eyes.

*"I see happiness, joy, and contentment. You have lived well, my friends! It is most pleasurable to be in your presence once again."* His manner, his tone, his very essence filled the moment. Nothing else was noticed or seemed to matter. His presence was life itself!

*"I come again, old friends, to remind you the time is now. As before so long ago, I say to you again, the time is now."* Dee and Frank gasped. The words filled them again, as when they were first heard. Perhaps, because the words had been heard before, they were more prepared to ask questions this time, so Dee proceeded.

"Are you telling us again that we have the option of going or staying, or do those words of urgency refer to something else of which we are unaware?" Her question pleased the man who looked upon them not unlike a parent adoring his children.

*"Your questions are based in wisdom,"* he said approvingly. *"The former does indeed provide the option of staying in your present experience or exiting it. The choice is yours. The latter pertains to either option that is chosen. If you remain in this experience, the relevant guidance is the time is now. If you exit this experience, the guidance remains the same. The time is now."* The couple sat in puzzlement. The old man, appreciating their confusion, continued.

*"My friends allow your minds to rest. It interferes with your discernment process. The mind cannot make this decision for you. The answer comes from within. Let your heart be your guide. Long ago, before you entered into this experience, a commitment was made. You came to be of service. I remind you again, the time is now. If you stay, your commitment will be fulfilled from this location. If you depart, your commitment will be fulfilled from another location. Either way, your purpose will be fulfilled.*

*Old friends, The Island is in great need. You must assist her. The time is now. Ponder this, please. When your decision is made, I will return."* With love in his eyes, he looked upon Deidre and Frank, and they knew he would soon disappear as before. This time they were able to say goodbye!

*A passage from*
***The Time is Now***
*(Chapter Twelve)*

*"And in knowing of the natural circumstances of the tragic situation, All experienced deep compassion for the Ones affected by the circumstance."*

The Sandersons continued holding hands, as they had done throughout the entire encounter. Questions raced through their minds, but neither Dee nor Franklin expected any instantaneous answers. They would do what the old man had advised. They would ponder what was said, they would seek within, and a decision would be made.

"It's been a long day, dear. Shall we motor home?" Dee responded to her husband's question by rising from the table, repacking the picnic basket, and sliding it over to him. She wrapped her arm about his waist, as they walked to the car.

Little was said on the drive home. It was one of those drives that happen, but you're not present during the experience. They got into the car, drove away from the roadside park, and then they were home. What happened in between was a mystery. And when Frank pulled into the driveway, they were both surprised.

"Do you mind if I go down into the workshop for a while, dear? I need to lose myself in a project. It will clear my head."

"Oh, please do," she urged him. "It will be good for you. I'm going to stay outside and water the flowers. I'll be in shortly." Frank headed toward the back door with the picnic basket in one hand and his handsaw in the other. He would retrieve the wood at a later time.

Dee meandered through the backyard assessing her potted plants, deadheading where needed. The garden, when it was started, was a mutually shared project, but in recent years, it had become a project requiring assistance from a gardener with a strong body and greater stamina. The real work was done by this 'gardening angel,' which left her to manage only the lighter work. What was required this evening was a good soak. She grabbed the hose addressing the potted plants first, and then went from bed to bed providing the elixir of life. And as she managed the yard, she pondered. *What are we to do,* she questioned.

Frank immediately picked up a small block of poplar. He loved working with poplar because it was particularly easy to turn. He had no goal in mind; he simply wanted to lose himself in the realm of art. Here in his sanctuary, he could ponder the encounter with the old man. *What are we to do,* he wondered.

Eventually, Dee tired of her task at about the same time as Frank was doing the same. They met in the kitchen each delighted to see the other. Dinner was discussed and dismissed for neither was hungry for a meal, which did not override their need for an indulgence. As often was the case for these two old friends, popcorn was the indulgence of choice. Frank made the best popcorn on the planet, and they were in need of such a treat. The fragrance overtook the house. Nothing was better than a home filled with the aroma of popcorn. Both agreed it was sign of distinction. Satisfied by their indulgence, they both admitted it was time for bed even though the night was still young.

They engaged in their nightly routines, changed into their pajamas, and slipped into bed. With the lights turned off, they each breathed deeply. It had been a long day.

# ~ Chapter Nine ~

"A beautiful day, it is!" I announced to the empty room. Enjoying the view from the large picture window facing east, I knew a decision must be made. "Do I head for the hills, or do I stroll the streets of the neighborhood?" The question asked every morning did not come with an easy answer. An energizing walk through the countryside was always satisfying and exciting, but a nice stroll through the neighborhood also brought great beauty to behold, particularly at this time of year. "Nature is at its best during this season of the year! Although every season," she added, "has its own unique beauty!"

Looking about the living room, I wondered if it tired of my idle conversation. "Perhaps dear home of mine, you are in need of some excitement!" A gathering came to mind, so I conferred with my home. "Maybe it is time for a social engagement, old friend! Would you like that? Would you enjoy having a party?" Silence echoed throughout the house. "Ah, my friend, your silence can be interpreted in many different ways. I choose to believe we are both in need of company." Surprised by and excited about the early morning decision to host an event, I went about preparing myself for a walk through the countryside. The latter decision to head for the hills was not a surprise, since it was the choice most frequently made and which always resulted in enjoyment.

As my mind is wont to do while we walk about, it cogitated. On this particular occasion its topic of distraction focused upon the gathering. Who, what and when? Those were the primary questions racing about. *Who should we, my mind and I, invite to this occasion? What is the purpose of the occasion? And when should the occasion be scheduled?* The questions brought recent events to mind. Somehow, the people involved in these memorable experiences needed to be brought together. It is a matter of timing and preparation. Ironically, the Smiths, the Joneses, and Marilyn Brown are all acquainted. And of course, there is nothing ironical about this, because as we all know, there is no such thing as a coincidence. The truth is, the six of us have been good friends for years, and it seems obvious we are intended to come together to speak of these unusual happenings. What is much more complicated is the invitation of those outside of our friendly circle. "This demands more thought and careful consideration," I spoke aloud. And then another thought came to mind. Another couple, the senior members of our circle of friends, must also be invited. The Sandersons, if memory serves me, also have an interesting event in their past, which may be relevant. Although, they never shared the details of their experience in the woods, something mysterious obviously happened to them.

I devised a plan. At the next meeting scheduled by the Smiths, I would advise Jan, Everett, Pat and Bill of my desire to host a gathering not only for them, but also, for any others who may have encountered similar experiences. Opening this discussion will allow me to acknowledge without divulging any identities that other events have come to my attention since our previous meeting. If they approve of the idea, then I will invite Marilyn and the Sandersons to the event as well, and the Smiths can extend an invitation to Wendy. Satisfied with my plan, my mind was finally able to quiet down. We walked in silence while Mother Nature entertained us with all her glory.

*A passage from*
***The Time is Now***
*(Chapter Thirteen)*

> *"As awareness of the tragedy continued to grow, more knowingness of the potential for the tragedy to spread throughout the Universe became apparent. What grew of natural circumstances on the newly evolving planet in the distant galaxy was of such lethal proportion that the contamination potential for other interstellar inhabitants was extremely high.*
>
> *As this awareness grew, so too did the commitment to rescue the children from the contaminating situation. What evolved from natural circumstances could not continue to evolve in this tragic way. An action of cleansing would need to occur."*

# ~ Chapter Ten ~

"Welcome! You've arrived at the same time. Do come in everyone!" Jan amiably greeted her old friends and invited everyone to the back porch. "You know your way. Everett is arranging things, as we speak. Please go out and make yourselves at home." As we paraded through the hall to the back door, I asked Jan if she needed an extra hand. She immediately sent me off to grab a tray from the refrigerator. It was easy to feel at home at the Smiths' place. After all the many years of friendship shared, they were indeed family. Snatching the tray into one hand, I also grabbed the pitcher of ice water with the other. And off I went! Everett quickly took the tray and placed it according to his design plan, and I, with his permission, filled the glasses. The evening commenced immediately. Pat posed the necessary question, and the conversation began.

"Well, I'm assuming we've all been possessed by the question, which ended our last meeting. So let's get on with it. What are we to do?" Her husband chuckled.

"Leave it to Pat to immediately call us to task," he saluted her with his wine glass. "Dear One, perhaps you should go first. Your energy indicates you've given the question a great deal of consideration." Embarrassed by her apparent zeal, Pat squirmed about in her chair.

"My energy," she admitted, "is an indication of my curiosity. I have given the question considerable thought, but frankly, my thoughts are still rather muddled. While I'm absolutely convinced we should be doing something, exactly what the something is still eludes me. So my brash behavior is evidence not of a solution, but of hopeful anticipation that one of you may have an answer." Similar comments circled the table. Jan, in acknowledging her personal thoughts, discussed the ethereal nature of the experiences.

"In the moment, one is filled with a sense of duty, responsibility, and desire. The desire feels so intense, as it wells up within that you are convinced an action must be taken, but as the moment wanes, it becomes increasingly more difficult to cling to the inspiration, which was originally experienced. The moment passes, if you will, and all that remains is a lingering memory, flickering off and on, trying to reignite the flame of awareness that once burned so brightly."

"Well said!" praised her husband.

And it was! Jan's testimony described the process for all of them, and for a brief, ever so brief, passing of time; there was a sense the moment had been lost. I observed what was happening and felt the energy switch from excitement to confusion, and it became apparent to me my time had come. The message of old, repeated over and over again in countless ways in endless settings, including the events experienced by my friends, was calling to me. *The time is now!*

"My friends, I too have given this a great deal of thought, and because of several interesting experiences, which have transpired since our last meeting, I come this evening with a proposal. What I'm about to suggest involves your participation, if you are willing, so I am very interested in hearing your thoughts about my idea. Actually, dear ones, it isn't just my idea. We talked about this at our last meeting, so it is an idea, which emerged from our conversation.

I would like to propose we have a gathering, which I would love to host. My house is distraught of late and is in need of company, so I would like to accommodate her needs for connection." Accustomed to my inclination towards anthropomorphism, my friends indulged me.

"The purpose of this gathering is to invite you, of course, and others who may have similar experiences to come together and share their stories. As we learned from our talks last week, sharing the stories roots them into reality. And as you have all just acknowledged, the memories fade. This indicates to me that gatherings of this nature will not only facilitate awareness of these events, but also assist those who have experienced the events to retain the essential elements of the events themselves. Bottom line," I said in summary, "sharing the stories will spread the messages, and by repeating the stories, the messages will be retained."

"Wonderful proposal, dear!" expressed Pat. "So, you're suggesting we function as a group and basically do what we did last week. We come together and share our adventures. And because we've already done it among ourselves, it will be easy for us to do with others."

"Yes, exactly. The trust you share with one another will foster trust within the newcomers, and the ease with which you share your stories will model for others that they too can feel safe to reveal their secrets."

"Sounds like a good idea to me," offered Bill. "Guess the only downside is we might get very bored telling and hearing our stories over and over again."

"I've thought about that possibility Bill, and you may be right. Over time, you may feel less inclined to share your stories, or not. We won't know until you guys give it a try. However, in the interim, you may discover repeating the stories to others may actually serve you well. The inspiration initially received when hearing the messages may evolve with each repeated telling of the stories and result in an actualization of the messages' intentions."

"Goodness, friend, you really have given this careful deliberation," commented Everett. "And it makes sense. I think we should give this a try. How about you Jan? What are your thoughts, dear?"

"I'm very impressed," she responded and paused for a moment. Then repositioning to the edge of her chair, she assertively declared, "Something important is happening, and for some reason still unknown to us, we are privileged to be a part of it. We cannot turn our backs on this. I will never believe we are meant to be tight-lipped about these events." Shaking her head to emphasize her disbelief in remaining quiet, Jan boisterously proclaimed, "How blessed are we! We have each other! Before Everett and I were feeling isolated about all of this. Now, we are joyous! We spoke our truth, and we were believed. I hope you (she pointed to Bill and Pat) are feeling the same. I'm not afraid of going forward now. The five of us can manage anything." Her confidence inspired the others and the energy of the group positively shifted. Once again, they were feeling uplifted.

"Jan, we are feeling comfortable now," Pat replied. "Once we learned about yours and Everett's experiences, we moved to another place. The worry about it just disappeared. The fact we are all involved in this weird situation is both comforting and evidence. For goodness sake, we've been mutually involved in activities for decades. Why wouldn't we join forces for this adventure?" Wine glasses were raised to accentuate Pat's last comment.

I was very pleased with the forward motion of our group, but more discussion was needed. Just as I was about to take the leap into the next phase of my proposal, Everett quizzed me.

"Earlier, you made an allusion to some events that transpired since we were last together. Would you like to tell us to what you were referring?" I smiled, tapping the fingertips of both hands before my lips. Excitement overtook me.

"My friends, I've enjoyed the most exciting week. First, I was blessed with the stories the four of you so generously shared. And if that were not enough, the week continued to unfold in the most delightful manner. I must speak very carefully now, for what I have heard is not mine to repeat; however, what I can say is there are others with similar experiences who may be interested in meeting with you." Curiosity heightened, as did everyone's posture. My friends were literally sitting on the edge of their chairs.

"Surely not!" declared Everett. "In such a short period of time, more have come forward?"

"Yes," I replied. "I know for certain one will wish to explore conversation with you. The other is complicated, because the story presented to me was about someone else's experience. So this person, whose identity I do not know, may or may not be interested in participating; however, the reality is, another event similar to yours has crossed our path. And the next issue I would like to speak of is a situation we all already know about, but some of you may have forgotten."

Jan quietly interrupted. "You're referring to Dee and Frank, aren't you?" I nodded in agreement. "Needless to say, I've been thinking a lot about them. Many a time, I've wanted to go talk to them about this, but uncertainty stopped me. They've been reserved about the incident for decades, which as you all know is not their usual manner of being. They are the most open, loving people one could even hope to know, except for the incident that happened in the woods."

Silence entered the discussion while memories were visited.

"We need to talk to them," stated Pat, "and apprise them of what's been going on with us, and let them know the purpose of our gathering." Everyone agreed with Pat's suggestion. The Sandersons needed time to consider the idea.

"Will you do this, dear?" asked Jan. "You have such a wonderful way with words, and maybe, they will listen to you, and see the merit in participating in our little affair. I think they would benefit immensely and it would be so grand to have them join us." A curious look came over Jan and she suggested, "You don't suppose Marilyn might have a story in her back pocket. Wouldn't that be great? Then our circle of friends would be complete, and our family would be off on another adventure." Smiling, I accepted the opportunity of meeting with the Sandersons. Inwardly, I chuckled about my friends' future delight upon seeing Marilyn at the forthcoming gathering.

*A passage from*
***The Time is Now***
*(Chapter Fourteen)*

*"When the time of the awareness grew to knowingness, and the knowingness became evident, the Ones of Ancient Age began their search for the ones who could lead the difficult mission to the third planet of the distant sun.*

*From this awareness came the selection of those who had served many times before and who were of ancient wisdom. All were eager to serve and All were worthy, but some were of more knowingness, and upon these Ancient Ones, much of the responsibility of this mission would fall.*

*These leaders would devise the plan and implement the plan, and upon their shoulders, the mission rested."*

# ~ Chapter Eleven ~

I waited for an appropriate hour to call the Sandersons. Even though I knew them to be early risers, good manners would not allow me to call before ten o'clock. At the allotted time, I called, and to my surprise Frank answered the phone. "Good morning, Frank! Why aren't you down in the studio?" he laughed admitting it was indeed unusual for him to be the one answering the phone. "No matter," I said. "I'm actually calling to invite myself over to your place for a visit. Have something to run by the both of you. Is it possible you might have room in your busy schedule to spend some time with me?" In his loving, gentle way, Frank answered they were never too busy to spend time with me, which of course, warmed my heart.

"Hold on, dear, while I walk us out to the porch. Dee's outside attending some matter of importance. Hold on!" I heard the back door open and close and then Frank calling out to his beloved. He informed her of my request and she quickly took over the phone.

"Hello there! So good to hear from you." I replied the same and cordially restated my request about a visit. "Well, when would you like to come?" she asked. "We're free today, nothing on our calendar."

"Well, I'm actually out walking now and only a few blocks away. Is now a good time? Please feel free to say no, Dee, if this last minute intrusion isn't convenient."

"You are never an inconvenience dear. And now, is the perfect time! Trek on over and we will put on a fresh pot of coffee. See you soon, dear?" Dee handed the phone back to her husband and asked him to attend the coffee. "I'll clean off the table out here. Such a lovely day to have a visitor!"

"Might be nice to have the umbrella set in place," he suggested, which met with Dee's approval. Frank addressed the task before disappearing to brew the coffee.

As I walked toward the Sandersons' home, I remembered to call the Smith's. "Jan, good morning. Do you have a minute?" She did, so I continued. "Jan, what about Wendy? I forgot to mention her last night, but she is another one who should receive an invitation."

"Oh, yes. Everett and I discussed that after you left. I plan to call her later today and explain the situation to her. She may not be able to manage it, but I think the invitation will be well received." With that task attended, I marched towards my destination.

"Hello, You!" came a cheery welcome. "Come over here and give us some major big hugs," declared Dee who was standing on the deck with arms akimbo. I approached and did as instructed.

"It is so good to see you," I said with the utmost sincerity. "Thank you for allowing me to barge in on your morning."

"We couldn't be happier about your impromptu visit. Come sit down. Frank will be arriving in just a minute. Oh, here he is now. Look who's here, dear!" And another round of hugs and greetings were enjoyed. We chatted about this and that catching each other up on our latest doings, which was good, because I needed time to settled in before my task was attended.

"So, Frank, what is your latest project?" I said with a gleam in my eyes. An avid fan of his artistic talents, I was always curious to see what he was up to. "Come on," I teased. "As your greatest fan, you must indulge me with a peak!"

"Oh, dear, you must see his latest woodturning! It is fabulous! Frank, do fetch the vase. Spoil your greatest fan, dear!" Frank obediently went into the house and quickly returned holding an object with a towel over it.

"One must be appropriately surprised," he smiled. "Please close your eyes, so the masterpiece can be suitably presented." I did as requested, listened to the object being placed upon the table, and then, heard Frank returning to his chair. Once seated, he announced my eyes could be opened.

I sat in silence, stunned by the spalted, white maple vase. "Frank, you are a genius!" Raising my right index finger to silence him, I continued. "I'm aware of the beauty of this particular piece of wood, but your workmanship has accentuated what was already divinely created. The shape is extraordinary. It reminds me of the pottery created by Native American Indians. Was this piece inspired by their work?" He acknowledged it had been.

"I saw a book at the library," he stated, "featuring pottery from the southwest, and I was particularly taken by this lovely shape, and it seemed right for this beautiful piece of maple. In fact, Dee and I went up to the hills yesterday and found the log from which this piece was taken. I managed to get two more pieces for additional experimentation. Looking forward to that!" he said with a boyish grin. We chatted some more. They told me about the lovely picnic shared at the roadside park and subtly indicated it had been a remarkable experience. From the tone of their voices, I wondered what remarkable actually meant.

"So dear, what brings you to us?" asked Dee. "Frank said you wanted to run something by us. What might that be?" The question asked; the time was upon me.

I began my story with a frequently overused four-lettered word. "Well," came forth the aforementioned word followed by a poignant pause. "I'm here on a mission. It seems some dear friends of ours are having some very unusual experiences. And these friends, namely the Smiths and the Joneses, have recently disclosed these events to one another and are stunned by the similarities. As their stories unfolded, it seemed apparent they were not the only people having these unusual experiences, and since it has been brought to my attention, I have encountered two other people with similar stories." The Sandersons listened with attentive ears. Their expressions revealed no information and left me wondering if my idea had been a mistake.

"So, I have come because we thought you might be interested in hearing the stories." For the first time in my life I came to understand the meaning of a pregnant pause. I waited. The Sandersons made no eye contact. I waited some more. Stillness prevailed. Beads of perspiration formed on my forehead, and when the tension within me reached its peak, Dee cleared her throat.

"Well dear," she said to her husband, "it appears the time has come. What are we to do?" The question spoken captured my attention, and then, I was certain. They too had encountered the mysterious fellow dressed in suit and tie. I wanted to beg them to join us, but knew it was not the approach to take. They needed time to digest the possibility of revealing their story. Only they could make the decision. No one had the privilege of imposing upon this very private matter.

Frank gently placed his hand atop Dee's and look deeply into her eyes. "Shall we, old friend?" Dee nodded.

"I think we must, Frank. After yesterday, we both know it is time."

Frank turned to me, took a very deep breath, and said, "Your timing is exquisite, dear. We are of an occasion to consider your proposals. We have carried in silence an incident of unusual circumstances for several decades, and have often revisited decisions made at that time. We are still unclear if our decisions were wise. And yesterday, as happenstance would have it, we were invited to review our plans for the future. Deidre and I do not believe in coincidences. Your arrival today is happening for a reason and we would be foolish not to notice." Frank indulged in another deep breath, and for a brief moment, turned to observe a monarch butterfly in flight. "Look dear, it's a monarch! Shall we take her appearance as a sign?" The couple held hands, smiled lovingly at one another, and leaned forward to share a kiss.

"So tell us," Dee took over the conversation. "What are you and our other dear friends planning?" I told them, without sharing story details, what had already transpired, and elaborated upon our idea to provide an opportunity for others with similar experiences to come together and share their stories.

"Naturally, we thought of you two and wanted to include you. If you prefer, we can all meet again before any others are invited. In fact, we would prefer to do that. We have enjoyed the luxury of bringing these stories out within our family of friends. Because you are a part of the family, we prefer to honor your wishes."

"Very thoughtful," replied Frank. "We do have a tale to tell, don't we, dear?" They giggled, which was nice to see and hear. "What do you think, dear? Shall we make our debut among those we love the most before we perform in front of others?" The decision was easily made.

"As you know, dear, we have honored this experience in silence for decades." Dee's gracious manner was one to model. She spoke with elegance and dignity. "Truth is, we are running out of decades. We both know it is now time for us to speak the truth. And we would prefer to do that with our dearest friends. Will you arrange that for us, dear? We would be ever so grateful?" I assured them I would handle the arrangements and asked if they would be comfortable coming to my home for storytelling time. They agreed it would be a lovely setting to share their story.

Walking home, I was once again overwhelmed by the courage exhibited by those who were willingly coming forward to share their stories. And I wondered how many other stories were waiting to be told.

*A passage from*
***The Time is Now***
*(Chapter Fifteen)*

> *"As the Ancient Ones agreed on those who would serve and in what manner, apparent it became that many would be required to assist the leaders for the plan to be of successful completion. And of the many that offered their services, more wished to assist in ways of complementary means. So many offered to leave their homes and families to participate in this mission while many others offered to remain to continue the plan from the source of origination.*
>
> *All assisted and All were impacted by this plan of rescue."*

# ~ CHAPTER TWELVE ~

"Dear Ones, another day has transpired and the process continues to unfold. I hope my services are in alignment with the mission you attempt to accomplish. While I do not pretend to comprehend the complexities of what is unfolding around me, I know it is happening for a reason. I am in awe of your masterful orchestration. I trust you will apprise me if and when I may be of assistance. I am forever grateful for the opportunity to bear witness to your work. In peace be, My Friends." I remained sitting wondering if a response to my prayer would be forthcoming. None was needed. It was simply an expression of gratitude and acknowledgement, not a request for a response.

*"Your words are heard, Dear Friend, and we are most grateful for your skillful means of facilitation. People are gathering, Old Friend, and this is necessary. Soon the masses will be prepared for what is next to come. Your assistance is needed, and we will continue to call upon you. Please know you are loved and cherished. In peace be, Old Friend."*

To say that I was comforted by the words from an unseen voice would be the greatest understatement ever declared. The warmth of gratitude washed through me. It was beyond my control; it simply was. I like to refer to this remarkable experience as the 'moment of overwhelm.' The precious, unforgettable moment when one fully comes into awareness that he or she is in the Presence of another. Overwhelmed by a sense of gratitude, love, and compassion, one's essence is enlivened to the reality that we are not alone. "What a wonderful way to end the day!"

For me, the day was complete. Much more remained to be addressed, but for the moment I was at peace with the greater way. Already prepared for bed, I slipped under the covers. Sleep came quickly for I was at One with All That Is.

# ~ CHAPTER THIRTEEN ~

A date was set, arrangements were made, and preparations for the gathering of our family of friends had begun. My house was ecstatic; she was spotless. Windows and glass tabletops sparkled, sneaky cobwebs were no more, and not a single dust bunny could be found anywhere. We, my house and I, were ready for the evening's affair. At the request of our older family members, we started early. Promptly at 6 o'clock, our guests began to arrive. We met in the living room where chairs were comfortably arranged for conversation.

It was a tender meeting of friends. Many hugs and fond pleasantries were exchanged as preferred beverages were poured and served. There was an air of excitement, and impatience. Everyone was eager to begin. As my friends began to sit themselves, I graciously excused myself and retreated into the bedroom. There, my surprise for the evening waited. Marilyn Brown, having arrived early as planned, went into hiding when the doorbell rang. After the meeting with the Sandersons had gone as hoped, I connected with Marilyn to apprise her of the upcoming gathering. We agreed her presence was absolutely necessary. It was time for the entire family to disclose with one another the special encounters they had experienced.

I entered the living room first and announced, "Dear Ones, I have a surprise for you, which seems appropriate for an evening that will be filled with surprises. I turned, and with a gesture of invitation, sang out, 'ta-dah!" And in waltzed, Marilyn! Instantaneous happiness filled the room and another round of hugs and greetings were exchanged.

"Oh, what fun!" declared Jan. "I just knew you were going to be part of this! Yeah!" Marilyn was pleased by the reception, not surprised, but happily grateful. It was good to be together and she said so.

"I am so glad to be with you! Our friend here," she said pointing to me, "has informed me something is going on with all of us, and I am so eager to be here tonight to catch up with everyone. I'm sorry to have been out-of-pocket lately, but life has been so busy. It is good to be back together again."

"I think when we hear each other's stories this evening we will have greater understanding why there has been less connection lately." My comment seemed to ring true for everyone. I briefly summarized for the Sandersons and Marilyn what had already transpired for the rest of us. "So, from our previous two meetings, we agreed we wanted to pursue the possibility of assisting others who may also have similar encounters. Which led us to this point. Dee, Frank, we all assumed you might have a need to be a part of this, and we are so happy you accepted our invitation. We need you! And because Marilyn and I had crossed paths on the trail after our first impromptu meeting, I knew she would be on board. So, here we are!

Our objective for the evening is to share stories, so as a group, as a family, we will have greater awareness of the phenomenal unfoldings, which are occurring around us. I think that about sizes it up. Does anyone have anything they would like to add?"

Jan addressed a question to me. "I've been wondering, dear, how you've been managing all this. It appears you have been the listener of many stories, and I'm curious. How are you being affected by these stories?" Her question aroused similar comments of concern, which is not surprising since we are a close and loving group of friends. I was pleased with Jan's question for many reasons. It gave me an opportunity to share my thoughts about recent events, and it also provided a means to gently move into the evening. *No coincidence,* I thought.

"I feel privileged! It is a remarkable gift to bear witness to anyone's experience, and as you know, this is an extraordinary grouping of events. I am living in gratitude." Glancing about the room, I relished the moment. "As you all know, I am a listener. It began at very early age and grew into a life-long vocation. I am always honored when someone shares his or her life with me. So, imagine my surprise and absolute delight when my dearest friends began telling me about these intriguing events that were happening. One by one, the stories were told, and with each story heard, I wanted to dance with joy. And then the unusual stories spread beyond my circle of friends, and I became even more curious.

And just as each of you have wondered about these encounters and strived to understand their underlying purpose, so too have I. Why have I been blessed to be in the right place at the right time to be a listener for someone's story? And the same question arising for each of you has also surfaced for me. What am I to do?" It felt good to share these thoughts with my friends, but the most important thought still remained to be said.

"I am so grateful to be a part of this!" Tears came forward as the moment seized me. "Something very extraordinary is happening and we are being called to be a part of it, whatever it is. And I'm grateful. Grateful you trusted me enough to share your stories with me, and grateful I am called to be the listener." With joy in my heart, I truthfully announced, "We are so blessed to be in this place at this time, and I'm just grateful we are sharing the moment."

"Well, we are grateful too, dear, for your wonderful listening ears. What a gift you are to us!" praised Jan. Similar compliments were extended. I breathed in every word allowing the energy of each compliment to fill my being. "You know, dear, I had secretly hoped you would begin the evening with one of your wonderful inspirational prayers. And you did! What a sweet way to begin our conversation!"

"Thank you, Jan, for opening the door for me to share my thoughts. And now, my friends, how shall we continue? Who feels ready to share their story?" Pat and Bill immediately stepped up. They beautifully related their adventure at the scenic overlook, and shared every detail as they had done during our first evening together. It was gripping, heartfelt, and illuminating. As Pat described the encounter with the old gentleman, I watched Dee and Frank. They listened attentively. The only demonstration of connection with the story came when they reached over and held hands. I wondered what their story would be.

After the Joneses completed their story, a round of discussion followed. Amazement was disclosed. Excitement energized the room and the significant pause followed, during which everyone wondered who would go next. Marilyn took the lead.

"Well, I am certainly in the right place at the right time," she announced with a smile. Thanking Bill and Pat for their remarkable story, she began hers by saying, "The story I am going to share with you is one that was shared with me. I have contacted the original storyteller and received her permission to relay it to you. She is, by the way, extremely interested in your idea of offering these gatherings and wishes to be apprised of their success. I know she is interested in attending if the timing works for her." This was exciting news and evidence the group was moving in right direction.

Marilyn's efforts were admirable. A superb storyteller, she honored the possessor of this tale by relating it with accurate detail, noteworthy mystery and intrigue, and most of all, with gracious dignity. When she was done, she praised the woman's courage. "I understand why she was reluctant to share her tale, and I am so grateful she did. Her story, not only affirms what you two just shared, but it also informs us of the expansive scope of these events. These unusual encounters are not limited in their location. We are witnessing a far-reaching mission." And as always with the telling of these tales, when the story is completed, a pause consumes the room allowing for a moment of reflection. Perhaps, the mind demands time to process its encounter with the unimaginable, or perhaps, the heart and soul simply need time to revel in the moment.

"This guy really gets around," chuckled Bill. And a glimmer of expression crossed Frank's face. I thought he and Dee might go next, but they remained silent. No one wanted to push them, so Everett began sharing their first adventure with the mysterious older gentleman.

"As Bill just indicated this fellow does indeed get around. Our first experience with him was in the Delhi International Airport. Everett and Jan took turns telling the tale. As they spoke, I observed. *Each time they share their story, it becomes easier. They are less apprehensive, their memories of the incident are precise, and they appear to be completely at ease.* It was also obvious their listeners were totally engaged with the story. When Jan described their mystery person, Frank was noticeably shaken. His response transpired in an instant, but the raising of his right eyebrow did not escape me.

"Everett," called the eldest of the group. "You mentioned this was the first encounter you and Jan had with this fellow, am I correct?" Everett immediately reassured Frank he had heard correctly. "So there are more tales to be told?" he asked.

"Yes, Frank, our experience seems to keep expanding upon itself. After we first saw him at the airport, then we had an experience where we overheard two women talking about an encounter one of them had, and the same fellow was described. Tag on to that, we met a woman on our favorite walk in the northeast, and she too had encountered him on a busy New York street."

"My word," uttered Frank. "Never heard of such a thing. This is truly quite remarkable." Turning to his beloved, he asked, "What do you think about this, dear? Isn't it fascinating?" Dee had been quiet throughout the evening, which is not to say she wasn't present, because she was. She hadn't missed one word of the stories told. Dee squeezed her husband's hand tightly and then responded to his question.

"What I think, dear, is this. We are in very good company!" Her smile brightened the room. As she gazed upon her friends, she continued to speak in the most loving, tender manner. "Dear ones, the truth is, we have known for a very long time that we are not alone. Having the opportunity to share this truth with our friends is a blessing. Because of the experience we shared in the woods over fifty years ago, we were changed, shall we say. Occasionally, when we have thought about our experience, we felt odd. Because we were unaware of anyone else having such an encounter, there were times when we did feel lonely even though we certainly knew we were not alone. It was the experience that separated us from others.

As I observe you this evening, it makes me question our decision to remain silent all these years, but you must understand it was a different time." Dee paused and then shifted her perspective. "Actually, I'm not certain things are any different today than they were back then. People are still afraid of the unknown and they still have prejudices based in misunderstandings. The fact is we were afraid to speak out. We were afraid of being ridiculed or discounted or all the other words one can choose to describe one's fears. So, we held our secret within all these years. But now, as we watch each of you express yourselves so beautifully, it is very impressive. I admire your courage, and recognize it is now time for us to be courageous, as well. Clutching Frank's hand, she looked deeply into his eyes. *We must do this, dear!* Their friends did not hear Dee's unspoken words, but Frank did. He smiled, nodded in agreement, turned to their friends, and spoke very softly.

"We would like your permission, dear friends, to tell you a story that began over fifty years ago." Needless to say, permission was granted.

"Some of you," he began "may have heard the story about our big adventure back east when we got lost in the woods. That was a very long time ago. We were in our early twenty's and fearless, as those of that age are inclined to be. When we first realized we were lost, we didn't think much of it. After all, we were semi-prepared for an overnight of camping. And honestly the idea of spending the night in the woods with this beauty was rather appealing to me." Frank sported a very boyish grin as Dee punched him on the arm. The image of the two of them ignoring the reality that they were lost was charming; their friends enjoyed walking down memory lane with them.

"Well, as I said, we were fearless and we were on an adventure, so what was there to worry about, right?" Shaking his head in disbelief, he grunted, "Youthful arrogance!"

"The first night, shall we say, was memorable," confessed Dee with embarrassment, which brought about a playful moment. Still blushing, she commented about the second night, which was not as free spirited. At that point, the daring duo, hungry and very cold, was aware of their predicament.

"By the third morning, we both awoke cranky and out of sorts with one of another, and being very headstrong individuals, we were not in a cooperative mood. Fear was taking hold, but neither of us would admit it. Unfortunately, we were so distracted by our obstinate behaviors that an accident happened. Deidre slipped on a lose rock and took a very bad fall. Could have been worse, but it was bad enough. Very nasty gash along the knee, lots of bleeding with rapid swelling, and the wound was just miserably painful.

So, here's the picture. The temperature is dropping significantly, snow is beginning to fall, we are out of food, my beloved cannot walk without assistance, and we are lost. Well, leaving Dee alone was out of the question."

"Frank was marvelous," interjected Dee. "The accident changed him. Before my eyes he transformed from a cocky kid to a young, responsible man. First, he bandaged my leg, then, he repacked the backpacks eliminating everything that was unnecessary and combining the remaining necessities into one pack. We strapped the pack on me, and then this incredible guy carried me piggyback up and down the hills of the forest. I'm not sure how he managed. By the end of the day, we were not happy campers. But Frank never stopped taking care of me. He constructed a fabulous shelter for us, and somehow we managed. The next morning we were scared. My leg had stiffened badly during the night, and Frank's body was wrecked from carrying me the day before. I wanted him to go ahead, but he adamantly refused. And admittedly, I was grateful, because I didn't really want us to separate. I was afraid of being alone out there. I think it's fair to say we were both feeling desperate. Frank tried very hard to be nonchalant, but I knew he was as frightened as me. He was confident we would run into a highway if we just kept going east, so that was our plan the morning of the fourth day. We had a plan, but we didn't have the gumption to follow it, so we got personal instead, and admitted how much we cared for each other. It was rather a special moment, when two children awaken into adulthood and know they are in love. And we were! We were looking longingly into each other's eyes, the way only the young can do, when we realized we were not alone. There standing before us was a fashionably dressed gentleman, looking affectionately upon us.

*'You are in a difficult situation, my friends!'* he announced. Well, we were confused. We thought we had been found, but this fellow didn't seem to be part of a rescue operation. He just stood there smiling, as if he knew us. Frank explained we needed help and the man nodded in agreement. Then he came closer and positioned himself on the ground in front of us.

*'You are in awkward moment. A juncture in time when you can choose to go or choose to stay.'* His expression was one of pure love, something neither of us had ever experienced. He gazed into our eyes. First, into Frank's and then, into mine, and we quieted. Fear was released, immaturity fell by the wayside, and we were simply there. The three of us were One.

*'Old Friends, you are here for a reason. This moment in time is a point of*

*discernment. You can remain here in this experience or you can proceed to another experience. The choice is yours. And regardless of the path you take, the reason for being continues.*

*The commitment made long ago remains the same. The Island is in great need. Her health declines. Assistance is necessary; do not delay. Go to The Island. The time is now.'*

Even in our altered state of awareness, we were unclear about what was happening. We understood his words, but really had no idea what the man was talking about. We tried to ask him questions, but he simply repeated the same message. Finally, Frank begged him to help us. He explained I was injured and he needed help to get me out of the forest. With those remarkable loving eyes, he looked into our souls.

*'All is well! The path lies before you.'* He pointed to the left and sternly declared, *'Follow the path! Help is but a breath away!'* "Then he looked into our hearts again, and said, *'Today, old acquaintances were renewed. As was long ago, so too is true today. We are Friends of Old. Do not fear, little ones. Help is near!'* And then, he gazed upon us again, and faded into nothingness.

And to quickly conclude the story, we followed his directions, which led to a parking area not more than hundred feet away. Thank goodness, he came when he did, because the direction we were following would have taken us deeper into the forest. He led us to safety. Several park rangers were congregated at the parking area and immediately came to our aid. Our adventure in the woods was over."

"My word, I'm stunned. The same message presented fifty years ago." Everett Smith, filled with emotion, was struggling for words. He leaned over and placed his hand on Frank's knee. "What courage it took to hold that secret for all these years. I'm amazed!" Facing both of them, he asked if they were okay.

"Feels good to share it," Frank admitted. "Appreciate the opportunity. What you're doing here is good; it's very important and people are going to benefit from your generosity. Trust me, this is going to change things."

"I agree," added Dee. "I cannot tell you how wonderful it feels to bring this event out into the open. I'm so grateful to all of you for reaching out to us." Looking towards me, she said, "This is a fine answer to the important question."

"What do you mean, dear?" I asked.

"The question!" she responded. "What are we to do? Well, you are doing it? Having these gatherings will have far reaching ramifications. I just know it."

"Thank you, Deidre." I responded. "I really do believe what we're doing here is an essential part of a master plan that is in progress. These gatherings are a pathway to expansion in ways, which we aren't clear about at this time. But this is a beginning. By opening the door for others to share their stories, they will benefit, as you said Frank. Both from telling the story, and by recognizing how many other stories of similar nature are also being told. They will benefit, and we, and other listeners, will benefit from hearing the stories as well. Each time we hear someone's story, I think we will gain greater clarity about the master plan including other ways in which we can participate. I suspect there are many avenues of service from which we can choose, and/or be led to do." Turning to Frank, and then to Dee, I said, "We are so grateful you joined us tonight. I can't imagine starting this new project without the two of you on board." Similar comments were voiced as well. Jan Smith heralded them as the backbone of the family and emphasized their family needed them. For reasons unknown to us, our kind words seemed to make Dee and Frank uncomfortable. They appeared to retreat into themselves and once again were tightly clinching each other's hand. I assumed the incident they had recently experienced at the overlook was the cause of their unusual behavior, but was reluctant to broach the topic. Fortunately, Everett was poised with a question.

"Frank, may I ask you a question?"

"Certainly," came an agreeable reply.

"Was that the only encounter, Frank, or have there been others?" The older man turned to his beloved, and again conferred silently. Then he turned back to his friends to address the question. "Two thoughts raced through my mind in response to your question, Everett. The first is this. The initial encounter had a lasting effect on Dee and me. Fifty years is a long time to think about something, and we have." Looking to Dee for confirmation, he added, "We never stopped thinking about that day in the forest." Frank paused, nestling closer to Dee. "Your timing is relevant, Everett, which brings me to my second thought regarding your question. We have had another encounter. Just last week, in fact." The energy of the group shifted. Excitement took the lead followed by curiosity, concern, and amazement. Personally, I was unable to contain myself.

"Please forgive me, Frank, but I am possessed by curiosity and this madness has stripped me of everything that once resembled good manners. I must know if the same older gentleman was in this recent encounter."

"Oh, pshaw!" exclaimed Dee. "Your forward manner has always tickled us, dear! And we are delighted to assuage your mischievous curiosity. Yes!" she declared emphatically, "the same well-mannered, dapperly dressed fellow appeared again." My mouth fell open, but no sound was uttered. Curiosity has been sated and silenced.

Everett sat forward in his chair, "And has his appearance changed at all?"

"Nope," replied Frank. "He looked the same as he did fifty years ago. And his manner was the same, as well. It was, as if, no time had passed except for us, of course. We certainly don't look the same. Well, that's not true for Dee. She's still a looker!" Rolling her eyes, his wife playfully slapped him of the thigh.

"And what was his message this time," Pat asked. The couple took deep breaths; their discussions about sharing the most recent experience hadn't reached a conclusion yet. It was a complicated matter. To go or to stay had a different meaning to them now, at this age. With Dee's memory becoming more worrisome and Frank's heart acting out, they needed to weigh their decision very carefully. They didn't want to worry their friends.

"Oh, my!" whispered Marilyn. "He offered you the same proposition, didn't he?" Marilyn's intuition was stellar, and the minute she expressed her insight, the group understood.

"Goodness, Dee! What are you going to do?" Jan's sense of alarm was exactly what Frank feared would happen. He stepped in quickly.

"Dear Ones, you must understand we have made no decision about this. Please know we do not take this situation lightly. We need time to process this, but for now, let's stay focused on the point of this evening's gathering." Dee was relieved and very proud of her husband. *You handled that beautifully, dear! Please continue.* A faint smile crossed Marilyn's face. Frank was not the only one who heard Dee's compliment.

"We were indeed advised we have the choice of remaining in this experience or exiting it, but he also apprised us of something rather interesting. He said we had made a commitment long ago and indicated we would fulfill that commitment regardless of the decision made. If we stay, he said, we will fulfill our commitment from this location, and if we exit, we will fulfill our commitment from another location. And then, he spoke to us with a sense of urgency about The Island. He said The Island was in great need, and that we must assist her. And several times, he repeated the message…the time is now. It was an extremely moving appeal. Leaves one in quite a conundrum. The question of the evening presents itself again. What is one to do?"

"We continue!" Marilyn asserted. "We continue to do our own inner work and we continue reaching out to others who may be in need. I want to be a part of this. Count me in!" The Smiths and the Joneses chimed in as well.

"What are your thoughts, dear? What do you think the next step is?" Dee's questions directed towards me opened the stage for another adventure.

"I think we should make our first attempt at outreach. We have three potential guests. Let's begin with them, but also encourage these three to invite anyone else they know who may also be interested. One of the things we must remember is inclusivity. Our gatherings cannot be limited to only those individuals who have experienced an encounter. Others will be interested. Initially, they will be listeners, but with permission from the storytellers, themselves, the listeners will help spread the message about this mysterious phenomenon. Spreading these truths will open the hearts of others, which perhaps is one of the reasons why this is happening. Ideas of importance cannot be effective unless people are willing to open their hearts to possibilities beyond their present scope of understanding." I paused to collect my thoughts and then summarized my plan.

"So, we need to connect with our potential guests and arrange a meeting that will be conducive with their schedules. At the same time, each of us needs to review our network of acquaintances and hopefully come up with a list of folks who might be interested in attending our gathering. And in terms of the meeting itself, I think it is essential we develop a structure that provides a sense of safety for our guests, which will also include a guideline for addressing and maintaining confidentiality. Basically, I think we will learn by doing, but in the meantime, let's strive for another gathering that's founded in curiosity, support, and love."

My suggestions were received with enthusiasm. I knew more ideas would naturally evolve as we moved forward, but for the moment, I was confident we were moving in the right direction. My confidence was abruptly shaken upon remembering Frank's youthful insistence in the woods regarding which direction was to be pursued. A smile washed within me. *I trust, Dear Friends, if my ideas are off the mark, a messenger will be sent to direct me back to the path of intention.*

"Those are worthy suggestions," asserted Dee. "Shall we gather again in a few days, for a progress report. Frank and I will be delighted to host the meeting." I was relieved. Dee's offer indicated they were on board.

# ~ Chapter Fourteen ~

*A passage from*
***The Time is Now***
*(Chapter Sixteen)*

*"When the Mission of Mercy initiated its journey to the faraway galaxy holding the ailing planet, the first wave of volunteers infiltrated the planet with amazing ease. So accepting of newcomers were the residents of the dying planet that no unrest occurred.*

*During this phase of initial entry, many volunteers established themselves as residents of the planet and began, unknown to the residents of the planet, to co-exist with the indigenous population.*

*This period of colonization occurred during the initial phases of the mission and continued throughout the entirety of the operation."*

"Good morning, dear house of mine!" I announced entering into the living room where the meeting with old friends had occurred the night before. "I hope you are feeling refreshed and nourished by the heartfelt connections achieved last night. I trust you enjoyed the stories. Quite an evening, was it not?" Pausing, my eyes perused the room. Perhaps, it was my imagination, but the room did seem happier and more alive this morning. "Your spirits are brighter today my friend. Thank you for welcoming our guests. A good time was had by all!"

Satisfied the house was right with the world, I left for the office. The stack of paperwork, still unattended, was taking on a life of its own. Committed to the task, I hopefully believed an early start would put an end to the rising mound of papers.

"Are you awake, dear?" whispered Jan, wondering if her daily question was becoming annoying. Truth be known, it was the appropriate question for the occasion. She sometimes wondered what would happen if the question wasn't asked. Would they stay in bed all day, or would Everett take responsibility for announcing the morning wakeup question? Perhaps, someday she might experiment, but not today, her mind was racing with ideas and she needed to talk.

"Yes," he replied. "I was waiting for you to ask," he chuckled. "I wonder what would happen if one day you refrained from whispering that question." Jan rolled over, righted herself on her elbow and stared at her husband.

"Have you been reading my mind, dear?" she probed. He laughed again, assuming her reaction indicated another experience of shared thoughts.

"Did I once again repeat your thoughts?" he asked. It was becoming a more frequently occurring experience, which was both amusing and curious.

"Yes, you did! And that brings up one of the things I would like to discuss. So, are you up for some conversation, and if so, where?" Everett assumed the last question was one, which would lead to getting dressed and going for a walk. He informed his lovely wife that conversation would be acceptable, and he left the where part of the question up to her. Much to his surprised, she chose to stay in bed.

"Everett, I'm almost certain Dee and Frank were communicating silently on several different occasions during our gathering. Did you notice?" Other conversations of this nature had occurred before. In fact, they had wondered for quite some time if the Sandersons were actually able to communicate telepathically.

"I did notice, and I think you're right. Something more than just eye talk was transpiring between them. We need to approach them about this, Jan. The worst that can happen is we are wrong, and then, we'll all have a good laugh and no more will be said about it. On the other hand, if they have learned how to finesse this ability, then maybe, they can help us."

"I agree! Let's call them later and see if we can stop by for coffee. We'll bribe them with fresh baked scones!" Delighted with her plan, Jan was ready to move to another topic.

"Well, this also involves Frank and Dee. Everett, should we be concerned about them? They were very private about their decision to go or to stay, and it worries me. I think they were trying to protect us. And I know you're going to tell me it is their business, which it is, but I just want them to know how loved they are and how much they mean to all of us."

"We're in sync once again. Let's reach out to them, and as you say, let them know how important they are to all of us, and also, reassure them we will respect whatever decision they make. We need to support them, Jan. We cannot allow our selfish preferences to interfere in this incredibly intimate decision." His wife sighed deeply, and a few tears escaped, but she knew Everett was right.

"I don't want them to go, but if it is their wish, then we need to celebrate the occasion with them. I do not want them doing this alone, Everett. We need to stand by them, celebrate their lives, and give them the best send off we can imagine." The words flowing from Jan's mouth truly surprised her. "I'm not sure where that came from, but I believe if their decision is to go, then the rest of us have to do the right thing." The couple rested in each other's arms both realizing their conflict of interest. On one hand, they truly wanted the best for Deidre and Frank, whatever that might be, and on the other, they did not want them to choose to leave.

*A passage from*
***The Time is Now***
*(Chapter Seventeen)*

> "*When the colonization of the first wave was complete, the second wave was in readiness to follow and as they settled into their new roles, more waves followed. All these participants offered their experiences to serve the innocent children.*"

"That was an exceptional evening, wasn't it, dear?" commented Frank as he placed his coffee cup back of the table. "There such a good group of people. We're lucky to call them friends!" Dee nodded in agreement, but remained silent, as if she were deep in thought.

"Look now," Frank asserted, "we haven't even made a decision. You're worrying about them and don't even know if it's necessary."

"You were worried last night, dear," she replied. "Their reaction was normal, Frank. They're our friends and they love us. Naturally, they are going to have concerns about this, and I can assure you they will bring it up, so we might as well be prepared for it. What are we going to do, Frank?" Before the question could be addressed, the phone rang.

"Good morning, Jan. So good to hear from you. No, we don't have any plans for the day. Scones? Oh my, yes! Do come over!" Turning to her husband, she smiled lovingly. "The issue is upon us. Let's brew another pot, dear. And perhaps, we should get dressed. Company is coming!"

The tower of paperwork was diminishing. First, the dreaded filing was addressed, which reduced the stack by at least fifty percent, then the equally dreaded monthly bills were paid, leaving the least favored task of all. Correspondence! It sat before me. I wavered. A quick walk around the block seemed like a marvelous idea, and then the compromise was struck. *Complete two pieces of correspondence, just two, and then a walk can be enjoyed.* Selecting two requests, which were the least demanding, I completed the tasks with a flare of competence. Impressed with myself, I took on another, and completed it with equal ease, and then felt extremely deserving of a walk about the neighborhood. The previously, formidable stack, now a mere shadow of itself, no longer dominated my life. And it was still early. Two hours before my first client. Grabbing my cell phone, I prepared to leave the office. Just as I reached the door, the phone rang. I glanced at the device with irritation.

"Oh, for goodness sake, this is a workday. Answer the phone," I scolded myself. And so I did, and much to my surprise it was Anne Billings. I greeted her warmly and acknowledged Marilyn had mentioned she might connect. "So glad you've called. Tell me what's going on with you."

"Well, something rather unusual has happened, and I need to talk to someone about it, and of course, you came to mind. I know this is very last minute, but my schedule just freed up and I was wondering if you might be available?" Obviously, the two hours had purposefully been set-aside for a visit from this old colleague and friend.

"Can you come now? I'm free for a couple of hours."

"I'll be there in ten minutes." With that settled, I returned to my office and pulled out another piece of correspondence and completed the response before my friend arrived. My confidence soared! I faced the tower of paperwork and lived to talk about it!

Glancing out the window, I saw Anne drive up and went to the door to meet her. "Anne, how good it is to see you!" Hugs and warm greetings were exchanged in the waiting room, and then, Anne immediately focused. Her sense of urgency was clear. We quickly moved back into my office and began our conversation, as if, no time had passed since the last time we were together, which is evidence of our long-standing friendship.

"I'm sorry to bother you, but I really need to talk with someone. Thank you so much for being here at this early morning hour." I smiled, pointed to my desk, and proclaimed paperwork as the culprit of my earlier than usual arrival to the office.

"Obviously, you are up and about at this early hour, as well. Something is up with you, my friend. Tell me everything!" And she did!

"The most extraordinary thing has happened, and I'm quite confounded by it, but it's very awkward to talk about. In fact, part of me is afraid to tell you even though trust is not an issue between us. This is a most curious matter." I listened. Of course, with recent events in my life, I wondered if Anne's discomfort was related to a similar experience. Regardless of her story, she needed my undivided attention.

"I've been very involved lately with my inward journey. Feeling called to go deeper I've been pursuing a more dedicated meditation practice. As you well know, the journey can be challenging at times, but for the most part, I really have been inspired. My meditations have been increasing from thirty minutes to an hour, and it's been going well." Our eyes met, and she quickly turned away. I saw a tear resting in the corner of her eye. She blinked, releasing it to create its path down the side of her face. Gently placing my hand on her knee, I urged her to continue.

"Please don't think I'm crazy, because I'm not, but what I'm going to tell you really sounds crazy." My curiosity was rising, but my heart was also aching for my friend. In my most professional tone, I assured her I did not question her sanity.

"We've known each other for years, Anne. I can see something deeply disturbing is going on in your life. Please tell me. I want to help, if I can."

"Thank you, for having faith in me! Something is going on! And as I said, it's very confounding. But quite frankly, it doesn't feel disturbing until I think about telling someone about it. Then, I get very rattled and afraid that someone may accuse me of losing my mind. And the irony is, I am losing my mind, and finding my heart. My meditation practice is truly helping me to have command over my unruly mind so that peace of mind is possible. And with peace of mind comes peace within. I'm happier now than ever before. Even though my present behavior is not evidence of that, it really is true."

"I do believe you, Anne. Meditation has the potential for opening us to all kinds of new and wondrous options. Initially, however, the newness can be very confusing because we are not yet accustomed to the new possibilities." Anne vigorously nodded in agreement. "So, undoubtedly, you have encountered something new." She nodded again. "I would love to hear about it."

"Well, okay. Here goes! Recently, a few weeks ago, I had a wonderful sit.

My mind didn't act out as it so often does, and I sank deeply into that precious inner sanctum that allows for expansion and connection. It was delightful. The hour passed in an instant and when I returned to the present and opened my eyes, I was not alone. Now, when I think about it, I am amazed by my reaction. I was totally calm. Isn't that absurd? Can you imagine coming out of a meditation in the privacy of your own home, and finding a man sitting across from you with the same meditative posture as your own?"

"No, I can't imagine that, Anne. What happened?"

"He stared at me for the longest time in a very kind, loving way. I felt no fear whatsoever. Eventually I said, 'Do I know you?' The expression that crossed his face was one of overwhelming bliss. *'Yes,'* he said with utter joy. *'We are friends of long standing. Your renewed openheartedness allows us to connect in this way. I am deeply grateful to be in your presence, my friend. It is good to see you again.'*

Obviously, I was stunned, curious, confused, all of the above. And speechless! Now, I can think of a thousand questions to ask, but in the moment, I literally was struck silent. And then, he continued to tell me more. He said, *'You must continue with your meditation. It facilitates closer connection and heightens our ability to communicate with one another. Please continue to go deeper and interactions such as this one will become an easier process. Old friend, your time has come. The Mission of Mercy advances and all who committed so long ago to this mission must now move forward. You are called, Dear Friend. You are needed to participate in the grand act of generosity. The time is now. Please do not allow this encounter to fade from your memory. Our reunion has transpired for a reason. Remember!'*

The reason I can repeat all of this to you is because I immediately took notes when the encounter was over."

Reasonably certain about the outcome of Anne's encounter, I quietly asked her what happened next. And it will of course be no surprise to any of you that the man faded from her view. When I asked for a description, it matched the ones previously heard.

"Well, dear friend, I am happy to announce your sanity is not in jeopardy. I believe you, Anne." Her sigh of relieve was audible and more tears welled up and streamed down her face.

"How can you be so certain? This is a crazy story! Why do you believe me?" Her appeal was one of woman who desperately wanted the truth. She didn't want to be discounted or discredited, but she also didn't want to be patronized.

"Anne, dear, I believe you for two very good reasons," I began. "First, because I absolutely trust you and know you would not lie about something like this. And secondly, my dear friend, I believe you because your story is not new to me. I have heard several other stories in recent weeks, which are profoundly similar to yours."

Needless to say, Anne was stunned and relieved to hear that others had encountered the older gentleman. I apprised her of the next meeting we were planning and encouraged her to come. "Our hope is to bring people together to share their stories and to process the messages he is presenting to everyone." At first, she was hesitant and then realized everyone else would have the same concerns as hers.

"I think it would be good to discuss these matters with others who have had similar encounters. Are the others as rattled as me?"

"They are both rattled and at peace. Does that sound familiar? Anne, you are in very good company, some of whom I think you already know. Suffice it to say, our goal is to create a safe environment for everyone to share their stories and their concerns.

These experiences are happening for a reason and the messages received must be spread. I think we have a responsibility to help one another and to keep the messages alive."

Anne agreed and asked to be apprised of the next meeting. Before she left, I sought her permission to share the fact I had met another person with a story. "I will not divulge your name or your story, but it would be good if I could inform the group that another person is on the invitation list."

"Absolutely! And thanks for maintaining confidentiality. For the time being, I still need my privacy."

*A passage from*
***The Time is Now***
*(Chapter Eighteen)*

*"In preparation for the primary leaders arrival, many actively participated in the colonization of the newborns' planet. Unknown this was to the newborns and of no interference to their experiences, for so subtly did the volunteers blend with the newborns' environment."*

"Good morning, you two! Do come in!" greeted Dee. "We've got a fresh pot of coffee brewing. And what is that incredible aroma following you,

Everett?" Holding up the bag of treats just purchased at the local bakery, their early morning guest announced the menu. "For your delight, dear lady, we have fresh scones, and or course, an apple fritter especially selected for Frank!"

"Hmmm!" she proclaimed. "Doesn't that smell yummy? Frank, certainly will be pleased. He's out back setting up the table for us. Let's go join him." They chatted about the beautiful morning as they walked through the house towards the back door.

"Good morning, Frank! Hope you don't mind us barging in at this early hour," declared Jan.

"Not at all. Glad you stopped by. Always nice to start the day with good friends! Please come make yourselves at home." The coffee was poured, treats were nicely placed as the centerpiece of the table, and small talk began. The weather was honored, the garden was praised, and Frank's latest project was admired.

"So, dear ones," Dee said, as she focused on her scone, carefully separating into four parts, "what brings you to our backyard this fine, beautiful day?" Jan and Everett squirmed in their chairs. *Straight to the point, Old Girl! Good for you!* Frank's comment was, of course, for his wife's ears only.

"Straight to the point, Dee. One of the traits, I've always admired about you!" smiled Everett.

"Oh, pshaw!" she responded. "You're here for a reason! You know it, and we know it. This isn't just a casual visit, so get on with it!" Dee's straightforward nature was not uncommon; however, this morning's demonstration was a bit more direct than usual.

"Well, you're right of course," acknowledged Jan. "We do have a few things we'd like to discuss with you." Jan was torn. *Which topic do we begin with?* She thought to herself. *I so wish Everett and I could do this telepathic thing. It would be so useful at times such as this.* My indecision was obvious, and finally, Everett leaned over and encouraged me to just pick a topic and go for it. Once again, he had replied to my thoughts, or so it seemed. I considered it a sign and broached the topic with our friends.

"Dee, Frank, I've wanted to discuss something with you for a long time, but was reluctant to do so, but now, I'm just going to take the plunge. The truth is, Everett and I frequently say things in unison, and then, we just laugh it off as a coincidence. But lately, we have noticed one of us will think something and the other responds to the thought. Again, we've just discounted these incidents as coincidences, but honestly, we don't believe in coincidences, and we are very curious." Laying the foundation for her question, Jan discovered asking the question was actually more difficult than she anticipated. As she reviewed her need to explore this with the Sandersons, Dee intervened.

"Not to worry, dear. We understand your curiosity. Frank and I went through the same phase you're in now. We discounted the little events in many different ways. 'Oh, it's just a coincidence,' we would laugh. 'It's an age thing,' we would quip. 'We've lived together for so long we just anticipate each other's thoughts.' Etc., etc.! Until we reached the point when we could no longer deny the reality of what was really happening. We were indeed tuning-in to one another's thoughts.

And then, we decided to practice. Of course, we didn't have a clue how to proceed, but we just started experimenting, and lo and behold, we began to have results, which encouraged us to pursue telepathy with greater zeal. And now, we find it very useful.

I noticed you watching us last night, dear, and you were correct. We did consult with one another on several occasions." Dee clapped her hands in praise of her younger friends.

"Good for you two! The ability is awakening within you! Pursue it! You can definitely develop the skill. We are living proof of that." At this point, the man dedicated to projects interjected.

"It's just like any other project you take on. If you give it time and attention, you get results. Looking back, if memory serves me, we enjoyed the process. Didn't find it frustrating at all, did we Dee?" She agreed the experience had been fun and entertaining.

"At first, I thought it might be rather tedious, but it never was. Truth is, it was an adventure we enjoyed immensely." Reflecting briefly, Dee took their conversation in another direction. "You know, Frank and I have come to believe telepathy is the next step in humankind's evolution. It's a natural ability that can be developed just like any other skill. If you want to become proficient in a certain area, you have to pursue it with gusto and practice, practice, practice. We sometimes ponder the ramifications telepathy will have on humankind. It gives one much to think about."

"Wow!" replied Everett. "I had no idea this conversation would lead in this direction. It's comforting to hear you talk about your experience in such a matter of fact way. And you've eliminated the idea that this is an impossible quest, and instead, present it as a very attainable goal. This is very inspiring. Thank you! And your thoughts about telepathy's future impact on humankind are fascinating. I would like to talk more about this, if you guys are open to it."

Frank responded, "Indeed! That would be a discussion I would much enjoy, but at another time, I think, because there is still another topic you two want to broach."

"Yes, that's true, Frank," agreed Everett, who decided to simply confront the issue head on. "As you know, we are concerned about this idea of staying or going. We don't want to interfere, but we do want you both to know how much you mean to us and to many others, as well." Jan's eyes began to well up again, but Everett pushed forward.

"We want you to know we will respect whatever decision you make, but we do not want you guys going through this process alone. We've been through all of life's ups and downs together, and we want to be a part of whatever comes next." Everett reached over and gently placed his hand on Jan's forearm making it clear he was speaking for both of them. "We love you guys. You're our family! Please let us be a part of this." Jan's tears flowed freely, as did Dee's. The men were too male to allow theirs to be seen, but the emotions were there, nonetheless.

Dee tried to speak but wasn't able. She communicated to Frank he needed to take the lead. "Well," he said tentatively, "you've touched our hearts. And we're both very grateful. As you might imagine, the incident at the roadside park has given us a great deal to think about, and at this point, we are still processing. It's going to take us a bit to work through all of this. But your words were well spoken, Everett, and heard. We appreciate the sentiment, and of course, it is mutual. We will definitely keep both of you apprised of our deliberations and also call upon you when we need an ear or a helping hand."

"Thank you!" whispered Jan. "My selfishness wants to take over and beg you not to leave, but I'm not going to do that. At least, I'm going to try to contain myself. But I do want to help in any way, which might be useful. This is a remarkable discernment process that's been presented to you and it demands careful consideration. It brings up a ton of emotions and bushels of questions for me, which must pale to your own process. Just know we love you and we want to help."

*A passage from*
***The Time is Now***
*(Chapter Nineteen)*

*"When the first wave arrived to the newly developing planet, in apprehension All were, for uncertain were the volunteers of the contagious effect of the disease contaminating the planet. Difficult it would be to assist the newborns, if the volunteers were susceptible to the illness.*

*Until the colonization occurred, no one could predict the impact of the illness on those of wellness."*

Marilyn rose early with good intentions of going for a walk. She dressed appropriately for a morning hike, headed for the door, and then stopped and turned back towards the kitchen. She felt compelled to check her messages. Although she wasn't tethered to her cell phone, she had learned over the years to trust her intuition, and this morning, Lady Intuition was calling her.

Surprised by one of the callers, she immediately listened to the message. "Well, this is no coincidence," she declared. It was too early to return the call, so she pocketed her phone and headed for the hills again. After walking for about an hour, her phone dinged indicating a missed call, a common thing that happens in the hills where service is iffy at best. She checked the source of the call, and found it was the caller of the earlier message. Marilyn hurried to the next rise hoping it might be a vantage point for service. It was! And she quickly returned the call.

The woman, who shared her bench at the conference, immediately answered the phone, and apologized for her early morning call. Marilyn assured her it was okay. "I'm very glad to hear your voice again. How are you doing?" The innocent question resulted in a plea for help!

"I've had another encounter," she said tearfully. "And I'm just so confused. I'm wondering if we can talk." Marilyn, explaining her present situation, made a plan for a video call later in the day. She was curious, but not alarmed. Walking a bit further, it was obvious her mind was running away with itself, so Marilyn decided to return to the house.

Bill and Pat slept late the morning after the big gathering. At least it was late for them. Finally, when their bed was covered with sunlight, they awakened to the new day. "Yikes!" exclaimed Pat. "What time is it?" She rolled over towards her husband to check the clock. "Goodness, Bill, it is after eight o'clock!'

"Isn't that grand!" he replied. Pat thought about his response and decided he was right. They really didn't need to be jumping out of bed. Nothing was on their calendar and they deserved a nice relaxing morning.

"I slept really well last night," she said. "I think it's because of the meeting. It was so comforting to hear other people's stories, and also to tell our own. How about you, dear? Were you able to get a good night's sleep?" Bill stated he had, and agreed with his wife's supposition regarding the meeting.

"Bill, are you concerned about Frank and Deidre?" Her question indicated she was worried about them. He thought about it for a moment and then solemnly answered.

"It's a very complicated situation, Pat." Bill thought about the situation and then acknowledged it bothered him. "My heart goes out to them, but I also do not want to interfere in their decision-making process. Seems a rather insensitive gesture, if you ask me. I'm not sure which is worse. Hearing that proposal when you're in your early twenties and lost in the woods, or hearing it now, when you're in your seventies with health issues on the horizon. Pat, it just doesn't seem fair…or kind."

"It gives one pause," agreed Pat. "The stories are so remarkable, I just don't want to believe there's something callous about them. We must remember, Bill, the old fellow saved their lives some fifty years ago. After he gave them the message about staying or going, he directed them to safety."

"Yes, that's true, we must remember this. Hopefully, it will help us understand the goodness in a message of this kind. Like you, Pat, I don't want these unique experiences to be spoiled. They seem so special, and purposeful. I've heard people discuss being called, but never really understood what they were talking about until now. Our message truly does feel like a calling, as if, we are intended to participate in something very important. And let's also remember Dee and Frank are called to assist The Island as well. Perhaps, there is more to their message than I'm realizing." Bill contemplated the idea and then expressed another thought.

"Sorry Pat, I went off on a tangent. My main concern is that we stand beside them throughout their discernment process. You know, they've been absent of late, and I think we need to remind them how much they really mean to us.

"Yes, Bill, that's my concern as well. We've all been preoccupied with our own comings and goings. I think we need to be more diligent at keeping in touch with them, and the rest of the gang as well. Coming together last night was an absolute joy. We need to renew our commitment to this family, Bill. I think they need us, and I know we need them."

*A passage from*
***The Time is Now***
*(Chapter Twenty)*

> *"The volunteers came and the mission commenced on the planet destined for destruction, and as the volunteers began their duties so diligently learned prior to their departures, the Ones of Watchful Care noticed a change in the volunteers. That which was most feared and dreaded was occurring. The disease, which infected the planet and its populace was spreading and infecting the volunteers.*
>
> *"Only time would reveal the impact this would have on the Mission of Mercy.*

Marilyn made good time on the walk home. Driven by excitement regarding the earlier phone call, her steps seemed lighter and easier on the return trek. She readied herself for the day, had a quick breakfast, and then, found she was free for several hours. Impulsively, she texted the new friend recently met at the conference to see if she was available to do the video-call sooner than previously scheduled. As luck would have it, the new friend was available. Marilyn immediately went to her home office, turned on the computer and waited for it to boot up. "This doesn't have anything to do with luck," she declared to her empty room. "And it isn't a quote-quote coincidence. This little orchestration of opportunity is about intention. This is happening for a reason!"

Marilyn pressed the call button on her computer and within seconds, her new friend appeared on the screen. "Isn't this a marvelous device?" she declared. "Tell me what's going on Casey?"

"Oh, Marilyn, once again I am in need of a listening ear."

"Good! I have two available at the moment, and I am filled with curiosity. So, tell me everything, please."

"The old man appeared again." Through the screen those deep dark eyes met mine and I knew another adventure was about to be revealed. "I walk every day; it is as essential part of my commitment to wellness. And I typically carry my journal with me in case the moment grips me. Well, that particular morning the need to journal was singing loudly within me, so my footsteps took me quickly to my favorite bench, which I have designated as 'my bench.' Fortunately, as fate would have it, my bench was vacant. I sat down, opened the journal, and the words began to flow from my pen. It was extraordinary, Marilyn. My heart spilled out onto the pages, and at times, it actually felt, as if, a conversation was underway. Time literally stood still as the pages filled. I didn't want to stop, and I'm not sure it was even a possibility. My hand was writing faster than my mind could think. I am still astounded when I remember the experience." She paused, not because she wanted to, but because she needed to catch her breath.

"Well, that was the first part of the story, which I want to talk more about later, but now, we must move onto the next part of my morning. Eventually, the writing waned and finally came to an end. I was exhausted, Marilyn, but also deeply saddened the experience was over. And then, I looked up, and standing in front of me at water's edge, was the man seen in Tibet. I was astounded, and extremely grateful for his return. I gestured to him to come sit beside me on the bench. And he did! So there we were, sitting sideways so we could face each other and he greets me in that lovely way he did before. *'I am pleased to be in your presence once again, Dear Friend. I hope it is agreeable to you.'*

I replied it was an honor to be in his presence again, and also indicated there were many questions I wished to ask him. He nodded and laughed, and then spoke again.

*'Your writing went well this morning. It is the way of the future. Many more experiences such as this one will come forward in the days ahead. You must attend this task. It is your calling.'* Needless to say, I was puzzled, but once again, no questions came to mind.

Marilyn, what's wrong with me? I had dozens of questions to ask him, but when he announced my quote-quote calling, I fell silent again." Her frustration was understandable. Giving her time to breathe again, I posed a question.

"Does this sound true for you, Casey? Do you feel you have been called to write or to receive messages, as the gentleman advised."

"Well, I certainly never considered this before, but in the last few days the journaling has continued in ways, which are unbelievable to me. I am truly astounded. And it does feel, as though, I am receiving messages as you inferred. Quite frankly, I'm just taking dictation, Marilyn. This is very odd, but it is also beautiful, and I don't want it to stop."

"I can certainly understand your reaction. Am I correct in assuming the writings are lovely and powerful."

"Yes, they are, but tell me please, why do you presume that?" she asked.

"I've read several books, Casey, by individuals who claim the material is channeled, and the messages are astonishing. Very deep, thought provoking, expansive, compassionate, loving, etc. Those are just a few words that come to mind. You may wish to explore some of these books for yourself. You may find it very comforting. From what I understand, when this happens to someone, they experience similar reactions as you are having now.

Casey, I'm so grateful you are sharing this with me. I am deeply honored, and I believe everything you're telling me. And I am really very happy for you." We were quiet for a few minutes both trying to absorb our conversation and then I encouraged Casey to finish her story.

"Oh, yes, there is more! He brought up The Island again. *'You must follow your calling for The Island needs you. The writings will help save The Island. Listen to me, Little One. You are here for a reason. Take the messages received and bring them forward to the masses. You must do this. The Island is in great need. The writings will help her. I must go now, but I will return again. Until then, please continue your work. It is of great importance.'* And then, he just faded away again."

"Casey, I'm going to say just one word to you. Believe!" She looked at me curiously, but at the same time understood.

"I do, Marilyn. I do believe this is real!" The two women chatted briefly. Both expressed their appreciation for the other and their desire to keep in touch. And then Marilyn remembered the group.

"Casey, I was so mesmerized by your story I forgot to tell you the group is moving forward. Our next step is outreach, so we are asking people, such as you, to join us for our next meeting. Presently, we have eight core members and our goal is to host these gatherings on a regular basis. It is an opportunity to meet others who have similar experiences, and also a chance to get validation for your own story. So, you are invited and we hope you can come. Do you think it would be possible? Casey, you're welcome to stay with me if you like. And another thing, if you know of anyone, who has had an experience or simply is interested in these types of events, we urge you to invite them, as well.

Our goal is to reach out to people from our present location, and hopefully create satellite groups in other areas, so that traveling doesn't become an issue."

"This really is a wonderful project, Marilyn. Noteworthy! I am curious where it will take you and the others. When you decide upon a date, please let me know and I will try to make arrangements to be there. Thank you again, Marilyn. Our conversation has been very helpful and heartwarming."

After the video call ended, Marilyn just sat in front of her computer staring at the blank screen. "Where is this taking us my friends?" She closed her eyes and opened her heart to connection. "I am so grateful. Your work is stellar to witness."

*"As is yours, Old Friend. You continue to be in the right place at the right time, and your facilitation skills in all situations are, as always, flawless. We are most grateful. Please continue to listen with the ears of your heart, for your assistance is needed. Rest assured, you are loved and cherished, Dear Friend.*

"Thank you," she whispered. "As always, you remain in my heart, and I look forward to our next visit. In peace be, Dear Friends."

# ~ Chapter Fifteen ~

*A passage from*
***The Time is Now***
*(Chapter Twenty-One)*

*"When all was said and done, the Ones of Ancient Age knew their plan must be enacted, for without action the innocent children of the dying planet would be lost. It was a time of great sorrow and solemn resolve. None wished to intervene, but All knew it was necessary."*

"Frank, do we have everything we need for the gathering tomorrow evening? I've checked our list twice. Will you go over it again, just in case I'm missing something?" They sat down together and reviewed the list, which seemed to be growing. Going over each item, it appeared every thing needed was already in house.

"Dee, accordingly to our list, we are in good shape for the meeting. Now, tell me if there is anything in particular you would like for me to do today so tomorrow is an easy day, rather than a hectic one."

Concentrating on various areas of the house, Dee reviewed each situation. "The living room is ready except for bringing in a couple of chairs from the den. That task could be done today. The bathrooms are clean and fresh towels are already in place. The kitchen is ready to rock and roll, and the deck will need to be freshly swept right before everyone arrives. Can you think of anything I may be missing, dear?"

"We're ready, Dee! You haven't forgotten anything and we can just go about having a nice day without stressing about the gathering." Her husband's words were very reassuring. Frank noticed Dee's concern about her memory and it worried him. She didn't appear to be losing ground, but she was so worried about it he feared she was losing confidence in herself. "Dear, you're doing fine. You haven't missed a beat. This event is coming together because of you, not me. You are the one who has orchestrated everything, and I'm simply double-checking your double-checking. Please stop worrying. You're doing fine."

"Okay," she replied. "I get it! Stop worrying! Will you remind me if I forget to stop worrying, dear?" And then she burst into laughter. "Oh Frank, all we can do is laugh about this, because it is what it is!" They hugged, kissed, and informed each other of their individual plans. Frank was headed to his studio. Dee was going to finish the book she was reading. And then the doorbell rang.

"My goodness, who can that be?" asked Dee. The aging couple went together to see who was at the door. "Oh my!" Dee exclaimed. "What a wonderful surprise! Please come in!" Pat and Bill entered their friends' home with a small bouquet of flowers in hand.

"And bearing gifts, as well. What are you two up do?" quizzed Frank.

"Well, we've been thinking about you and decided to behave impulsively. So here we are dropping in unannounced!" declared Pat. Dee graciously accepted the flowers and praised them for their spontaneous behavior.

Leading their friends, Bill and Pat, into the mainstream of their house, Frank asked, "What's your preference? Indoors or outdoors?" Everyone agreed the deck was the place to be. As they moved towards the backdoor, Dee inquired about refreshments. It was difficult for her to accept that no one was in need. After three offers and three declines, she finally adjusted to the idea.

"Let's put the umbrella in place, dear?" proposed Dee, as she and Pat brushed leaves off the table and chairs. Bill motioned to Frank that he would manage the umbrella, and within a couple of minutes, they were all seated around the table.

Frank and Deidre knew what was coming, but they waited for the Joneses to begin the conversation. The usual, and presumed necessary small talk that typically precedes heartfelt conversation was thankfully brief, and then, the true purpose of their friends' visit commenced.

"We are here for a reason, as you both know already," Pat began, "so there's no point in us beating around the bush. The fact is we love you very much, and we need to talk with you about the message you received from our mysterious stranger."

"Yes," replied Frank. "He is a curious fellow, but obviously well meaning. Dee and I are sorry everyone is in a stir about this, but the truth is, we are grateful for your concern and your support."

"Well, we are concerned, and that's why we're here," stated Bill. "I hope you both know we do not want to interfere in your lives, but at the same time, we don't want you to be dealing with this dilemma alone. We want to support you in any way we can."

"We know that, Bill," responded Dee. "And we are so touched by your offer. We really do need our friends support. As you both know, the possibility of remaining or leaving has many ramifications, and we're just beginning to realize how powerful and important this decision is. So rest assured, we will reach out to you, as we try to make our way in this new territory."

"We want to do the right thing," asserted Frank. "It's very comforting to hear we will fulfill our life purpose regardless of our decision; however, we would like to have clarity about our life purpose. What is it? What are we to do?" Turning to his beloved wife, he lovingly continued. "Dee is my priority! I need to be certain whatever we decide to do is in her best interest." Turning to Bill, he questioned, "You can understand that, can't you?" Both Pat and Bill reassured Frank his priorities were also theirs.

"Perhaps," started Pat, "we need to remind one another of the meaning of this friendship. We are a family, which means we are going to take care of one another. I hope you guys understand this. Our preference is for you to stay, but if you choose to move on, we're going to be a part of that process. And if you choose to stay, we're going to be a part of that life process as well. You are not alone." Once again, Frank and Deidre were overwhelmed with gratitude. So much love had come their way in the last week. Dee prayed she would remember these moments. And her beloved silently responded. *You will, Dee. You will remember!*

# ~ Chapter Sixteen ~

*A passage from*
***The Time is Now***
*(Chapter Twenty-Two)*

> *"With the decision made and the plan initiated, the Ones of Leadership Roles continued their studies of the people inhabiting the distant planet.*
>
> *"Never before had such a massive intervention been undertaken and All were concerned for the care and safety of the Ones of Innocence. Their continuance was the purpose of this mission and their continuance was of the deepest concern to the members of the Universal Family.*
>
> *All efforts made were on their behalf, and of this, no one was ever in unawareness."*

"Well, here we are!" greeted Dee. "We are so pleased to have all of you in our home again. And very eager to hear about what has transpired during the last week." Excitement filled the room. Marilyn described the energy of the group as happy energy. Although I remained silent, my interpretation of the group's energy was similar. Excited, curious, and hopeful. We were all glad to be in one another's company. "So, when our last meeting ended, we all agreed it would be wise to have a follow-up meeting to update each other on progress made, as well as, any situations that may have arisen. Are we all still on track with this?" Everyone agreed and were eager to begin. "So, who would like to go first?" Much to Dee's surprise, Frank volunteered.

"Well, I would just like to say Deidre and I are still reeling from the outpouring of support we've received from all of you. And we want you to know how grateful we are. As we prepared for this evening, we were reminded how much we have enjoyed out get-togethers over the years, and we want to renew our commitment to gathering more often. We've been rather self-absorbed lately with our aging process, and I guess we retreated, not even noticing we had done so. But we want more contact with all of you, and we're very grateful you're in our lives." Frank stopped briefly, and then muttered, "Well, that's where we are. Thanks again, to all of you!" Looking toward her beloved, Dee accessed her inner voice. *Thank you, dear, for making those loving comments. Well done!* Marilyn's attentive ear concurred with Dee's praise for her husband. To keep herself from speaking back in like manner, she offered to go next.

"As the universe prefers, the woman who I mentioned last week, called me before I had a chance to call her. It seems she has experienced another encounter with our mysterious fellow and she needed to talk about it, which my friends, speaks to the importance of having a group available for people in need. I updated her about our progress and she is very interested in coming to our first meeting. So as soon as we know a date, I will let her know and she will attempt to adjust her schedule accordingly. By the way, she too believes this group idea is wonderful and important. She's looking forward to meeting everyone, and is also very grateful for our sensitivity to the confidentiality issue."

"That's wonderful news," expressed Bill. "Without giving any of the details, Marilyn, can you tell us if the second encounter was as remarkable as the first?" She indicated it was and suggested the second message had expanded upon the first.

"I'm wondering," Marilyn continued, "if these experiences are so energetically charged that they must remain relatively short for the recipient's sake, and perhaps, for the mysterious man himself. I also wonder if the recipient of the message is given only that, which he or she can presumably handle in the moment." Her thoughts aroused curiosity.

"I've had similar questions and thoughts," added Bill. "I'm very curious to know if it's common for people to have more than one encounter. Maybe, I'm planning ahead," he said not knowing if he really wanted another encounter. "I'm also very curious about this man. Who is he? What is he? And why are we all encountering him now? Don't you think it's strange we are encountering so many people who also are encountering the same little old man? Really makes you wonder. I also wonder if he is the only messenger. Has anyone else had one of these encounters with someone other than the old man in suit and tie?" Bill's last question startled the Smiths. They turned to one another in surprise and then Everett spoke.

"Yes, we have! Your question brought it back to us, Bill. The man we saw on the beach was not dressed in suit and tie. I remember he was dressed in white." He looked to Jan for affirmation.

"Yes, it was a loosely fitting garb that was flowing freely in the wind, and I'm trying to remember his face, but it's gone. I cannot see him clearly, but my sense of him was very different than the man in the airport. Do you remember, Everett?" Her husband was also confused. "I can't see his face either, but in our conversations, I never thought of the man on the beach as being the man in the airport. It is very interesting that neither of us have a clear picture of him, yet we have a very clear image of the man in the suit."

Listening with extreme interest, Frank interjected his thoughts. "Well, I too wonder about the presumed increase in these encounters, and I say presumed, because we really aren't certain there's been an increase. What we do know is our first encounter," he said pointing to Dee, "was over fifty years ago, so these events have been going on for a long time. Was it also happening to other folks back in the day? We don't know. And we also don't know what's happening in other parts of the world. I find it hard to believe we are the only people involved in this."

After Frank's last comment, Marilyn piped up. "Again, I cannot reveal details, but I do want to remind everyone our encounters already include faraway lands. Everett and Jan were in India and on an island in the Pacific when they had their encounters. The woman who I met was in a distant land during her first encounter, so, I think it is fair to say this is not a local affair."

Dee had been watching me for some time as I was observing everyone else. At one point, I looked in her direction and winked at her. *She knows my wheels are turning*, I said to myself. And then, she acknowledged my thoughts, by quietly addressing me.

"Dear one, your wheels are turning full speed ahead. Would you like to share your thoughts about this discussion?" I nodded acknowledging her telepathic abilities, and then, took a deep breath.

"Well, I share similar thoughts and am asking similar questions, with one additional one, which has not yet been spoken. My question is, 'Why us?' Why have the eight of us been brought together to address these encounters? And when I think of this question, it makes me start wondering about the process from a bigger picture. How did we all come together in the first place? How did we meet? When? Where? When did our friendships merge together into this long-standing arrangement that brings us to this point in time as a group facing a very peculiar situation? And thoughts, such as these, make me believe we are involved in a very elaborate mission that has been in operation for a very long time, and which is now advancing forward. For reasons, we are yet to understand, it appears we have all agreed to participate in this mission and we agreed to come together as a team to address whatever the issue is.

I don't really know how to articulate this, because honestly, it sounds weird, and yet, it feels right. We are here for a reason. We are together for a reason. And whatever is happening, we are being guided, led, and/or called to move forward. I feel, as if, we are being primed to go into action. And as I hear myself speaking about this, there's a part of me diminishing every word coming out of my mouth. But I'm trying really hard not to give into that part, because, my friends, we are needed. Every message received, has mentioned, 'You are needed!' We must trust this message. I don't think it is time for us to listen to the nonsense of our minds. We really must trust the other component of these repeated messages. 'The time is now.' I think it is time for us to trust what's going on here and to support one another through the process. When one of us falls victim to our doubts and fears, someone else has to stand strong. Hopefully, we won't all have a sinking spell at the same time.

My friends, we know something unique and important is transpiring within and around us, and we cannot allow ourselves to deny this is happening, because if we do, we will lose our focus. Even though, we do not have precise understanding of what is happening, we know we are being called and we feel the energy associated with this calling. When doubts invade our thoughts, our energy diminishes and our ability to hold onto the calling wanes. Perhaps, one of the reasons we have come as a group is to overcome this perplexing dynamic.

I am so grateful to be a part of this mysterious mission, for which we have undoubtedly volunteered. I truly cannot imagine anywhere I would rather be. Here in this setting, at this time, with my family of choice working towards something, which is to benefit humankind. This pleases me! I'm grateful for the opportunity to be of service and I am eternally grateful to be facing this situation with my best friends." Falling into silence, I breathed deeply and prayed my words were assisting.

Bill leaned forward in his chair with elbows resting on his knees. *There has to be a way,* he thought, *to get more information. If we're here on a mission, there must be a means of opening lines of communication.* Before he managed to articulate his notion, Frank Sanderson replied to his thoughts.

"I wonder the same thing, Bill. How do we increase our ability to receive additional information so that we can function more efficiently?" Frank's response startled Bill. He was certain his thoughts had not been spoken, and yet, Frank addressed them, as if, they were vocalized. "I would like to put that question to you two," Frank said looking towards Marilyn, and then, to me. "You two have abilities that are beyond the rest of us here. Your intuitive skills are keen, and Dee and I both know you are able to communicate in ways that we cannot. Perhaps, one of the reasons we have come here as a team is so that we can share our gifts with one another. So, tell us," he said assertively, "What do you have to say about this?" Bill, continuing to look extremely perplexed, was becoming overwhelmed by curiosity. Rather than addressing Frank's interception of his thoughts, he chose to listen carefully.

Marilyn and I just smiled at one another, each inviting the other to go first. "Well, Frank, you speak frankly," chuckled Marilyn. "What I have to say is this. I agree with you! It makes sense we have all come together to learn from one another, which will inevitably enhance our developmental process. Frank, you and Dee are very perceptive, and our friend here," she said pointing to me, "is profoundly connected in ways I am just discovering. As for me, my intuitive skills are trustworthy, and I do have a burgeoning telepathic ability, which has allowed me to witness the beautiful telepathic communication the two of you enjoy. I think you and Deidre can help the rest of us tap into our own telepathic abilities, and by working on this as a group, our skills will advance quickly.

I am also very happy to share with all of you what I know about intuitive awareness, which by the way, is similar to telepathy in that, it is also a natural ability, which is possessed by everyone. If we attend our natural abilities, they will flourish, if we don't, they will fade, and we, as a species, will forget these abilities ever existed in us. Well, the truth is, these abilities do exist, and it is our responsibility to learn how to access them." Marilyn turned to me with a look that said, "Go for it, Girl!"

"Frank, you amaze me!" I heard myself say to him. "When you decide to come forward, you do it with gusto!" As Frank turned several shades of red, I thought about his courage and wondered if I could do the same. Quietly, a whisper was uttered, "What a role model, you are Frank Sanderson!" Assessing the situation a while longer, I finally realized and accepted there was no way to speak the truth, but truthfully. Facing Marilyn, I began with the over used four letter work, "Well, my friends, for years, I have hoped some day, topics such as this one would happen freely and openly without fear of retribution, and here we are now pursuing said topic. This is a day to remember! So, I will try to be as brave as my two friends here, and acknowledge I too have learned to access some skills of old, which have certainly served me well. For reasons I cannot explain, my ability to hear and receive messages from those who do not reside on this plane of existence was activated in my early thirties. Fortunately, my grandmother also had this ability so she assisted me through the earlier phases of confusion and disbelief. And most importantly, she reassured me the experiences I was having were simply a natural ability capable of being developed and refined. What a gift, she was! And over the years, the ability to communicate with others has become more and more accessible and proven to be incredibly useful to those who are willing to open themselves to the information provided.

The ability to communicate telepathically is the means by which I am able to communicate with those in places we cannot imagine, and others can access this ability as well. I would love to tell you that I am special, but it just isn't so. I am, however, dedicated. And once I accepted this was intended to be a part of my life, I went after it. I pursued it, practiced it, and made it a part of my life. Bottom line, if you want to refine a skill set, you must practice.

Each of us will bring our own unique essence into the pool and we will all learn and benefit from the mixture of resources we share. This is very exciting, my friends, and once again, I must express my appreciation for what is transpiring among us, and acknowledge how happy this makes me. This is a dream coming true!"

"Isn't this fascinating?" remarked Dee. "We certainly are learning new things about one another, aren't we?" Her attitude was playful. She and Frank were thriving. I wondered if they might be finding a purposeful reason for staying.

Jan shook her head in disbelief. "My goodness, what a talented group we have here! So, the four of you," she said pointing to the Sandersons, Marilyn, and me, "are all practicing telepathic communication. And you dear, are able to communicate with those from beyond. Is this the correct way of speaking about these forms of communication?" she asked specifically of me. Without waiting for a response, she turned to Marilyn and noted, "And you are highly intuitive to the point that you really trust your ability."

"Let's just say," Frank intervened, "we all have abilities, which are continuing to develop."

"Nicely stated, Frank!" interjected Everett. "I'm intrigued, and surprised so much has been happening among us, and yet in general, we knew little if anything about what was really going on." Everett's comment was well taken. Many truths had been hidden for a very long time.

"I'm glad our secrets, our fears, are finally out in the open. It's refreshing!"

Marilyn looked about the room, making eye contact with everyone. "Thank you for allowing this to happen! This is such a relief!"

"Well, I don't think any of us anticipated this happening tonight," Dee declared in surprise. "I wonder what else will come out of these meetings?" Other members of the group muttered similar comments. "Shall we return to our progress reports? Does anyone else have something to add?"

Jan Smith reported they had made contact with the woman called Wendy who is very interested in coming to our meeting. "She indicated a weekend would be better for her, but she would try to be flexible. Marilyn, what about your person? Did she indicate a preference for weekend or weekday?" Marilyn admitted it hadn't been discussed, but said she would email the woman when she returned home.

I then reminded my friends there might be another possibility, but I still needed to contact the person in question. I raised another thought. "Is there anyone here locally we can think of who may have an interest in what we're pursuing. Let's put our fears aside for a moment and see if we can come up with any names." No names immediately came to mind, so we all agreed to put that task on our respective To Do lists.

"Let's think about timing," asserted Dee. "Dear, since you are hosting, you need to decide what is good for you." I indicated complete flexibility. We finally decided upon three different dates to offer our out of town guests and sighed a relief.

Dee asked us all to stand in a circle and to join hands. We did as directed. Then she asked us to plant our feet solidly upon the floor and to take a long deep breath. Again, we did as suggested. "Beautiful Presence, who is responsible for us all, we come in gratitude. Thank you for bringing the eight of us together. Thank you for watching over us all these years. Thank you for providing this opportunity to work together on this new adventure. Thank you for making us a family. Thank you for all you do for all that is. In peace be!"

Heartfelt hugs were exchanged, goodbyes were offered, and the meeting came to an end.

woman looked about the room making eye contact with everyone. "How could you allow this to happen? This is such a relief!"

"Well, I don't think any of us anticipated this happening tonight," Deb declared, [illegible] "I'm not sure what she will [illegible] of these meetings." Other members of the group muttered similar comments. "She [illegible] [illegible]. Does anyone else have something to add?"

[illegible] they had made contact with the woman called Wendy who is very [illegible] [illegible] [illegible] she indicated a weekend would be better for [illegible] [illegible] to be flexible [illegible] what about [illegible] [illegible] indicated [illegible] forward to [illegible] [illegible] said she would [illegible] until the woman when [illegible]

[illegible] there [illegible] not possible, but I still need [illegible] the [illegible] thought [illegible] there [illegible] [illegible] [illegible] [illegible] [illegible] [illegible] and [illegible] [illegible] immediately came to mind [illegible] [illegible] [illegible] lists.

[illegible] since you are [illegible] what is good for you [illegible] [illegible] [illegible] three [illegible] out of [illegible] [illegible]

[illegible] [illegible] [illegible] is declared. [illegible] [illegible] [illegible] suggested [illegible] who is responsible for [illegible] we [illegible] [illegible]. Thank you for [illegible] [illegible] us together. Thank you for watching over us all these years. Thank you for [illegible] support [illegible] on this new adventure. [illegible] thank you for [illegible] [illegible] all the [illegible]

[illegible] were changed [illegible] and the meeting came to an end.

# ~ Chapter Seventeen ~

*A passage from*
***The Time is Now***
*(Chapter Twenty-Three)*

*"As the time grew near for the Ones of Leadership to join the volunteers already in place, it was a time of great anticipation. All who had participated awaited their arrival.*

*What was next to come rested upon the shoulders of the leaders and their presence and guidance were necessary to fulfill the rescue."*

"My Dear Friends, your work astounds me. The revelations in tonight's meeting were timely and beautiful. I am so grateful for everything you are doing. We are coming together as a very refined instrument of service. The release of decades of fears and doubts lifted this evening. And we all came away lighter and brighter. Please guide me as needed. I desire to be of assistance."

*"Old Friend, we too are grateful for the turn of events. How quickly things change, and in the process, transformation unfolds. Greater peace lies within this cluster of friends, and now the work that is done will be of a higher quality, for less burdened are they by the human condition. Please continue to listen with the ears of the heart and maintain a sense of opening for all who approach you. Another will come forward in mere days. Know this one is intended to join the group for this one will serve as a core member, as will the original eight.*

*All are most pleased, Dear Friend, with the unfoldings occurring at this location and in other locations. The Mission of Mercy is moving forward and there is reason for hope. Please continue, Old Friend. Your assistance is needed! In peace be!"*

"Frank, dear, you were marvelous, this evening. Now don't you roll your eyes at me! I'm serious. You took charge and led the group into an extremely important conversation. And it was marvelous. My goodness, dear! Our secret about our telepathic abilities is finally out. Isn't it just wonderful? Our friends know we are telepaths, and they also know about the old man in the woods. It's so freeing!" She sighed with relief.

"I think we did some good work, Dee! And there are many more possibilities that may come out of these meetings. If we decide to stay, we may have a very busy future here. Are you up for that, Old Girl?" They both remained silent still thinking about the possibilities and then Dee asked.

"Do you think we have the energy to be actively involved in this new adventure?" Frank did not say anything for what seemed a very long time and then he replied.

"Yes." Dee waited for an explanation of some kind, but done was forthcoming. Eventually she asked.

"Would you like to expand upon that, dear? I know there's more to this than a simple yes, so please enlighten me." Frank's quiet nature was a blessing at times, and other times, very frustrating. A thoughtful man, he often got lost in his ruminations. Tonight, she prodded him to speak aloud.

"Sorry, dear. I've done it again, haven't I?" She nodded in agreement. "Dee, in the last week, we've experienced renewed energy. Obviously, our encounter with the mystery man played a role in that, but there's more to it than just his timely reappearance. Reconnecting with our friends also put a spark under us again, and it's good for us. We're feeling alive again, Dee.

I think we allowed our aging issues to get us down for a while and we started believing the idea we were limited, and as a result, we began limiting ourselves in ways, which may not be necessary. We certainly have to make adjustments in accordance with our aging bodies, but we do not have to stop living. These meetings and the connections with our friends have really brought us back to life. So yes, I do think we have the energy to be involved, and I also think we have a lot to offer. We're still sharp, Dee! You did a beautiful job of facilitating the group tonight, and I am pleased with my contributions. The point is, maybe we have found our purpose. We are still useful, Dee, and by participating in this new adventure, I'm certain we can be of service." His wife listened carefully and was pleased by what she was hearing. She too felt ignited by the events of the last week, and she had so enjoyed hosting the party and facilitating the flow of the meeting. It was enlivening, and reassuring. She wondered if their reclusive behavior of late was contributing to her memory problems.

"I've wondered about that, as well," responded Frank, not even noticing he had once again responded to her unspoken words. "You were brilliant tonight, Dee! I believe engaging with our friends and having this new project to pursue will do both of us a lot of good, and in turn, we will be helping others."

"Are you awake, dear?" whispered the loving wife of Everett Smith. He chuckled. *Surely she doesn't want to go for a walk in the moonlight.*

"We just got into bed, Jan. I'm still wide-awake."

"Can we process the gathering for a few minutes?" Everett agreed it might be helpful and invited her to go first.

"I'm just curious about this notion of telepathic behavior. This is going to sound demanding and childish, but the truth is, I want to be able to do this! If our friends can do it, then we can too. Let's start practicing, Everett." Her husband laughed again and teased her.

"Jan, are you feeling competitive?" His question startled her. Even though she knew Everett was teasing her, she took a moment to think about his suggestion. The idea of competition had never entered her mind, but Jan wanted to be certain it wasn't an underlying factor in her zeal to learn how to communicate telepathically.

"Geez!" she finally responded. "Everett, this is an extremely important question." He tried to minimize his suggestion, but Jan dismissed his attempt. "I'm serious Everett. I know you were just teasing, but it is a very powerful question. I want to understand what is motivating me, and the truth is, I don't want to be left out. If telepathy becomes the new way of communicating, I want to be part of it, and when it became evident tonight that four out of eight of us are already practicing telepathy, it made me feel like we are missing the boat." Jan quietly reflected upon her response and then emphatically announced, "I don't want to miss the boat, Everett! This isn't about being competitive; it's about taking action. Excuse the pun, but we need to get on board with this new way of being." Listening to his wife's response, Everett realized the impact of his question made in jest.

"Your point is well taken, Jan, and I agree with you. We need to take this seriously and we need to start now. Perhaps, we can see if Dee and Everett can give us some tips on how to begin. Let's give them a call in the morning!" Jan was pleased, but she wasn't finished. The disclosure made by their friend about using telepathy as a means of communication to talk with those from other planes of existence peaked her imagination and she wanted to know her husband's opinion about such possibilities.

"I know nothing more about this than you do, dear, but I'm open to new possibilities. Just look at how much we have learned from our friends in the last couple of weeks. The diversity in our small network of friends is amazing. Because we've known each other for years, history tells us we can trust one another, and because of the trust we share, we openheartedly believe each other's stories. Jan, just imagine how many other experiences are happening around this planet that also need to be shared, and likewise, need to be trusted and accepted. We need to open our hearts to new ideas and to the people who bring the new ideas to the forefront, even though we don't presently know these people. These unusual experiences, as we keep calling them, may become less and less unusual as more people come forward to share their stories. I don't understand what's happening, Jan, but I want to remain open, because whatever is unfolding is real and it's happening for a reason."

"That was well said, Everett and I agree with you. We've been very fortunate to be among friends during this process. It may become more complicated for us when we share our stories with strangers, but strangers will hopefully become new friends when we realize we have something in common. These experiences may serve as a bridge between cultures. Wouldn't that be wonderful?" The possibility inspired more new ideas, but the hour was late and this new topic needed fresh energy.

"Everett, before we end, I have one more question. You didn't respond to the possibility that telepathy could be utilized to communicate with others from planes different than ours. What do you make of this, dear?" The room became silent. Jan wondered if her husband had fallen asleep, and then, he answered.

"I believe!"

"Bill, let's sit on the porch for a while. I think swinging will help me to wind down. Do you mind?" inquired Pat who was still wired from the meeting.

"Not at all. Sounds like a wonderful idea. Are you still processing tonight's conversations?" he asked as they both seated themselves on their porch swing.

"Over and over again!" she responded. "We have the most remarkable friends, Bill, and yet, tonight we learned things about them we never knew before. It is mind-boggling!"

"Yes, it is! And it's very exciting. Little did we know just how remarkable how friends really are. Fifty percent of us are able to communicate telepathically. That's absolutely amazing! When Frank responded to my thoughts tonight, it blew me away. Pat, I want to learn how to do this! Will you join me? Please say yes, dear." The swing quietly swished back and forth, as Pat pondered her husband's request. She wasn't at all reluctant. In fact, she was eager to pursue the intricacies of telepathy, but her thoughts took her in another direction. Their dear friend's comment about using telepathy to access those from other planes tugged at her. She wanted more information about this.

"My answer is yes, Bill. I do indeed want to explore this possibility with you. Let's add another adventure on top of the adventure we are already undertaking." Her husband was delighted.

"And by the way," he added. "Let's also find out more about accessing telepathy to communicate with individuals on other planes of existence." Pat stopped the swing and stared at her husband.

"Did you just access my thoughts, Bill Jones?" Her question surprised him.

"Not that I know of," he responded inquisitively. "Why do you ask?"

"I was just thinking the same thing." They sat still, each indulging in their own thoughts while wondering if the other could overhear what was being contemplated.

"Beloved Friends, I come in gratitude," whispered Marilyn. "The wisdom shared this evening astounds me, and I am grateful for the privilege of being a part of the conversation. I am grateful for these wonderful friendships that have sustained me for decades and which still nourish my heart and soul. I am grateful for the opportunity unfolding before us, and for the privilege of experiencing this adventure together. I am grateful for the sense of family existing among us, and I am most grateful for your ever-present presence. You were with us this evening. You are here now. And I know you will be with me through the night and all the days ahead. I am grateful for all that is done on behalf of all that are, and I am grateful for this quiet time to express my appreciations. My heart is full, Old Friends." Marilyn sat quietly wondering if those who surrounded her were able to hear her communiqué. She hoped they could. She prayed they knew her words were sincere. She chose to believe connection had been successful.

*"As are you grateful, Dear Friend, so too are we. Your words of gratitude honor present friends and friends of old and all who are of listening ears appreciate the kindness conveyed. Your gratitude shifts the energy surrounding you allowing us to connect with you in this unique, yet ordinary way. We are most grateful for this communication and desire to have more connection with you in days ahead. The time is now! You are now ready for frequent contact and we ask you to develop a regimen that will allow such interactions into your daily schedule. Through repetition, your ability to communicate with us will rapidly advance. This is needed! We repeat…the time is now!*

*Dear Friend, long have we waited for this moment in time. As the Mission of Mercy advances forward, those who can, must do what they are intended to do. You are here to advance the cause of transformation. Be not afraid. You are ready to proceed and we are ready to assist you!*

*Please heed our words! The time is now! Rise early, please, for our next session of communication.*

*In peace be!"*

Marilyn, sitting perfectly still whispered, "Thank you!" The prayer long requested was answered. Contact had finally been made. Her heart was racing. She jumped up and grabbed her journal, recording everything just heard, and in big letters wrote. REMEMBER! Remember the expressions of gratitude shifted the energy facilitating this connection. Remember to rise early as was requested. Remember the time is now! Remember you recorded this in your journal and read it every day if you must to remember this really happened.

Marilyn wondered if she would be able to fall asleep. She did…with ease and grace.

# ~ CHAPTER EIGHTEEN ~

*A passage from*
***The Time is Now***
*(Chapter Twenty-Four)*

*"And so they came. She, the One of Ancient Age and Ageless Wisdom led the way and of her protection, the volunteers were most careful. So vital was her role, essential it was that she remained free of the contaminating disease. Great care and consideration was taken to protect her from the infection, for from her would come the guidance to proceed, and for this role, she must remain of clear mind and open heart.*

*This One of Leadership Role knew far more than others, for of such ancient knowingness was she and of such clarity of mindfulness and heart that her perceptions of service were most pure.*

*Had she not been of such profound clarity and awareness, she would not have been chosen for this role, for in readiness, she would not have been. It was her ancient wisdom and her clarity of All That Is that gained her the role of such importance.*

*And of this responsibility, which she accepted with humility and with focused intentions, she openheartedly requested guidance from All That Is to fulfill her purpose."*

The early morning call was a surprise. Rarely does anyone call me before eight o'clock, but when I saw the time was actually only seven, I feared it might be an emergency. "Hello," I said hesitantly.

"Please forgive me for calling at this obscene hour, but I must talk with you." The caller was Marilyn Brown. I immediately asked if something was wrong and much to my surprise and delight she responded. "No, nothing is wrong!" she sang out loudly. "Everything is wonderful! Unbelievably wonderful and I simply must share my news with someone or I am going to burst."

"Tell me what you need, dear. Do you want to come over, or shall I come to you? What is your preference?"

"I can't leave the house," Marilyn declared. "I have a date. Do you believe this? I have a date!" Her joyful energy was boundless. My heart was filled with happiness for my friend, who had been widowed for many, many years. "But I need to talk before the date arrives, so can I tell you what has happened?"

"Goodness, yes," I replied. "Please tell me everything! Give me all the details!

"Well, you not going to believe this," she said with exuberance. "Are you sitting down?" she asked. "If not, grab a chair, because you are going to be flabbergasted!" Reassuring my friend, a seated position was taken, I informed her I was braced to hear her news.

"It's happened, my friend," she began her story. "It's finally happened!" Presuming that Marilyn had finally met someone, I sat still waiting to hear the words come from her mouth. As usual, presumptuous behavior got me nowhere. "Last night after the meeting, I came home and immediately went to my sacred space. I just needed to be alone and spend some time expressing my gratitudes for everything that is going on with all of us. It's how I pray." At this point, I knew my friend's story was headed in a very different direction than earlier anticipated. My happiness for her reached a new level.

"Anyway, I spoke my gratitudes aloud, as is my preferred way, and then fell silent. My heart was so full; I could do nothing else, but bask in the radiant energy of the moment. And then, it happened." I waited for Marilyn to continue. The silence on the other end of the phone seemed endless, but eventually, I heard the deep breath that precedes the next spoken word.

"You know how you've always told me that some day I would be able to communicate with 'others.' Well, it's happened. What a divine experience it was! I'm giddy with excitement. And there's more! I've been asked to pursue this daily. I was told I am here to advance the cause of transformation. Not exactly sure what that means, but I assume more information will be forthcoming. So, I'm supposed to set aside time every day to communicate with them. The time is now message was repeated several times, so I guess my time has come. Anyway, I'm so excited, I just had to share this with someone who would understand!"

"Marilyn, this is wonderful! I am so happy for you and honored that you shared this great news with me. Wow!" I declared. "There really is something major going on in the universe. I'm so glad we're walking this path together, dear friend. Thank you; thank you, for telling me! You have made my day!" We spoke for a few more minutes before Marilyn excused herself.

"Gotta go! Can't be late for this date!" And off she went for a date that would never be forgotten.

Marilyn's call set the mood for the day. I walked about the house with a smile on my face, and was certain the house had also enjoyed the phone call. "Thank you, Marilyn, for this day filled with joy and happiness. I wish you well, my friend."

Later in the day, more phone calls were exchanged among our group of friends and the first outreach meeting was officially scheduled. We were all ecstatic...and a wee bit antsy. Another group meeting was also scheduled to plan the outreach event.

*A passage from*
***The Time is Now***
*(Chapter Twenty-Five)*

> *"As leader of this most important endeavor, this One came purposefully and with clear intentions of what was to be done. Her mission clear and her commitment high, she entered the new environment and began her acclimation process."*

As my workday came to a close, the path called to me. Please understand I am referring to my favorite walking trail not my spiritual path. Truth is, the two are often one in the same, but at this particular moment in time, I felt an incredible urge to walk for miles. I hurriedly left the office, returned to the house, changed into appropriate walking attire, and was out the door in less than twenty minutes. *Amazing how quickly I can move when a walk is calling me.*

In no time at all, I was at the foot of the hills, and as is always my response when reaching this point on the trail, excitement overwhelms me. *Why do I always react this way? Every time, the question is the same. Perhaps, I will never know the answer.* "And perhaps, you don't need to know the answer," I responded aloud to myself.

The walk took me deeper into the hills, and with each one traversed, another one waited up ahead. The hills appeared to be endless, which provided me the challenge of achieving another after another in hopes that one day, I would meet the last hill. I wondered what would happen if the last hill was actually encountered. *Would it be the end of my journey or the beginning of another?* Again, I had no answers to these questions. I walked happily and gratefully. "My life is rich. I have wonderful friends, work which brings me great pleasure, and adventures that keep me forever guessing. This is a life that will be remembered, I'm sure of it!"

Another ridge reached, I paused. "Okay, self, do I continue, or do I turn back?" Not expecting an answer, I check my watch to see what time allowed me.

*"Continue!"* came an answer from seemingly nowhere. And so I did. The downward slope went quickly and brought great beauty. In a clearing to the right of the path was a small group of deer. They were less excited with me than I was with them. *Beautiful creatures. Be at peace, I mean you no harm!* They resumed their grazing and paid me no mind. I sneaked another appreciative look and continued on my way.

Atop the next ridge, I wondered again if I should continue, or begin the trek back home. And the voice again replied, *"Continue!"* Needless to say, my curiosity was rising, as was my concern for the time of day. *"Be not afraid. You are not alone!"* I proceeded down the hill, and again, was treated to nature's best. The stream, normally not noticeable at this time of year, was adorned with wild flowers all along its banks creating a winding parade of beautiful colors in the pasture below. "What a blessing it is to be in the right place at the right time." My words echoing down the hill expected no answer. But one was forthcoming.

*"Yes,"* came the reply.

"Yes?" I asked.

*"Yes, it is a blessing to be in the right place at the right time!"*

"And is this the time and the place you desire me to be, or shall I continue forward?"

*"Yes, this is the time and place you are intended to be, and you must continue forward."* At this point, it was evident my earlier assumption about the path calling me for a vigorous, long walk was an assumption made in error. The walk did indeed get me to the right place at the right time to receive the message, which was, of course, all about the spiritual journey.

"My friends, how may I be of assistance?"

*"Another awaits! Approach the one who experienced the encounter in the church. She is needed. Reach out to her and invite her to the initial meeting. The task is given. We express gratitude for your assistance and will accompany you on the path back to your home. In peace be!"*

As always, the return trip passed quickly. Upon reaching the foot of the hills, I turned back for another breathtaking look. I was not the only one who gasped at the beauty of this remarkable planet. Gratitude was silently expressed.

The last thirty minutes of my walk were restful. My pace slowed and I pondered the call that needed to be made. When I arrived at the house, I went straight to the phone and called the client who had shared the story about her friend's encounter in a church. I was still unsure if the story was really about a friend's experience or if it was indeed a personal experience that she shared. In truth it didn't matter. Whether it was her story or another's, she obviously was a believer, and our group was in need of believers.

She answered, I provided her with information about our group, and invited she and her friend to our first outreach meeting. She was quietly pleased, and acknowledged the idea was suitable to her. She agreed to relay the message to her friend and would let me know her response. And so it was done.

"My friends, thank you for pushing me forward. The task is done. I await your next assignment." I listened for a reply, but none was heard. *Attending other matters,* I thought, and bid them fond farewell.

# ~ Chapter Nineteen ~

*A passage from*
***The Time is Now***
*(Chapter Twenty-Six)*

*"Upon her arrival, the volunteers of previous arrival attended her with great care. Deliberate they were in protecting her while she gained awareness of her surroundings, but for her, the transition was less difficult, for of such knowingness was she that in awareness of her mission she was from the beginning. Little transitioning was required for this One, but protect her they did from the contagion to which many had fallen prey.*

*Pure of mind and heart would she need to be to lead the mission effectively."*

The organizational meeting for planning our first outreach gathering was hosted by the Sandersons. They were insistent about hosting the meeting and we all arrived promptly at 6 o'clock as instructed by Deidre. "Come in everyone! We have the dining room table set up for our meeting." Dee's manner was one of an authoritative, master teacher who had objectives to achieve. Her agenda was brief, but explicit, and in short order, tasks were clarified and assigned.

"Dee, my word, you are an absolute marvel! No wonder the school administrators were so upset when you retired. You bring new meaning to efficiency, my friend. We have come, we have met, and we are done!" pronounced Everett. "Thank you for your preparations for this meeting, Dee, and for your leadership."

"Amen to that!" declared Marilyn. "I expected this to be a long, tedious meeting. Thank you for making a planning meeting pleasant. I vote we put Dee in charge of all planning meetings!" A round of applause was given, and more appreciations were voiced. Frank observed his beloved's confidence returning. *Thank goodness,* he thought. *She's back!*

"Your words of praise are deeply appreciated," responded Deidre. She glanced at her husband and beamed with happiness. "I must admit it felt good to be in charge of something again. I needed this," she admitted to her friends. "Thank you for helping me to remember who I am." Her voice, cracking a bit, led Dee to a moment of reflection. "I remember a line that was heard sometime in the past, which seems appropriate for this moment. 'I am not who I once was, nor am I who I am yet to be.' Perhaps, this is a message intended for all of us, since each of us in our own way seems to be in some wonderful phase of transformation.

Again, my dear friends thank you for allowing me to contribute in this way. My confidence is returning." Another glance in her husband's direction acknowledged his silent expression of gratitude.

"Well," intervened Frank, "since our meeting was so efficiently managed, we have ample time for conversation. Does anyone have anything to report?"

"Yes," exclaimed Everett and Bill simultaneously. They each urged the other to go first, and then, as men will do, they resorted to flipping a coin. Bill won the toss.

"I will bottom line this," asserted Bill. "Pat and I have been talking about the possibility of learning how to tap into our telepathic abilities, and we are psyched. We want more information!" Bill's comments aroused an immediate reaction from the Smiths. Everett, waving his hand, confessed that he and Jan were having similar conversations.

"We are in the same place as you two. We want to know more and we want to get started. So we are wondering how to proceed. Are there books to read, classes to take, or what? Dee, Frank, we would really like to work with you two if you are up to being mentors?"

"Yes, we were hoping for that as well," expressed Pat. "We meant to call you, but time has gotten away from us, which is part of the problem. We need something regimented, I'm afraid. Because left to our own devices, we will allow our attention to go elsewhere.

"The same is true for us, as well," added Jan. "I think we are afraid this will be tedious and very time consuming, even though we really have no idea what to expect. So, we need help. We need guidance, and also ideas about jump starting and advancing the process forward. Do you have any thoughts about this?" I watched the interactions taking place before us, and knew with absolute certainty it was intended to be. My heart was filled with joy as I reviewed the dynamics of this unfolding situation. Those new to the idea of telepathic communication revealed excitement and eagerness to know and learn more about the process. Those experienced also experienced enthusiasm and demonstrated gratitude, optimism, and willingness to share what they already knew. What was transpiring in our small core group would spread to other groups, which would spread to more, and more. Indeed, what was happening was intended. It was transformation in the making.

"Dee and I have discussed this, as well, and we would be delighted to talk more about this. We don't consider ourselves experts, because we're not, but we figure we have some ideas to share that may be useful. Perhaps, Dee can come up with some ideas to present to you four and then we can proceed from there." The four aspiring telepaths were extremely excited, as were the aging Frank and Deidre, who were both realizing they still had something to offer.

As conversation about telepathic abilities lulled, I seized the moment. "Dear ones, may I change the topic?" My friends generously encouraged me to proceed. "I just wanted you to know we do have confirmation from the person I previously spoke to you about, and she may be bringing another. One for sure, maybe, two."

"Oh, my!" expressed Dee. "Let's review for a minute. The Smiths have invited Wendy. Marilyn has invited her bench lady. And our dear friend here has invited three candidates, two who have already accepted. Have I remembered correctly?" She looked about the room and all concurred with her count.

"I think this is a very good start," Marilyn remarked with enthusiasm. "If only one or two came, they might feel outnumbered by the eight of us, but four or five feels like a nice way to begin our outreach efforts. I'm so excited about this! Doesn't this feel right to you?" Her question demanded no response. "I really think we are doing something important here." Wondering if Marilyn would tell the group about her latest experience, my thoughts were interrupted when she changed the topic, and revealed her story.

"I also have something to report that's related to my own personal development. For years, this one," she said pointing to me, "has told me I would be able to communicate with the voice within, but as the years passed, hope waned. But our meetings reignited that desire in me, and my friends, it has finally happened." Tears of joy streamed down Marilyn's face. "I have actually received inner guidance and I am now diligently pursuing and practicing maintaining this connection that came about after our last meeting. It has been a remarkable few days, and I am grateful to all of you. Your openheartedness has opened my heart." More tears appeared. No one doubted Marilyn's experience. Her sincerity revealed the truth.

"Marilyn, may I please ask you a question?" inquired Jan. "When you say you have received inner guidance, what exactly does that mean?" Jan's question was one Marilyn would hear from others, and ask herself for years to come, probably the rest of her life.

"I'm not sure how to answer this, Jan. And I suspect different people who have had similar experiences will have different ways of articulating what transpired, but all I presently can say is I heard a voice within me that shared love, wisdom, and guidance in ways never experienced before. I was engulfed by an energy of such purity that it felt divine. As I say this to you, I am disheartened because my futile attempt to describe my experience pales to the actual experience. With all my heart, I wish everyone could experience this."

"Marilyn, I appreciate how difficult it must be to try to describe the indescribable, and yet, your words have registered," responded Jan. "I feel the truth in what you say, and I believe you. I am mystified, and want to understand more about this idea of being able to communicate with those from other planes of existence. That's the impetus for my question, dear." Marilyn looked in my direction. I knew she wanted me to expound upon the topic. I was reluctant. *How can one discuss the unknown as if it is known, and still, the attempt must be made!*

I turned to my friend and acknowledged Marilyn's appeal. "I agree with Jan, dear, you have made a valiant effort at sharing your experience. The tears you share with us are evidence of the truth existing within the mystery." Facing my friends, I said, "Dear ones, my words are no better than our dear friend's and my attempt to clarify the mystery will not surpass hers, but perhaps, in situations such as these, anything said may have the potential for igniting a spark within a particular listener thereby revitalizing a memory, an insight, a knowingness, which may for one brief moment bring a heightened level of awareness. So with that potential in mind, I will try to share some ideas I think are true."

Catching my breath, I wondered where to begin. *Speak of those from other planes,* I heard the message clearly, and wished my companions could hear the words, as well.

"I heard it, dear!" exclaimed Marilyn.

"So did I!" added Dee. Frank waved his hand acknowledging he too had heard the words of guidance. "For those of you who didn't hear what just happened, let me describe the situation. Our friend here," Dee said pointing to me, "was wondering how to begin this discussion and a voice replied to her thoughts. 'Speak of those from other planes,' stated the voice. To which, our friend responded, 'I wish my friends could hear the words, as well!' So, our responses were to confirm that we did indeed hear the message. This, my dear friends, is an example of telepathic communication with someone from another plane." With a mischievous look, Dee chuckled, "Rather a timely incident, wouldn't you say?"

"Thank you, Dee. That certainly was a serendipitous teaching moment." Smiling at my friends, I continued, "Welcome to my life! When these experiences first started happening, I must admit it was startling. But over time, this so called unusual type of communication became ordinary, as well as a very important and trusted resource in my life." I paused hoping my words would reflect the invaluable gift this form of connection had been for me.

"In general, I want you to know what a positive experience it has been and I also want to encourage you to think expansively when we talk about the idea of communicating with others from planes of existence we presently cannot identify. Although my understanding about these topics is at best miniscule, it is, nonetheless, food for thought and worthy of sharing. Hopefully, the more people we encounter through our adventures and the more conversations we have regarding these topics, the greater our foundation of understanding will become."

Settling myself with a substantial breath of good energy, I trusted the importance of this occasion. An opportunity to share what had been learned through previous collaborative communications had unfolded and it was happening for a reason. I was at the right place and the right time. "Communication with those who have departed our plane of existence is not rare, as many would have us believe, but is in actuality, commonplace. Likewise, communication with those who are sometimes referred to as angels, guides, protectors, and many other names of which I am personally unaware, is also common, but such experiences are not openly proclaimed for reasons we all understand. Just as we have been private about our own experiences, so too are others who have experiences with these types of communications.

It is purported that ancient wisdom is received through some of these communiqués. Who provides this wisdom? I do not know. It is a mystery! From what I understand, there are times when the presenter of the communication desires to be identified and provides information to that effect; however, on other occasions, no such intentions are given and the mystery remains alive. Are we communicating with Archangels, Spiritual Guides, Biblical figures, Beings of Ancient Age, Beings from other times and locations or are we speaking to the One whom we all seek?" Another pause was warranted. I gave it time to mature.

"My friends, I don't have the answer. But I can tell you with absolute certainty, life is fuller when you open your heart to the mystery." Purposefully making eye contact with each one of my friends, I truthfully announced, "I hear voices. And I am so grateful for their presence. Sometimes I know who the guest speaker is; sometimes I do not. And sometimes, I am almost positive the voice heard is the One who is sought by all. My life is richer because of these connections, and it is deeply comforting to know I am not alone. And it's nice to have a helping hand, or should I say a helping voice, along the journey of life." A sigh escaped followed by embarrassment and an apologetic concluding statement. "My discourse has been like a meandering stream. I hope it was helpful."

An overwhelming sense of exposure triggered great fear. *What have I done? What have I said? Have my meanderings pushed these wonderful friends away?* I looked to Marilyn for reassurance. Her eyes were filled with tears.

"What you have done demonstrates great courage. What you have said, gives us pause. You have given us much to think about, and we have learned because of your willingness to speak your truth. Thank you, old friend." Marilyn's words touched me deeply. Tender comments from my other friends also provided heartfelt reassurance. The vulnerability that consumed me began to dissipate.

*A passage from*
***The Time is Now***
*(Chapter Twenty-Seven)*

> *"And so it came to pass, She arrived and prepared the way for He who would follow."*

"Apparently, we have much to learn from one another," remarked the teacher of many decades. "I'm curious. How much time are you willing to devote to this pursuit of higher learning?" Dee's question encountered blank stares. She wasn't surprised. Often during her years as a teacher, she would see a robust interest in a topic quickly fall by the wayside when the interested parties realized how much time and work were involved. Her friends needed to face the issue and move beyond it. "This is not an idle question. I'm serious, my friends." Dee waited, hoping that someone would make the first commitment.

"You're bringing the point home, Dee." Everett's expression was one of man deeply engaged in conflict. "It's time for us to make a decision. Are we going to take the next step or not? We want to know more. We want to learn more. But are we going to do the necessary work to gain the next level of understanding we desire? Isn't that the bottom line, Dee? We can talk about this forever, but are we going to take the next step and meet whatever challenges come our way to learn these new skills?" Dee nodded in agreement.

"It seems we are facing our first challenge. How much time are we willing to give to the pursuit for higher learning?" Everett quieted as he thought about the challenge. Eventually, he began to laugh. "Part of me wants specifics. How much time and effort is this going to demand? It doesn't matter, folks. We're all here for a reason, and we are going to do whatever it takes, so we might as well stop listening to the ruminations of our minds, and just take the next step. I'm in!" he proclaimed.

"Everett's right," concurred Bill. "I'm in too!" Around the table hands were raised to acknowledge the commitment made.

"Great!" Dee was pleased by the quick response. "Everyone in this room has something to offer, so your work for the upcoming week is self-awareness. What do you have to bring forward to the group? Give this careful consideration, please. We have a group populated by eight students and eight teachers. Figure out what it is you want to teach!" Frank looked upon his wife with great pride and respect. *She's back!*

# ~ CHAPTER TWENTY ~

*A passage from*
***The Time is Now***
*(Chapter Twenty-Eight)*

*"And now with the assistance of the many volunteers already in place, She again is in readiness to present clarification to the People of the ailing planet called Earth."*

My day was to begin with an early morning energy session. Preparation for the session began the evening before. I went into silence, as is my way, and received a message for the client, as well as essential information for attending her during the session. I arrived at the office early, arranged the office in alignment with this particular person's energy, and conveyed my messages of gratitude to those who were the true energy facilitators. With the necessary tasks completed, I basked in the presence of those who I would be assisting during the session. It was a special moment, an intimate moment when hearts align, and the essence of Oneness fills the space. The moment of overwhelm was enjoyed, commitments to the highest good were made, and the time of readiness was upon us. I rose from my seated position, bowed to the sacred space, and exited to the waiting room where I expected to find the client.

Upon entering the room, I found two individuals waiting rather than just one. My scheduled client quickly introduced me to her friend, the woman who had experienced the encounter in the unidentified church. Her name was Mary.

To my surprise, Mary and my client, who from this point forward will be identified as Adeline, had changed the purpose of today's session. "I'm sorry about this, but we really need to talk with you before we can commit to coming to the gathering you're offering."

"We certainly can do that now, but are you comfortable forfeiting your session? We can schedule another time to talk if you prefer." There was a sense of urgency emanating from the two women who clearly had already discussed the situation and firmly made their decision to meet in the allotted time slot schedule for Adeline's session. I invited Mary and Adeline into my private office.

"How can I be of assistance?" I inquired. Mary spoke first.

She leaned forward in her chair and looked me straight in the eye. "Why do you believe me?" she asked. I was taken aback. The intensity emanating from her energy field confused me. Fear, distrust, defensiveness, all of the above! *Deeply afraid is she. In kindness be!* The words of wisdom settled me. I took a deep breath and responded with honesty.

"I believe you for many reasons, Mary. The first of which is based in fundamental self-care. Why on Earth would anyone make up a story like this? Let's face it Mary, this is not a story that will win you applause and accolades. The second reason is based in years of experience. And my experience tells me when a friend trusts in someone so much that they will risk telling the person's story for them, then the person in question must be worthy of the friend's trust. And the third reason is founded in recent experience. Your story, Mary, is not new to me. In recent weeks, several other stories similar to yours have come to my attention. It seems this older gentlemen dressed in suit and tie gets around. And because of these stories and the messages being provided, we are arranging this gathering. My friends and I think it is very important for people who have encountered this fellow to come together for support and validation."

"But what if I am crazy? Maybe I am making this up and don't even know I'm doing it."

"May I ask Adeline a question related to this?" She reluctantly said yes.

"Adeline, has Mary's behavior changed lately? Is she acting oddly? Are you concerned that she is having some type of breakdown?" My questions startled Mary, but she bravely wanted to hear her friend's response.

"Absolutely not! Mary's story is odd, but like you, I completely believe her. She's the same old Mary, I've always known, loved, and trusted." Adeline's words were medicinal. Mary wept. We sat quietly while the pent-up tension was released through her tears. Several deep breaths alerted me that Mary was regaining her composure.

"One of the things you have in common with the other people just mentioned is the concern you just voiced. Everyone knows their experience was real, and still, they worry something is wrong with them. They're all afraid of being ridiculed, discounted, and or discredited. These are legitimate concerns, Mary. We believe these incidents are evidence that something very important is happening in our universe. And we want to provide a safe place for people such as you to come and share your stories and to receive the love and support you deserve and need."

"Have you encountered the old man?" asked Mary.

"No, I haven't, but I am eager to meet him. Looking forward to it!" I smiled hoping my words were being of service. "Mary, although I haven't had the privilege of meeting this gentleman, I have many stories of my own I can and will share in the group. There is a reason we are coming together. What are the chances that you just happen to know someone who just happens to come to me for energy work and I just happen to be someone who has encountered several other folks with similar experiences? I don't know about you, Mary, but I don't believe in coincidences. Something is going on here that's bigger than all of us. I think we're all in the right place at the right time!" I glanced over to Adeline. She smiled and gave me a nod, which I interpreted as a thumb's up.

"How do you feel about the things I've said, Mary?" She was not an easy person to read, at least in the moment. I hoped for the best.

"Your words are very comforting. I understand why Adeline is so fond of you. I appreciate your candor. The truth is, I know I'm not crazy, but I'm afraid someone else might label me in that way. It's been such a blessing to share this experience with Adeline; she's been so supportive. What happened to me was a wonderful experience. It's been life changing, and when you experience something so remarkable, so beautiful, you want to share it with others, but it really isn't safe to do so. And that's sad, really sad. If everyone could experience what I experienced, the world would change. What I'm saying may sound ludicrous, but it's true. Encountering the old man made me a better person, a kinder person, and the experience inspired me to become a more loving and compassionate person. I'm not saying I'm there, but at least the path is before me now. I think I can get there." Mary's story about being inspired was inspiring. She was a perfect addition to the group. I hoped she would come. While Mary took a moment to recover from her story, Adeline presented her story.

"Mary's encounter has also changed my life. When I listen to her story, I feel the benefits of her experience. Because she shared her story with me, I also feel the sense of awe and wonderment she describes. I am so grateful. The group you and your friends are starting is important. These stories must be told. People have to know these incidents are happening. I agree with Mary. The event is life changing, and I can attest to the fact that hearing about the event is also life changing. My heart has opened to new possibilities. I want to know more about all of this and I want to be part of the process. I definitely want to attend the meeting. I hope the invitation still stands."

"Absolutely, you are welcome and you are needed! And Mary, so are you. Will you join us?"

"I am so grateful for this opportunity. Thank you! I will be there!"

Adeline and Mary were in a good place. I smiled as they exited the office. "Well, that happened for a reason!" I declared to my empty space. "Jeepers! This is amazing!" Relocating to my sacred area, I sat cross-legged on the floor. Breathing deeply, I realigned myself.

"Dear friends, your work continues to present itself. Mary is a very powerful energy. Are we now ready for the gathering?"

*"Old Friend, we are most pleased with the interaction just had. You facilitated the change of plans with grace and ease. And you spoke the truth truthfully. We are deeply grateful for your assistance. The gathering is already in good standing; however, another possibility awaits in the wings. Connection is possible. Remain open to all opportunities. In peace be, Dear Friend."*

*A passage from*
***The Time is Now***
*(Chapter Twenty-Nine)*

> *"Dear People of the planet Earth, I come to you through pen and verse to clarify the many misunderstandings created by our first visit so very long ago.*
>
> *In times of great difficulty, We came with the hopes and expectations of assisting your ancestors so that you and your descendants would have more time to correct the problems of your ailing planet, and so that you might be prepared and in readiness when the time of the unfolding event occurs.*
>
> *Unfortunately, our first arrival did not serve as clarification, but instead created misunderstandings, which have lasted for millennia, and for this, we are most regretful.*
>
> *Often we have attempted to clarify these misunderstandings, but to no avail. Each attempt served to create more confusion and more misunderstanding resulting in further distance from the original message and its intent.*

*Of this miscommunication, which began so long ago, we are here to right the situation with this story of the Truth of our purpose, so that the People of Earth will know who we really are, how it was we came, and why it was we came.*

*It is our sincere hope that through the telling of this story, the misunderstandings of our coming will at long last be corrected and the Truth will be known."*

In a community not too distant from the one where the eight friends reside, another sits quietly on a favorite bench with a journal in hand. She who is called Casey patiently waits for a message from one who is unseen and presently unheard. She strives to remain peaceful and calm, but as the silence continues her patience wears thin. She frets. She attempts to improve her listening skills by sitting rigidly stiff in hopes that it will somehow bring the words into focus. She continues to fret. She opens the journal, and bares her soul to its pages. *What am I doing wrong? I'm sorry, but I cannot hear you. Please tell me what to do. Tell me what I am doing wrong.*

Casey sat for over an hour waiting for a message. The day began in excitement and wonderment and turned bleak as the possibility for receiving a message became hopeless. She thought the worst. *I'm not good enough. They are tired of me. I didn't advance as rapidly as was needed.* Her mind raced with negative thoughts, none of which was true, but once in motion, a wayward thought is difficult to restrain. She felt desperate. Eventually, Casey returned to her car and drove home. She wanted to call Marilyn, but did not want to burden her, but she needed to talk to someone, and she knew no one else who would understand the situation. She closed the door to her home office and made the call.

The phone was immediately answered and Marilyn happily greeted her new friend, "Casey, I was just thinking about you! How are you?"

"Marilyn, please forgive me, but once again, I call you in need of a listening ear. Are you available?"

"Yes! Please tell me everything!"

"I am very distressed, my friend. Since we last talked, I have been practicing every day, and each day I have received brief, but significant messages. Today, I arrived at my favorite bench with the same intentions, but Marilyn, I heard nothing. Nothing! I stayed for over an hour in hopes that something would happen, but it didn't. I am so afraid, Marilyn, and I don't know what to do." Casey's sorrow was palpable.

"My friend, I believe you are trying too hard!" Marilyn's suggestion was not acceptable.

"No, that isn't true. I must be doing something wrong. Or perhaps, they have given up on me. Perhaps, I am not developing as well as they had hoped." Casey's negative mind was over functioning once again.

"Casey, please listen to me. I need you to take several deep breaths. Do so now, please." Marilyn listened carefully to be sure her instructions were being followed. "And now, I want you to visualize your favorite bench and remember the special moments, you have experienced there. Remember, encountering the gentleman first seen in Tibet. Recall the message he delivered to you and how ecstatic you were about being called to receive messages. Remember this! Bring it to the forefront of your mind. And now, remember the recent days when you successfully received other messages. Breathe this in Casey, and remember." Marilyn waited allowing time for Casey to recall the good memories in hopes they would override her recent misinterpretation.

"Okay, Casey! Now, I need you to trust me for a minute. Your experience today is normal. I understand it was extremely disappointing and a distressing surprise, but it really is ordinary to have days when you simply cannot connect with those who are sending the messages. I hear this from folks who have years of experience doing what you are just learning how to do." A loud sigh of relief came through the phone.

"Casey, I am so sorry you have no one to mentor you through this learning phase."

"You just did, Marilyn! Once again, I am in your debt. I feel very foolish and embarrassed, but I thought the gift was being taken away from me, and I panicked. I am surprised by my over reaction, and equally surprised to realize how strongly committed I feel to this. I so want to be able to fulfill this role, which apparently has been assigned to me.

"And you will, Casey! Please have compassion for yourself. This is all new to you. You're still in the very early phase of your training. From what I understand there will be good days and there will be days that are less productive than you prefer, but it is what it is. And it doesn't mean you are at fault. Sometimes, frequency disruptions just don't allow for connection to happen."

"My dear new friend," exclaimed Casey, "you are an angel in disguise!

Gratitude abounds, Marilyn. Many thanks to you!" Casey's frantic phone call reminded Marilyn of the complications associated with new skills, particularly skills founded in mystery. As she thought about Casey's situation, she had another idea for their group.

"We need a hotline service! And a mentorship program!" She would add these two new ideas to the growing list of opportunities for their group to attend.

*A passage from*
***The Time is Now***
*(Chapter Thirty)*

*"Let it be known by All who read these pages that we are here to serve, but never were we meant to be adored or worshiped by those for whom we came to serve. Our existence is of such long standing even we do not remember our beginnings, but of our existence and its relevance to your existence, let this be known. We are All One."*

# ~ Chapter Twenty-One ~

"Beloved Friends, thank you again for a most remarkable day. The time spent with the one called Mary and the one called Adeline was time well spent. They are women of extreme goodness and they are guided by their hearts. They will be great additions to our cluster of friends, and we will bring familial ties to them. You spoke of another waiting in the wings. Do you care to elaborate?"

*"Old friend, we are most grateful for a day well lived. The cluster comes together and with each addition, more opportunity for outreach is created. The other who is coming is close. You will feel this one's presence, before the presence is seen. Trust your intuition. When the presence has arrived, you will know with certainty, because there will be no doubts, no questions. You will simply know the other has arrived. A new day is coming, old friend, but for now, it is time to rest. In peace be!*

"Old Friends, thank you for this precious time together. As always, it is comforting to be in your presence. I will remain attentive to the arrival of the other and look forward to welcoming this one into the cluster. In gratitude, my Friends!'

I meandered about the house trying to decide how to address the suggestion of rest. Rest encompassed many different meanings for me. I deliberated to no avail. I asked the house for its advice, but no words of wisdom were provided. Apparently the house was already resting. My mind juggled several different ideas at once, but the notion most appealing was a quiet, stroll through the neighborhood. Requiring no effort other than grabbing a light jacket, I found this choice the one that spoke to me.

For thirty minutes, I leisurely walked up and down the streets surrounding my home. It was a quiet neighborhood, where people lovingly attended their yards and gardens. And for some serendipitous reason, I had the streets to myself. *How do you manage this, my Friends? Are you providing this peaceful moment just for me, or are you also in need of precious alone time?* I laughed at the thought. *Is it possible that those who accompany others at all times in all places also require quite moments for reflection?* Ironically, it was a thought that never crossed my mind before. *Goodness! I act, as if, you are available for me whenever I need you.* I shook my head in disbelief. *Another idea founded in presumptuous self-centeredness. Sorry, Dear Friends, I hope my thoughts and my frequent demands do not intrude upon your personal needs.* As I continued to meander about the neighborhood, a mental note was made to pursue more information about the needs of my companions.

*"Old Friend, your concern for our wellness pleases us, but does not surprise us. Always, you have held our interest in the highest regard. Although you may not remember this, we assure you it is the truth. Our preference is to be available to you at all times in all places. Our commitment is to do so. Please know and accept this arrangement is one that was chosen and which is of long-standing."*

"Thank you, my Friends!" I continued to amble about. Lost in my aloneness, and yet, fully aware my companions were with me. *We are not alone.* My mind flashed back to the moment when this realization finally registered. At first, there was great joy! Without any doubts, I believed and accepted the concept that we are not alone. I still remember how glorious it was on the early morning walk when awareness filled my essence. Knowing my companions were walking up and down the hills with me was remarkably comforting. Actually it was a joyous experience, one that has come to be known as a 'big smile experience.' Indeed, my first reaction to the awareness of not being alone remains a significant moment in my life.

But in days that followed, other reactions surfaced. Privacy issues arose. I became hypersensitive about my behavior and the thoughts in which my mind indulges itself. The idea of someone observing my antics and listening to my outrageous thoughts was very upsetting and made me feel as if I needed to be on my best behavior at all times, which I believed was impossible. At times, ideas of rebellion mounted within me. Grand pronouncements were made, which in retrospect were ridiculous. I demanded private time as if one needed to do so. So little credit did I give my companions in those days. One does not need to insist upon respect from those who live life from this perspective.

Eventually the awareness of not being alone led to a question demanding great consideration. *Why are you fighting this opportunity for improving yourself?* The question was a turning point for me, and it is one I frequently must revisit, because my behavior and my thoughts are mine to command. If my behavior or my thoughts are of a nature causing me shame, then it is my responsibility to make changes. I choose to improve myself.

*Goodness, my Friends! Simply stated, you have been influential in my life. Admittedly, I am a work in progress, which constantly needs attention, but I am a worthy cause, and because I choose to be a respectful presence to those around me, I remain committed to the process of bettering myself.* I laughed aloud and then announced to those with listening ears, "Maturation is a difficult process! Thanks for your help!"

*"It is a pleasure to be of assistance!"* came a reply from behind me. I quickly turned around, and much to my surprise, came face to face with a well-dressed, older gentleman with dark complexion and graying hair. Shall we say, it was a big smile experience! *Finally,* I thought to myself. *At last we meet!*

*"It is very good to be in your presence again, Old Friend."* His unspoken response did not escape me, nor did his welcoming greeting.

*I take it we have met before in some other place at some other time.* His expression was one of sheer joy. As my friends had reported, his eyes were captivating, but so too was his essence. An image of the two of us sitting on the curb talking through the night rushed through my mind. Before I could invite him to join me in that vision, he invited me. There we sat, staring at each other. Many thoughts and questions raced through my mind, but caution drove my first inquiry.

*Are you visible to any others who may pass by?* I asked.

*"No,"* he replied. *"Wise it would be for you to continue using your inner voice. A misunderstanding could arise if anyone saw you sitting here talking to yourself."* We both laughed at the idea, and my mind quickly asserted in that arrogant tone it sometimes uses that my insanity would at long last be confirmed. My companion, whose hearing was acute, looked at me and responded to the naughty mind, by moving his right index finger back and forth. *"Do not listen to the nonsense of the mind."*

Smiling in agreement, I broached the topic most present in my mind. *I take it you are here to impart great wisdom.* He laughed jovially, and in turn, I laughed with him. Being in his presence was completely comfortable. It reminded me of those wonderful moments when two old friends come together and immediately take up as if no time had passed. I wondered if this was our situation, or if the stories shared by my friends had prepared me for this moment. Whatever the reason, I was at ease with this wonderful gentleman.

*"We are indeed old friends, My Friend, and I am here to be of assistance. It pleases me that you recognize our connection, even if my appearance is not one to which you are accustomed."* He paused, reflecting upon something I was unable to hear, and then turned to face me once again. Looking deeply into my eyes, his heart and soul spoke to mine. *"The time is now, Old Friend. As agreed so long ago, those who came to be of assistance must awaken to the task. The Island is in great need. An infusion of energy is necessary to revitalize her. Remember, Old Friend. Do not delay! The Island needs assistance now!"* His words spoke to a part of me I no longer remember. They made me want to weep, for reasons

I did not know or understand. And yet, part of me did! Tears streamed down my face. I knew with absolute certainty I was being called to duty. Fear welled up within me, and as I wept, my silent voice pleaded.

*I do not remember, My Friend. Please help me. I want to be of assistance, but do not know what it is I am to do. Please, tell me, Old Friend. What am I to do?* I wanted the old man, my friend, to hold me, but knew he could not do so in his present form. The child in me wanted to crawl in his lap, but the adult knew it was time for me to grow up. Something very important was happening, and my heart ached to be a part of it. *I am here. And I want to be of assistance. Please tell me how to proceed. Please tell me what it is I am to do.*

*"Your tender heart aches because you erroneously believe you are not participating in your life purpose, yet everything you do and have done is in alignment with your reason for being. You are one who shows up, and for this, those who work in conjunction with you are most grateful. You are at the right place at the right time, which is what you are intended to do. When another needs to talk, you are the listener. When another needs to share his or her story, you are available. And because of you, those of like mind and heart are coming together to initiate changes that will assist many others who also are needed to participate in the evolutionary development of humankind. Old Friend, you are already doing what you are intended to do, but your work is now becoming more expansive. Do not fear this idea, for you are ready, and truthfully, fear will only add to the deceleration of energy that is creating great havoc upon this beautiful planet.*

*Hear me, and hear me well! You are ready to proceed, and already you are ably moving forward. I come this day to commend you and your associates. Your assistance is deeply appreciated. I also come to inform you that we are but a breath away. Whenever you are in need of assistance or guidance, do not hesitate to call. We will hear you.*

*My Friend, it pleases me to be working with you once again. Always, I am near, but now, the Mission of Mercy moves into another phase of implementation. The time is now. All are needed. All must participate. The Island is in great need."* His voice was waning. I knew it was time for him to leave. Tears once again began to flow. I explained they were tears of joy.

*My Friend, I am eternally grateful for this experience, and I will do as you say. I will reach out to you when we are in need. And I trust you will do the same. As you know, our cluster of friends is eager to be of assistance. We will be here, My Friend.* Our eyes met again, smiles were exchanged carrying the love we felt for one another, and then he faded into nothingness.

I sat on the curb watching the fireflies flicker in the yard across the street. Their presence was as ephemeral as the Old Friend just encountered. I considered getting up, but then decided the light show was worthy of more attention. I lost myself in the wonderment of it all.

"Hello there!" Once again, I was caught off guard by the voice of an old friend. Looking up, there stood Marilyn Brown. She looked down at me and gave me a Marilyn smile, which is not like any other smile. As far as smiles are concerned, Marilyn's are over the top, the best in the world!

"So, tell me," she asked, "have you claimed the entire curb for yourself, or can someone join you?" We both laughed as I motioned her to come sit beside me. We nestled close together looking like children, both needing to talk, and each not knowing where to begin.

"So, how was your day?" I asked with a twinkle in my eye, and we both burst into laughter.

"About as interesting as yours, I suspect!" and we laughed some more. Marilyn urged me to go first, but I declined. "You always do that," she asserted. "What would it be like for you to go first sometime?"

"Oh, please! You have listened to me so many times, who knows whose turn it is to go first, but my friend, I'm still processing something that just happened, so if you would go first, I would really appreciate it." Marilyn honored my request, even though her intuitive skills sensed something was going on with me. She told me another conversation had taken place with the woman met at the conference. She gave me the details and expressed concern for the woman.

"It really was a mini-crisis session," she acknowledged. "I felt so bad for her, because she has no one to mentor her. I'm afraid she's feeling very isolated."

"You mentored her, Marilyn and you did it beautifully. My friend, you simply do not give yourself credit. And please don't diminish my words," I said emphatically. "Because I'm right about this!" She giggled about my mighty forcefulness and then concluded by telling me about her ideas regarding a mentor program and crisis hotline service.

"Marilyn, what brilliant ideas! Have you written this down, dear? This will certainly assist the outreach program. Congratulations, Girl!!!" We sat quietly for a bit before a big sigh was released from within me. Marilyn, taking advantage of my innocent sigh, posed her question.

"Was that enormous sigh indicative of your day?"

"I suspect it was, my friend. You know, there are no coincidences. Your interaction today happened for a reason. The script between you and the woman who invaded your bench is playing out. First you connect, then the idea for a group is developed, then she has a mini-crisis from which your brilliant ideas arise. These are not coincidences!" I adamantly pronounced.

"And my day was similar, but different." I told her about the impromptu meeting at the office with Mary and Adeline, without sharing their names, and explained how their situation was also evidence of divine orchestration. "I am amazed! Who is directing this magnificent play called life, Marilyn?" Again, we sat quietly, each processing in our own way.

"May I disturb you?" she asked politely, knowing full well I would say yes, which I did, so she continued. "What happened here this evening? You were in another world when I approached you. Something happened. Want to talk about it?" I reached over and wrapped my arms around hers.

"You're such a good friend—and a very good intuitive! And yes, I would love to talk about this." With a deep breath taken, my intentions were to forge ahead. "Where does one begin?"

"Anywhere you like," my friend encouraged.

"I like that response, dear. It's so permission giving." Turning to face her, I was surprised by another large inhale. "Marilyn dear, guess who I met this evening?" Even in the poorly lit setting, I could tell she was staring at me. Her silence surprised me. Her outburst did not!

"Oh, my goodness!" she declared. "You didn't?"

"Yes, I did!"

"Here on the street? Did the two of you just sit here on the curb?" Yes was of course, the response given to both her questions. "How long did you talk?" she asked. The last question caused me to think.

"Marilyn, I have no idea. My experience was similar to the other stories we've heard. Time just seemed to stand still. We sat together here just as you and I are doing now, and we communicated telepathically. The message was similar to those already heard. The time is now. The Island is in great need. But there was more, Marilyn. He said it was time for those who had come to assist to awaken to their tasks. And the outreach plan we're developing will help with that, as will the new ideas you just told me about. He said we will bring people of like mind and heart together, which will help with humankind's evolutionary development. He also said The Island was in need of an energy infusion, and she needed it now. There was tremendous urgency in his tone.

Oh, yes, there was another message. He said, he was but a breath away and could be called upon at any time. That was very comforting. It was a wonderful experience. I'm still resonating with his energy." Marilyn wrapped her arm around my shoulders and we just swayed together on the curb.

"Look!" she exclaimed. "Fireflies! A perfect ending to a perfect day!"

*A passage from*
***The Time is Now***
*(Chapter Thirty-One)*

*"As we evolved over ages and ages of experiences, our skills and our abilities also evolved in remarkable and delightful ways. And with this evolution, our commitment to care for all others of evolving nature also grew into existence.*

*Over the ages, the care and protection of All in the Universe came to be the primary purpose of those of elder evolution. And through this purpose of being ever watchful and protective of others and their evolution, we continued to grow in our own evolution.*

*The process, we came to know was ongoing, never-ending."*

# ~ Chapter Twenty-Two ~

A muffled, but audible humming noise brought Deidre to attention. Awake, but still resting with eyes closed, Dee realized the faint sound probably meant she was alone. She reached over to find Frank, but he was not there. *He's in the basement,* she thought. *I wonder how long he's been up.*

She arose, quickly attended her morning rituals, and dressed for the day. An extra moment was taken while making the bed to complete an unspoken commitment made long ago. Carefully situating the cobalt blue, crystal heart on Frank's pillow initiated the long-standing, daily demonstration of a relationship founded in love. This act of love would continue to unfold throughout the day, as she and Frank would take turns slipping into the bedroom to relocate the heart to the other's pillow. Dee loved this tradition. She prayed she would never forget this simple, but meaningful act of cherished love.

Stopping by the kitchen first, she noticed her husband had made only a single cup of coffee before entering into his inner sanctum. *Hmmm,* she mused. *This means he's been up for a long time.* Frank never brewed a whole pot of coffee when he rose early. He was convinced the only exceptional cup of coffee was one freshly brewed. So, when his projects called to him in the wee hours of the morning, he made only his single cup, and then waited for his beloved's arrival before making the special brew they would enjoy together. Dee deliberated. *Should I make us a pot now? He may not be in a stopping place.* As she attempted to make a decision, the humming noise of the lathe stopped, which indicated his estimated time of arrival was soon. She became a taskmaster. Selecting their favorite blend called Morning Decadence, she confronted their new coffeemaker and successfully met the challenge. She then placed two croissants in the warming oven and a small container of raspberry jam in the microwave. The couple believed warm jam added another level of decadence to the morning ritual.

And then the decision of all decisions had to made. Where would they dine? Eating in the kitchen nook was the easiest choice, but not necessarily the best, so she rushed to the porch and the decision was made. It was a beautiful morning with a view that demanded their attention. She arranged the table in a way that accentuated the view, but also facilitated intimate conversation. Dee anticipated an important discussion was on the menu.

"Good morning, Love!" The best friends exchanged a warm embrace, as was done every day since they were married. On the first morning of their honeymoon, Frank established this daily routine. "I want to hold you in my arms every morning of every day, so I never forget what a lucky man I am!" His pronouncement was expressed with such tenderness and sincerity that it made a young bride blush.

"What were you working on this morning, dear?" Dee's question was intended to open the door for discussion. Frank may have arisen early to address a new art project or he may have been distracting himself to get away from the overriding question that was possessing both of them. Dee didn't want to intrude upon his privacy, but the question about staying or going still remained an unresolved topic.

"You know how I am, Dear. Sometimes, I wake up early and just can't get back to sleep. Hope I didn't disturb you, Dee." She dismissed the idea.

"Not at all. Didn't even hear you leave. Have you been up long, Frank?"

"Yes, I have. Since about 4:30 a.m. And you're right, dear. I couldn't stop thinking about our encounter and the so-called opportunity we've been given. Puttering about in the studio helped me to escape the question for a while, and then I decided to tackle one of those pieces of maple. It isn't finished yet, but I'm optimistic." Dee smiled in acknowledgement of his optimism. The "O" word meant another masterpiece was in the works. Placing the croissants and raspberry jam on a tray, she motioned for Frank to grab the coffee pot. He did so and followed his wonderful wife to the porch, and was delightfully surprised by the simple, but sophisticated table arrangement. "Beautiful, Dee! Thanks for making everything so special."

"You're very welcome, dear. Thanks for being the love of my life."

"Easiest thing, I've ever done," replied Frank as he leaned in for another kiss, which was mutually enjoyed.

"We need to talk about the future, Frank." Dee pushed the issue forward. "I suspect avoiding our friend's proposition is more cumbersome than just looking at the issue and making a decision." Frank agreed and admitted trying to run away from the topic. Dee grabbed his hand, held it to her cheek, and kissed it.

"Let's pretend to be brave and just go for it!" she said in a lighthearted manner. "Frank, I don't like the idea of becoming frail and dependent. And the thought of losing my memory is the most frightening part of growing old for me. Our memories are so wonderful; I don't want to lose even a moment of the good times we've shared. And my dear, dear Love, I don't want to become a burden for you." Frank turned rigid, and adamantly announced she would never be a burden, and Dee responded in like manner.

"And taking care of you would never feel like a burden either, Frank. But the reality is, as we both grow older, we will become less capable of managing, and we have to take that into consideration. I love you Frank, and the idea of being dependent upon you frightens me for myself, and for you." Dee paused for a moment. Talking about this was trying, even more difficult than she had anticipated. "The bottom line, Frank, is this. I am not ready to leave. We're both afraid of what may happen down the line, but right now in this moment, life is fun again! And I'm just too selfish to turn my back on it. Maybe later, but not now!

I've been thinking a lot about our mysterious man. This is the second time he's made us this offer. Perhaps, he will do it again. If one of us takes a turn for the worst, then let's accept his proposition, but not now. We're old, dear, but we still have much to offer!" Reflecting upon what she had said, Dee realized she had dominated the discussion in such a way that she sounded totally inflexible.

"Frank, I've spoken out more forcefully than intended. Please know I just blurted my thoughts out, but it doesn't mean I'm not open to your ideas and preferences. I want this to be a mutual decision, one that serves us both." She shook her head in frustration. "Forgive me, dear. My delivery was very clumsy." It was Frank's turn to take his wife's hand to his cheek. He loved the way her hand so comfortably rested against his cheek. It was a perfect fit. He loved her more than life itself.

"My Love, you are so dear to me. It will be no surprise to you to know our thoughts are in alignment about this topic. I worry about the future and our declining health; I can't deny that. My biggest fear is going out before you. Our friend's offer appeals to me when I worry about you being alone. And I also like the option of going out together. But I too am not ready to say goodbyes to our friends. Something very important is happening and I'm curious. I want to know what the heck is going on. We seem to be holding our own in these meetings and I think we are contributing well, so why would we leave now?

I've also wondered about the old man's proposition. It obviously wasn't a one-time offer. We're living proof of that! And I also wonder if we can somehow access this fellow and share our thoughts with him. The truth is, I don't want this ticker of mine to play out on us. I just cannot fathom leaving you behind, Dee. But I also don't know how to finesse a send-off party for ourselves if we don't accept his offer. Perhaps, we can still do some more research about that for the future. Anyway, my Love, for the present, I also prefer to stick around. We have many more good times ahead of us, Dee, and many more good morning hugs."

"Well, isn't this a lovely way to start the day?" declared Dee. "We've made a huge decision. And once again, we've professed our love. My goodness," she sighed. "Perhaps, it is time for another cup of Morning Decadence."

"Are you awake, dear?" came the whisper that always arrives at the same time of day. *How does she do that,* wondered Everett.

"Don't worry, Everett. I'm not going to coerce you into going on a walk with me, but I would like to talk if you are up for that." Her husband agreed conversation would be a pleasant will to start the day.

"What's on your mind, dear?" he inquired.

"I think this is more heart related, Everett. I'm feeling out of sorts!" Jan searched for a better way of articulating herself, but confusion prevailed. "I think it's fair to say we are blessed at the present moment. Our family of friends is flourishing again, mystery fills the air, and we are embarking upon exciting new adventures, which have the potential for significant influences. These are very exciting times, and I am grateful to be alive and a part of everything that's going on. Life is full!" Jan sat up and turned around so she could face her husband. "I don't understand what's wrong with me, Everett. Why am I so restless?" Jan leaned against his reclining body. Just bringing the topic to the forefront made her feel vulnerable.

"Doesn't it seem to you that everything happening with us and our friends is happening for a reason?" Everett readily concurred. "And doesn't it feel right for us to be here?" Her husband agreed again. "Then why do I feel so lost? My heart is aching!" She shifted about on the bed in frustration. Everett reached over and turned on the bedside lamp.

"Is the light okay, Jan? It's still too dim in here; I can barely see you."

"Oh that's much better, dear. I need to see you as well. Please don't be alarmed Everett. I'm really all right, but something seems amiss, which is ridiculous when you assess the beauty of our lives. My goodness, we are on such a high! Who could ask for anything more? And yet, something is missing.

Everett, are you identifying with any of this? Is it just me? Or are you also feeling odd, awkward, or whatever descriptor is appropriate? I feel unsettled. It doesn't make sense to me; I can't articulate it, and yet, here I am."

"Actually, I do resonate to the sense of restlessness and confusion. Like you, Jan, it seems to me that we belong here at this point in time, but part of me feels we need to be returning to The Island." Everett's demeanor changed when he brought up The Island. Jan looked on, hoping he would talk more about it. "It's odd, dear. When we first shared our story, or better said, our stories, it was such a relief, and when the other stories came out into the open, I was both relieved and energized. The excitement of mutually shared experiences was riveting, as was the development of the outreach ideas that evolved. Everything about this is good. It feels right! And still, I wonder if we've drifted from the path we were following."

"Exactly!" affirmed Jan. "Oh, thank you for saying that Everett. I've been having similar thoughts, but didn't want to admit it, because it feels out of alignment with what's evolving. As you said, everything feels right, and it really is great to be working collaboratively with our family of friends, and yet, I feel torn! Part of me wants to continue this work with our friends and part of me aches to return to The Island. Although at this point, I'm not certain what returning to The Island actually means. Do we return to our favorite island in the northeast or do we return to the island in the Pacific? Or is The Island some other island that we haven't encountered yet. Everett, we really don't know where this alleged island is located."

Silence engulfed the room as the couple fell into deep thought. "Jan, do you ever wonder if we misinterpreted the messages from the mysterious man at the airport and the strange guy on the beach? Perhaps we have misunderstood what is meant by The Island. Maybe, we are interpreting things too literally and limitedly. Who knows, Jan? Maybe this entire adventure is a figment of our imagination." Everett's question hit home.

"Yes, I have wondered about that, Everett. In fact, I've given it a great deal of consideration. It's all so odd. So unbelievable! And yet, we now have validation from numerous other sources. So it isn't just our imaginations anymore. Many other people are also involved in this mystery, so I don't think we can or should diminish the reality of these experiences. Everett, when we talk about this with others with similar experiences, we feel strong and confident. But in moments such as these, our trust in the experiences and in ourselves wanes. We must remember all the validation, Everett. We must!" Her husband agreed and commented on their rampant diminishment of confidence when consumed by confusion.

"Jan, I also wonder if we need to expand our way of envisioning our work in the future. Obviously, we are still being pulled to The Island. Our heartfelt connection with the message about The Island is what got us involved in all of this. The connection, although inexplicable, is powerful and it's real. And we cannot turn our backs on that calling, even if we do not have full understanding of what the calling truly is. Likewise, the encounters, which have brought all of us together, are also real and I don't think we are supposed to abandon those efforts either. My muddled conclusion at this point is that we must remain open-minded to all possibilities and not limit ourselves to what we originally thought a calling was. Perhaps, our moments of confusion are allowing us time to redefine our understanding of what a calling really is, and maybe one of the ramifications of this discovery period is a greater understanding that we have multiple callings that demand our attention and commitment."

"Everett, you are so clever, dear. What you describe is what we are now witnessing, experiencing, and discussing. And if I may add another point, Everett, what I am learning from this discussion is the need for defining healthy self-care and balance when trying to effectively manage multiple callings. So basically what we're saying is that we must figure out a way to participate in these local affairs and at the same time continue to explore why we are being called to The Island, wherever that may be."

"Jan, thank you for initiating this conversation. You're the clever one, dear. This was an extremely important discussion. I'm up for a walk now, if you like." Jan smiled.

"The idea speaks to me, Everett, but I think it is time to journal. We learned a lot in the last few minutes. I need to take notes and then do some reflection."

"What a creative concept, Jan! Let's do it!"

"What a great idea! I'm so glad we're doing this, Bill," exclaimed his wife. William J. Jones had awakened earlier than usual and couldn't stop thinking about the Sanderson's recent experience at the roadside park. A need to have another encounter with the unusual visitor was growing within Bill. He had thought about returning to the scenic overlook where he and Pat had met him before, but it was a multi-day road trip, which seemed out of the question at the moment. Bill wondered if the nearby site with the view overlooking the valley and surrounding hills might bring about another encounter for them as it had for the Sandersons. The more he thought about this possibility, the more excited he became. After lying quietly for what seemed like hours, he had presented the idea to his beloved the moment he heard her stirring.

"I'm really grateful you were open to doing this, Pat," he said placing his hand on her knee. "I have no idea if we will actually have another encounter, but we can hope. I need to talk with this guy again, Pat. Can't really explain the desire, but I feel it nonetheless. How about you? Do you want more contact with him?"

"Oh, yes, Bill, the desire has been mounting, but driving all the way back to the overlook on the slim chance we might see him again just didn't feel reasonable. So, I've been vacillating about making a return trip, and pouting about having to do it." Pat chuckled at herself. "Why isn't there a handbook on this? Perhaps, we should write one, dear. We could call it, *How To Connect With The Invisible Man.* Catchy title, uh?" They laughed about the title, which led to more conversation about the idea of connection. "Anyway, after hearing everyone's stories, it made me wonder if there is a way to connect with him rather than just waiting for him to show up. So I'm very glad we're taking this drive. If he doesn't show, we will enjoy the outing anyway." Agreeing with his wife's thoughts, Bill planted another seed for thought.

"Pat, if this doesn't work, I think we should seek some other avenues. And in fact, I think the group, as a whole, should do so as well. Obviously, this fellow is reaching out to people, and he certainly seems to be well intended, so isn't it reasonable to expect we should be able to reach out to him as well? Seems to me we have as much responsibility for connection, as he does. Let's bring this up to our friends and see what they think about the idea of initiating contact." The couple agreed and Pat jotted the idea down in her pocket notebook. As she did, another idea floated through her mind.

"Until a handbook is written, we need to come up with some ideas and ways of trying to engage with our new friend, and maybe, in so doing, we will actually develop the resource materials for a handbook. Isn't that an interesting idea?" Pat contemplated the idea, and marveled at all the new possibilities that were arising from this new adventure. "This is such a lovely drive, Bill. I'm really glad we're doing this." Their short drive brought back wonderful memories of the many road trips taken. "We're at our best on a road trip!" she declared.

Bill nodded in agreement and followed with an affirming acclamation. "I think we're growing into a new level of being at our best!" With the exception of numerous oohs and ahs in response to the beautiful scenery, the Joneses enjoyed the remainder of the drive in silence.

"If memory serves me, the roadside park should be around this bend," stated Pat. Bill decelerated the car, put on the right blinker, and entered the park area. The view was spectacular. "Wow!" exclaimed Pat. "I had forgotten how beautiful this setting is. And it so close to home! We need to remember this, a lovely scenic drive and a perfect setting for a picnic without an eighteen hundred mile road trip." Bill parked the car opposite the viewing area. The couple walked hand-in-hand to the edge of the overlook.

"Geez! This is amazing. We travel all over the place, and this glorious beauty is practically in our own backyard." Wrapping his arm around Pat's shoulders, Bill whispered, "I am so glad we're together. Thank you for all these years of happiness." His beloved wife returned the sentiment. They stood in awe for time unknown and eventually decided to rest in a shady area with an equally impressive view. They talked about the recent weeks, expressed much gratitude for all the opportunities, which were arising, and then waited.

"Do you think he will show, Bill?" Her husband raised his shoulders indicating that he was uncertain. "Perhaps, we might sit here and practice meditating," she suggested. Glancing curiously toward Pat, he posed an interesting question.

"Well, what if he comes by and we miss him because we're sitting here with our eyes closed?" Bill's innocent question demanded attention.

"Remember, Bill, we heard his voice before. If he comes by today, we will hear him again, at least, I think we will. However, one doesn't have to close your eyes during a meditation. There are many different ways to approach meditation, so I propose we try sitting with eyes closed, and then, with eyes open. It might be a useful experiment for us. Besides I am so overwhelmed by all the beauty just witnessed, I think it would be a nice break to close my eyes for a moment or two. So, I'm going for it!" She gave her husband a peck on the cheek before situating herself in a comfortable position. Bill followed her lead. And for a brief moment in time, they intentionally explored the silence. Time passed without their awareness, and eventually, each returned to the present.

"Well, that was lovely," proclaimed Pat. "I feel rested, how about you?" Bill didn't respond at first. He seemed rather disoriented. Pat became concerned and asked him if he was okay, but he just stared at her.

"Bill, look at me, dear." Pat gently stroked his left cheek. "Tell me what's going on!" Simultaneously, he took a huge breath, blinked his eyes several times, and shook his shoulders as if to bring himself back into reality. Then he looked deeply into Pat's eyes and spoke.

"Remember who you are!" the words struck her as if she had been slapped in the face. A memory surfaced. She remembered hearing a voice, reminding her to do exactly what Bill had just mentioned. And then she remembered more.

"You are more than you appear to be," she added. The couple stared at one another with curiosity, with wonderment, and with many questions.

"Pat, what just happened here?" asked Bill. She took both of his hands in hers and just held them tightly. And with a lovely reassuring voice, she replied.

"We're okay, Bill. And I think our road trip was a success. We've had an encounter, via the meditative journey, and thanks to you, the encounter came to the forefront." Bill's look was one of puzzlement, but he wanted to hear more.

"I personally don't remember seeing our mysterious friend, or anyone else for that matter, but I do remember hearing a voice informing us that we are more than we appear to be and which also said remember who you are. The memory hadn't surfaced for me until you spoke the words first. Then it came forward for me. Thank you dear, for remembering!"

"Is this what happens in meditation? I mean, was this real or did we just imagine it?"

"Bill, when I responded to your initial comment, did you remember the words that I presented to you?"

"Yes, absolutely! I assume we heard the same message. And if that's the case, then this must be real. We couldn't be making this up."

"I think we were just shown how to maintain connection. But I also think we need to practice this so the skill is mastered. Honey, I don't know much about the ins and outs of meditation, but I think we just experienced one of the benefits of this activity. Do you remember anything else about your inner road trip?" she inquired.

"No, I don't, not at this time, but Pat, this is very exciting. We have experienced another encounter. It just wasn't what we were expecting." They laughed with childlike glee. Bill and Pat enjoyed the view a while longer before deciding to return home. Pat offered to drive; she wanted her husband to have more time to process his experience.

*A passage from*
***The Time is Now***
*(Chapter Thirty-Two)*

*"As the Universe grew in its own ways of beauty and mystery, so too did we in our process of evolution. And at some time in ancient past, an awakening occurred, and in that awakening, consciousness was birthed. And from that consciousness, All That Is began and from that time forth, All That Is became All That Was and All That Was To Come."*

# ~ Chapter Twenty-Three ~

"Welcome, Dear Ones! And thank you, for coming to this impromptu meeting! My agenda for this gathering is purely selfish. I want to be with you!" I raised my glass in honor of these dear friends, and proclaimed, "To friendship!" The toast was greeted with cheers, and then followed by another, heralded by Frank Sanderson. "To Family!" Murmurs of affirmation circled around my living room. Satisfaction inspired by gratitude filled the hearts of everyone present.

"Thanks for bringing us together, dear. I was hoping we would gather again before our outreach meeting." Marilyn's intuition, which was extremely trustworthy, indicated the meeting was not only needed, but it was essential. *My goodness,* she thought, *things are popping for these folks.* "Do we have a topic this evening or are we going to simply enjoy conversation?" I was very pleased and relieved by Marilyn's question. She facilitated the group towards a focus.

"Truthfully, my primary goal for this evening is to share time with everyone; however, something tells me new stories have developed since our last time together." Expressions, both verbal and non-verbal, confirmed Marilyn's intuition and mine as well. "So," I said in my most cheerful voice, "let's enjoy another wonderful conversation from the heart, and include our latest happenings." The invitation met with everyone's approval.

Marilyn excitedly volunteered to go first. "Well, I have something to report," she acknowledged. "I've had another interaction with the bench woman, whom you will soon be meeting. Without revealing her story what I can say is this. Two new ideas came up as a result of our conversation." Marilyn elaborated upon her thoughts about a mentorship program and a crisis hotline service. The ideas were well received.

"Marilyn, these are wonderful ideas," affirmed Dee. "Frank and I now realize how isolating it was for us to privately carry the woods incident for all these years. Our lives have profoundly changed since sharing that event and the latest one with all of you. We are so grateful; it has truly changed our lives. I think these two ideas are essential components to the outreach program. Well done, Marilyn! And by the way, I would like to be a part of the planning committee, if you're accepting volunteers." Marilyn was pleased with the feedback and delighted to hear that Dee was interested in being on the committee. She hoped Dee's offer meant she and Frank had made a decision about the so-called proposition presented by the mystery man. Her hopes were soon to be addressed.

"Well, Dee and I will go next, if that meets with everyone's approval." Marilyn wasn't the only member of the Family of friends who was eager to hear what the Sandersons had to say. Ample encouragement was uttered, so Frank began to speak.

"We have some news to share with all of you, so it's best to just say it and get it over with. We've made a decision. At this point in our lives, Dee and I are not ready to say goodbye to all our friends, so we're going to be hanging around a while longer." Cheers echoed throughout the house, hugs were exchanged, and tears of joy fell. Before Frank could continue, another toast was given.

"To long and healthy lives!" declared Everett. Glasses were lifted and expressions of appreciation circled the room.

"Thank goodness," whispered Pat. "I'm just so pleased you've made this decision." Pat had more she wanted to say, but emotions stilled her voice.

Blushing and overwhelmed by their friend's reaction, Frank tried to resume their story, but found himself speechless as well, so Deidre continued. "As you might guess, this was a complex decision-making process. We had our 'older than dirt' conversation, where all our fears, worries and concerns came out in the open. For quite some time, we've both agreed that our preference is to exit at the same time. Our mysterious friend seemed to be offering us an avenue for that type of departure, and we really had to give the idea a great deal of consideration. We're both so afraid of being a burden to the other, and neither one of us wants to leave the other alone. So you can see, this dying business is such a complicated affair.

But the truth of the matter is, we are really enjoying life presently and we just aren't ready to leave. We don't want to miss this adventure we're all involved in, and we don't want to say goodbye to each other or to all of you. So dear friends, it appears you are stuck with us for a while longer." Again, cheers filled the room and resonated to all parts of the house. Having gained his composure, Frank added on another part of the story.

"We also gave a considerable amount of attention to our wandering messenger, and we decided maybe his offer isn't as black and white, as we were interpreting it. This is the second time we've been given the chance of staying or leaving, so maybe, we may have another chance at that when our health begins to fail. We'd really like to talk to him about this, but until such a time comes, we're going to stick around, and contribute in whatever ways we can." The Sandersons' friends breathed a sigh of relief.

"Dee, Frank, your news warms our hearts. We are so pleased about your decision," I spoke as if I were speaking for the entire Family, and essentially I was, because numerous conversations about assisting the Sandersons through their aging process had already begun. "Several thoughts come to mind, so I'm going to jump in for the moment. We, meaning the members of your Family, plan to be part of your declining years. And I know you don't want to be a burden on us either, but the truth is, we want and we intend to be a part of this phase of your life." Frank tried to interrupt me, but I appropriately shushed him. "So, we hope you will find our offer to be of assistance comforting, and we expect you to accept our offer. We will not take no for an answer." My friends chuckled at my attempt to be forceful.

"And there's another point we want to make. If at sometime in the future, you decide it's time to exit, we want to be a part of that as well. So, if the mystery man doesn't show up, please know we believe you have the right to make your own decision about this, and we will support you." Tears streamed down Dee's face while Frank stoically listened.

"One more thought, please, and then I'll be quiet. I don't think we've seen the last of our gentleman friend. In fact, I suspect we may be having a lot more contact with him." My insinuation puzzled the Sandersons and peaked the interest of other Family members, but the elders of the clan were momentarily distracted by additional words of support supplied by their dear friends. Suffice it to say, Dee and Frank were reminded how deeply loved they were.

"We would like to tag on to this conversation," announced Pat, "because we had another encounter we want to share with all of you. Bill, would you tell the story?" Bill took over immediately.

"Yes, as Pat said, we have had another experience, and it may be significant to this current topic. What happened is this. We've also wanted more contact with our vanishing fellow and both of us were separately thinking about driving back to the scenic overlooked where we first met him, but then, we thought of Dee and Frank's experience. So yesterday, we drove out to the roadside park area and were blown away by the view." A thought breezed through Pat's mind and she interrupted her husband.

"Some day, let's all go out there together and have a picnic. It is so lovely and only a few miles away. Oh, excuse me," she said. "Obviously, I never tire of being with you guys." Her exuberance was well received and comments were made to pursue the idea. "Please continue, Bill."

"Well, we got so wrapped up in the view that we didn't even notice the old fellow hadn't shown up to greet us, so we found a nice boulder to rest on, and Pat suggested we do a meditation, which is not a skill set for either of us, but we decided to give it a go. And something rather remarkable happened. It turns out during the meditation, we both heard a similar message. I say we both heard it, but I mean to say we each individually heard the same message. Actually, it was two messages. First we heard, 'Remember who you are.' And the next message was, 'You are more than you appear to be.'

As you might imagine, we were shocked by the experience; however, we firmly believe this was another form of an encounter. We didn't see anyone in our meditative state, but we did hear the same message. And because we intentionally went out there in hopes of having an encounter, we believe our hopes were answered. We're very excited about this, and propose that we, as a group, do similar experiments to attempt connecting with this guy." Bill's rapid fire delivery was evidence of his excitement, which was infectious.

Everett turned to Marilyn and me to seek validation about the possibility of using meditation as a means of connecting. Marilyn answered first. "I absolutely believe Pat and Bill received a message, even though the source of the message remains unknown at this point. With practice, the ability to meditate can be refined and the possibility of receiving messages is enhanced. This is not uncommon. I agree with their suggestion. Let's do some group meditations and see what happens. And in between our group sessions, we can improve our skills by practicing daily. This is one more possibility worth pursuing. I'm in!

Jan turned to me and asked, "What about you, dear? What do you think about this?

"I'm in agreement with Marilyn. Meditation opens the door to many new possibilities. We will benefit individually and as a group. What exactly will happen only time and effort will reveal; however, in the meantime, we will gain greater command over our wayward minds. That possibility alone makes the exercise worthwhile." I paused for a minute trying to strategize my next step. Turning to Marilyn, I silently asked her if it was time to tell our friends about the encounter. She returned my look, smiled lovingly, and nodded yes.

"Something happened a couple of nights ago that relates to our present topic, so I need to let you all know what happened. First, I will tell you the day began with an interview with one of the people who I've been trying to contact. We now have confirmation that she also will be attending the gathering. The interview went well. It was exciting and inspiring and by the end of the day, all I really wanted to do was stroll up and down the streets of the neighborhood. So I did, and as the evening light paled, I had the privilege of meeting our mysterious, well-dressed friend." My friends' reactions were similar to Marilyn's that evening when she joined me on the curb.

"Tell us everything, dear," declared Dee in her authoritative voice. And so I did.

"The part of the encounter that directly relates to our present discussion is what he said shortly before he vanished. He was very pleased with our efforts and said we would bring people of like mind and heart together, and because of this, we would be helping humankind with their evolutionary development. He said he is but a breath away and we can call upon him at any time."

"Goodness," replied Dee. "It sounds like he plans to continue having contact with us. That's good news!"

"Yes, that certainly was my sense, Dee. He's been the one reaching out to us, but my understanding of his message is that we can learn how to reach out to him. And Bill and Pat have proven it can be done."

*A passage from*
***The Time is Now***
*(Chapter Thirty-Three)*

*"Since consciousness began, our journeys to seek all there is to know began. In ways of many kinds, we experienced more and more, so that we might learn all there was to know. And from our intense curiosity to know all there is to know, eternal life evolved, providing endless opportunities to experience new experiences, over and over again, for all ages.*

*In this way of experiencing many experiences, we learned more about all there is to know through each opportunity experienced. And each time we experienced new experiences, we learned that more there was to experience. So this has been the evolving process from the beginning to the present."*

"This may sound odd, but then again everything we talk about sounds odd, so what's new? But it feels as if we are part of a team." Marilyn glanced at her friends, to see if they were following her train of thoughts. "We are here on the human plane being guided, in the most synchronistic ways, to certain activities and people, while others, such as our mystery man, are on another plane of existence trying to guide us to the right place at the right time for some presently unknown purpose we mutually share. We seem to be associates, teammates, with growing responsibilities we are intended to manage. It's exciting and a bit humbling, because our responsibilities seem to be growing at a very rapid pace. At times, it feels overwhelming. Either we need more teammates, or we need some very clever management skills." As Everett and Jan listened to Marilyn, they knew it was their turn to take the lead.

Everett began by acknowledging the synchronistic unfolding of the evening's conversation. "It really is like watching a play. One of us shares a recent experience, which just happens to coincide with someone else's recent experience, which broadens the learning experience for all of us. This entire conversation has been one experience augmenting another experience and now, in like manner, it is time for Jan and me to follow through with another scenario, which just happens to relate to Marilyn's comments.

"The truth is, we've been struggling. Jan and I feel completely committed to this project with all of you, and yet, we still feel very drawn to the messages about The Island. So, we have felt torn. Our commitment to these local activities is resolute. We feel a part of what is transpiring here and we want to continue, and at the same time, we feel pulled to the mysterious island that we all now refer to as The Island. So, we believe we are being taught to redefine our previous definition of what a calling really is. We both thought that a calling is a calling, meaning you feel called to do a certain activity for reasons you may or may not know. But now, we have come to believe we may be called to participate in numerous callings, which will necessarily demand we have a healthy wisdom about self-care, and also the ability to find balance while serving multiple callings.

We don't believe we are being asked to do more than we are capable of doing; however, we do believe our callings must be managed well or we will become depleted before projects are completed. We agree with Marilyn's assessment. It does seem as if we are part of a network of people who are being drawn together for some yet to be defined purpose, which evidently has something to do with humankind's evolutionary process, and as we've discussed before, it is highly unlikely we are the only group involved in this emerging project. So, if you are accustomed to leaping to conclusions, one might conclude many other clusters of folks are coming together to address additional projects for similar reasons. The idea that something big is happening in the universe seems to becoming more and more evident."

"And yet," Jan interjected, "we still remain rather clueless about everything. Everett and I have had many chuckles about the vague, mystical aspects of our present pursuits, and what's even more humorous is we are actually becoming comfortable with our confusion. We're operating from faith. We truly believe something is happening, which we are intended to be involved in, and we trust the way we are to be of assistance will continue to be shown to us."

"Yes, it's true," confirmed Everett. "We really are pursuing life from a faithful perspective, which is new for us. But we believe we are truly being called, and we want to faithfully respond. We believe another aspect of our outreach program, which would nicely complement Marilyn's ideas for mentoring and crisis hotline programming, should include providing assistance to people who need help regarding self-care issues, as they pursue their callings and move forward towards fulfilling their faithful journeys. I think with careful consideration and planning, we can provide valuable information and assistance to people entering into this adventure." Everett turned to Jan, "Have we covered everything, dear?"

"Everything, but the thank you!" Jan gazed upon her friends, and once again, was stunned by the beauty of this union of goodness. "We are so grateful for all of you! Being in your presence is a delight and a blessing. We have no idea what's going on here, but we do believe whatever is happening is happening for a reason, and we are so happy to be involved in this adventure with our very best friends. Whoever designed this play in which we are all participating is an absolute genius. Thank you! Thank you! Thank you!"

*A passage from*
***The Time is Now***
*(Chapter Thirty-Four)*

> *"So long has this been our way of existence that eternal life is of natural circumstance to us. Difficult it is for us to remember existence before eternal awareness, for it has been of our awareness for so many ages.*
>
> *To encounter those in unawareness of this existence surprised All in knowingness, for so difficult it is to imagine life without this awareness.*
>
> *When our kind came to know your kind, unaware were we of your unawareness and there began the first misunderstanding."*

"Well, my dear friends, we certainly know how to have a stimulating evening! I think we have successfully mastered the art of heartfelt conversations." Looking around the room, my heart filled with gratitude. "Indeed, we are blessed to have one another." The intensity of the moment overcame me as I grasped for the right words to communicate my feelings to these dear friends. "I find myself becoming very emotional knowing our time this evening is drawing to an end, and yet, I know we will come together again very soon. What my reaction tells me is we are in very good company. Our friendship is a blessing! This remarkable adventure, which has somehow landed in our laps, is a blessing. And the new connections we are making are also a blessing. We are embraced by love and surrounded by blessings!

Why us? Why are we so fortunate?

These questions take me back to the messages received by Bill and Pat on their mini road trip yesterday. 'Remember who you are!'" Glancing about the room, I made eye contact with several of my friends. "Who are we?" A pause overtook me, and then, I was able to continue. "What a question! Who are we? Appearances indicate we are just ordinary people living ordinary lives, and yet, we appear to be involved in some extraordinary adventure, or so it seems today. Perhaps, some day this adventure will appear to be as ordinary as our lives were before the adventure began; but for the moment, I think we would all agree our lives of late have become extraordinary.

'Remember who you are!' Is our adventure, as we presently define it, assisting us in remembering who we are? Have we come together for the purpose of assisting one another in remembering our elusive identities? And what of the next message?

'You are more than you appear to be!' We've known each other for decades and we presumed we knew each other very well. And in general, we do; however, in the last few weeks, we have learned how much we don't know about each other. Oh, my friends, our foundation of knowledge about one another is expansive, and yet, this message tells us, we are more than we appear to be. I cannot begin to imagine what this means for myself, much less for the rest of you." My spoken words silenced me. "Actually, what I just said may be in error. Perhaps, we can see the true self in others better than we can see it in ourselves, which would be another reason why we have been brought together.

Dear Ones, when I look into your eyes, I am filled with wonder. You truly are more than you appear to be, and each of you is here for a reason. How blest we are to be in such good company!"

*"Hello, Dear Friends, it is good to be in your company again!"* Much to everyone's surprise, the mysterious, well-dressed man stood between Marilyn and Jan. He laughed with great delight. I rose, offered him my chair, and joined the Sandersons on the sofa.

*"I come with love in my heart,"* he expressed. *"You have gathered as was intended and you have heard the messages. You are here for a reason. You are more than you appear to be. And you must remember who you are. The messages of old call out to those who are here to assist the peoples of Earth. Hold these messages in your heart and share them with others who will also awaken to the cause.*

*Dear Friends, much work lies ahead. We gather on behalf of humankind and The Island upon which humankind resides. Both are in great need and their wellness is dependent upon the other. Humankind must rise to the occasion. For the sake of self, and for the sake of The Island, humankind must evolve. You are here, Dear Friends, to effect great change, and will do so by assisting humankind in their evolutionary expansion.*

*Please know you are not alone. Many are here to assist you and we are but a breath away. Please call upon us when you are in need.*

*My heart is filled with gratitude. In peace be, Dear Friends!"*

And with that said, their guest began to fade. His departure left the room silent and still. No one moved except to close their eyes, and without any direction, the eight friends entered into a meditative state. They sat without awareness of time, for time did not matter in their present state of existence. They simply were!

*A passage from*
***The Time is Now***
*(Chapter Thirty-Five)*

*"It is most regrettable that when we came so long ago to assist your people that unaware we were of this circumstance. Had we known of this evolutionary mishap, we would have acted differently."*

Eventually, movement returned to the group. Eyes opened, sighs were heard, and looks of bewilderment were exchanged. And then laughter filled the room. The energy generated by healthy, joyous connection rejuvenated the friends.

"Looks to me like he's part of the team," declared Marilyn. I smiled in agreement.

With tears in his eyes, Frank turned to his beloved wife. "He's here, Dee.

We will be able to connect when we need him. Everything's going to be fine, my Love!" The tender moment was witnessed by the Sandersons' friends, and by many other unseen guests.

*"Life is, and always will be, eternal,"* came the now familiar voice. The message was comforting to everyone, but it was particularly timely for Frank and Dee.

"Another blessing!" whispered Marilyn.

I sat quietly wondering if there was anything remaining to be said. It had been a very full evening. "We must continue," the words came flowing from my mouth. My friends came to attention. "We must continue," we all said in unison.

*"Indeed, you must continue!"* came the voice again. *"And remember, you are not alone. Many are here to assist you, and more are amassing every day. The time is now!"*

*-More To Come-*

# PART TWO

# ~ CHAPTER ONE ~

"Well, my dear house, how are you this evening?" Waiting for an answer that was not forthcoming, the narrator of our story, who also happens to be a very active participant in the story itself proclaimed, "You appear to be in good spirits!" Courtesy demanded the narrator pause briefly, just in case the house wished to offer a reply, but when silence persisted, the resident of said house continued the one-sided conversation. "I am happy to announce our meeting this evening was indeed a success. Of course, you already know this, dear house of mine, but please bear with me. I need to hear the words flow from my mouth. The meeting was a success!" I purposefully raised the volume of my voice during the second delivery of this celebratory message so it would fill the room, which it did! This act of boldness was my way of saluting what had transpired during the meeting while also heralding in what is yet to come. Admittedly, and with all honesty, what is coming remains a mystery to me, but in this particular moment at this particular time, I am comfortable waiting for the mystery to unfold.

Satisfied with the evening thus far, I bid my living room adieu, and ambled leisurely back to the bedroom. For a brief moment, my mind entertained the idea of a walk through the neighborhood. It was a tempting thought, one which ordinarily would be difficult to resist, for evening strolls are especially alluring, yet for some reason the usual tendency to follow my mind's lead was rejected. Instead, I heeded the present state of being currently engulfing me and trusted my inclination to remain quietly at home. The decision seemed to affirm an inner knowing that the evening was far from over. Anticipating, but not knowing what to expect, I entered the bedroom and moved directly to the far end of the room, which years ago had been purposefully created and designated as a personal sanctuary. Before crossing the threshold of this Sacred Space, I did what is always done. I paused. With eyes closed, a deep breath was taken, while prayerful hands rested near to my heart. Eventually, when the opportune moment was instinctively known, my arms moved outward in invitation welcoming whatever was intended to come forward. It was no surprise when the now familiar older gentleman materialized in my Sacred Space.

His delight was apparent as he excitedly invited me to take a seat in my favorite chair, which has served me tirelessly for the last two decades.

I did as requested while also extending similar hospitality. He responded in like manner and seated himself across from me in the equally over used companion chair. *"Indeed,"* he announced, as if he were responding to my earlier comment made in the living room, *"the meeting was extremely successful, and for this, all are grateful! We are most pleased! Hope abounds!"*

His smile filled the room with light, or so it seemed. Perhaps, it was his essence. I do not know, for it was like nothing ever seen before. For a moment, I thought the gift of exceptional sight had been granted, and then just as quickly, the moment passed and all was as it was before. The elder gentleman once again sat before me, and the light previously engulfing him was no more. What happened, I do not know, but whatever it was, will never be forgotten. All I can say is this. I believe for one brief moment in time, I witnessed what is…what really is…and then, the world we presume is our reality returned to the forefront, and what truly is dissipated from my human eye.

*A passage from*
***The Time is Now***
*(Chapter Thirty-Six)*

> *"Our Dear Children of the Earth, such sadness we experienced when of your situation we came to know. And for your circumstance, All were of compassionate concern and because of your circumstance, we chose to come and offer assistance."*

"Your comings and goings are a sight to behold, my friend. Surely you must know," I said peering deeply into his eyes, "your manner arouses many questions. And your comment that alludes to the presence of others cannot help but stir one's imagination."

*"Indeed, your questions are plentiful,"* he said acknowledging the aforementioned behavior, *"as are the unseen companions about whom you are most curious."*

His affable nature invited more connection, so I broached the topic of the invisible companions to whom he referred.

"You speak in plural form, and yet, before me sits only you. Who are these others to whom you are alluding?"

*"They are Dear Old Friends, whose commitment to those of this beautiful*

*planet has existed since your species came into existence. Just as I am able to appear before you, so too are they; however, manifesting into a visible form demands great expenditures of energy, and because of this, we do so sparingly. Pardon our frugality, but materializing is not as easy as it seems."* With that said, my guest paused allowing me time to grasp the importance of the information he had just imparted. My naïveté blossomed into a somewhat larger, but still remarkably limited understanding of the efforts this mysterious Samaritan had been making on our behalf. Swallowed by embarrassment, my eyes closed in an inane attempt to create distance from my ungracious behavior. Recognizing one has taken another for granted is an unpleasant realization that demands amends. Ready to do so, I opened my eyes and found my guest gazing lovingly upon me. Before an apology could flow from my mouth, he reassured me no indiscretions had been committed. *"Your assumption that you have, as you say, taken me for granted is a misunderstanding, when in truth, your open acceptance of my presence and my limited abilities has been most gratifying. I most assuredly have enjoyed our time together and hope we will have many more opportunities for discussions of similar nature."*

"So do I, my friend!" To emphasize my sincerity, I instinctively reached over to place my hand upon his knee, and then realized the gesture, though well intended, was not suitable for the situation. I wondered if in another time and place such a demonstration of appreciation had been common between us. His gentle nod affirmed my thoughts.

*"Our forms are presently different,"* he commented, *"which actually is not new to us, for we have existed similarly in many other experiences; however, since we are both accustomed to existing in forms that afford us physical touch, reunions such as these are typically awkward in their beginning stages. Just know, my friend, your gesture was appreciated and empathically enjoyed."*

"Thank you. Even though your keen awareness of my thoughts and feelings is evident, it is comforting to hear your validating words. At times my curiosity gets the best of me and my desire for immediate answers overwhelms the reality of our circumstances. In my finer moments, rare that they are, I understand the complicated nature of our situation and realize information will be provided when needed and necessary. Suffice it to say, my seemingly endless questions are driven by an extraordinary inquisitive nature and an equally expansive impatience; however, on occasion, patience can and does prevail." Chuckling quietly at myself, I openly admitted, "I am very skilled at being impatiently patient." Our eyes met, and once again, it was apparent my visitor required no explanations. His understanding of my intentions was revealed through his loving, compassionate manner, but the desire to express myself verbally led me to continue. "I am very grateful to be part of this inter-dimensional exchange, and I want to be of assistance."

*"Indeed, we are aware of your desire to contribute. Always, you are one who is a dedicated and enthusiastic participant. Rest assured, old friend, our paths have crossed for a reason, and much work lies ahead. We are most grateful to be working with you as we have so many times before. It is good to be in your presence once again."*

*A passage from*
***The Time is Now***
*(Chapter Thirty-Seven)*

> *"Unknown to you was our assistance in your earlier time of evolution. As on many other evolving planets, our kind offers aid in the beginning stages of the evolving process by providing genetic enhancement to the species most likely to gain intellectual means.*
>
> *In so doing, we bring intelligence to planets capable of sustaining higher functioning life forms. For time on end, we have provided this assistance throughout many galaxies on many planets, and once done, we leave the evolving species to develop freely in their own ways and at their own pace. But from a distance, always we keep a watchful eye over Our Children, and of their care, we are most attentive."*

*"The time has come for you and your companions to move forward with your plans. You have risen to the occasion and now you must proceed. You will not be alone in your endeavors. Many, operating from the celestial realm, will be available to assist you. We hope that our presence is reassuring, for assisting the peoples of Earth has always been a priority and a joy. Because you have opened your hearts to our presence, others will open their hearts to the possibility as well. As awareness of our existence grows, our ability to be of greater service will also. Circumstances unraveling upon this beautiful planet demand the aid of far more than just her inhabitants. Although decisions must be made and actions initiated by the indigenous population, additional assistance will be needed. We are prepared and ready to act on your behalf. Through the project you and your friends have embarked upon, many more will become aware of their friends from other realms of existence. We stand ready to aid the peoples of Earth."*

As I listened to the generous offer being presented by my guest, numerous thoughts raced through my mind. The first of which will not surprise you, my Dear Reader. I wondered why me? Why us? Who are we, my friends and I? And my mind also wanted to know how many others around the planet were being informed of this incredible offer of global assistance?

*"My friend, we have visited these questions before, and again, I wish to reassure you that others are being contacted, and we will continue to do so through our efforts to inform the peoples of Earth of our desire to help with your present crisis. We will connect with everyone who is willing to listen. Our messages are not for a select few; however, getting the attention of humans who are remarkably distracted by other matters is not a task easily achieved. Therefore, when we are able to connect with those such as yourself, we work hard to create a collaborative union that will inspire others to open their hearts to our presence. And we will assist you, and others like you, to find one another. It is imperative the people of Earth become aware of the assistance available to them. You are not alone. Many, who desire to help you with this unfolding crisis, are waiting to be of assistance."*

"Your words are extremely comforting, my friend, and also puzzling; however, I am content to simply be with the information you have provided. My curiosity need not be addressed at this point in time; it can be attended at a later date. Do you have any specific thoughts or ideas that you would like me to convey to my friends, or are you satisfied with the steps we are presently pursuing?" My guest's response was not immediate. Whether he was individually pondering the question or telepathically conversing with his invisible companions, I could not tell, nor did I need to know. I was at peace, engulfed in a sense of well being that allowed patience to be my guide. Eventually, after an unknown amount of time passed, his response became known. How it was received is difficult to describe. He sat before me in his gentle way, looking upon me with those adoring eyes, and I simply knew his intentions. He did not speak, yet a voice was heard within, and I knew what was transpiring was real. There were no doubts about the process; I simply knew it was real and completely trusted the experience. His message was succinct but prophetic.

*"Please remember, you are not alone! And you must continue! Convey this to your friends, and express our sincere respect and utmost gratitude. In peace be, my friend."* And with those words shared, the evening came to a close.

Much to my surprise, sleep came easily. One minute my guest sat before me, and the next, I awoke without any memory of falling to sleep. The new dawn making itself visibly present through the pale blue sheers covering my bedroom windows called to me. I could not ignore the invitation. Tossing the bed covers aside, the wanderlust walker within me hurriedly dressed in anticipation of a trek into the hills. As I reached under the bed to recover my favorite walking shoes, the cell phone already safely tucked away in a cargo pocket vibrated. The message shining brightly in the dimly lit bedroom brought a smile to my face. "Are you up? I'm headed for the hills! Want to join me?" A quick reply affirmed I was on my way.

# ~ Chapter Two ~

"Good Morning!" The voice breaking the early hour silence was music to my ears. Hastening my pace, I wondered if my friend, who was yet to be seen, had intuited my presence, or if her auditory skills were so adept that she could actually hear my footfalls approaching. With a few more steps taken, our paths intersected. The hugs exchanged would have led onlookers, if any had been available, to believe we hadn't seen each other in a very long time. In truth, our greeting was indicative of the excitement we shared. "I'm so glad you were up," declared Marilyn. "After debating whether or not to call so early, I decided to chance it. How are you this morning? Are you still supercharged from last night's meeting?"

"I think it's safe to say my energy is soaring!" My words came as quickly as Marilyn's. "I am so glad you reached out…your timing was perfection!"

*A passage from*

***The Time is Now***

*(Chapter Thirty-Eight)*

*"As with other planets, so too with yours, we visited you long ago, and from our assistance, man evolved."*

With eyes still closed, Dee identified the humming sound coming from beneath the bedroom. Though it was unnecessary, she reached over to Frank's side of the bed to affirm what she already knew. Her dear husband, best friend, and the love of this lifetime, and possibly more, was already down in his basement studio creating some soon to be revealed masterpiece. The image of Frank happily working at the lathe brought a pleasant smile to Dee's face. *We've been so fortunate,* she thought. *A life filled with good times and wonderful memories.* As Dee listened to her inner talk, the notion of 'wonderful memories' gave her pause. "Please let me have these memories forever." The prayerful plea whispered quietly reminded Dee of the visitor at last night's meeting. *Yes, I do believe my memories will continue as long as they are needed, and then, what will be will be.* Sighing loudly enough to surprise herself, Dee continued her inner conversation aloud, "Friend, if your listening, I want you to know Frank and I are very grateful for the role you've played in our lives, and we will be keeping in touch with you regarding future decisions. When the time comes, we will call upon you." Dee's recollection of the previous evening was very comforting; she remembered how much lighter they both felt after the meeting. Rather than worrying about the future, they were excited about it, and with this shift in attitude, they were both feeling extremely optimistic.

Dee's thoughts circled back to the present moment. As she contemplated Frank's early rising, it made perfect sense to her. *He needs an outlet for his creative energy*, she thought. "And so do I. It's time for me to get moving!" she announced spiritedly. And with that said, a flurry of activities began. Within minutes, Dee dressed, tidied up the bedroom, and with pen and tablet in hand, scurried towards the kitchen to actualize the tantalizing aroma of coffee emanating from the chambers of her mind. As the coffeemaker magically transformed roasted beans into the precious morning elixir, Dee busily jotted down ideas. Delighted by the efficiency of her mind this morning, Dee took notes as fast as her hand would allow. The 'To Do List' quickly expanded into three columns as her sharp senses functioned in a manner she hadn't enjoyed of late. Feeling productive, useful, and alive, Dee excitedly exclaimed, "The old girl still has some spunk in her!"

*"Of course, you do, dear friend!"* came an unexpected validating voice. Assuming her husband had surfaced from his studio, she turned to greet him, but found her assumption was in error. She, and she alone, occupied the room. Puzzled, but not at all afraid, Dee, under the guidance of another assumption, responded to the empty room.

"Thank you for your kind words."

The voice, attached to no form, continued the conversation. *"Please do not presume that your aging process diminishes who you are. Remember, you are more than you appear to be. Though this message may not be fully understood at this time, just be with these words for they speak a truth that is known by you from deeply within. You remain a vitally important member of this Council of Friends. Your assistance continues to be needed. You are here for a reason and the time is upon you. Rest assured, you are capable of fulfilling all the tasks, which will be asked of you. You are ready, old friend. The time is now!"*

Dee recorded every word as it was spoken. When the message was apparently complete, she carefully placed her pen upon the tablet. "You're right," she began. "I don't fully understand the meaning of your message, but it feels right to me. I sense, or perhaps, it is better to say I believe you are providing me with a truth that resides within me, which for whatever reasons I can no longer clearly remember. I'm grateful…very grateful. It's very comforting to hear I still have something of value to offer. That's very good to know." Dee's commentary seemed to lead her into a contemplative place. Silence befell the room, but the essence of those in attendance remained. Eventually, after an unknown amount of time passed, a word was spoken.

*"Yes!"* The word, appearing to be an answer to an unspoken question, was evidence that much more transpires in one's surroundings than is apparent.

"Thank you for verifying my thoughts," Dee smiled. "I assumed it was you, dear friend. Did you hear my message earlier expressed when I was still in the bedroom?"

*"Yes! And I too am grateful for the connections we have shared in this lifetime. Suffice it to say, we are friends of long standing."* The sentiment warmed Dee's heart and brought another smile to her face.

"Well, my dear friend of long standing, it is with great embarrassment I must admit to a failing in our relationship. For the life of me, I cannot remember your name. What shall I call you, my friend?"

*"By many names have we addressed one another throughout our many experiences, but always the name that pleases us most, we already utilize. My dear friend, please continue to call me your friend."*

"Thank you, dear friend, your request is one I am pleased to oblige. Safe journey, my friend, until we meet again."

*"And to you, my friend. My heart is filled with gratitude for this time together."*

*A passage from*

***The Time is Now***

*(Chapter Thirty-Nine)*

*"And as the evolution of man came into existence, so too did our union. For it is through our assistance that You became One with All and through Oneness, we are All related in the Universal Family."*

Completing another round of sanding, Frank turned off the lathe. He carefully and methodically examined his latest project. This was the moment he had been waiting for…the time when he could step back and bear witness to Nature's artistry. It was, as always, a humbling experience. As Frank is well aware, Nature's craftsmanship needs no assistance. First, she grows a magnificent forest, which serves all who have the privilege of encountering it, and within the core of each standing tree, a painting is birthed developing over the expanse of a lifetime until the opportunistic day when it is time for the tree to fall. Through its passing, the painting residing within waits for the moment of its debut. The grain of the wood exquisitely designed throughout its years of growth evolves into its own masterpiece, and then, an aspiring artisan, hoping to create his or her own work of art, comes along and assists the unveiling process by simply revealing the natural beauty of that which was already created. Frank, a humble man who holds great respect for Mother Nature, has no illusions about his own handiwork; he knows who the true artist is. "Thank you for the privilege of working with you," he whispered. "I hope you are pleased with our collaboration." And then, Frank backed away from the lathe and did what he always does before completing a project. "I'll give you some time to think about this," he said to Nature's artistic creation. "Let me know if you're ready for me to present you, as is, or if you prefer some kind of modification. I'll leave the light on for you." And with that said, Frank headed up the stairs to greet the one who makes his heart sing.

As he entered the kitchen, Dee welcomed him with a cup of coffee, "Heard you coming, dear! So what's been happening in the Den of Creativity?" Questions about his work always sparked Frank's shyness. Even with his beloved, he found it extremely difficult to talk about the intimate connection he experienced when working in his studio. He had attempted on several occasions to share his feelings with Dee, but never really succeeded in articulating the depth of emotions inspired when participating in the creative process.

"It's another extraordinary piece of wood, Dee." His eyes moistened, as Frank's passion for his artwork welled up inside of him. He distracted from the moment by having a sip of coffee.

"Are you giving the piece time to adjust to its new form?" Dee's sensitivity did not go unnoticed. Her question honored both the artisan and the object of intention, and it freed Frank from the overwhelming sense of inadequacy that sometimes grips him in moments such as these.

"Don't know why it's so hard for me to talk about this, Dee, but I just want to be respectful of Nature's majesty. I don't ever want to forget who the real artist is in this process."

"I don't think you need to worry about that, dear," she responded. "Your regard for Mother Nature is admirable, Frank, and the humility exuding from you concerning your own work is refreshing. People could learn from you, my dear gentle friend. They could, indeed!" Dee's kindness touched her husband very deeply, which set off another round of internal emotions. Again, he struggled to maintain some self-inflicted notion of composure, which inhibited rather than facilitated the real connection he desired. Finally, with the aid of a deep breath, he was able to reply.

"You're the real artist in this house, Dee. Your inspirational demeanor, the way you naturally are with people, is life altering. You assist others in reaching their dreams, and that is a work of art in motion. You provide wisdom and encouragement, while those you support go about creating their own masterful lives. It's good work, dear! I respect who you are and the way you are. I love you, Dee!" Now, it was Dee's turn to be overwhelmed with emotion. For the second time in a day that was just beginning she had received wonderful, complimentary remarks, which were vital to her well being.

"My goodness!" she stated, as her little finger quickly whisked a tear from her left eye. "Well, perhaps, I should feign unworthiness, but honestly, I don't want to. Your reassuring words come at a very important time, Frank. I really need to hear this, and because, you are the messenger, I can allow myself to trust this message." Dee closed her eyes and inhaled deeply, as if she were trying to consume the message, which indeed she was. She so wanted to believe she was still useful, and for the second time on this remarkable morning, she had received confirmation that she was. Frank placed both his hands atop hers and waited for her to return. When her eyes opened, she witnessed a beautiful sight. Her dear husband was gazing upon her with the most adoring look. It was a look she had seen many, many times before, and one she prayed would never be forgotten.

"I'm so grateful you decided to be my bride!" Frank's comment was accompanied by the boyish grin, which had initially grabbed Dee's attention so many years ago.

"The best decision I ever made," she asserted confidently. "I knew you were a keeper the minute I saw you."

"Any regrets, Dee?" asked her husband.

"Never! Not once!" she adamantly replied. "And you, Frank? Do you have any regrets?"

"Absolutely not! Couldn't have asked for a better life. I can't think of one thing I would change. And that's the truth, Dee! Life with you has been an absolute joy!"

"Likewise!" she spoke emphatically. Conversations such as these were not unusual in the Sandersons' home, and were, perhaps, one of the solidifying components of their long lasting relationship. The tender communication lulled and Frank took advantage of the moment to refill their cups. As he did, he noticed Dee's 'To Do List.'

"Goodness, Old Girl, you've been busy!" At which point, Dee glanced over her tablet and beamed. She was very pleased with her morning's productivity.

*A passage from*
***The Time is Now***
*(Chapter Forty)*

> *"As such, when we speak of "Our Kind," included are You in this descriptor. For in Oneness, we are All of the same kind, for we all came from One. In many different forms have we evolved over the ages, and though our appearances appear to be different, it is not the shell, which defines the Oneness, but that which resides within the shell that signifies our Oneness."*

"Dee, what brought on this burst of energy this morning?" inquired Frank, who was curious about her extensive work list. "This is impressive, dear!" Once again, the boyish grin illuminated his face, as he encouraged his Beloved to fess up, "Me thinks you're up to something, Old Girl! Spill the beans!" Frank's playfulness made them both chuckle.

"Well, let's just say the morning has been full!" Dee described her early morning encounter, as best she could, and found sharing the story enlivened the experience for her again.

"This is delightful, Dee! I'm so happy you received such wonderful affirmation from our friend. And it's very encouraging to know he really is going to be available to us. This interaction is proof of his intentions!"

"We are so blessed!" acknowledged the Sandersons simultaneously. The coinciding reaction tickled both Frank and Dee, who were always pleased by such incidents. Of course, some would say their timely remarks were a coincidence, while others would disagree, which made no difference to the aging couple. Regardless of one's beliefs regarding such phenomena, the appreciation expressed was the point of importance.

# ~ CHAPTER THREE ~

*"Dear Old Friend, the time is now. Our Mission of Mercy requires the attention of all who participate in this life saving experience. We must advance our efforts to a new level of connection, thus we wish to apprise you of new recommendations."* The elder gentleman known by many different people from many different settings around the globe came to immediate attention.

*"Please join me, my Friends. I am honored to be in your presence. How may I be of service?"*

*"Your service is exemplary, Old Friend, and we are most grateful for everything being achieved, and yet, we must ask more of you. Please know you are called upon, because it is necessary. The Island demands immediate relief and we must take action on her behalf."*

*"The urgency of your visit is apparent, my Friends. My vow of commitment made long ago still stands firm. How may I be of assistance?"*

*"Although we are not surprised by your loyalty, Old Friend, we are indeed inspired by your affirmation of commitment to the Mission. As you know, our efforts to assist those in need continue to encounter serious delays. For reasons directly related to their perilous predicament, the inhabitants of The Island continue to live in denial of their circumstances. No longer can we wait for them to accept their reality. Although some progress is being made, their actions are too limited and their focus does not include the most critical aspect of their dilemma.*

*We have no choice, but to speak more bluntly with them. Although we do not wish to create fear among these good people, they must be apprised of the truth of their situation. Therefore, we will be bringing more messages forward through you and others who serve in similar ways, which will emphatically inform them of the primary issue of concern. This will be a challenging feat, but one that is essential to the well being of all who reside on The Island.*

*The Children of Earth must come to accept that energy, founded in and generated by hatred of self and others, is the primary factor in the decline of The Island in the Sky. No one individual is to blame for this hazardous situation, but the contagious nature of this toxic energy makes it more destructive than any other disease or natural event previously known, and unfortunately, everyone and everything is susceptible to this toxicity, including the Earth herself. Everyone is a carrier of this toxin, thus everyone is involved. The situation cannot be denied. Too much is at stake. A planet and all her inhabitants are at risk. Although these words are unpleasant to hear, they speak the truth. This reality must be faced. The time is now.*

*Dear Old Friend, this is not a message that will easily be received, nor is it one we wish to deliver, but we will. For the sake of the Life Being Earth, her residents, and all who will experience the aftershock of what is coming, we will address this most difficult task. Many are contemplating this situation as we speak, and more information will be provided as discernments are made. Please know you are not alone. You will be assisted in this process. Please ready yourself for this next phase of the Mission of Mercy."* Listening carefully, the elder gentleman knew the message from his Companions was truthful, and still, he did not want to accept the severity of the situation. His heart ached for everyone involved, and in a desperate moment of clarity, he comprehended the reasoning underlying the need for denial.

*"Old Friend, the awareness just illuminated within you, unfortunately, is accurate. Fear inhibits one's ability to face the truth, thereby blinding one to possibilities capable of altering an unfortunate situation. The unfolding tragedy is unthinkable; and yet, these circumstances demand the undivided attention of all involved. And let us speak truthfully, everyone is involved. The primary factor in the decline of the planet Earth is the negative energy created by her inhabitants. Decelerating energies generated by anger, hatred, and violence impact everyone—all life beings, including the planet herself. Until this reality is accepted, our efforts will not be sufficient to alter the present course of decline; however, with the cooperation of everyone involved, there is reason for hope. This is the message that is paramount to the success of the Mission of Mercy. There is reason for hope!*

*We must proceed, Old Friend, by speaking the truth truthfully. The truth must be heard and accepted for the necessary changes to occur. The truth is the people of Earth are the creators of their futures. They can choose to continue on their present course and the future will be very unpleasant or they can choose to alter their present behaviors and create an existence founded in peace. No one will be exempt from participation. Everyone, we repeat, everyone must seek within and honestly review his or her inner feelings. The thoughts and emotions that brew disdain for self and others must be confronted and released. No one deserves to be hated by anyone. Until this truth is comprehended, the fate of the people of Earth is tenuous at best. These are words we do not wish to speak, and yet, it must be done. So much goodness resides on this planet. So much kindness resides within all her inhabitants. We pray the Children of Earth will believe this of their fellow beings, for it is the truth. We pray they will see the goodness in everyone and release the nonsense of the mind that fosters ill will towards another. Goodness does exist and because of this truth, there is still time for hope!*

*Old Friend, we ask much of you. Please continue your work. Please impress upon the peoples of Earth that their Island is in great difficulty, but they have the power within them to alter her situation. By accessing their own goodness and by releasing their fears, doubts, and particles of ill will, they can heal the planet and thereby assure their own continuance."*

The truth was realized to the depths of his being. The elder gentleman comprehended the situation and the enormity of this mission. For a brief moment, fear rushed through his essence, but he refused to dwell there. He believed the truth, as it was presented, and he had faith in the peoples of Earth. He believed they would awaken to the reality of their circumstances and he trusted their goodness would prevail. He trusted the good people of Earth would choose the right path, and this gave him tremendous hope. *"I am humbled by your commitment to the Children of Earth, and I am honored to be a part of this Mission."* His words, though barely audible, were distinguishable to his Companions. Their response was no surprise.

*"The time is now!"*

# ~ Chapter Four ~

Not wanting to disrupt her husband's sleep, but at the same time wishing he would wake up so they could discuss the previous evening's meeting, Jan Smith noiselessly rolled over on her back, only to find that changing positions didn't help matters at all. Having been awake for what seemed like hours, her ability to remain still was faltering. As impatience mounted, thoughts raced about, each competing with the other for her attention. Then suddenly, a debate between selfishness and generosity ensued in the stellar auditorium of her mind. Part of her truly wanted to honor Everett's need to sleep peacefully until he awoke on his own accord and another part of her wanted to honor her own needs. *I really want to talk with Everett now*, she spoke silently but insistently.

As if her thoughts were heard, a voice responded. "Are you awake, dear?" Jan immediately rolled over and rested her torso upon her right elbow. Looking down at her husband, she replied excitedly.

"That's my line, dear! And yes, I am awake! Were you listening to my thoughts, Everett?"

"Well, I'm not sure. Maybe, maybe not! You know, Jan," he responded truthfully. "I'm finding telepathy rather difficult to understand. I can't say your voice was physically heard, because I'm rather certain you haven't vocalized anything except your reply to my question. On the other hand, I was wondering if you were awake and wanting to talk. Is that telepathy, or simply anticipation of what is usually the case when you awaken in the morning? Is it telepathy or coincidence?" Everett paused as if he were considering his question and then followed with another. "Were you trying to communicate with me telepathically, dear?"

Her husband's question required some thought, which for Jan resulted in external processing. "That's a very good question, Everett, and it forces me to give this topic more thorough consideration. The truth is I wasn't deliberately trying to communicate telepathically; however, the desire to talk with you was certainly mounting internally. And my desire, I must admit, was a bit insistent, which makes me wonder if indeed my thoughts were actually penetrating the void between us, which somehow reached into your range of sensory reception allowing you to access my thoughts." Jan shook her head and laughed aloud, "This is truly fascinating, Everett. Trying to discuss a topic, for which you have no language, is very complicated. Please excuse my clumsiness, dear, but this is a humbling experience. I feel both inept…and exhilarated at the same time."

Everett, recognizing a lengthy conversation was underway, adjusted his position. As he sat up and comfortably rested against the cushioned headboard, Jan also rose and turned to face him. "We really must seek guidance from Dee and Frank regarding this telepathy issue," he announced, "but in the meantime, I choose to believe our interaction is indicative of the fact that we both wish to review last night's meeting. So, dear, why don't you continue?"

"Thank you for so cleverly bringing us to task, Everett." The truth was the two old friends could have talked endlessly about telepathy, because it was such an exciting possibility, but other concerns also demanded their attention. However, before switching topics, Jan accepted responsibility for calling Dee and Frank later in the morning to schedule a 'training session' with them. She knew this would please her husband since he was not one who enjoyed arranging details. Jan then quickly acknowledged how excited she was about the turn of events the evening before.

"We really have a wonderful opportunity unfolding before us. The prospect of being a part of this potentially life altering experience is…" Jan hesitated. Her mind searched for appropriate descriptors, only to discover she was denied access to her internal dictionary. Frustrated by the inconvenience, she finally gave up the search and forged another path. "Well, dear, the point is, we are extremely fortunate, and even though I am acutely aware of our delightful situation, I am still conflicted." She paused again, and then laughed at herself.

"Everett, I can't believe what's coming out of my mouth, yet it is the truth, and must be said. The need to return to The Island is burning inside of me. I wake up in the middle of the night hearing 'You must go to The Island.' And that same phrase is the first thought to greet me in the morning and the last registered before falling asleep, and if I am to be perfectly honest, I hear those same words countless times during the day. It's like having a broken record in your head that keeps repeating itself over and over and over. It's confusing… compelling!"

"And persuasive!" Her husband's affirming declaration quieted Jan's oratory.

"Yes," she whispered. "Everett, are you receiving similar messages as well?" Jan's question stimulated more thoughts, followed by more questions.

"Interesting articulation, dear! Are we receiving messages?" Inquisitive glances passed between them, but no words were spoken as each deliberated the idea. Eventually, Everett continued. "This does feel like a message, doesn't it? And each time it is heard anew, it is more convincing than the time before." Everett's response affirmed he too was repeatedly hearing the message. "We're not accomplishing anything by perseverating about the oddity of this situation. Even though we don't understand what is underlying this message, we both know we cannot turn our backs on this request." Jan nodded her head in agreement. "It's time for us to make a decision. Are we going back to the island in the Pacific or are we going to our favorite island on the east coast? Or are we going to choose another island? Until we know which island is The Island, all we can do is make a decision and hope for the best."

"I agree, Everett. Although our situation lends itself to endless conversations, we must move beyond that inclination and discern what steps are to be taken next. I am open to all possibilities, which also includes participating in the projects developing locally with our friends. It appears we are intended to pursue both avenues, don't you think?" Before her husband could respond, Jan proposed another idea that grabbed his attention. "I believe an interesting opportunity was presented to all of us last night. Our visitor seemed to insinuate we are part of a collaborative operation. If my interpretation is correct, then perhaps we can ask him for more information. Surely, it is not in anyone's best interest to have us running about in circles. If we are intended to participate in some type of mission on behalf of The Island, then it is efficacious for us to know how to proceed. We can discuss this possibility with the Sandersons when we meet with them. Since their experiences with the elder visitor are more extensive, perhaps we can glean some words of wisdom from them regarding connecting and interacting with him."

*"Would you enjoy conversation now?"* came a voice from the corner of their bedroom. Startled, but not frightened, the Smiths immediately turned in the direction of the voice, and there before them materialized the now familiar gentleman first seen in the airport on the other side of the globe. As he approached the foot of their bed, exuberance filled the room. *"Many questions, you have, old friends. Shall we address your concerns and explore the future?"* Too excited to speak clearly, Jan and Everett clumsily stumbled over their words, but eventually managed to convey their consent.

"The Island," uttered Everett. "Please elaborate! We do not understand where you want us to go. We want to help, but we are unclear. Which island are we to pursue?" The couple sat atop their bed eagerly awaiting answers, while their amiable guest enjoyed the moment. As he carefully listened to their concerns, his delight with their interaction was obvious.

*"My friends, I am eager to speak with you about the circumstances of The Island so that you will be able to share this truth with others you encounter. I speak for many who come on behalf of The Island, and it is with the utmost humility that we extend words of gratitude for your willingness to be of assistance.*

*The Island is in great need. The Heart of the Universe aches for her. She valiantly continues for the sake of her inhabitants, but her situation declines. She cannot continue to sustain the needs of all who make demands of her. For so long, The Island has served supremely. Because of her gracious generosity, the inhabitants have thrived and multiplied, but she cannot continue to manage the needs of others at the cost of her own existence. Unfortunately, those who have benefitted from her kindness have not learned to mutually coexist with her; thus she has suffered greatly from the consequences of their misguided behaviors. The burden has taken a toll, and her decline can no longer be denied. She desperately needs help. Many friends and relations from other realms of the universe are amassing and are ready to provide assistance, but the ones most important in aiding her situation still remain oblivious to her state of ill health. Although conversations are now underway and limited progress is in motion, the unfortunate truth must be faced. The primary issue of concern is not being acknowledged or addressed. Without accepting the reality of their situation, the peoples of Earth will not be able to alter the course of her decline.*

*The truth is The Island in the Sky can no longer withstand the bombardment of negative energy created by unkindnesses perpetrated by the human species. The daily maltreatment by humankind upon humankind renders her great pain, and her own energy is weakening as a result of the constant ill will she witnesses and to which she is subjected. Her heart is breaking, her spirit is waning; and yet, her messages of suffering are ignored by the ones who are responsible for her declining condition. The circumstances are most unfortunate. The disregard for one's own species, as well as other species, is unconscionable. Humankind must awaken to their misconduct. Within you is goodness; it has always existed within, but you must reawaken to its presence. The present behavior exhibited by your kind must be personally addressed by each of you. The Earth's wellness depends upon your willingness to do so. Please look within and find the real you that lies within, the part of you that exudes love and kindness and which appreciates all life of all shapes and forms. For the sake of Earth and all her inhabitants, including you, please attend this vitally important issue.*

*Look within, the peaceable you is there! The goodness with which you were birthed still burns within. Never were you intended to treat another unkindly, and never were you intended to be treated unkindly. So commonplace is your misbehavior that your species no longer notices it as a problem; yet, the extent of your ill-fated conduct has reached plague proportions. Old friends, this illness is treatable. Though highly contagious, the disease that infects your peoples, and which is contaminating The Island in the Sky, is curable. Please hear this truth. The destructive misconduct of your species is curable and by addressing the issue, not only will your species continue, but the Earth will also be restored to good health."* Jan and Everett sat rigidly still. Each dwelled in their own thoughts while the presenter of the sobering news wisely gave them time to digest the information. At some point in time, the Smiths instinctively reached out to one another. Hand-in-hand, they faced the truth.

*"My friends listen to me, please. Do not mistake the intentions of this message. Though the news is most difficult to hear, it must be heard and accepted before changes can be made. To fully comprehend the severity of this problem, everyone must accept their role in the solution. No one is excluded from this situation. Everyone plays a role in acts of misconduct and everyone is needed to correct the problem. The maltreatment of fellow beings must end; no other solution to this problem exists. And as stated earlier, the infectious unkindness expanding across the planet is curable. There is reason for hope! Please hear the entirety of this message! Do not get lost in the heartache, but rise to the possibility. Be part of the transformation. As an active participant in the resurgence of goodness and kindness, you will be the vaccine that brings a halt to the spread of meanness and cruelty belaboring humankind. There is reason for hope!*

*My friends, because of you and others similar to you; there is reason for hope! Indeed, you must honestly review the unpleasantness of the Earth's situation, but you cannot lose yourself to the fears of the mind. The tasks are plentiful, and they are doable. Let these words become your new mantra. There is reason for hope!*

*Quiet your minds, Dear Friends. Do not allow the nonsense currently swirling about in your mind to be your guide. Your present reaction is indeed an understandable response to such a message; however, do not dwell in the shock of this undesirable news. To do so will effect no positive change, and it will most assuredly worsen the situation. For change to transpire, you must first accept the reality of your situation, and then, necessary steps must be taken to alter the present course of decline.*

*Understand this truth, please. The Island in the Sky, this planet known as Earth, is a remarkable Life Being. She is resilient, and even now, in her state of unwellness, she is capable of returning to good health, but she cannot do this alone. The primary factor in her decline at this time is directly related to the negative energy created by humankind's ill will towards one another. It must stop; it cannot continue. Each individual who hears this message must personally accept responsibility for changing his or her negative thoughts, intentions, and actions, and for every person who participates in this transformational process, a noticeable difference will transpire within the healing process of the Earth. Issues of sustainability are critical and must be addressed and followed by appropriate actions; however, in this present moment, the issues of blatant and covert unkindnesses must be curtailed immediately. This reality is not debatable. The energy of ill will severely sickens the Earth and she cannot continue to withstand the cruelties that humankind perpetrates upon themselves and other species. The changes that must occur must be addressed by everyone. Each person who inhabits this beautiful planet must face the truth of their behaviors and make the necessary changes to correct the ill will manifesting within you. To do this will demand honesty and a greater understanding of the definition of wise conduct. So long has humankind behaved in unkind ways they no longer recognize their misconduct as a problem; thus, let it be known clearly and succinctly. Any thought, any intention, and/or any action taken that does harm to self or another is an act of ill will.*

*Dear friends, I speak bluntly with you because there is no other way to address such urgent matters. The message that repeats itself within your mind is real; it is not imagined. The calling echoing louder and louder is a plea for assistance. You are indeed being requested to assist The Island. Quiet your mind, and allow your heart to respond to this communication."*

Stillness engulfed the room. Momentarily lost in their own silence, the Smiths were completely unaware of a greater response transpiring about them. Unbeknownst to them, the message delivered by their visitor also was being received by countless other listeners located in faraway and yet to be known places. All who heard his message were also captivated by the inspirational words. *There is reason for hope!*

As the Smiths gripped each other's hand, a sense of peace enveloped the couple that effectively dissipated the overwhelming anxiety each had experienced earlier. They sat quietly together enjoying the wondrous space of serenity embracing their room. "We are here for a reason," each simultaneously whispered.

*A passage from*
***The Time is Now***
*(Chapter Forty-One)*

*"As are You, so are We, and as are We, so are You."*

"I'm so glad we're here, Bill. This was a brilliant idea!" Wrapping her arm around his, they both scooted closer to one another without taking their eyes away from the horizon. The couple had awakened very early, around four o'clock, which was a surprise to both of them, and after a few minutes of self-examination, each determined that getting up and engaging with the day was far better than remaining in bed in their present restless state, so Bill cleverly suggested an early morning drive to the roadside overlook. Upon hearing her husband's idea, Pat leaped out of bed, rushed off to the kitchen, and switched the coffeemaker on. They were both dressed and ready to leave before the aromatic brew was ready, which gave Bill a few minutes to bag a couple of day old muffins while Pat scurried about searching for an ancient thermos that continued to serve its purpose well. Within twenty minutes from when the suggestion was made, the Joneses were in their car and pulling out of the driveway. Conversation was uncharacteristically minimal. A deer standing near the side of the road inspired a brief exchange, but for the most part, Pat and Bill each seemed to be lost in their own thoughts during the drive. As the car turned into the parking area at the overlook, their excitement returned. They arrived at their destination with plenty of time to get comfortably settled upon their favorite bench, which offered the most spectacular view of the valley below. Pat poured two steaming cups of coffee, as Bill retrieved the lemon poppy seed muffins. The predawn picnic was thoroughly enjoyed as the couple eagerly anticipated the arrival of their honored guest.

Much to their surprise, another guest appeared before the awaited rising sun. *"Good morning, dear friends! May I be in your company?"* The familiar, but unexpected voice startled the couple from their morning reverie.

"Oh my!" declared Pat. "It's you, what a wonderful surprise! Yes, please join us." Bill gestured to their visitor inviting him to come and sit beside them. Pat continued to ramble on a bit, before she was able to quiet herself. "I'm sorry," she concluded, "but I am just so glad to see you again that my mouth is running away with itself." Her words instantly inspired a cartoon like imagery in the minds of her companions and everyone giggled with delight.

*"I am most pleased to be with you as well, and also eager for conversation;*

*however, for the moment,"* he paused, pointed to the horizon, and then, whispered, *"perhaps, we might invite our words to be patient."* Minutes passed, as the trio sat spellbound by the sun's first command performance of the day. Together, they lingered in the moment, cherishing the kaleidoscope of vibrant colors; while from another perspective, the magnificent sun witnessed its own reflection in the onlookers' eyes. Humbled by their loving gazes and respectful admiration, the Sun sighed and whispered words that were not heard.

*"What an honor, my dear friends, I am in awe of your kindness!"* The threesome gasped in unison, as if the Sun's sentiment had instantaneously extended across ninety million miles to touch the very core of their being.

"Goodness!" exclaimed the feminine member of the party. "What on Earth was that?" asked Pat while looking to her companions for an answer. No immediate response came. Bill continued to breathe in a noticeably deliberate way. Pat assumed her husband was trying very hard to manage his emotions. Their guest, on the other hand, sat calmly. His eyes remained closed, as his chest raised and lowered slowly and smoothly. He was at peace with the situation and appeared to be absorbing the moment, perhaps, in hopes it would sustain him throughout the day, or even a lifetime. His peaceful presence quieted Pat, and she found herself once again being held by the moment as she recalled the metamorphosis of masterpieces just witnessed. Within her mind and heart was an album of images and feelings that could indeed nourish her for a lifetime, and more. She, too, was at peace. Time passed.

*A passage from*
***The Time is Now***
*(Chapter Forty-Two)*

> *"Of this Oneness, All are participants. No matter what planet, what galaxy, what species, what form, we are All One. Of this Oneness is the Truth of the Universe."*

*"Dear friends, perhaps it is time for conversation."* Having broken the silence, the gentleman from parts unknown patiently waited for his Earth-bound friends to return to the present. Pat, whose curiosity quotient was second only to her husband's, began to stir first. She had many questions,

probably more than Bill, but for no reason other than love, Pat decided to postpone her need for answers. Comprehending her intentions, their guest intervened. Leaning forward from his seated position, he peered around Mrs. Jones and made eye contact with Mr. Jones. *"It is my intuitive understanding that your lovely spouse desires you to take the lead. Is there anything I may do to assist you?"*

"Yes," replied Bill. "If you would be so kind, please explain to me what just transpired while we were viewing the rising sun."

*"Each experience was unique to the beholder, dear friend. Simply stated, our reactions were most likely similar and different because of our individual developmental paths, which have brought us to this particular place at this particular time. At one point, my friend, I believe you experienced a powerful source of connection. Is my interpretation correct?"*

Pat had never seen Bill so reluctant to speak. *What is going on,* she wondered. Her husband placed his hand on her knee. She initially interpreted his gesture as a plea for support, but then quickly recognized her deduction was incorrect. He actually was attempting to comfort her, to reassure her that everything was all right. With similar intentions, Pat responded by placing both of her hands atop his. *You can do this, Bill! Just go for it!* She wondered if her silent encouragement would reach through the ethers and actually reach his consciousness. Pat doubted the possibility, but a gentle, mostly concealed smile, indicated her real thoughts. *Hope burns eternal!* Their honored guest, who shall remain nameless, since his name has still not been mentioned, observed the interaction between the couple. His all-knowing smile, which was not hidden, but also went unnoticed by his companions, revealed he was privy to the inner workings of Pat's mind. He wondered how long it would be before these two good people would master the ancient art of silent communication.

"My experience was life-altering," Bill announced, finally having found his voice. "I don't really know how to talk about this," he admitted truthfully. "I just know something happened that I've never experienced before." Hesitating again, his internal struggle became apparent. Pat desperately wanted to help him, but instinctively knew her role was to practice patience. So she sat quietly hoping her impatience wasn't revealing itself.

"You know while we were waiting for the sun to peak over the horizon, I was excited, but I wasn't expecting anything other than a panoramic display of a beautiful scenes, one morphing into another. Needless to say, that expectation was certainly fulfilled! But there was more. Something else happened. At one point, I felt as if we were being watched," Bill shook his head in frustration. There were no words to describe what he had felt or what he thought he had heard, and yet, what happened did happen and he knew the experience was real. Agitated, but determined, he turned around and faced Pat and their companion. "Look!" he declared. "I heard something and I felt something and I know it was real!" Bill's pronouncement was quietly and respectfully received, which took him by surprise. Because he was internally admonishing himself for his reactions, he unwarrantedly anticipated rejection and ridicule. Unfortunately, Bill momentarily had forgotten the good company he was keeping. His wife, whom he completely trusted, loved and adored him. And their new 'friend' who seemed a very good sort. Fear had taken over his senses and caused him to expect the worst. *Nasty business, fear is,* he commented to himself.

"Bill, please do continue. I'm very curious to hear more about your experience, and dear, please stop worrying about describing the situation perfectly. Just throw some words out and let us try to make sense of it." Pat's lighthearted manner was exactly what her husband needed. She understood he needed to be distracted from his self-consciousness, which once again had overtaken him. Sadly, this was not an uncommon situation for Bill. Often when confronted by emotions, particularly powerful emotions, he would lose his confidence, and then, erroneously judge himself incapable of handling what in the moment felt like an insurmountable dilemma. Pat, on the other hand, never lost confidence in Bill and knew he simply needed time to adjust to his emotions. "Bill, you said you felt as if we were being watched, and also that you had heard something. Can you say anything more about that?" Pat posed her questions hoping they would help Bill focus, and also, she selfishly wanted to know more about his experience, for she too had encountered something unfamiliar and she was eager to discuss it.

"Well," he began slowly, "as we were observing the sun, I sensed someone was observing us and it seemed this 'someone' was extremely grateful for our presence. And," Bill paused shaking his head in disbelief, "I know how odd this is going to sound, but I'm going to say it anyway. I think the Sun was communicating with us, and I believe it was as grateful for our presence as we were for his, hers, its—I'll let you choose whichever pronoun suits you. I remember feeling overwhelmed by an immense energy of gratitude that seemed to reach in and touch every cell within my body. It was a remarkable sensation...and it was real."

"I believe you!" exclaimed the person he trusted more than anyone in the world. "I believe you," she repeated softly. "You also said the experience was life-altering. Can you elaborate upon that, dear?" Looking towards their guest, he commented on a remark the elder gentleman had mentioned earlier.

"You insinuated we had encountered a powerful source of connection, and you were right. I've never felt anything like this before…and I will never forget it. The sense of presence was vast…infinite…and the sincerity of spirit was so pure it resonated throughout my entire body. It brings tears to my eyes; it was breathtaking!" With a deep sigh, Bill fell into silence. His companions followed his lead, as each recalled their own experiences of the morning sunrise.

*"A blessing, it is, to experience such remarkable connection, and even more so, because it was shared with friends. I am most grateful we experienced this encounter together, dear friends."*

"Have you ever experienced anything like this before?" asked Pat curiously.

*"Yes, I have had the good fortune to enjoy similar experiences, and I can attest,"* he said looking directly at Bill, *"the experience was indeed real."*

"So, I'm not crazy. I'm not having some weird kind of hallucination." Bill's assertion indicated both his vulnerability and his certainty that the experience was real. Pat grabbed his hand to offer reassurance of her faith in him, while their guest smiled and nodded affirmation.

*"I remember,"* he spoke thoughtfully, *"the first time I had such an encounter. Like you, I doubted my sanity, and at the same time, I was absolutely certain the experience was real. It was a different setting and occasion, but the connection was the same. The profound impact of that heartfelt, boundless connection was unforgettable and it does, as you said, change you, and each time you have the privilege of experiencing this type of connection again, it is as new and fresh and as unbelievable as it was in your first encounter. What words cannot describe is real, nonetheless, and within you, this is known at a level of certainty which is equally indescribable. So blest are we to enjoy this encounter together."* Silence again overtook the threesome until words became impatient.

"Sir," inquired Pat, "is this why you joined us today?" The question brought laughter to their guest.

*"No,"* he replied gleefully, *"this was a complete surprise to me. As encounters such as these always are,"* he added in a matter of fact manner. *"I came in hope of conversation; however, dear friend, you have not had the opportunity to discuss your experience this morning. Am I correct in assuming you also had an unusual experience?"* His question was accompanied by a smile indicative of one who

enjoys life to the fullest. Pat was extremely curious about this enchanting fellow.

"My experience was very similar to Bill's, but you already know that," she said returning his smile. "I was stunned by the depth and breadth of the connection, and also, the sentimentality that penetrated my essence. It was a stellar experience, an awakening, if I may be so bold to describe it as such, which left me with many more questions than awareness. Were we in connection with the Sun itself, or a Higher Power, or God, or what? I have no answers," she openly admitted, "but I want to know more. And I believe, dear sir, you are one who knows much more about the mysteries of the universe than anyone else I have ever encountered." Pat's audacious manner surprised and pleased her husband. "I am curious," she continued. "What is your understanding of the experience we just shared? With whom or what were we in connection?"

*"How do I answer this extremely important question?"* whispered the guest of unknown origins. To whom the question was asked remained unrevealed. Perhaps, it was an inward question spoken aloud, or perhaps it was a question posed to another. Neither Pat nor Bill was certain of the answer. They feigned patience as they waited for a response. Good manners would allow nothing less.

*"I am not certain,"* he eventually replied. *"I have thoughts, ideas, and opinions, but they are no more than that. One cannot be sure, or so I presume, but then again my supposition may be founded in my own limitations. Perhaps, at some point in one's evolutionary development, absolute clarity is gained; however, I am nowhere near that level of acuity; thus, I can only ponder possibilities. Just as you desire answers to the mysteries of the universe, so too do I, but in cases such as this, I find it agreeable and most comforting to trust the sense of wellness I experience during and after an event of extraordinary connection. What I presently believe is this. For a brief, but significant moment in time, I encountered profound goodness to an extent that seems unimaginable, but which was palpable, nonetheless."* His eyes met theirs and a look of extreme gratitude washed across his face. *"I believe the three of us were granted an audience with the Divine Mystery,"* he delightfully announced. *"So blest are we who rise early to greet the Beloved Sun!"*

"What a remarkable thought!" mused Bill. "An audience with the Divine Mystery...what a beautiful way to describe our experience!

"I agree! It was a lovely description of our encounter. Thank you for sharing your impression of the situation. I would prefer more information, more specifics," Pat acknowledged sheepishly, "but as you said, perhaps, clarity will come with time and maturity."

*"Yes, my friend, I believe this is true for all of us. Learning, growing, and developing are never-ending processes, as is our ongoing curious nature, which continues motivating us to seek more possibilities. Fortunately, we have infinite time and opportunities to explore this reality."*

"Are you suggesting life is eternal?" Bill posed the question to which both he and his beloved wanted an answer. Their companion seemed surprised by the question, but quickly recovered.

*"My friends, I am not suggesting this, I am living proof of it. Whether one chooses to accept or deny the reality of eternal life, is of course, in the purview of the beholder. Many from this beautiful planet still remain conflicted about this reality, and yet, eternal existence is, has been, and always will be. It is, as it is, and will be forevermore!"* Their unnamed confidant hesitated briefly as he contemplated the underlying disbelief in the concept of external existence. *"One wonders why such a remarkable gift is so difficult for its beholders to accept. It is odd, don't you think, that those who do not agree with the concept of infinite life experiences cling to this limiting attitude, when in actuality, simple acceptance of the truth of eternal life not only enhances each and every moment, but also accelerates one's evolutionary development and expansion. So much easier it would be, if everyone would simply embrace the magnificence of their true essence."* A smile brightened his face as their guest once again did what he does so well. Pure love emanated from his eyes engulfing Pat and Bill in a cocoon of absolute joy. Both were overwhelmed by a sense of inclusion and acceptance, but before either could express their gratitude, the elder gentleman continued.

*"Each of you now has another question answered. Indeed, life is eternal, and it is in your command to share this good news with all you encounter. Quietly, graciously, in a manner that is not imposing, share this truth with everyone, and then allow the Divine Mystery to take its course. When one unobtrusively expresses his or her belief in and acceptance of a possibility, more possibilities become possible. Ponder this, dear friends!"*

"Goodness!" whispered Pat. "Divine Mystery, eternal life, what next?"

*"You must continue! The next step is to continue! Dear friends, there is no perfect way to proceed. What is intended has commenced; keep the momentum moving forward. Call another meeting with the cluster of friends and continue the good work already in progress.*

*I am grateful for our time together. In peace be, dear friends."* With palms pressed over his heart, he bowed to Bill and Pat before fading away.

*A passage from*
***The Time is Now***
*(Chapter Forty-Three)*

> *"As has man evolved in many sizes, shapes, colors, and forms on your planet, so too have others species of similarity evolved elsewhere in the Universe. From this evolutionary development throughout the vast Universe have come creations of much diversity and much similarity, for no matter where one evolved, no matter how one evolved, no matter what form one was evolved into, All evolved were One, and of One, and from One."*

"Marilyn, now it is your turn! You've graciously allowed me to go on and on, but now, I want to hear from you." Marilyn Brown was an avid listener and a great friend. Unfortunately, her exquisite listening skills were so highly refined she often delayed her own needs for the sake of those to whom she was listening. Today was another example of her generous nature. As we trekked towards the hills, she listened to my thoughts about last night's meeting, which then led me to elaborate upon the conversation shared with our mysterious elder gentleman after the meeting. I talked; Marilyn listened. "Enough of me!" I declared assertively. "Tell me where you are with this amazing experience we are all sharing. I want to hear your perspective!"

"Well, first let me begin by saying last night was incredible! The sixteen year old inside of me is really excited about all this, and even though my adult is trying to be calm and collected, I'm not! I'm just as excited as the kid in me who would love to let loose with a stream of somersaults!" A flash of this feat jetted through both of our minds resulting in a chorus of laughter. After a few minutes of encouraging each other to attempt this acrobatic maneuver, we both agreed it was an effort best left to imagination.

"I'm also very curious and would love to sit down with 'you know who' and ply him with a few dozen questions. My list, by the way, continues to grow with each encounter. Realistically, I understand our circumstances are unusual and I appreciate the fact we need to be patient, but for goodness sake, more information would be helpful. I know this must sound selfish, but my intentions are coming from the right place. Undoubtedly, we have work to do, so let's get moving. And the more information we have, the faster we can move forward." Before I could agree with Marilyn's point of view, another voice intervened.

*"Perhaps, now is a good time to engage your questions, dear friend."* As we turned toward the voice, Marilyn and I witnessed our amiable friend materializing near the edge of the trail. His smile expanded as he took in the vista. *"What a lovely setting for a morning walk! May I join you?"* Marilyn graciously welcomed our guest and pointed to the hills that were our destination. His gaze was one of awe and longing. I suspected walking might demand more energy for our guest than it would for us, so I suggested an alternative. Located a few yards away was the giant beech tree where another significant conversation had been enjoyed not too long ago. It was an optimal setting for a heartfelt conversation. Our visitor agreed it was a sanctuary suitable for our needs. In an instant, he was standing under the massive tree waiting for us to join him. Shaking our heads in wonderment, we hurried towards him. He was chuckling as we reached the shade of the tree. *"Exercise is much easier now that I am in this form, but I do miss the physicality of the embodied form."* Sitting in lotus position on the plush carpet of grass, he invited us to join him.

"You do know another question has just been added to my list," Marilyn teased. "How in the world did you do what you just did?" Her inquisitive nature excited a ripple of laughter among the three of us. "That was absolutely awesome, and you know it! You were showing off!" she joyously declared. "And I want to know how to do what you are doing!" Amused and delighted with the camaraderie, the elder openly acknowledged he was indeed demonstrating his limited skills.

*"Your question is more relevant than you realize, dear friend, for my instantaneous movement from one location to another is indeed related to my present composition in the world. Suffice it to say, I am extremely agile in my present form, which allows me to navigate the world differently than you are presently capable of managing, but do not despair, with practice you too can acquire this skill."*

"Are you insinuating we can master this type of translocation, while we are still in human form?"

*"Yes, yes! That is what I am saying! All humans are capable of this, but for some reason, it is a skill that has been forgotten. And it is one which must be retrieved quickly and soon, for this ability may be needed in the very near future."*

"Why?" Marilyn and I asked simultaneously. The demeanor of our guest turned serious, and for a moment, there was uncertainty in his gaze. We sat quietly wondering if he would continue.

*"The Island in the Sky is in great need. If the people of Earth refuse to alter their course of behavior, she will endure great disruption. If her health deteriorates to this tragic state of unwellness, it will be necessary for the residents of Earth to relocate instantaneously. Hopefully, this will not come to pass; however, we must prepare for the possibility."*

"We really are in a crisis situation, aren't we?" Knowing what was stated was true, but not wanting to believe it, I longed for reassurance. When no response denouncing my spoken thoughts was immediately forthcoming, my joyous mood sank. The shift, felt both psychologically and physiologically, was profound. In an instant, I witnessed myself transforming from the highest of highs to the lowest of lows. Turning towards Marilyn, I saw her sitting rigidly still with her hands clinched in fists and her eyes tightly closed as if she were braced for the worst. The joy we were sharing just moments before was gone. Although this transitional experience felt like an eternity, it actually happened in the blink of an eye, and during the excruciating moment, I lost myself to fear.

*"Breathe deeply, dear friends, and listen to my words with the ears of your heart. There is reason for hope! Do not allow fear to become your guide. There is reason for hope!"* Audible gasps were our reactions to the sound of his comforting voice. Many prolonged breaths were required before either of us could speak, and even then, no words came to mind.

*"Forgive me, my friends, for speaking so bluntly with you; however, the truth must be heard and accepted before change is possible. Calm yourselves, my friends, and accept these words that are also truth. There is reason for hope!"*

"There is reason for hope," whispered Marilyn.

"We are not alone," I whispered back. Hearing each other's voice seemed to fortify us and we were finally able to be present again. "Tell us more, if you well. Needless to say, your words are not pleasant to hear, but as you said, we must accept the truth before we will be able to change." Reaching out to Marilyn, our hands clasped together in solidarity, "We're ready for this, aren't we?" She nodded in agreement.

"We need more information," Marilyn stated firmly. "What we just experienced here was a small, yet exacting demonstration of what will happen when this news goes public. We must gain command over our own emotional reactions before we can comfortably assist others with their responses. This was an incredible wakeup call for me, which has shifted my awareness of the magnitude of upheaval we can anticipate. My initial reaction to our previous discussions about The Island's situation was naïve to say the least. We need more information so we can prepare accordingly."

"Yes, I agree. I was stunned and mystified by my reaction." Looking directly into our visitor's eyes, I asked, "Have I been asleep during our previous conversations? You've spoken before about the precarious circumstances of the Earth's health; and yet, the severity of the situation was not grasped…until today. We definitely need more preparation. Of course, you already know this, don't you? Now I understand why you have been so careful in approaching us. How long have you been attempting to get our attention? And how long have we been disregarding your messages?"

*"Longer than you or I can remember, dear friends. Many different approaches have been attempted, but few heeded our warnings and little progress was made. Still we remain hopeful and resolved. And with the assistance of people like you, this time a critical mass will be gained so that the necessary changes will transpire. Please know we are hopeful about the continuance of the beautiful Life Being Earth. Even in her ill health, she is still resilient and with proper care her energy will be revitalized."*

"Why are you so positive the pendulum will change this time, my friend?" inquired Marilyn. "As you well know, there is great division among the peoples of Earth regarding her state of wellness, and those who do not believe she is in jeopardy are not impressed with or persuaded by the scientific evidence that indicates otherwise."

*"Yes, unfortunately, you are correct. Even as scientific advancements are made verifying her precarious condition, the controversy rages on. Intentions founded in greed and also in ignorance are placing her in harm's way. This cannot continue. She has sacrificed so much for so many, and still, those who are dependent upon her generosity treat her with utter disrespect. Such cruelty is unfathomable."*

"And yet, you have hope," I interjected.

*"Yes,"* the elder gentleman replied. *"The Earth is a Beloved Child of the Universe and many are gathering on her behalf. They are not inclined to allow a Dear Old Friend to be ravaged by unkindness and misguided behavior. They are here to assist the peoples of Earth and to aid the planet back to good health."*

"Who are they?" inquired Marilyn.

*"They are your Family, dear friends!"* exclaimed their guest. *"You are not alone in this grand existence. Many others, similar to you, exist throughout the endless number of galaxies, and even more Beings, who are dissimilar to you,*

*also exist in our infinite existence. And all of us, regardless of our differences, are One."* As if experiencing a humorous insight, their companion chuckled for a moment before continuing, *"Indeed this is another controversy for humans to contemplate. You are One with all others in existence. This is another truth, which has been denied for ages. And speaking of denial, one of the existences with whom humankind co-exists is the Life Being Earth, whom you refuse to accept as a sentient Life Being. Regardless of humankind's unwillingness to accept ancient truths, they exist nonetheless. We are all One and many more Life Beings are included in this magnificent Oneness than humans can presently imagine."*

"We are all interconnected," Marilyn stated quietly.

*"Indeed, we are! And the peoples of Earth have reached a moment in time when they must faces these realities. Fortunately, your Family is comprised of Beings imbued with loving-kindness and they are eager to make your acquaintance. Much can be learned from these benevolent Beings."*

"Obviously, we have much to learn, but I suggest we continue this conversation in the company of our other Earth bound friends. Don't you agree, Marilyn?" She nodded her consent. "We are so grateful for this connection this morning. It has been most informative; however, for the sake of efficiency, let's continue this conversation in the presence of our entire group."

*"It is a plan with merit,"* agreed their other worldly guest. *"Please schedule another gathering, and we will learn more about the days ahead."* Smiling in his usual warm, gracious way, he concluded the conversation, *"I have enjoyed this time together. In peace be, dear friends."* And with that said, he faded into nothingness.

# ~ Chapter Five ~

*"We seek an audience, Old Friend. May we come forward?"*

*"Indeed,"* responded the one who served as an intermediary to the cluster of friends situated on The Island in the Sky. *"I am most grateful for your presence. Please join me!"*

*"Your work this morning was inspirational. Each encounter imparted new wisdom founded in the Mission of Mercy. You guide them well, Old Friend."*

*"Very little is required of me, My Friends. They are people of goodness who have naturally evolved to this point in time when the need to fulfill their purpose is awakening within them. We are most fortunate. They are able assistants and they will serve well."*

*"As do you, Old Friend. You have our gratitude. Please remember, we are but a breath away. In peace be!"*

Although the elder gentleman, as his companions from The Island referred to him, could not see his ancient companions, he respectfully bowed to them as they departed. Their praise filled is heart. He rested in the quietude of his surroundings appreciative of the opportunity to serve in his present form and location. *Indeed, life continues,* he silently spoke as if answering the ageless question for all those who could not remember the truth of their circumstances. *"Life is, life was, and life will ever be. Remember, dear friends. Remember!"* he whispered into existence for any listening ear to hear.

# ~ CHAPTER SIX ~

Marilyn arrived early to help with the evening's gathering. As we rearranged the living room furniture, she joked about the regularity of our meetings. "Maybe, you should just leave the chairs positioned like this. After all, we'll probably be calling another impromptu get-together in a few days, if not tomorrow."

"You're right about that!" I replied with amusement. "We really are enjoying each other's company, aren't we? In all the years the eight of us have known one another, we've never visited this frequently. It's really been lovely."

"It has been very special," added Marilyn, "and timely, I think. Even without the excitement of our new mutually shared adventure, it seems as if all of us were in need of connection." As the last chair was planted in its appropriate place, I nodded my head in agreement. "We are so blessed to have one another!"

"Amen to that!" I exclaimed just as the doorbell announced the arrival of our cluster of friends.

"Okay, you two," declared Dee as she marched through the door, "tell us everything!" Dee's authoritative manner set the tone for the evening. Favorite chairs were quickly selected and the meeting promptly began.

"Welcome back, dear friends!" I began with a chuckle. "Well, it's been twenty-four hours since our last meeting and I suspect each of you has something new to report." Looking around the room, excitement was evident. "Is it correct to assume each of you has had another encounter with our mysterious friend?" The answer was not a surprise to anyone.

"Well, it looks like this may be a lengthy meeting," Marilyn's gracious smile brightened the room. "Any suggestions as to how we should proceed this evening?"

*"Perhaps, I may be of assistance,"* came the familiar voice of the yet-to-be seen guest. Words of invitation and gratitude circled about the room while the voice materialized into the form of the now well-known elder gentleman. He quickly occupied the extra chair, which had been specifically placed for him. *"I am most grateful for this opportunity to be in your presence once again, and I ask permission to facilitate this meeting."* No one challenged his request. In fact, we were all very pleased he willingly took the lead.

*"My friends, many conversations were shared this day, and from these heartfelt connections, it has been determined you are all ready to move forward. To do so, we must have yet another significant conversation. Hopefully, this discussion will*

*enable you to fully comprehend the importance of the calling to which each of you has responded.*

*On several occasions, dear friends, you have heard mention of a Mission of Mercy. It is of this mission we must speak, for this endeavor involves the greatest rescue attempt ever before conceived. For millennia, Friends of the Life Being Earth have attempted to inform her residents of the negative impact they were having upon their host planet. Unfortunately, only a few heeded our messages and these were unable to create the massive changes necessary to alter the course of an entire civilization. Our efforts continue to fall on deaf ears as the careless maltreatment of the planet persists with ever increasing destructive results. No longer can the truth be ignored and denied. The beautiful Island in the Sky is waning and no longer is she able to sustain the needs of her inhabitants. She has done too much for too long for too many, and she can no longer bear the consequences of her generosity. Her valiant attempts to continue for the sake of her residents have been in vain, and at this point in time, her own survival is endangered.*

*Her declining health is real. One does not need to be a scientist to recognize the injuries she has incurred. One does not need a medical degree to determine she is an ailing life being, and still, endless debates continue while her condition worsens. While evidence verifying her decline mounts, denial of her situation continues to delay actions that are critical for her continuance. If the people of Earth do not take immediate action on her behalf, they will unfortunately suffer the ramifications of their neglectful ways.*

*My friends, I take no pleasure in being the bearer of such devastating news, but the truth must be spoken. The situation of the Life Being Earth is perilous, and the consequences of her continued decline are unimaginable. Denial is no longer an option. Hear my words, dear friends, the people of Earth must change their violent, destructive ways or their home will collapse beneath them. No longer can she be subjected to the negative energy created by humankind. No one can survive such abuse. No one should be the victim of such extreme disrespect and no one has the privilege of participating in such vile perpetration. The angry energy thriving within the human species must cease to exist. This reality is not debatable nor can it be denied. The negative energy generated by the ill will of humankind is destroying their species and the Life Being that granted them residence. This is the unsightly truth of your circumstances, and each of you, every human residing upon this planet, must accept responsibility for this crisis.*

*It pains me to bring this message forward, my friends, but our previous attempts have not gained the attention of your people. Now, the truth must be heard, understood, and accepted. There is still time to reverse what is happening;*

*however, this message is timely. Please do not presume that time will not run out, for it will, and the time when time no longer matters approaches rapidly. Please heed this message, for your lives depend upon it."* The messenger paused allowing time for his words to be digested. His breathing was slow and deliberate, as he too absorbed the enormity of the message he was called to deliver.

*"My friends, please be with me. These words are most difficult to hear, but you must do so for the sake of humankind. The Mission of Mercy includes not only the rescue of the inhabitants of Earth, but also the rescue of the Life Being Earth from those who are unwittingly destroying her life force. There is still time for the Mission of Mercy to be accomplished. We cannot succeed without the assistance of the people of Earth, nor can you succeed without our assistance. We stand ready to aid you. Please accept our offer."*

*"As you might imagine, Dear Reader, this message silenced the meeting and halted time. Each member of our cast of characters grappled with the devastating news, and each one survived the initial impact, as will you. We say this with certainty because we have faith in you. In recognition of the complexity of this moment, we elect to pause for the purpose of addressing your present state of being. Unlike the characters in our story, who had the good fortune of receiving this message in the company of friends, you Dear Reader, most likely are alone as you read this book. Our concern for you is sincere, thus we stand by your side as you internalize the regrettable news. As you well know, the intention of this message is to awaken humankind to the reality of their circumstances. Even though this most unfortunate news is presented through a fictional story, the message regarding the declining health of the Life Being Earth is the truth. You know this in your heart or you would not still be reading this book.*

*Remember, Dear Reader, you are not alone. Many others are also reading this book and they too grasp the seriousness of this dilemma. This time the message is being heard, and the message will spread. People like you will stand ready to assist the Earth. People just like you will make the necessary changes to aid her back to good health. There is reason for hope, Dear Reader. While assimilating the difficult news, please do not forget the entirety of our message. There is reason for hope.*

*When you feel ready to continue reading, please envision other readers around the world joining you in the process. Enjoy this camaraderie! Take comfort in knowing that others of like mind and heart are moving forward in their efforts to assist the beautiful Island in the Sky, the Life Being Earth.*

*With gratitude in our hearts, we remind you, we are but a breath away."*

After an unknown period of time, Frank Sanderson interrupted the silence. "I'm guessing you drew the short straw," he said addressing their somber guest. Not understanding the meaning of Frank's comment, the elder gentleman sat with a quizzical look. With great empathy, Frank elaborated. "I can't imagine what it was like for you to deliver this message to us. I assume you were called to do this." Frank's gesture of kindness brought everyone back from their internal journeys of exploration. He somehow managed to move beyond his own discomfort and was able to identify with their companion's situation. Dee was extremely proud of her husband. His tender heart was becoming more demonstrative.

*"I am deeply comforted by your consideration of my needs. It was not a pleasant task to be the bearer of such profound sadness, but it was necessary. Because of the strong bond all of you share and also because of the success of our recent connections, I was confident in your abilities to handle this news. And I believe we can move forward now that the truth is out in the open."*

"Thank you for your confidence in us," interjected Dee. "Your frequent visits prepared us for this. I can't say it was easy to hear this message, but because you were the presenter of this unpleasantness, it was more palatable." Dee hesitated and then returned to her husband's question. "I'm curious," she said. "Were you called to do what you are doing?" Their visitor had a pensive look as he considered the question.

*"Was I called to do this work? The calling is an interesting concept, is it not?"* He hesitated and seemed to go within again. *"We are very similar, my friends. Even though, we presently reside in different realms of existence, we are all motivated by similar mysteries.*

*The passion demonstrated by the eight of you is worthy of your attention. To witness such passion in one individual is amazing in itself, but to see it play out in a group of people is really remarkable. Each of you, in your own unique way, feels driven by 'something' that you cannot identify. You sense there is 'more' to life than you presently experience, and you feel compelled to pursue this mysterious driving force. You feel 'called' to pursue some unknown source that presumably holds answers to the heartfelt questions regarding your reason for being.*

*And in this particular situation, the eight of you have apparently, in some mysterious manner, been brought together to assist with an issue of mutual concern. Have you all been called to this particular place at this particular time?"*

Shrugging his shoulders and sporting a childlike grin, he giggled with delight. *"My understanding of the calling is no greater than yours, my friends; however, my intuitive sense of it as a tool of distinction may be more finely tuned. What I know in this moment in time is this. I am called to be here in this particular place, at this particular time to be of assistance to you. I am an intermediary between the eight of you and Those Who Came Before. I understand this is my truth, because when I serve in this way, I am at peace, and if I stray from this path, my heart begins to ache. Over time, I have learned my heart is a source of great wisdom."*

"Your presence is such a gift to us," Jan sincerely declared. "Since the first day we encountered you, our lives have been significantly enlivened. Although your comings and goings have been confounding at times, you have certainly brought greater meaning and purpose into our daily existence. And because of this, as Dee said, we are more able to hear the fullness of today's dreadful message. I heard the difficult part and will not forget it, but I also heard your words of inspiration. There is reason for hope! I'm grateful you had the courage, the resolve, to share this truth with us. I'm grateful you are following your calling. Thank you! And we definitely want to participate in the Mission of Mercy. We're still unclear as to how we are to proceed, but we want to be of assistance." Jan's commentary instigated a round of similar commitments by the other members of the Cluster of Friends.

*"Your acceptance of the truth regarding Earth's declining health touches the hearts of many, my friends. And the sincerity of your vows to participate in her recovery process is most comforting. Finally, the Children of Earth are responding to the call to save their host planet. Gratitude abounds throughout all existence."*

"My friend, your words honor us…and as usual, they create many more questions. However, let me put the questions aside for a moment while I attempt to respond to the sentiments of gratitude you shared with us from others whom we cannot see. We too are grateful we have heard the calling, but it would not have happened if you and 'the others' had not persisted. While it is not my place to speak for the peoples of Earth, I must express my appreciation, the group's appreciation, for everything being done on our behalf. I know we will never know the extensive efforts made for us and for our planet, but all I can say, is thank you." Other members of our group also expressed their gratitude, and for a brief moment in time, if one listened carefully you could hear a faint echo reverberating throughout the cosmos.

"May we assume we will learn more about Those Who Came Before in the near future?" Bill questioned in a lighthearted manner.

*"Oh, indeed yes! As are they in need of our assistance, we are very much in*

*need of theirs. Suffice it to say, my friends, we are in very good company.*" His brief response was satisfying. In truth, little more could be assimilated at this point. Everyone was exhausted. *"My friends, much was achieved this evening and there is reason for celebration. A message of grave importance was delivered, and you survived the message with grace and resolve. Let us applaud this achievement as we advance to the next phase of our mission. Rest now, my friends. In peace be!"*

After their friend translocated to parts unknown, the Cluster of Friends lingered. "Okay, tell me the truth! Did you guys really handle this evening with grace and resolve?" Pat's inquiry unintentionally set off a much needed round of laugher. After several attempts were made to rein the frivolities in, everyone realized the tension they had been containing throughout the evening had to be released; the outburst of laughter simply had to play itself out. With the release, a sense of calm overtook the group and they were finally able to address Pat's question.

Marilyn responded from an energetic perspective. "Well, considering the circumstances, I think we did the best we could. Obviously, our energy levels shifted profoundly, but they did not turn frenetic, which was a testament of our ability to be with the devastating news. I also think we exercised noticeable resilience, as demonstrated by our compassionate response to the bearer of bad news. And our commitments made certainly appeared genuine and sincere to me. Is anyone having doubts now since we are more removed from the moment?"

"I'm not," responded Frank. "I have many questions, but that seems to be standard operating procedures with this fellow. And of course, there are concerns related to my age and stamina, but I don't have any doubts about participating. I will do what I can do to the best of my ability." He hesitated for a brief instant before he boldly announced, "I do feel resolved about my commitment." Frank's determination was inspiring and his firm declaration strengthened the resolve in others. "Pat, if you're doubting yourself because you've got the shakes, just know that we're all feeling shaky. Seems to me, it's a logical response to the situation." Not only Pat was reassured by Frank's demonstration of strength. His words were comforting to the entire group.

"Actually, this is very helpful, Frank. What you refer to as the shakes, I call the jitters and when Pat posed her question, I was acutely aware of feeling jittery. I was a breath away from misinterpreting my jitters as a collapse of my resolve. I am so grateful for this discussion," asserted Jan. "I'm learning so much about myself through our conversations."

"Me, too!" acknowledged Pat. "This is invaluable, and what we're learning will be extremely useful as we begin planning our outreach groups.

"My sentiments exactly," Dee chimed in. "Tonight's meeting is the schematic for our upcoming group meetings. Before we meet and greet, we must be prepared for everything we encountered this evening. What we've heard, what we've witnessed, and what we've experienced are the foundational elements for our tasks." Dee's eyes sparkled with awareness. "Aha!" she voiced loudly. "What amazing teachers our invisible friends are! Through their intermediary, contact was made and trust was gained. Over time information of relevance and significance was shared, and assessments were made, and then, at an auspicious moment when their students were presumed to be ready, critically important, life-altering information was divulged. Reactions were carefully monitored, more assessments were made, the results were positive, and success was declared. The students were determined, ready to advance to the next phase of the operation. My friends, our colleagues are master teachers. We will be wise to follow their lead."

*A passage from*
***The Time is Now***
*(Chapter Forty-Four)*

> *"As the evolutionary process grew in its ways of delightful wonder, the Ones of most evolution came to understand the process of evolution more than those of less evolution, and in knowing more of the evolutionary process, more they wanted to know. And from this desire to know more about the evolutionary process came the desire to experience more of the evolutionary process, and in experiencing more evolutionary processes, more evolved. We became."*

Everett, in a very matter of fact manner, turned towards me and stated what everyone was thinking. "I presume we're meeting again tomorrow evening. We'd be glad to host if you would like a break."

"You know, as we rearranged the furniture a few minutes before everyone arrived, Marilyn suggested we just leave the chairs positioned as they are, because she anticipated we would be having another meeting very soon. And here we are again, scheduling another meeting. Her intuition is mind-boggling!" I noted in a teasingly way. In good fun, Marilyn responded by playfully placing her right hand to her forehead, as if she were attempting to divine some mysterious information. "Everett, thank you for the offer; however, since everything is already in place, we might as well just meet here again, if that suits everyone."

"I have a suggestion," Dee announced assertively. Her demeanor had completely changed in recent weeks. Her confidence was back. The commanding nature so deeply imbued in her professional self was fully activated again. Frank loved seeing this side of her again, as did her friends. She was powerhouse! "I know we will need to process what has happened here tonight, but as we all know, our wonderful conversations can take over the evening. Because of the amount of information we were imparted with tonight, I believe tomorrow's meeting really must be task oriented. We need to address not only the information we've received, but also the fine points of role modeling demonstrated. I encourage everyone to make notes about your experience tonight, highlighting the points which were most poignant for you, but also, noticing all aspects of the discussion you feel may potentially and significantly affect a participant. Each of us will have our own unique perspective and by combining our experiences, we will be able to develop a program that is as powerful and influential as the experience we just shared." With business attended, Dee turned to me. "Will you bring the meeting to a close, dear?"

Grabbing my favorite brass Tibetan bowl, I faced my friends. "No more words need be said this evening. Shall we conclude with five minutes of silence?" With their approval, I gently tapped the side of the bowl producing the lovely sound that instantly calms the soul. Time passed, as we each meandered our way into the quiet. Together, yet separate, alone, but not, we existed in the moment of timelessness.

*A passage from*
***The Time is Now***
*(Chapter Forty-Five)*

*"From the simple cell amoebae, We evolved into creations of remarkable knowingness, and from this simple cell, All came, and All are One."*

# ~ Chapter Seven ~

*"Well done, Old Friend! These fine people have developed very quickly under your tutelage, and with your continued guidance, they will be effective and influential advocates for the Mission of Mercy."*

*"You are most kind, My Friends. I am eager to continue; however, as you already have observed, they are remarkable individuals, and the camaraderie they share strengthens them as a whole. They are motivated more by kindness than ego, and their curiosity and openheartedness make them natural leaders. We are most fortunate these old friends have awakened."*

*"Indeed, you are correct, and their compassionate, amiable ways will assist others to awaken as well. Just as you quietly reached out to them, they will follow a similar path and as their numbers grow, additional clusters will form and through these agents of peace, messages defining the Earth's precarious condition, as well as the means for healing this precious Life Being will spread across the planet.*

*We are most grateful and pleased these good people heard our message. As you witnessed, they did not falter when they heard the disparaging news. It was difficult for them to hear, as well it should be, but they recovered quickly and immediately were inspired to action. Now, we must provide them with the information, which will assist the peoples of Earth in healing their beloved planet. The Mission of Mercy advances forward."*

# PART THREE

# ~ CHAPTER ONE ~

Hurriedly shifting the laundry from the washer to the dryer, I was not surprised when the sound of the doorbell drifted down the stairwell. My guests were exceptional in many ways, including their keen sense of timing. As always they were diligently prompt. Rushing up the basement stairs, my mind entertained itself with a critical account of my tardiness. *Why didn't you just leave the door open? Why didn't you think about that earlier? Perhaps, you should make life easier and just give all of them a key, or better yet, assign them a bedroom.* The dialogue running between my mind and itself didn't seem to be accomplishing anything, so I increased my pace only to arrive at the front door huffing and puffing. "Sorry to keep you waiting friends, I was down in the basement."

"Not a problem," replied Frank Sanderson as he ushered everyone in. "We just got here."

"You might as well just leave the door open," snickered Dee with a sly look on her face. "Or give all of us keys to your house, since we seem to be spending so much time here."

"Better yet," remarked Marilyn, as she winked at me, "why don't we just move in? It would be so convenient for all of us and our conversations could go on and on endlessly. Great plan, don't you think?" she muttered while poking me in the ribs.

As everyone moved towards their favorite chair, I quickly flashed on Dee and Marilyn's comments. *This cannot be a coincidence!* Shaking my head in disbelief, I burst out laughing. "You rascals! You've been listening to the nonsense of my mind. Now, don't deny it. You fess up to this in front of friends and family! And then you tell us exactly how you did that!" Surprised by my outburst everyone was looking about trying to figure out what was going on.

"Oops! She nailed us, dear!" admitted Dee gleefully.

"Gotcha!" I responded.

"Okay, okay, you caught us!" Marilyn was having far too much fun to feel the least bit guilty. "Let's just say we were overseeing your movements."

"What on Earth is going on?" inquired Everett. "What is happening here?"

"Tell them," I insisted, pointing my finger at both of them and pretending to be miffed. "Tell them what you've been up to!" They deliberated for a few moments, and then, Marilyn pretended she was flipping a coin. Catching the invisible disc in mid-air, slapping it on the back of her opposite hand, and then sneaking a peak, Marilyn happily pointed to Dee indicating that she had lost the toss. Dee bravely accepted the ostensible loss.

"Well, dear," she said looking in my direction, "since you are the injured party, perhaps, you would prefer to go first." My inclination was to decline her offer, but then I thought better of it. Realizing everything happens for a reason, I decided to use this opportunity as a teaching aid for all of us.

Letting go of the humorous approach, I responded in a more serious tone. "Dee, perhaps it is wise if I share my perspective first." Gathering my thoughts, I informed everyone of my experience while rushing up the stairs to answer the door, and particularly elaborated upon the thoughts racing through my mind at the time. "So you can imagine why I was taken aback by Marilyn and Dee's comments when they entered the house. What we have here, my friends, is another example of silent communication. Obviously, the two of you intercepted my thoughts, which by the way, I am not at all concerned about, but I am extremely curious about the process. How do you do this? Let's take advantage of this incident and learn from it!" Looking toward Dee, I acknowledged my intentions. "I know telepathy is not in alignment with the evening's task, but it seems important. Can we spend a few minutes discussing this?"

"Who knows, dear? Perhaps, this topic is in alignment with our needs for this evening and we just don't know it yet. Everything happens for a reason, so maybe we are intended to talk about this."

"Let me get this straight. You two heard the thoughts of our friend here, as she was bolting up the stairs." Looking to Dee and Marilyn for verification, Bill received nods from both of them. "Okay, ladies, explain yourselves!"

"For me," Marilyn began, "the process is multi-faceted. While we were waiting on the porch, I felt a rush of energy and saw a flash of our friend climbing up the stairs, and at the same time as the image appeared, her words were faintly heard. I don't really know how this happens, but I presume she was expending so much energy attempting to respond to our arrival that her energy field collided with mine providing me with a very brief glimpse of her situation. I also believe long-standing relationships, such as our heartfelt friendship can enable and enhance these types of experiences. I didn't think anything of it until I saw Dee's playfulness, and then I just went along with the banter. Of course, if we had intercepted a private matter, our reactions would have been very different."

"Yes, of course," agreed Dee. "With this privilege comes responsibility. The playfulness you witnessed was the result of precious connections. If I had overheard a private matter, as Marilyn referred to it, I would have held the experience close to my heart. The privacy of someone's personal thoughts is a delicate matter, which will require great consideration and discernment, as this ability becomes a common form of communication.

My own experience with these types of events is still very limited, except with Frank. Our thoughts merge more and more frequently now, and actually, I think the ability has increased since we've started having these regular meetings. I'm not sure if we are really more skilled at this than any of you, but perhaps over time, we have become more attentive and trusting of these exchanges. When these events initially began, we were too distracted to notice, and when we did notice, we gave the event very little credence, because some other event quickly captured our attention, and the moment passed without thought or consideration. However, as the events became more frequent, curiosity compelled us to pay attention, and eventually the idea of a coincidence was no longer acceptable as an explanation for these otherwise inexplicable events. I think it's fair to say we are vigilantly in tune to these events nowadays. We enjoy them too much to let them slip pass by without notice.

I'm not clear why this chain of events has happened this evening, but I think it is highly unlikely we are witnessing a coincidence. My friends, this topic surfaced for a reason, and it will be most interesting to see how it plays out tonight."

*A passage from*
***The Book of Joy: The Invitation***
*(Chapter One)*

*"Seek within? This directive seems simple enough, does it not, but what does it actually mean? How and where does one begin? If you are someone familiar with the inward journey then most likely some modicum of awareness regarding the significance of these two small words is already in your possession. And perhaps from previous experiences you have witnessed the never-ending qualities related to this profound guidance. No matter how far your expedition extends or how long the journey has already endured, the words of wisdom "seek within" are forever relevant and poignant. Whether you are a seasoned seeker or just beginning your inward pursuit, hold these precious words of guidance near to your heart. Seek within."*

"That was very informative; thank you both for sharing your perspectives. I suspect numerous questions are looming, but perhaps, we can save them for a moment." Feeling responsible for getting the meeting on task, I suggested we table the telepathy topic for the moment and turn our attention to the evening's agenda. "Dee, your summation of last night's experience was extremely impressive. You seemed to have a clear idea about how we should proceed. Would you like to facilitate the meeting?" Dee did not hesitate.

"Yes, I would! I realized last night the experiences we've been having the last few weeks were the model for advancing our tentative plans forward. This may sound ridiculous, but it seems our lives have been carefully choreographed lately in ways, which have brought us all together to pursue a mutual purpose. When I think about this, it seems absurd and egocentric, and yet, here we are. In truth, we've been drawn to one another for years. Our life experiences have been sweetly interconnected with times of intense closeness and other times with less intensity due to various life circumstances, but always, regardless of our personal and familial involvements, our friendships remained solid and heartfelt." Dee made eye contact with her friends, and asked, "Why is this? Is it merely a coincidence? As you all know, I don't believe in coincidences. So here we are again sharing another period of intense camaraderie, making sincere commitments to pursue a life of service, which may substantially alter our own lives and change the lives of others we encounter. And all this is happening because of an amiable gentleman who intentionally engaged each of us and gathered us together for the purpose of participating in an endeavor intended to save the Earth.

Well, it seems to me the way we were approached, the manner in which information was carefully and deliberately shared, and the time allotted us for assimilation of the provided information, all of this transpired with great consideration. This was not a coincidence. We are part of a process much bigger than we presently understand, and it seems to me the way we have been attended has been admirable and extremely successful. Having experienced this first hand, I think it is a model for us to pursue as we reach out to others."

"I agree with you, Dee," affirmed Marilyn. "The synchronicity of our mutual experiences is beyond anything I've ever witnessed or heard about. It's fascinating! And when I allow myself to really ponder what is happening with us, among us, and seemingly for us, it is truly humbling. I can't pretend to understand everything that is going on, but what is happening is real, and I want to be an active participant in this project. Obviously, we are people who want answers, and hopefully more clarity will come as we become more involved, but for now, I have enough information to know I want to be a part of this. Our mentor delivered us a blow last night. The news was devastating, and yet, it wasn't anything we don't already know. We all know the Earth is in serious trouble; he just spoke the truth truthfully and forthrightly. But what we didn't know about were the efforts being made on her behalf by others who consider themselves long-standing Family and friends of the Earth, and that news was incredibly uplifting. I trust what's happening and I want to do my part."

*A passage from*
***The Book of Joy: The Invitation***
*(Chapter One)*

> *"Many of you already know this truth, yet it is one worthy of frequent visits and considerable attention. The truth about existence is this...there are many, many truths that exist in existence! Although many of these truths have been known for ages, even more have existed for ages that are not yet fully understood, and even more, which are yet to be discovered. Compound this reality with another truth that often results in substantial complications among those who believe they know the truth. Not everyone who knows the truth believes the same truth, nor do all believers of the same truth believe it in the same way. Unfortunately, this inevitable reality can be tedious at times, as well as, precarious; however, this is an aspect of truth that will be addressed later, for at this point in time, we are assembled to focus our intentions upon the truth of joy."*

Marilyn's display of confidence and determination aroused the group, as had Frank's, the evening before. Momentum was building as grateful eyes from afar were carefully observing the unfolding development that was long in the making.

"I'd say you two did a very good job of explaining yourselves." The compliment from Bill was happily received. "And if your premise is correct Dee, which I believe it is, then we are already moving forward. During these weeks of reconnecting and sharing our stories about recent experiences, we've come to a greater level of acceptance regarding the unusual circumstances in which we seem to be involved. And we've grown because of our camaraderie.

We've gained confidence and strength, and it seems to me our attitudes have also changed. Of course, I can only speak for myself, but I feel better about 'me' and more excited about life. The idea that I am actually here for a reason pleases me. It's a bit embarrassing to acknowledge this aloud, but it's true, and I really want to help in whatever ways I can." Nods and similar sentiments circled about the room confirming Bill's observations, while Marilyn sat quietly, inconspicuously watching the energy fields of her friends shifting in ways that confirmed the positive acclamations being articulated. Individually and collectively, the group was growing stronger and healthier. Physically, they all looked younger, and energetically, they appeared to be rejuvenated and more vibrant.

"And the commitments we've avowed to each other and to our mentor," Bill continued, "also indicates we have risen above our doubts and fears, and our incessant questioning has quieted. This meeting tonight is evidence we are already taking action. Good for us!" he declared with gusto, and after a few moments, he added, "And thank you. Thank you all for many years of friendship, and for this adventure we are embarking upon together." Bill's sentiments succeeded in deeply touching the very core of his friends. Operating from a place of selflessness, the Cluster of Friends was indeed openheartedly pursuing a purpose that had awakened within them.

*A passage from*
***The Book of Joy: The Invitation***
*(Chapter One)*

*"You, Dear Reader, whether you are presently aware of this or not, are an instrument of joy.*

*When this statement was received, my wayward mind stepped forward with words of caution. What if the reader of **The Book of Joy** does not resonate to this bold declaration about being an instrument of joy? What if said reader does not experience life from a joyous perspective or even identify with the concept? What if, Dear Reader, your life circumstances are presently complex, and because of your situation, it is extremely difficult for you to connect with the joyful resident existing within you? As you can see, my mind quickly ascertained a need to prepare for contradictory reactions to*

> *this delightful statement of possibility. And my mind's response gave me pause.*
>
> *If your mind experienced similar "what ifs" when it encountered the pronouncement of your joyful potential, then perhaps it might be beneficial for each of us to explore why? Why, Dear Reader, might we react hesitantly or perhaps even feel resistance to the idea of being an instrument of joy?"*

*"Good evening, my friends, may I join you?"* The invisible voice, greeted with a gracious welcome, materialized near the remaining empty chair. Their guest bowed to his companions before taking his place among the group. *"Already, your conversation is exceptional, and it is noticed by those from far places. I bring sentiments of gratitude and joy."* Placing his palms together under his chin and near his heart, he respectfully bowed again. Marilyn responded in like manner, and then, other group members did the same.

*"Ah! You adopt the manners of gentle courtesy. I am grateful. It is a small gesture with profound impact, and one that benefits both the donor and the recipient."* Once again, our new friend mentioned 'others' who are obviously intricately involved in this unusual scenario we find ourselves in, and I felt inclined to pursue more information.

"Friend, I wonder if you will tell us more about our unseen guests tonight. Undoubtedly, they are observing our meeting. Will they be participating in our discussions?" The question asked had been brewing for some time and this seemed an opportune time to give it voice. Our visitor paused for a moment, which made me wonder if he was presently in communication with them. The answer to my thoughts came quickly.

*"First, I will reply to your unspoken question. Yes, I am presently in communication with our Beloved Friends."* He spoke softly while scanning the room with those remarkable eyes that dissolved any notions of concern lingering about in the cavernous spaces of an apprehensive mind. *"Dear Ones, they oversee these meetings and guide me when necessary. As said before, I am merely an intermediary, and like you, the opportunity for participation fills me with gratitude. I too wish to serve as best as I am able. Our Ancient Companions are Those Who Came Before and they will indeed be monitoring our meeting, but they prefer not to be the focus. Through our continuing work together, trust will be nurtured and a fond relationship will actualize; these Ancient Ones have great love for the Children of Earth. In essence, my friends, you have been working with them since our first encounter. And before,"* he added quietly. *"While you*

*came to know and trust me through our numerous encounters, so too were they part of the unfolding process, even though you were unaware of their presence and their contributions. As you said, dear friend, they are intricately involved in our interactions and in the welfare of humankind and the Life Being Earth."*

*A passage from*
***The Book of Joy: The Invitation***
*(Chapter Two)*

*"The energy that constitutes joy and which dwells in every existence existing in existence is, was, and always will be present, and since you are an existing existence within this remarkable existence then you too are a carrier of the energy of joy. What does this mean to you? Regardless of your present circumstances, what does this thought provoking statement mean to you? How does it effect your perceptions of self, others, and everything else with which you co-exist?*

*Pause for a moment if it will be helpful. Reading **The Book of Joy** is an act of active participation and there will be times when discernment will necessarily be a part of this active process. Knowing when to pause is an essential part of all aspects of life and it stands true for this reading activity as well. The questions above warrant your consideration. Discern what is more important for you… racing through these pages for whatever purpose, or pausing when the moment demands further contemplation.*

*As you reflect upon the aforementioned questions, you may find it beneficial to journal about your thoughts, as well as the mannerisms of your thoughtful mind's process. The human mind is a marvel to witness and a challenge to command. Hopefully, through this and many more contemplative investigations to come, you will indeed gain greater understanding of the mind's capabilities including its brilliance and its limitations."*

*"Dear Friends, I come this evening to request your participation in an act of generosity. Your vows of commitment made last night already speak to your willingness; however, today I wish to introduce two compelling factors, which may significantly influence your participation. Please understand this generous act is essential for the Earth if she is to successfully regain her health. If it meets*

*with your approval, this will be the primary topic for our meeting tonight."* His request was met with enthusiasm.

*"Before we begin, I remind you there is reason for hope. The changes required, which are necessary for the revitalization of the Earth, are within humankind's capability. Simply stated, elimination of the negative energy produced by aggressive intentions and actions is not only in humankind's best interest, but it also can effectively and expeditiously restore Earth back to good health. That said,"* his voice strengthened, *"our primary obstacle is convincing an entire populace they are personally responsible for the Earth's declining condition. Unfortunately, there is a fear-based inclination among the human species, which inhibits their natural ability for accepting culpability in any given situation. Resistance of this kind leads one to blame others for wrongdoings while denying responsibility for one's own actions. Because of the catastrophic implications of Earth's present condition, misguided immaturity cannot be the approach taken when addressing this crisis. Each member of the human race is responsible for this situation, and every individual must take part in rectifying the problem.*

*A passage from*
***The Book of Joy: The Invitation***
*(Chapter Two)*

*"The art of reflection is a skill of mindfulness that demands the cooperation and assistance of a contemplative mind. You possess such a mind, as does everyone else, but alas, many have not yet encountered the contemplative mind residing within them. Perhaps now is a good time to change this unfortunate circumstance. Dear Reader, seize the moment of opportunity. Now is the time to meet your beautiful mind, for it is an essential companion on the journey ahead...*

*Of course, you are invited and may choose to read the plethora of books and articles available about mindfulness, meditation, and/or relaxation techniques, or you may choose to take classes that can offer assistance in learning various styles and approaches to the contemplative process, or you may instead seek the counsel of a learned friend. Whether you are one who is blessed with friends and enjoy the camaraderie and growth experienced in the community of others also seeking contemplative practices, or if you are one who prefers the solo path, there is another learned friend you may wish to pursue for guidance. Dear Reader, your most competent and able friend resides within you, and it is this learned friend who is most capable of providing assistance. No better or more meaningful guidance will you ever receive than "Seek Within!"*

*Before pursuing this seemingly simple direction, let us first recognize another honored companion that is indispensable to the inward journey. The mind, masterful as it is, can be profoundly handicapped without the amiable and compassionate assistance of the open heart. Obviously, when speaking of the open heart, our focus is not the physical heart, but the essential essence within that is the driving force for every existing being. Serving as an entryway to connection, expansion, and evolution, the open heart is a portal leading to greater understanding of the infinite mysteries that call to all of us thus learning to access this pivotal port of call is critical. In truth, without your open heart's presence, the process of seeking within will seem so much more tedious and cumbersome than is necessary.*

*Separately, both the mind and the open heart are accomplished at being creatively and productively stellar; however, when the two join, their outreach can extend beyond the stars. Earlier in our conversation you were encouraged to think expansively about existence and now you are gently and rather subtly advised that you indeed have the means and capacity to stretch beyond your present surroundings and encounter more than you presently can see. In truth, your potential for expansion towards and connection with "more" is unlimited when these two remarkable companions cooperatively combine their essential elements to your journey within. Both will require your undivided attention, for you must thoroughly comprehend the inner workings of each to fully grasp their complementary effect, as well as, the disruptive influence each can yield."*

A discordant tune of reflexive gasps and extended exhalations reverberated around the circle of friends. Their eyes turned empty and distant as if stilled by the magnitude of the Mission of Mercy enveloping them, but their minds refused to be stilled. Flittering from one 'what if' to another, their unruly minds frantically searched for an escape plan. Witnessing the downward swing of energy, Marilyn quickly initiated action.

"Friends, I need your assistance. Please help me to quiet myself, by joining me in several long deep breaths." Marilyn's friends responded immediately. "Even though, I know you are here beside me, I need to feel your presence. Breathing together will restore our unity and bring us back to center."

*"Ingenious!"* The observation made from an unknown destination

complimented the swift and pertinent action taken to stabilize the group's sudden decline of energy. A smile brightened the face of the elder gentleman who also noted the rapid recovery of his students' momentary encounter with shock. He patiently waited while they lovingly cared for one another.

*A passage from*
***The Book of Joy: The Invitation***
*(Chapter Two)*

> *"You, Dear Reader, are a carrier of joy. Although this truth is true for each who reads this book (and all who do not), it is likely that many of you may have doubts…questions…and varying degrees of cynicism. If this is the case, then investigate your doubts. Question your inquiring mind and study the reasons behind your cynical nature. Likewise, if you already accept your status as a carrier of joy, examine why this is as well. Whether you are a doubter or a supporter of the notion of being a transporter of joy, take advantage of the moment. Pursue greater awareness!*
>
> *As you may have already surmised, this is an opportunity to practice engaging with your contemplative mind and your open heart. Quiet your beautiful mind, open your receptive heart, sink into a state of peaceful serenity, and ponder. Just ponder any doubts, concerns, or joyfulness you may have about being a carrier of joy, and as you do, observe your mind, experience your heart, and assess your state of tranquility."*

*"Well done!"* their mentor declared. *"Well done indeed! Very clever you were to engage your friends through the natural agent of recovery. The breath, in all its simplicity, is the quickest path to peace and right-mindedness. You also demonstrated wisdom when you invited your friends to assist you. So very quickly did they respond to your request! People are much more inclined to help another than they are to receive help. This mannerism is prevalent throughout the human species. Pride is the underlying reason for this behavior, which unfortunately deprives them of the courtesies they willingly offer to someone else. This is another aspect of humanity that you must keep in mind when planning future outreach interactions."*

"Thank you, Marilyn," uttered Jan who deeply benefitted from the impromptu breathing exercise. "I'm curious dear, did you initiate that session because you truly needed help, or did you launch into it because you knew we needed help?"

"Both!" responded Marilyn. "My mind was chasing after itself, engaging with one scary scenario after another, which is an indicator for me that I'm headed for a tail spin. So, I did a quick scan of everyone's energy and it was obvious all of us were going down a path we really didn't need to take. I know from previous experiences the benefits of utilizing this exercise, and as you witnessed, it's easy and extremely effective."

Seizing the moment, I interjected a perspective believing and hoping it would be helpful. "What's important for me to remember in situations such as these is the reality that I am safe. Similarly to you, Marilyn, my mind took off in directions that may or may not come to pass, but the fact is, these scenarios are not happening now, and we do not need to respond as if they are. When the mind creates these stories, our body reacts to them, as if they are actually playing out, and as a result, fear and stress related chemicals are produced by the body to assist us in protecting ourselves from a situation, which is actually being orchestrated by the mind."

"Goodness!" declared Dee. "This is fascinating! Thank you both for talking about the antics of the mind in a way that is easily comprehended. And I like what you said Marilyn about recognizing this kind of behavior, albeit, silent and hidden, as an indicator that the mind is off course. Very helpful!"

"I guess an issue of relevance is the ability to discern when the mind is running amok versus when it is appropriately distinguishing information." Frank mulled over his statement. "Well, this takes me back to your comment," he said looking towards me. "Is the situation actually happening or is it being devised by the mind?"

In response, I suggested another point of significance. "For me Frank, the most critical aspect of our discussion is the reality that the mind is incredibly skillful at creating stories, and many of us aren't paying attention to this, which leaves us vulnerable to the mind's whims."

*"Wonderful!"* exclaimed our teacher and mentor. *"We candidly speak of one of the compelling factors, which may significantly influence your participation in assisting the Life Being Earth."*

*A passage from*
***The Book of Joy: The Invitation***
*(Chapter Two)*

> *"Only you can do this inner work. Although your outward appearance may provide some information to others regarding your peaceful resonance or lack there of, only you can accurately attest to your true state of being. So, please take advantage of the moment and learn more about yourself.*
>
> *Consider this useful and worthwhile training, because it is. Through this mindful and deliberate process of observing and interacting with your mind and open heart, you are moving forward with your guidance to seek within."*

*"What you discuss now must be conveyed to others. The undisciplined mind wields far too much influence, and as you just witnessed and experienced, this is not a type of influence you wish to possess. The human species is ready to advance to another level of existence; however, for this evolutionary leap to actualize, individuals must have authority over their respective minds. This is not a difficult task to achieve. Many already have command of their minds, but many more are not even aware a problem exists. Perhaps even you were surprised to discover that your mind was not functioning at its best. Not to worry! Once the issue is identified, one becomes motivated to change. Fine tuning the undisciplined mind leads to higher functioning, less distraction and aggravation, and results in a cooperative mind that is far more reliable and assisting than a mind operating in response to its own preferences. Dear friends, as the children of Earth become inspired to nurture and discipline their minds, they will be prepared for their evolutionary expansion and they will be able to heal the Earth."*

*A passage from*
***The Book of Joy: The Invitation***
*(Chapter Two)*

> *"As is existence unimaginably expansive…so too is the energy of joy that exists within you. For the sake of your advancement, the following is reiterated. Joy exists within every existence residing in existence. Although this may seem incomprehensible to some*

> *of you, it is a truth that resounds for all throughout all existence. If you presently resonate to this message and already live your life from this optimistic and joyful perspective, then your challenge is to continue. Maintenance of your present status is essential; however, advancing your present state of being to even greater heights of joy and gratifying tenor by attending it through a daily practice is necessary. Develop a discipline…a commitment to self…that nurtures you and allows your inner joyfulness to flourish. Open your heart to the possibility of a plan for self-care and request the assistance of your beautiful mind in developing a personal regimen that complements your style and needs. Make it simple, make it easy, and most of all, make it joyful."*

"Friend, are you and your invisible companions concerned about our meandering minds?" My question was not easy to ask, but it was sincere. I was not seeking praises or reassurances, and even though I was mildly worried about their response, I really wanted to know the truth. Our mentor remained quiet, raising my concern; and for a brief moment, I regretted asking the question. And then, I realized my mind was creating another scenario that was not founded in reality. His silence did not mean something was wrong. I took a deep breath and released the anxiety my mind was activating.

*"Well done,"* he whispered. *"By monitoring your mind, you successfully overrode its tendency towards worriment, and you saved yourself some needless heartache."*

"Did you delay responding on purpose?" I asked curiously.

*"Yes!"* he acknowledged. *"Please forgive me, but I thought it was another opportunity to practice. As I suspected, your mind began to wander to a place of discomfort, but you commanded the situation well."* Looking to the other members of the group, he continued, *"Your companion quickly recognized what the mind was doing and successfully counteracted it with another breathing exercise."* Compliments were issued and received and then we all waited for the answer to my question.

*"The answer to your question, dear friend, is yes…and no! The issue of your undisciplined mind is definitely a concern that requires immediate attention; however, we have faith in humankind, and we trust you will address this problem."*

*A passage from*
***The Book of Joy: The Invitation***
*(Chapter Two)*

> *"As you engage with the reality that joy truly does exist, your perceptions of life and your position in your life will naturally change, because encountering joy is a life-altering experience. For this to transpire your heart must be open and your beautiful mind must also be an active participant. Perhaps you may accept this reading project as one of the self-care activities you will pursue.*
>
> *Seek within for guidance regarding how to proceed, and as you do, carry this awareness with you. Joy does exist, and as you become increasingly more familiar with this Companion of Old, the benefits of its presence will become evident, and you will spread these benefits to all you encounter."*

*"Please understand, dear friends, we are deeply committed to the peoples of Earth. Your indomitable spirit is greatly admired and your lust for life inspires all. You are cherished by your Family in existence, and we are extremely proud of you."* The voice heard came from an unknown location. We all heard the words, yet our guest did not appear to be the presenter of this heartfelt and intriguing message. We sat in silence, pondering both the message and the messenger. Time passed as we reveled in the love expressed through the unseen voice.

# ~ CHAPTER TWO ~

*"May I invite you to discuss what you just heard?"* inquired the gentleman from unspecified origins. His question aroused a wave of movement among the circle of friends.

"Well, I heard a very loving and warmhearted message," announced Dee, "and I'm certain the message was not spoken by you, unless ventriloquism is a hidden talent you possess."

*"No!"* Our honored guest chuckled in denial, *"No such ability is in my repository of skills, but perhaps it is one worthy of consideration."* His jovial manner was a marvel to watch, and more so, because it was authentic. I wondered how he was able to maintain such a consistently affable manner. Even in those moments after he had delivered a particularly difficult message for us to hear, he maintained his hopeful, cheerful comportment, which enabled us, his listeners, to assimilate the messages with only a modicum of discomfort. Our friend was a remarkable individual, and yet, we knew so little about him.

"I have a couple of thoughts," asserted Everett. "First, I want to be certain everyone actually heard the same message, and secondly, I'm curious if we all received the message as an auditory experience or did some of us receive it telepathically. The group quickly ascertained everyone indeed had heard the same message; however, questions arose regarding the means of reception. Everett was reassured he was not the only one struggling with the concept of telepathy. He turned to Dee, and asked, "How do you know if you're really hearing a message from within or if you're just hearing your own thoughts?"

"It just takes time and practice, dear. Initially, I recommend you approach this challenge as an observer." Dee's demeanor, both compassionate and encouraging, was exactly what her friends needed. "Just now," she admitted, "I was confused as well, and resorted to sneaking a peak to verify if our friend here was the source of the message we heard. Although, I didn't think he was the speaker, the voice seemed to be coming from outside of me, not within. So, in this case, it was necessary to rely upon my other senses; my vision served an important role in my discernment process. I know all of you are curious about existential communication, and you have doubts and questions of various kinds and nature, but I ask you to be patient. This ability is real! Although it may seem elusive at times, it is real! And if you need a gentle reminder, just recall the exchanges we've already participated in with our friend and mentor! There are times when we hear his voice before he materializes, there are other times when I feel certain he reaches out through the silent means of connection, and then there are times such as now when we have the luxury of talking with him just as we do with one another. And perhaps, he will take the lead now and speak more of this, and also," she said in a very suggestive manner, "please include a bit of information about the messenger of our recent communiqué." Eight heads turned simultaneously in the direction of the elder gentleman.

Once again, I wondered what it must be like to be this fellow. Who is he? From where does he come? Why is he spending so much time with us? Does he also attend other groups in similar fashion as he addresses us? Why has he been assigned to us?

For a brief moment, his smile relaxed, his eyes closed, and his breathing became deliberate and measured. *"So many questions,"* he murmured. *"Old friend,"* he said while bowing to Dee with his palms pressed in prayer position, *"I am honored to resume the lead for the moment, but before doing so, I applaud your able skills. You are an admiral teacher."*

Dee's face registered the surprise of his compliment. It had been many years since she had received such praise, and it felt good. She nodded and quietly whispered, "Thank you!"

*"Perhaps, my friends, it would be wise to focus our attention upon the extraordinary message just received. Let me begin by clarifying: the message was indeed audible. Just as you have heard my voice numerous times before witnessing my presence, this evening you have heard the voice of another."*

"Who is this other?" inquired Frank insistently. "Will we be meeting this individual at some point?"

*"That I cannot answer,"* replied our friend, *"for I have no dominion over such matters."* More questions rushed forward.

"Is this the one you are in contact with? The one you consult with during our sessions?"

*"Yes...and no! The voice heard was one, and it was many. Although the concept is confusing, it is the truth. When communicating with Those Who Came Before, one is often in connection with many. The speaker may vary from time to time; however, the speaker comprises many. It is not unlike the experiences we share. When you speak with me, I am accompanied by others; thus, you are essentially speaking with many. Much more will be learned about this as we continue our conversations.*

*Regarding the message just received, dear friends, it was most supportive. Both complimentary and informative! The reality of your situation has been announced. You are not alone!"*

*A passage from*
***The Book of Joy: The Invitation***
*(Chapter Three)*

> *"Dear Reader, thank you for reading our story, which as you might imagine is provided for a reason. "You are not alone!" Just as existence was given pause so very long ago when this reality was first expressed, so too is it true now when heard again. The personal impact of this thought provoking statement is yours to explore. Please do so, because it may be an evolutionary experience for you as well. Examination of this fascinating, yet perplexing declaration will naturally stimulate your mind, which of course will be an active participant in this discovery process. Your beautiful mind's presence will indeed be necessary, for it must join with your heart's intentions in this journey to ascertain the full personal effect of this purposeful message. Capturing the essence of this communiqué upon one's being must come from within…anything less has the potential for diminishing its effect. Once again, you are encouraged to pause for a moment and seek within for clarity."*

"We are not alone! A very small statement with expansive possibilities!" exclaimed Marilyn. "Do you have any idea how many questions are racing through my mind?"

*"Yes!"* he laughed cheerfully. *"If we could download the questions from each of your minds, we would have a sizable document. Be that as it may, I ask you to focus upon only one question at this time."* He scanned the room, invited everyone to close their eyes, and then encouraged them to follow their breath. *"Join me, my friends. Breathe deeply, quiet your minds, and allow a state of peacefulness to fill this space of sacred conversations. Do this for yourself, and do it for one another. Move into a place of deep, heartfelt serenity."* The group cooperated for the sake of each other and quickly found themselves in a delightful state of relaxation. *"Now, dear friends, as you rest peacefully, please listen to this question with the ears of your heart. Just listen to the question; do*

*not strive to formulate an answer. Simply allow the Self Within to be with the question. How does it feel to know you are not alone?"*

As is often the case when one enters into the province of silence, time becomes a distant memory of another time and place. A visitor who sincerely seeks the silence may lose all sense of time, while the silence, which has no attachment to time, patiently awaits the arrival of a visitor who truly is silent. While engaging with the perplexing territory of timelessness, unknowns are sometimes encountered. Clarity of mind is just one of the mysteries that may surprise a visitor who frequents the silence. Such was the case on this occasion.

*"My friends, may I welcome you back to the present? Follow your breath, Dear Ones, and allow this able guide to bring you back home."* Their mentor's voice was received telepathically. It happened so easily no one even noticed or gave it any attention. Simply stated. No words were spoken, yet the message to return home was received. Each responded slowly, yet deliberately. Withdrawing from their inner sanctum aroused confusion. A desire to remain in the silence was fervently experienced, as was the longing to return home. The confusion was overridden by the Call to come home. Time passed, as it is wont to do, while eight different adventures transpired without time even noticing their transformational experiences, but another noticed. Indeed, that which called the friends home noticed, vigilantly watching every moment transpiring for each returnee with protective care and a loving heart. Yes, another noticed, for this Other always notices the passing of time for every participant experiencing in the grand adventure. This One notices all manner of things, for this One cares about and for every existence existing in existence. Indeed, this One noticed everything…and remembered.

*"My friends, may I invite you to return?"* The familiar voice, always gentle, ever welcoming nudged his friends to return from their journeys. Silence prevailed for an indistinguishable amount of time before movement slowly became noticeable among the group members. Unsure of their location, their actions were tentative. Where were they? Where had they been? Their minds wanted answers, but their mentor wisely advised each of them to quiet his or her curious mind while they simply reintegrated into the present moment. And this they did.

*"My friends, I am glad to be in your presence once again!"*

"Have we been gone?" inquired Dee who personally wondered if she had been to heaven and back. Her thoughts were plenty, but her need to 'know' was surprisingly patient, almost to the point of not really needing confirmation or clarification of any kind. For the moment, Dee was at peace with her experience.

*"Your question is one of merit, my friend, and the answer is yes...and no."* Frank shaking his head in response to their mentor's answer quietly and respectfully interrupted with another question.

"Are there no answers in your realm of existence that can be offered with certainty? I don't mean to be pushy, but Dee's question seems rather simple. Either we were here or we were elsewhere. So which is it?" Frank, fearing his manner was a bit forward, hoped he had not offended their mentor, but before he could qualify his statement, an answer was forthcoming.

*"Few questions have a singular answer, my friend, for it is the introduction of a question, which brings forward the opportunity for expansion. So in attempting to answer your question, I would be remiss to say there are no questions with a single response; however, for those who embrace the exploration of possibility, it is the question with multiple answers that provides the greatest adventure. So, in addressing Dee's question, the answer is both yes and no. Yes, all of you were elsewhere while exploring the reality that you are not alone, and at the same time you were involved in your adventure, you were also here, embodied within this room.*

*Perhaps, my explanation will be better understood if each of you shares your experience. Although, my suggestion may seem intrusive at the moment, please excuse my impertinence. When an extraordinary connection has been experienced, one sometimes for a variety of reasons feels shy about sharing it with another. Remember please, you are in the company of very good friends, who will support you in moving beyond your present moment of discomfort. By sharing these experiences, you will actually effectively ground them into reality. Because these inexplicable adventures are still interpreted as unusual events, they can unfortunately be elusive and may quickly be forgotten if one does not give them credence through some means of acknowledgement. Journaling is a beneficial means of documenting the incident for future reference, and I encourage you to do so; however, when in the company of trusted friends, it is wise to share the experiences for the sake of all involved. The possibility for broadening one's own experience is enhanced when listening to another's experience."* The invitation, intended to inspire conversation, seemed to have the opposite effect. Silence engulfed the room. Unconcerned about his students' reticence, the elder gentleman joined the silence and patiently waited for the first courageous move. His patience was rewarded within an unnoticeable amount of time. No one was surprised when the matriarch of the group took the lead.

"Well, I'll go first!" declared Dee. "I appreciate your candor regarding my earlier question. And I almost understand what you said!" she said with a smile. "I do believe my adventure took me elsewhere, yet I'm clear my body was here during the entire experience. And the truth is the location of my body didn't seem to be a factor of relevance. I had a glorious time! And I saw things…no let me find a better word. I saw 'beauty' beyond my imagination. Landscapes like never seen before with rich fertile lands, incredible water masses, and nature both similar to and different from ours. It was marvelous! Colors were more vibrant, sounds were more distinct, and sensations were brilliantly responsive and precise. And," she continued, "I saw the emptiness and fullness of the Universe. I believe I witnessed both the microcosm and macrocosm of infinity. Is that possible? It seems grandiose to express my journey as such, but what I describe is true. It really happened." Dee paused, both exhilarated by sharing her story and also depleted by doing so. *Is there more to share? Have I accurately shared my adventure with my friends?* Before she could ascertain an answer, her beloved husband nudged her.

"Dee, dear, did you encounter anyone during your experience?" Frank's question jarred her memory.

"Oh my, I forgot the most important part of my story. And the answer to your question, dear, is yes…and no!" She smiled lovingly towards her companion and best friend of this lifetime. It was the same wonderful smile he fell in love with the first time they met. "I was not alone, Frank! I can say this with absolute certainty; however, it must also be said that no one was physically seen. But the presence of another was definitely palpable. I was not alone!" she repeated. Sighs of relief echoed throughout the room as individual stories were validated before they were even told.

*A passage from*

***The Book of Joy: The Invitation***

*(Chapter Three)*

> *"Sit quietly just for a moment…no more is needed unless you prefer it so. But now, just for a moment sit quietly and merge your presence with its natural state of your being. Notice your breath flowing inward, then outward and simply become comfortable with its rhythm. Be comfortable. Be at ease. No great effort is necessary to*

*attend yourself. Simply be. Practice this for a moment, longer if you desire, but know that a moment is significant and can have lasting effects. Proceed now with this loving, gentle act of self-care; you deserve to be attended in this way."*

Peace befell the group. Dee's description of her travels inspired a sense of anticipation and confidence within her friends, which had not been her intention. She spoke first, or so she thought, simply because of her readiness and eagerness to share her story. After revealing what had transpired during her experience, Dee realized the wave of relief that washed over her companions indicated they too had interesting tales to share. Although she wasn't certain how the moment of self-assuredness had awakened within her, she was grateful it had. Apparently one person's story has the power to facilitate the revelation of stories for others.

"As some of you already know, my beloved is much more at ease with these types of experiences than am I. At times I have both marveled at and been skeptical of her simple acceptance of events that appear to be inexplicable; nevertheless, over the years, her unwavering trusting nature has repeatedly proven to be noteworthy. Today, I am once again reminded of Dee's powerful sense of knowing that we are accompanied in these life experiences, and her certainty of this truth, her confidence that we are not alone, gives me strength to feel confident as well. Of course, our friend here," Frank pointed to their guest, "is certainly confirmation of Dee's convictions, but she's been believing without any visible evidence for a very long time and her faith is inspiring." Shifting to face his wife, Frank lovingly expressed words often thought but never spoken. "I'm so grateful to you, Dee. You've taken the lead regarding this aspect of our lives ever since we met, even before we encountered our friend here in the forest. I haven't done my part in the past, Dee, but I'm on board now. We're walking the rest of this path together." Dee's eyes expressed everything that needed to be said. Gratitude, excitement, playfulness, and hopefulness...all were conveyed and received.

*"The energy of tenderness is exquisite to witness,"* acknowledged their guest in a volume not much more than a whisper. *"Such incredible power the human heart can generate, and yet so few of your kind are aware of this natural ability. But this will change soon, my friends, and then, all of you will be able not only to witness this energy, but also you will gain command and authority over this inner power existing within you."* He paused momentarily before adding, *"That day is coming soon."* His comment quietly stated had a prophetic ring to it.

His students noticed but refrained from pursuing the curious suggestion. Still deliberating over their recent travels, they remained focused, each anticipating what might be revealed next. The teacher was pleased with their attentiveness, as were others who were observing the session from unknown locations. Addressing Frank specifically, their mentor continued, *"I wonder, Dear Friend, if the story shared by your beautiful spouse has inspired you to share yours. Perhaps, it is your time to take the lead."*

Frank sat rigidly still for a moment before shifting about in his chair. "Yes, you're right," he declared. "Commitments are useless unless you follow through with your intentions." Glancing towards his wife, Frank took a deep breath and then shifted his eyes to the floor before finally admitting he was afraid to share his story. "Please forgive me. This is about me, not you," he confessed to his friends. "I find it difficult to share what I do not understand, and yet, I want to try. I think it's really important for us to do this." Frank paused again, and as he did, his friends empathized with his hesitancy. Everyone shared his reluctance each in his or her own way. "Well, the truth is," he began, "I feel really good about what happened, even though it's difficult to tell you exactly what was experienced. But it was good!" A smile brightened Frank's face, one that made him look twenty years younger. He was radiant. "I had an encounter," he continued. "Well, it was more like a visit that entailed a meandering stroll and pleasant conversation with someone you've never met, but you feel like you've known all your life. It was simple, but extraordinary...and it makes me feel good just to think about it." Tears welled up in Frank's eyes, and he bravely shared them with his friends. "I don't ever want to forget this experience. And I suspect if the story is shared I will have a greater chance of holding onto it. And if for some reason I forget it, then perhaps one of you can remind me of what happened." Frank's friends quickly assured him they would carry his story with them. It was a tender moment. And once again, the visitor who still remains nameless enjoyed observing the energy of tenderness shared among these friends.

"Frank, what did you and your visitor talk about?" inquired Bill, who quickly followed with another question. "Was your visitor a man or a woman? Guess it doesn't matter, but I'm just curious."

"We're all curious, Bill. In truth, those were my first two questions as well. I'm glad you asked them." Marilyn's manner was gentle and reassuring as always, but internally, her excitement was boundless. Her heart was pounding so loud, she was afraid her companions would be able to hear it. This was a dream come true for Marilyn. Being among friends and openly sharing these experiences was the greatest gift she could ever imagine. "So Frank, tell us everything!

"Everything! Goodness," Frank exclaimed while swallowing a very large, audible breath, "that's a big charge, but one worthy to pursue." Dee, observing protectively, restrained herself from encouraging her husband to proceed. She resisted her immediate inclination to help him share his story. *Give him room, Old Girl. He can do this!* Frank turned and winked at Dee. "Not to worry, dear, I'm just cogitating." Returning his focus to the group, he chuckled, "In case you missed that exchange…my beloved is worrying about me. She's trying to figure out a way to assist me in telling my story." Patting Dee lovingly on the knee, he reassured her that he was fine. "I can do this, Old Girl. Just trying to figure out how to begin." The tenderness exchanged between the elder couple sparked another energy acceleration among the group members, which was noticed not only by their resident teacher, but also by another within the group. The teacher smiled with satisfaction.

"Well," Frank began, "it seems my adventure took me to a forest, which felt familiar, but was unknown to me. Of course, as we all know, this isn't an unusual reaction even in a wooded area that you walk every day. Things change so quickly in the forest," he mused. "Anyway, the point is, I found myself walking along a wide, nicely cleared path that was wandering hither and yon through a thickly wooded area. The trail was well lit, which surprised me. Usually landscapes with lush growth can lose the sunlight, but that wasn't the case in this unique setting. Even though the area was heavily forested, light filled the surrounds and every tree, every bush, every life form regardless of size or shape was easily seen. It almost seemed as though each individual plant was being spotlighted. Interesting," Frank reflected. "I didn't realize it until now, but my adventure really did seem to illuminate, to highlight every object that was observed, which is why everything was so vivid and why I can remember it all so well. What a remarkable experience!" Frank's realization validated his experience while making it a reality for his friends.

"Your description makes it visible for me, Frank," remarked Jan. "I truly feel as if I am seeing the path with all its beautiful plant life and vibrant colors. I feel like I'm there! Wow! Thank you, Frank!"

"Me too!" added Marilyn. "Please continue." Their comments reassured Frank who was feeling more comfortable telling his story.

"Thank you," he replied. "Sharing my experience is actually helping me to remember it with greater clarity. It was a wonderful experience. I remember simply enjoying the walk and reveling in the beauty of each plant, when from out of nowhere, I heard a voice." Frank paused, deliberately making eye contact with his friends before continuing. "I had just stopped to examine an especially beautiful colony of ferns. Mesmerized by the size and majesty of these exceptional flowerless plants, my perception of reality appeared to change. It seemed as if I had been transported into a forest of gigantic ferns with fronds larger and taller than me. I was surrounded by these amazing architectural life forms and embraced by their subtle, yet revivifying colors. Simply stated, I was lost in the moment, when the comment was unmistakably heard.

*"Life in all its gracious presentations is a marvel to witness, is it not?"*

"The voice brought me back to reality. The fern forest was still before me, but the size and brilliance of the moment had returned to what I presume is its normal state. Perhaps, I am mistaken about that," Frank noted. "Maybe, what we believe to be the distorted reality is the real reality, and this reality, which we think is the real reality is actually the distorted reality. Or perhaps, they are both real realities and we're just not aware of it at this point. Guess we can all ponder this for a lifetime or two." Frank's puzzling thoughts triggered many more ideas and questions among his friends, but no one pursued the tempting opportunity for distraction. Everyone knew Frank's momentary lapse into reflection had not taken him astray from the primary topic.

"Well," he proceeded, "without hesitating or taking my gaze from the fern garden, I affirmed the voice's comment." Pointing to their resident visitor, Frank added, "Suppose I've gotten so accustomed to our friend's comings and goings that an unidentified voice doesn't take me by surprise anymore. Eventually, I turned about, not really expecting to find anyone, but sure enough, there was a pleasant looking fellow observing me from the trail. His smile was welcoming, and I just immediately assumed he was intended to be part of my experience."

*"I too am particularly fond of that variety of plant life,"* he remarked. *"Seemingly delicate, yet tenacious in its intentions to survive and thrive, which it has done here and in many other settings."*

"His eyes, beaming with curiosity, reached for the sun and mine followed his. Watching him, I wondered if this was his first visit to the forest or if he was a frequent visitor appreciating sights seen before. Quickly responding to my thoughts, he indicated his journey had brought him to this setting many times before and he assured me he was always eager for another opportunity to return.

*"Your presence, Mr. Sanderson, provides me with such an opportunity,"* he

expressed. *"I am grateful to share this experience with you. Shall we stroll down the path while we discuss your present circumstances?"*

"His manner was not unlike our own visitor…courteous, gracious, and honorable. You just knew the minute you met him, he was someone you could trust. And also like our friend here, he inspired countless questions. As you might well imagine, my mind was rapidly racing from one question to another. Who are you? Why are you here? What is going on here? Etc. etc. etc.! And of course, before any of these questions were articulated, my Companion began to answer my thoughts.

*"Mr. Sanderson, I am here to accompany you during this phase of your journey. You are having this experience because you are ready to do so, and it is transpiring in this manner, because for you, this setting is a safe place. Perhaps, this may seem ironic because of the experience you and your beloved shared so many years ago in a very similar setting. However, the result of your very unsettling event established a foundation for all experiences that followed. Through the experience of a crisis, the two of you were presented with a choice of a lifetime, and you both chose to continue your present experience rather than exiting into a new experience. You were accompanied during that experience and successfully guided to the circumstances resulting in your rescue. Such an experience deeply changes one's view of existence.*

*For you, Mr. Sanderson, you maintained a sense of connection with that profound experience through your artwork. Your frequent excursions into the forest carefully looking for the perfect piece of fallen wood for your next creative project are for a reason. These interludes are your pilgrimages…your way of reconnecting with the energy experienced that day so long ago, and the artwork you create is your expression of gratitude for what transpired. Think about this, my friend, the emotions that well up inside of you when you find the ideal piece of wood, the conscientious retrieval and safe passage of the selected specimen back to your workshop, and then, the actual creative engagement with the prized object itself. Is this not a ritual of extreme care and tender love? Does this not remind you of the deep, heartfelt connection you experienced during that period when you and Mrs. Sanderson were lost in the woods?"*

Frank, having shared his story as best he could with his friends, feared his rendering did not give justice to the experience itself. "It's odd," he remarked breathlessly. "My experience seemed timeless. We talked about so many different topics and seemed to walk for hours ever deeper into the forest. I distinctly remember walking a very long time and was surprised not to feel any sense of fatigue, and then suddenly, we were back at the colony of ferns again." Dee sensed her husband's frustration with himself. Rather than being satisfied and pleased with what he had remembered, he was instead disappointed by what he feared was forgotten. She felt the need to intervene before he slipped away from the truth.

"Frank, dear, do you realize what you just shared with us?" Her question, although not anticipated, was a relief to their friends. They too recognized Frank was veering off in the wrong direction.

"You received an incredible insight, Frank," exclaimed Everett. "What a gift!"

"Yes," agreed Dee. "Frank, please be happy with what you've remembered and shared. Because it is huge, dear, really huge! This is so much more expansive than you realize. At times, the connection you experience through your creative process silences you. I witness the flush of overwhelm each time it happens, and it occurs, Frank, because the intimacy experienced is so deeply heartfelt that it propels you beyond your mind's need for understanding into a realm of acceptance. Acceptance, Frank! Acceptance of the truth that there is more! Even though the experience itself is indescribable, it is real! It is, Frank! It simply is!

All these years you have been giving me credit for taking the lead regarding our spiritual endeavors, when in truth, you're the one who has been actively seeking and engaging with the 'more' that we all seek."

At this point, having remained quiet throughout most of the evening, I had to speak. Leaning forward with elbows upon my knees, I made my intentions very personal. "Frank, I hope you are taking Dee's words to heart. And before you cut me off," I asserted with humorous authority, "let me say, I agree with you about Dee. She is an active seeker as well, but her point is well made. What I learned from your story, Frank, is the profound and lasting effects of that frightening ordeal you and Dee shared in the woods. And it seems the Companion you encountered today was helping you to understand the earlier experience. I am deeply touched to hear about your pilgrimages. Although your artwork has always been impressive, now, I have a greater understanding regarding the shyness associated with your work. Passion is an extremely intimate experience, a private affair, if you will, which demands modesty and decorum. Frank, I just want to applaud you. No greater respect for the ultimate connection could be demonstrated. Thank you for sharing your experience with us." Other members of the friendly clan also expressed their appreciation for Frank's story as well. Receiving their support was initially very difficult, but his friends' sincerity couldn't be denied and eventually with considerable effort on his part, gratitude registered and reached a level of sensory overload rendering him speechless except for a grunt, which was barely recognizable as a thank you. Dee was extremely proud of her husband and his friends understood Mr. Sanderson was done for the moment.

"Well, I would like to go next if that's all right with everyone," declared Jan as she reached for husband's hand for support. "As you all know, Everett and I have been torn about our role in this project. Although, we are committed to working with all of you, we still feel pulled to understand what calls us to our favorite island retreat. It's been very confusing and unsettling for us. Well, my adventure took me to the island. Perhaps, my need for clarity was the driving force behind this exploration, but I certainly was not in command of the experience." A quick glance towards Everett intending to reassure him that all was well was received. Interpreting the look correctly, he eagerly waited for Jan to reveal what she had discovered.

"My journey commenced very quickly. There was no time for anticipation or concern about my technique. It seemed as if I was gone with the first deep intentional breath. One minute I was conscious of being present with all of you, and the next moment, I was walking the beach in bare feet. It's so odd! I knew my body was here in this room, but I was there on the beach as well. This wasn't a dream!" Turning towards the group's mentor, she appealed, "How can that be? How can we be in two places at the same time?"

*"Your experience was real, my friend, and your confusion is understandable. May I ask you to put your confusion aside for the moment and simply continue sharing your story? It is the experience that is relevant, not the confusion. Your confusion leads to endless conversations; whereas, your experience leads to expanded awareness. You have already spoken your truth with certainty; do not be distracted by a confused mind. Trust yourself, and also trust your friends to accept your story."* His words, though directed towards Jan, were not for her alone. Each student knew this and accepted their teacher's sound guidance.

"Goodness!" Jan exclaimed. "That was profound…and it relates to my experience." Jan gazed at her friends, and just shook her head in amazement. "You guys aren't going to believe this!"

"Sure we will!" laughed Marilyn. "Sounds like we're going to be entertained with another great story. Please go for it, Jan! Tell us everything!" Marilyn's lighthearted manner changed the mood of the group, as others followed her good spirits. Each was becoming increasingly more comfortable with their quote-quote unusual experiences, and as a group, they were now able to enjoy the stories with greater delight. Their stories and the experiences themselves were becoming commonplace.

"You're right, of course," agreed Jan. "We're not novices anymore! I think it's fair to say we've graduated from Unusual Experiences 101 to Unusual Experiences 201!" The levity demonstrated by the group pleased their guest, as well as others who observed with keen interest.

*"How quickly they adapt to these new situations,"* conveyed an unheard voice. *"Our expectation of their capabilities is coming to fruition."*

*"Indeed,"* replied the mentor. *"By sharing their stories, they advance rapidly and they gain confidence through their encounters with new acquaintances. There is reason for hope."*

*"Yes!"* affirmed the unknown communicator.

"When I arrived at the beach, I was immediately captivated by its presence. The sounds, the smells, the breezes, the reflected light, the ocean herself! It's always the same; I become one with the ocean. Suppose this sounds ridiculous but it's true. And if I were a poet, perhaps I could articulate my feelings in some magnificent way; but the truth is, I simply am when I'm near oceanic waters. I am the sounds! I am the smells! I am the breezes! I am the light! I am the ocean! This sounds grandiose, but it isn't. I simply am. Everything else seems grandiose, but I simply am. The ocean touches what is best in me; it brings the real me to the surface, and when I leave its presence, I feel very disoriented, as if some very important part of me was left behind. It always takes me a while to recover from leaving the ocean, and it's why I long to be there. When I'm there, by the ocean, I am me." Jan paused, and her friends simultaneously took a deep breath. A few tears were noticed about the room, but no one spoke. Each was living Jan's experience, and the moment was indescribable; yet each understood their friend in a way they had never known her before, and each also knew more about themselves. Suffice it to say, it was a poignant moment.

Everett's personal involvement with his spouse's story forced him to interrupt the silence. "Excuse me Jan, but as you know, I find your experience riveting and I am selfishly in need of information. Were you accompanied, Jan? Did you meet the same fellow on the beach again?" His questions, an extension rather than a hindrance, opened the door for Jan to move more deeply into her story. As she faced him, Everett saw the twinkle in her eyes, and his own excitement raced forward.

"At first," Jan continued, "I had a long, seemingly endless engagement with the moment. As already said, I merged with the ocean and just savored the sense of Oneness. I can't even guess how long that luxurious moment lasted. Again, it was an experience of timelessness. For me, the moment felt like a lifetime, but perhaps from our perspective of reality, it was truly only a moment or two. In essence, it probably doesn't matter, except to aid your understanding of the experience. Anyway, after whatever amount of time passed, I began strolling along the beach. It was wonderful." Jan's voice sounded dreamy. Sharing the story literally took her back to the moment when she could feel the sand beneath her feet and the breezes embracing her as if welcoming her home. "Yes," she mused, "it was an experience of coming home to a place you have been a thousand and more times, and each time you return, it is as if you were never gone. You are immediately encapsulated in a womb of existence with which you are completely, rhythmically in tune." Pausing, Jan closed her eyes and breathed in her memories, and as she did, everyone in the group could feel the moment with her. The sense of existential rhythm resonated throughout the room. And once again, the sharing of one's story expanded the life-enriching experience to and within others. Time passed without their awareness while each benefitted from the moment in his and her own unique way.

"At some point, I noticed the footfalls of another, and as you might imagine, another was walking beside me. I have no idea how long we had been walking together. One moment, I was in my personal reverie, and the next, I was in the company of a barefooted fellow in flowing white robes. Surprisingly, I wasn't surprised." Jan looked about the room at her dear friends, and chuckled. "Of course, he would show up!" Jan openly laughed at herself. Her acceptance of the unusual was truly becoming commonplace. "Let's face it!" she exclaimed. "At this point, his appearance was to be expected!"

"Did you receive any guidance or hints about what your role is intended to be?" An answer to Frank's question was eagerly awaited. Everyone in the group was personally attached to the ramifications of Jan and Everett's calling. Marilyn inwardly acknowledged she didn't want them to leave. Dee had similar feelings, but also knew they must do what was necessary. Everett, sitting pensively, felt apprehensive, but refused to be distracted by unwarranted concerns.

"Well, what I learned from the experience is similar to what we have already gleaned from our lessons shared with our wonderful mentor; however, I think this experience helped me to understand the energetic aspects of our goals. Is it correct to say that all of you experienced the peaceful rhythmic connection I enjoyed at the ocean side?" Her friends quickly affirmed her assumption. "Good! The then we all know another factor of our mission of work. The sensation we experienced is vitally important to the wellness of Earth and to all her inhabitants. However the experience is described, which will vary within each individual, we now have a more expanded idea of what we are seeking. Descriptors are always problematic because each individual will resonate to a word or phrase that most touches his or her own manner of being, but we will find a way to utilize descriptive words and experiential exercises, which will elevate one's ability to understand what they are seeking. The sense of peacefulness, connection, and oneness that I enjoyed inspires me to seek those attributes and incorporate them into my life on a more consistent basis. Imagine feeling that relaxed and 'at ease' throughout the day. Jeepers! How wonderful would that be! Our goal is to assist individuals in experiencing such moments so they too will see the benefits of this way of being. Ultimately one's own experience will lead to more such experiences increasing that person's desire for more of the same. Expansion of this awareness within will spread to others, thereby assisting each new participant while enhancing the health and wellness of all life beings on Earth including the Earth herself. The ramifications of increasing this essential calming life energy, in contrast to the present chaotic energies that run rampant across the globe, will literally change the energy of our planet and beyond.

What we're talking about is not new information; however, much of this knowledge has fallen to the wayside as humankind has evolved into their present distractible way of being. We have lost a very important part of ourselves during our evolutionary process, and it is time that we regain what remains an essential element of who we really are. As we know, there are many on the planet who do continue to live their lives from a consistent peaceable state, but far too many do not. And we need to play a part in bringing this practice back to the masses. Our wellness depends upon it. Our future depends upon it. Making changes that enhance a peaceable approach to life will enhance our existence and assist the Earth's recovery process. This is not rocket science! In truth, what we are discussing is something every person can participate in. Changing the energy of the planet begins within. It costs no money. It demands nothing of anyone other than a commitment to participate. And the result will literally be peace on Earth.

This sounds so simple, and in essence it is, but we know there will be resistance. Resisting appears to be a particularly unhealthy aspect of human nature. Even when the obvious lies before us, we find ways to reject the opportunity to improve the situation. So, if I were to bottom line this," she said exhaling and inhaling in the blink of an eye. "This is our reality. The Earth is in serious trouble. There are simple and complex ways of aiding her. Even though the resisting forces don't want to acknowledge her precarious condition, the reality of her declining health remains the truth. Evidence exists all about us, and those who choose to deny and obstruct her recovery process must be left behind until they choose to join those who are already working on her behalf. The complex approaches that will result in sustainability require initiatives that indeed will be costly. This is also reality and it must be done. However, the response that will immediately assist the Earth's situation and which will cost nothing is the commitment to alter one's personal energetic impact. As we strive collectively to reduce our carbon impact upon the planet, we must also individually pursue reduction of our personal negative energetic impact upon the Earth. Like it or not, believe it or not, our negative energy is the primary diminishing factor in her decline. And we can help the Earth's situation by sharing this information and recruiting others to participate in cleaning up our individual negative energy." Jan stopped abruptly; she was exhausted. So much information had streamed through her so quickly that she needed a break. The information had been heard and each group member knew the truth had been spoken.

*"May I make a suggestion, my friends?"* voiced the venerable teacher. *"Is it possible for us to indulge in some restorative treats. Our energies have been spent through the excitement of sharing these stories."* Turning to Marilyn and me, he proposed, *"Water and perhaps a light protein of some kind. Is that possible?"* We immediately retreated to the kitchen, found an assortment of nuts and cheeses, and prepared two pitchers of ice water. Within minutes refreshments were brought into the living room and served. It was a wise suggestion. A break was needed and the protein quickly reenergized everyone.

*"Better!"* sighed the elder. Whispers and nods indicated agreement by the group of friends.

"That was incredible, Jan!" commented her husband. "So, regardless of where we choose to live or travel, we will be able to impart these messages to anyone interested. Am I interpreting this correctly? Whether we are here or visiting our favorite island on this Great Island, we are called to bring this information forward to everyone who will listen?" Rather than answering Everett's question, Jan and her friends turned to the amiable visitor for guidance.

*"Yes!"* he replied with a glorious smile illuminating approval to all his

students. *"Yes,"* he said again. *"You perceive the message correctly. All of you are here to assist in healing this incredible life being called Earth. Rest assured, she is a sentient being, even if members of the human species do not grant her this distinction. Long before humans were a part of her existence, she existed, and her presence fostered growth for billions of other residents. These other living beings were and continue to be completely aware of the symbiotic relationship existing among all who occupy existence not only on this planet, but also within existence itself. Only humans have forgotten this truth about existence. So sad, this is, for never was it intended for any species to evolve in ignorance of this remarkable reality."*

"Well," announced Everett, "this is exciting! It seems we have ample work to do wherever we are at any moment."

*"Yes, that is correct! Whether you are offering a scheduled event or simply chatting with someone on a plane or while visiting another location. The word can and must always be spread to those who are of listening ears."* Their teacher's presence was a gift. His affable manner, the warmth of shared connection, the laughter, his smiles, the curious nature of his comings and goings, everything about his presence was uniquely special, even the pauses. Yes, maybe the pauses were the most riveting of all, because you knew something was about to happen, leaving you in delightful anticipation. Regardless of the message delivered, whether it was uplifting or puzzling, his presence did not disappoint. Such was the case during this exchange as well.

"And what of those who do not want to hear about our responsibility to the Earth?" asked Marilyn. "And how do we know who will listen and who will not? Determining someone's interest in a particular topic is not always easy?"

*"No, this endeavor will not always be easy, but each of you in your own way will grow into the experience. May I encourage you to expect the best outcome? If you dwell in worriment and fear of upcoming encounters, you will bring your discomfort to the situation. However, if you trust what is coming and proceed with an open heart, the results of your interactions have a greater potential for success."* Another pause came at just the right moment providing time for the listeners to grasp his intentions. *"We are seeking readiness,"* he remarked. *"Within each individual there is a level of readiness that must be engaged. One either is ready to hear this message or they are not; it is as simple as this statement. Some are ready to hear the truth about Earth's crisis; others are not. Your role is to casually introduce the topic, and if the listener appears ready, you provide more information through friendly engagement. If not, do not intrude upon their*

*present state, for the seed has been planted. Gestation will occur more rapidly if it is allowed to experience its own maturational process. If you try to impose your beliefs upon another when they are not ready to hear your perspective, you simply waste precious time, and too often antagonism is created as well. Unfortunately, we do not have time for any more senseless arguments or debates about Earth's predicament. Indeed denial and delays will continue; nevertheless, action must be taken by those who are in awareness, even as those who are not continue their personal struggles with the truth.*

*By seeking readiness, we invite possibility. Our goal is to broaden humankind's awareness of the environmental impact they have upon this beautiful Life Being. Poor stewardship and mismanagement of the planet's resources are issues currently well documented by scientifically proven measures. This information is available. What is less known to the peoples of Earth are the undocumented truths, which must also be addressed. As already stated, the primary factor of influence in this disastrous environmental equation is the toxic negative energy emitted by humankind. We have faith in the human species and believe once they are aware of this reality they will respond with gracious generosity. So little is required, but it is a choice that must be made by every individual when they are ready to do so. We hope the masses will rise to the occasion when this new information is understood and accepted. Only a few can create great change, but more than a few are needed to aid a Life Being as large as the Earth. She feels the change coming and she is optimistic, and this emotion in itself alters her wellness. With each additional individual participating in this act of generosity, peace will become a reality, and this energetic alteration will restore the Earth to good health.*

*So you see, my dear friends, your role is significant. As you have opened your hearts to this information, so too will others, and in this way the message will spread across the planet."*

As was often the case after words of wisdom were shared, the group of friends lapsed into contemplation. On this occasion, unable to embrace the moment of introspection, my mind racing with questions led me to an impolite act. Breaking the silence, I barked, "How many will it take to make a significant amount of change?" Even my embarrassing behavior did not squelch my need for an answer. "Sir, there are over 7 billion people on this planet. Can we really expect to change the energetic nature of every person? Is that possible?"

*A passage from*
***The Book of Joy: The Invitation***
*(Chapter Three)*

> *"If perchance your mind generates reasons why this is neither a good idea nor a convenient time for such a hiatus, pursue clarification. Can your mind truly deny you a moment of peace? The mind of other intentions certainly can and will try to dissuade you from any act of self-care that includes peace of mind, but is this in your best interest? Hopefully, your mind is under your own command and is not causing you distraction; however, if it is, then your task of seeking within will include inviting the cooperation of your mind's beautiful side. Rest assured your mind truly does have a remarkable demeanor, which flourishes when disciplined and guided from within. Ironically, training the mind to reach its full potential requires that you and this beloved companion become skillful at the practice of seeking within, resulting in increased peace of mind, which leads to further expansion. Unfortunately, the undisciplined mind finds peace of mind disruptive to its preferences, thus it may require numerous cajoling acts to convince the mind that peace of mind has value. Do not despair. The energy and time spent in creating a regimen of your choice will bring an abundance of information about your mind, your heart, and you to the forefront, all of which will prove beneficial and productive."*

*"Difficult it is to be in silence when the mind demands its own agenda."* Whispers and sighs of agreements circled about the room indicating more than a single mind was in quest for additional information. *"Indeed, you are not the only one present with an inquisitive and insistent mind. So many questions! Will you indulge me for five minutes?"* asked the learned teacher. *"For a brief five minutes will each of you quiet your mind so that the benefits of your shared stories can be enjoyed?"* Around the room, eyes closed while the eight students honored their mentor's request, and as this act of kindness was offered, time stood still, as the silence rapidly engulfed the group and granted their requests.

*"May I welcome you back?"* spoke the friendly visitor. *"And how was your brief interlude with your disciplined mind?"* His smile expressed curiosity and all knowing at the same time. Dee responded first.

"Do you already know what each of us experienced, because your smile makes me believe you do? Am I right or wrong?" she playfully asked.

*"Yes,"* he replied with equal delight, *"you are correct and you are wrong! Allow me to elaborate. I am aware silence was achieved during this experience whereas, it was not during the previous contemplative moment. Because you successfully reached the silence, I am confident each of you encountered some type of connection. Exactly what was experienced, I do not know, but I am very curious and hope you will share your findings with one another."* Dee took it upon herself to bring the focus back to me by immediately asking if I had found the answers to my questions. My response was immediate.

"Well, I didn't receive a precise answer, but I certainly acquired a sense of hope. It seems positive energy exerts greater influence than negative energy; therefore, a few participants truly can effect significant change. Evidently, positive energy begets positive energy. And as changes become increasingly more apparent, more people will be inspired to participate. With each new participant, momentum will build and involvement will spread. As the numbers increase, so too will the proliferation of good will and healthy influence. We will benefit from this change of energy and so too will the Earth.

The goal posited must include participation by every person on the Earth, because negative energy is contagious, and it is capable of spreading rapidly, as we well know. However, once the transformation of negative energy to positive energy is undertaken, the benefits for this action become so profoundly evident that observers will be inspired to explore the possibility for themselves. What is so remarkably encouraging is how rapidly change can occur. Look at us! Although our perceptions of time have frequently been distorted during this learning phase, in actuality, we have advanced very quickly. We have received instructional guidance and will continue to do so. We have practiced what we have learned and are becoming increasingly more skilled in our endeavors. We have reached a level of acceptance regarding everything we are learning, and as a result, commitments to continue were asserted. And we have all experienced the rewards of our participation. We have benefitted from the changes transpiring within and about us." I paused primarily to catch my breath, but the passing moment provided additional insight.

"Yes, I think my questions were answered. What we are doing, my friends, is significant. I say this with humility, for we all know it is a privilege to be a part of this transformational experience. The positive energy we are creating here within our circle will spread and those we are fortunate enough to touch will reach out and touch others. The potential for global involvement is high and I think there is reason to feel optimistic. In fact, I think we can feel confident about our participation. So rather than worrying about exact dates for completion of this project, we must proceed with the understanding that each day matters. Every connection we make, every opportunity we utilize to spread positive energy matters." Perhaps my plea for answers influenced my friends before we entered our 5-minute journey into the silence, or perhaps our unseen friends simply took advantage of the opportunity to provide encouraging information. Whatever the truth may be, we all seemed to return from our journeys with a similar sense of intention. Everett summarized the situation nicely.

"My friends, we seem to be at peace with our present and future roles. We know we must live one day at a time, and we must greet each day by intentionally managing our own energy. We must create, maintain, and sustain positive energy within and about us." Turning to Jan, he assertively acknowledged, "We can do this! We can help one another and we can speak of this to others here locally and everywhere we travel. Regardless of the setting, we can share what we are learning with everyone who is willing to listen." Everett's reassurance spilled over to Jan culminating in an impromptu hug that delighted their friends.

"I think we're witnessing a beautiful expression of relief," suggested Marilyn.

"Yes!" the Smiths replied simultaneously. Asserting herself, Jan carried on, "We've been really conflicted, as you know, so this new sense of flexibility is liberating. Wow! A few minutes of silence can be life changing." Her remarks generated a round of similar commentary among the friends, as their guest and others quietly observed the exchange. Eventually, Everett offered another comforting summary.

"We're living into our new roles," he stated. "What was once very unusual, just a short while ago, is becoming the norm for us. Every day we are learning something new about the world we live in, and each time, acceptance of the new information is becoming easier. It's rather remarkable, isn't it? We truly are transforming!" Everett thought about the idea of transforming and realized it was appropriate for him to take his turn at storytelling. "Well, friends, if you don't mind, I think it is time for me to share my story." Needless to say, his friends encouraged him to do so.

"My journey into the silence just happened. I didn't do anything but close my eyes, take a few deep breaths, and I was gone. Haven't the slightest idea where I was, but wherever it was, I was at peace. If there are words to describe what happened, they escape me. The best way I know of articulating my adventure is to say I visited a state of being, rather than a place." Everett put up his hands as if to say he knew how lacking, if not crazy, his description sounded, but his friends didn't doubt or question him at all. In truth, they were intrigued.

"Tell us more, Everett," urged Dee.

"Dee, I had no sense of place at all. I saw nothing. No visual images. No sounds of birds, water, or trees blowing in the wind. I simply was. I distinctly remember trying to feel my body, but I couldn't. And I remember wondering if I should be concerned about that, but concern didn't manifest. Although I didn't understand what was happening, I wasn't concerned about it. I simply was at peace."

"Were you accompanied?" Jan asked the question everyone was curious about. Her husband smiled.

"Yes, I was! And again, I cannot explain how I knew this, but I did. Because I had no sensory awareness, what was perceived was distinguished inwardly. Does that make any sense?" Everett asked somewhat desperately. "Please excuse me, but I really want to share this experience with all of you. I think it was important, one of those events we can all benefit from, and I don't want my ineptness to deprive you of the joy of experiencing this opportunity." Everett's plea was heard, understood, and quickly responded to by his friends.

"Don't be hard on yourself, Everett. We are listening!" Frank stated firmly. "And we are benefitting from your story. Remember who your audience is! Inept is not a word that would ever come to mind as an applicable descriptor for you, Everett. In fact, I think you've just experienced something the rest of us haven't encountered yet. So you just keep plodding along and we'll keep holding the space for this story." The encouragement propelled Everett forward.

"Thanks, Frank, and all of you! My impatience is getting the best of me. So, back to the story! This state of being I'm trying to describe simply was, and I simply was in it or within it, whichever is the correct way of saying that. Again, I saw nothing, I heard nothing, I did not physically feel anything, and yet, I experienced a wholehearted sense of knowing during my time spent in that remarkable state."

"What do you know, Everett?" interjected Dee. Before continuing, the storyteller closed his eyes, took a deep breath, and remembered what he had experienced during his journey into the silence.

"I know everything is going to be okay," he spoke softly. "I know we, all of us, are going to be fine. Our lives will be lived in meaningful ways.

We will impart messages of truth to all who will listen and our work will influence many. And we will all live happily and contentedly. I also know the Earth will survive and she will regain the vibrant wellness she once possessed. And humankind will continue. I remember wondering when the awareness regarding humankind entered into me how this could be known with certainty. And then, in an instant, I knew there are some truths that are known while other truths remain to be known, and the truth about humankind's survival is a known." Everett inhaled loudly giving his friends a chance to catch their breath as well.

"The journey will be tedious at times, but humankind is intended to continue. Goodness will surface again and humans will find their way. I find that comforting," he sighed. "Goodness will surface again," he repeated. "Isn't that a lovely thought?" Everett sighed again and then faced his friends. "I don't know how I know this, but I do. And I am so grateful to be able to share this good news with you." Tears filled Everett's eyes, and the eyes of his human companions as well.

"What an incredible experience!" Similar declarations accompanied Marilyn's. Although she didn't want to impose upon Everett, she could not contain herself. "Everett, first I want to say Thank YOU! And secondly, I want you to know I believe everything you shared with us. Can I say that I understand the state you experienced? No, I cannot, but I can tell you with absolute certainty, I believe you! And I want to visit that state of being!" Her voice increased in volume as if she were requesting an invitation. "What an adventure! I am envious!"

*"No need is there for envy, my friend! This experience awaits all of you. In truth, each of you has already experienced such an event."* The teacher's comment surprised some of his students but no one interrupted. The proverbial pin could have dropped as they awaited more information.

*"Rest assured, each one of you has had a moment of instantaneous knowing numerous times during your life experience. Sometimes the knowing was so subtle you were unaware of it, and other times you did not give it credence, or recognize it as anything other than a thought popping into your mind. The point I am trying to make is this. One must be present in the moment to appreciate such events. Also, one must be open to these experiences, so when they transpire you recognize that something significant is happening. By opening your heart to this type of connection, you are more fully engaged with the world about you. Much can be learned about self, others, and more when you are accepting of such interactions.*

*In this particular situation, you were so engaged with your state of being that you were exquisitely aware of what transpired and your message was indeed profound. On other occasions you can be equally aware of even the subtle messages, which may or may not be as powerful as the message just received; however, each message provided is one that serves the recipient. By leaving oneself open to such assistance, you also learn more about your mind. With practice, you can become acutely capable of discerning when a thought is merely a thought versus when a thought is something more than a thought. What I say to you now is extremely important. Please listen with the ears of your heart. Always are you accompanied! Regardless of where you are at any given time, you are, shall we say, in very good company."* His smile brightened the room and was contagious. Without even knowing it, each student was returning his gesture. *"If only the peoples of Earth would accept this reality, so much more delightful would their lives be. Is it not wonderful to imagine this reality? Is it not comforting and reassuring to know you are never alone? This is the truth of all in existence, and yet, those of the Earth have forgotten about their companions."*

"As always, your teachings impart great wisdom, which inspires many more questions." Marilyn's comment was delivered with a twinkle in her eyes. She adored being in their mentor's presence and wondered if he was one of the companions being discussed.

*"Yes, I am!"* he happily responded to her unspoken thought. *"But I am simply one of many. More exist than you can imagine, and we all desire to be of assistance."*

"And are you assigned to us permanently. Or are we assigned to you?" Marilyn laughed at the possibility, but then thought better of it. "Perhaps, you are upper level management and we are here to serve you?"

*"Actually, we serve each other in accordance with agreements made long ago. Because I retain memories, which have escaped you, I am able to reeducate and assist you in regaining missing memories and skills you already possess. At the same time, you are able to engage and interact with this plane of existence in ways I am not capable of managing. Thus, we work in union to serve the highest possible good for all intended."*

"And am I correct in assuming you work with others as well?"

*"Yes, that is true. From my plane of existence, I am able to multi-task in ways you cannot achieve on your plane of existence. It is very efficient. Although this seems confounding from your present perspective, rest assured, this ability is known to you. You have also enjoyed the luxury of interdimensional multi-tasking in other times and places, and you will again."*

"Well, now that you've brought up this intriguing possibility," stated

Marilyn insinuating a link to her next train of thought, "perhaps it is appropriate for me to share my story, if that meets with everyone's approval.

"I can't wait to hear your story," Pat's enthusiastic response included a quiet clapping of her hands. "Please tell us everything!"

"My story is similar to those already shared, and yet it is different. I think what is wonderful about sharing our stories is how much we are learning about possibilities. Which I'm sure," she said glancing towards their mentor, "is a primary reason for this activity. Not only are we learning for ourselves about possibilities of engagements, but also we are practicing how to share this information with others. By sharing our own stories people's curiosity will be piqued, and then hopefully, they will share their own stories with one another just as we are doing now. This is an old and cherished teaching tool…learn by doing!" Taking a deep breath, and briefly closing her eyes, Marilyn prepared herself. She wasn't afraid of sharing her story. She trusted these friends without reservation; but for some inexplicable reason, shyness was gripping her. *What is this about? Why am I hesitating?* Several of Marilyn's friends heard her unspoken thoughts, but no one intervened. To do so would have interrupted her inward process.

"Excuse me, dear friends, I seem to be struggling with a bout of shyness. Not exactly sure what this is about, but just acknowledging it aloud is helpful. Let me calm myself with a few deep breaths." Role modeling for her friends, Marilyn demonstrated the art of self-care. "My journey also took me to another place, but I don't think it was a place here on Earth. Of course, I may be wrong about that, but it was different from anything I've seen before. Not unpleasantly different, just different. Oh," she noted indicating a new memory. "Yes, now I remember why I was certain the setting was not on Earth. My destination had two moons. That's a clue!" Marilyn chuckled at herself. "Rather conclusive evidence, don't you think?" Closing her eyes again, Marilyn reached inward trying to remember everything about her recent adventure. Like Frank, she didn't want to forget any part of this experience.

"Wherever I was, it was spectacular. Similar to your story, Jan, I was on a beach. The view was amazing. To my right the beach seemed to go on forever, and the sand was white as sugar, refined sugar, that is. It may have been the most beautiful beach I've ever seen." Just remembering that moment took Marilyn back to the same sense of belonging and familiarity she experienced before. It was a powerful moment; one she hoped would never be forgotten.

"The view straight before me," she continued, "looking out over the water, was definitely an award winning photo. There, above the horizon line, were two immense moons seemingly floating in mid-air. These satellites were so close you could actually see land formations upon their surfaces. This was a very different experience than viewing our moon from here on Earth. By the way, let me be more specific. This was not a nighttime event. I was not looking at two glowing orbs in the dark sky. What I'm describing occurred during the day and the moons were so enormous it was like looking at another planet. It was fascinating." Marilyn paused for a moment wondering if her description of the scene was adequate. "Wish I had a video of this adventure," she remarked. "Afraid I'm not doing it justice. I guess this is one of those times when the phrase 'You had to be there!' applies.

Anyway, let me attempt to share with you what I saw off to the left of my location. Again, the beach seemed to stretch out for eternity but in the distance," Marilyn paused again and took another deep breath. "You won't believe what I saw, as if two moons weren't enough." Glancing about the room, she made eye contact with each of her friends. "I saw a community! It was too faraway to distinguish features precisely, but there were tall structures, similar to, yet different from, our own cityscapes. The point is…this place was inhabited." For a brief moment, Marilyn appeared perplexed. Before sharing her story, she was convinced her perception of the experience was real, but now having spoken it aloud, she found herself having doubts.

"Goodness!" she exclaimed in disbelief. "Well, this is an interesting development!" She looked a bit dumfounded. Her friends recognized the expression and understood her dilemma. Dee was the first to respond.

"You're doubting yourself, dear. Please share with us what is racing through your mind." Dee's acknowledgement quieted Marilyn's downward spiral.

"Thank you, Dee! You are absolutely right. My mind was taking me off into a direction I really don't believe is accurate. Let me tell you my emotional reaction during and immediately after the adventure into never-never land. While the event developed before me, I was certain what was being witnessed was real. Even though I couldn't explain what was happening or how, I had no doubts about the reality of the experience. In truth, it seemed as if I was being permitted to view a true to life documentary of another land in another world. And I continued to believe the experience was real until I began sharing it. Then this mind of mine was flooded with worriment perseverating about how my story was being received and how I was being perceived. In that brief moment of self-consciousness, the mind ran away with itself."

*A passage from*
***The Book of Joy: The Invitation***
*(Chapter Three)*

> *"Seeking within is indeed a skill, but more importantly, it is also a natural ability that has simply been overshadowed by the wonders of existence. External stimuli are so delightfully abundant that the mind prefers to observe outwardly rather than inwardly. Conceivably during its evolutionary development, the mind forgot about the wonders lying deeply within as it grew more and more fascinated with the world about it. And why would it not? With so much to see, explore, and enjoy, why would the mind not embrace the moment and indulge in every opportunity it encountered. The mind attended what it does best; it registered every aspect of existence it witnessed. A laudable achievement! Perhaps, the mind during this development phase became so adept at and enamored by observation that it neglected other equally impressive means of engaging with the existence in which it resided. Whether this is a plausible bit of reasoning or not remains to be seen; however, in the quest to seek within, observation alone will be insufficient to attain the magnitude of possibilities available. Thus, it is in your best interest to expand your present mind's potential, which, as you already know, is unlimited."*

"The mind is an incredible manipulator," continued Marilyn. "It overwhelmed my sense of truth and usurped my trust in our relationships, as well as trust in myself. Realistically, I understand my mind created this disruption, but the impact was powerful nonetheless. Jeepers! My friends, we must be alert to the clever misdirections of the mind."

"Indeed!" confirmed Dee. "This is another teaching moment! What just happened with you Marilyn happens for all of us and we must assist one another through these unfortunate moments. Your story was invigorating… and believable. And then, the doubts washed across your face sabotaging the delight and the beauty of the moment. We all witnessed the shift occurring by the change of expression flashing across your face." Dee checked about the room for verification of her assumption and received instant affirmation.

"Yes, this truly is a lesson for all of us. Because of the nature of vulnerability associated with sharing these stories, we truly must accept responsibility for monitoring one another during these storytelling events. And we must remember this for the future. As we reach out to others, it will be essential for us to be vigilant, as newcomers begin sharing their experiences. We are so blessed to have one another, and soon, it will be our turn to be there for others. These are very exciting times. It makes me eager to greet the future." Witnessing Dee's masterful summation of Marilyn's experience inspired me to check in on Marilyn's present state of mind.

"Dee, your reflection upon Marilyn's experience was a teaching opportunity in itself. Very helpful! Thank you! But I want to know how Marilyn is doing now. How are you, girl? Where's your mind? And where's the rest of you?" I asked with a playful tone.

"Actually, I'm doing well," she replied. "And you're right. This has been an extremely valuable teaching experience, both helpful as the storyteller and as a future assistant. Dee, your discourse about my shift in demeanor helped me to calm down and collect my sense of self, and it also demonstrated for me how each of us can readily step in and aid someone who appears to be waning. I am so grateful for these gatherings. We are growing in the most delightful ways. Expansive and heartfelt, yet gentle and grace filled." For some reason, it seemed wise to push Marilyn a bit so I asked her if any new thoughts or ideas has arisen.

"Well, my curious nature has surged again," she laughed. "And of course, my list of questions has lengthened. You know me!" Marilyn happily admitted her obsession for information. Turning toward their esteemed teacher, she sought answers. "I believe what was witnessed was real. I believe it was information regarding other life in the universe. And I believe this happened for a reason. Are you aware of what I saw during my meditation? And can you validate or negate my thoughts?" Marilyn's enthusiastic and courageous self was back as she pushed forward with her questions.

*"Yes!"* came the quick reply from their visiting preceptor. *"The location you visited in your adventure is indeed a place you are familiar with and one which you have enjoyed many lifetimes before. It is a home away from home that you prefer and often choose to frequent. And yes, you chose to visit it now, because it is time for you to remember you are not alone in this marvelous universe. Many more inhabited planets exist throughout countless galaxies in this presently existing universe, and as your scientists now acknowledge, the universe is ever expanding. As humankind evolves upon this planet, similar life forms evolve on*

*planets throughout the universe. Is it not reassuring that other life forms similar to your human species exist elsewhere? Is it not comforting to remember you are not alone?"* Marilyn's curiosity could not be contained. Although she was deeply appreciative for the information provided, it was inevitable the new information ignited more questions.

"And are there other intelligent life forms existing that are not similar to humans?" she asked.

*"Diversity is one of the greatest gifts of the universe,"* came the response. *"Throughout the entire universe, intelligence exists. Even here on this planet, there is intelligence beyond what humans define as intelligence. It is one of humankind's most unfortunate misunderstandings about their existence. The planet Earth is occupied by countless numbers of intelligent species, some of which are far more intelligent than humans presently are, but at this point, humankind is not receptive to this reality. But your species is advancing, and soon will realize the abundance of brilliance existing all about you. So much more exists than you are presently aware, but the time is coming for greater illumination, and with this will also come monumental transformation. Humankind is on the brink of exceptional change, and you, dear friends, are a part of that process."*

"That's a humbling thought!" Bill's comment seemed more like a thought released by chance than an attempt to communicate. Once he realized his thought had been expressed aloud, he stuttered shyly before continuing. "Of course, it's exciting as well, but the idea of being involved in something so profoundly important is humbling." Stroking her husband's shoulder, Pat affirmed her support of his comments.

"I had the same reaction Bill. Even though this suggestion is not new information for us, each time it comes up, I'm taken aback. But we're in a hundred percent, aren't we, Bill?" Pat's question set off a chain reaction. Not only did her husband nod in agreement, but nods and whispers also came from the other group members as well. Those who observed this behavior from afar stood in gratitude.

"Honored Teacher, are whales more intelligent than humans?" inquired Marilyn. "I apologize for my insatiable appetite, but I'm almost done, I promise."

*"Whales have exceptional gifts. They are among the most compassionate beings upon the planet. Humans would be wise to study these magnificent creatures, for there is much to be gained by using them as models of exemplary behavior."* A wave of dissatisfaction not witnessed before from their guest washed across his face. *"Their mistreatment is unconscionable. Words fail to express the sadness*

*the universe feels for these beloved friends. Such cruelty is inconceivable."* Their guest fell quiet in an effort to collect himself; however, it was obvious he had more to say. No one interrupted or attempted to console him.

*"Intelligence is defined differently in other realms of the universe than it is here on this planet. The peoples of Earth are still very young in comparison to other residents of the universe, thus perceptions and associated behaviors grounded in misunderstandings remain opportunities for improvement. Evolution unfortunately is at times extremely painful. We hold our dear friends, the precious whales, in constant prayer. Rest assured, their species will not be lost. Such grace is never lost!"*

Marilyn's question, innocently born in curiosity, had unwittingly created tension. An urge to apologize rushed through her, but words would not come. *Just be with the uncertainty,* came a voice of wisdom. *This is happening for a reason.*

*"My friends, I beg your forgiveness. Painful emotions have surfaced and must be addressed. To pretend these feelings do not exist is a disservice to myself and disrespectful to you. So, I will attempt to explain my present state of discomfort. Perhaps, it is my turn to share my story with you."* The serenity the group had become accustomed to returned, as their respected teacher regained his focus. *"Another noteworthy teaching experience just transpired, my friends, and it is in our best interest to take advantage of this situation."* Turning to Marilyn, he gently acknowledged, *"I am grateful for your kindness, but an apology is not necessary. Your beautiful curiosity successfully tapped a sensitive chord within me. An old heartache encompassing the injustices perpetrated by youthful innocence escaped to the surface and spilled out in a manner that was unkind and lacking in compassion. An error of the moment,"* he acknowledged quietly before continuing in an easily audible tone, *"which deserves reflection, adjustment, and honorable discussion. My truth is this,"* he humbly admitted. *"I have a particular fondness for the species of whales. Their intelligence is of a kind that is desperately needed by the peoples of Earth. A compassionate heart can alter the energy of the beholder and has a capacity for great outreach. Just one compassionate thought has the potential for creating a tidal wave of goodness."* Glancing about the room, he proceeded with confidence, *"I believe it is fair to say that each of you has a story in which one good deed fostered another, which led to another and another that continued spreading additional positive energy beyond your own reach of observance. This is how the energy of good will multiplies. One act of kindness inspires another, manifesting a momentum of positive energy with unlimited potential.*

*The whales, benevolent creatures that they are, have assisted humankind in ways that are unknown to the recipients of their generosity. For millennia they populated oceanic waters serving as generators and distributors of compassionate, healing energies to locations all across the globe. Facilitated by their innate abilities to transmit these energies through ultrasonic means, they continue these efforts even today. Although their numbers have been severely reduced by the brutal, violent acts of those they attempt to assist, the whales valiantly continue to serve the human species through their evolutionary upheavals. Such compassion and determination to aid a developing species is as incomprehensible as the behavior of those they attempt to serve. I am in awe of their goodness and of the sacrifices they have made for humankind. As said before, much can be learned from the magnificent beings."*

Time passed, as is often the case when another breath of awareness has been shared. In revealing his heartfelt connection with the whales, their esteemed teacher had opened the hearts of each member of the unique cluster of friends. Not unlike a pod of whales, this family of friends was evolving in many ways including greater capacity for openheartedness and wholehearted concern and interest in others. By sharing their stories, these old friends were becoming even closer than all the years of connection had already made them. And with the introduction of another, this new friend from another time and place, their understanding of the universe was expanding exponentially.

Dee eventually broke the silence. "I suspect there are many other beings on this planet who also are trying to assist humankind as well." Her comment was both a statement and a question, but before an answer was offered, she continued. "Of course, the Earth is perhaps the most important benefactor of all. My goodness, she provides us residence and supplies our needs in countless way. And just look how we treat her and all the other beings she accommodates. Humans really are quite oblivious of those around us. We assume everything is ours to utilize and we never question our actions or even consider the well being of those we unconsciously take advantage of without regard for their needs or preferences. We are a tragically selfish species." Dee's comments were not laden with contempt or judgment, but simply stated a truth indicative of humankind's profound lack of awareness of its fellow life beings.

*"Indeed, humans evolved in a singularly focused manner centering around their own personal needs while disregarding the needs of other species. And simultaneously, as the human species expanded and became increasingly more diverse, their intolerance for others of their own kind, but different from their image of themselves, resulted in selfish, exclusionary mannerisms within their*

*own species. Hence, humankind has an unkind and unrealistic worldview where their disregard for other species continues while the same disrespectful behaviors for members within their own species has also become more pronounced. This is not the desired way for a species to evolve. They have become lost in their individualism at the expense of their own collective well being, as well as that of countless numbers of others species with whom they coexist."*

"Why have we gone so far astray?" inquired Frank. "Have we always been like this? I know this sounds like one of those old codger's statements that were spoken by our parents' generations, but now it seems they were acknowledging what we are witnessing and experiencing now. Dissension truly does appear to be escalating at a frightening pace. Open hostility seems much more prevalent now than when we were young." Frank looked toward his beloved for validation, which he readily received.

"And it seems," Dee contributed, "this undesirable behavior is so commonplace it is now accepted as the norm. This is very disconcerting."

Carefully listening to the exchange Everett leaned forward to add his thoughts, "I agree! I know we are speaking in generalizations here, and of course, we all have numerous examples of scenarios depicting the abundant goodness still existing around us and throughout all lands across this remarkable Earth. But the circumstances we're focusing upon certainly make one wonder. What ever happened to love thy neighbor? When did kindness and openheartedness turn into suspicion and distrust? And I suppose the most important question of all is how do we get ourselves back on track?" Although everyone presumed their teacher would respond to Everett's questions, he remained silent, allowing his students to contemplate solutions for themselves.

*A passage from*
***The Book of Joy: The Invitation***
*(Chapter Three)*

*"So once again, you are invited to pause for a moment and follow your breath to a more restful state. If one moment does not satisfy you, take another. These are, after all, your moments to enjoy and since you are engaging with a book about joy, is it not fitting that you might explore one of your precious moments "in joy?"*

*"Perhaps, my friends, we can approach this conversation with optimism and joy in our hearts,"* once again the teacher had targeted a shift in his students demeanor. "*The mind is a remarkable tool, is it not? And it is one that demands vigilant management. For left alone to its own inclinations, it will quickly take you down paths that do not need to be investigated. Indeed, our discussion of the misguidedness of humankind is difficult to engage without a change in one's mood; however, we have choices. The topic is complex; it is unsettling, and still, each of you has within you the opportunity to approach the subject with your heart filled with joy and optimism. Remember, my friends, the evolutionary process has its challenges, but it also is an extraordinary journey leading one to ever-expanding possibilities. Because of this existential truth, an attitude of hopefulness and joy is one wise to pursue and maintain."*

As everyone looked downward in thought, Marilyn gazed around the room and noticed her walking buddy looking dreaming eyed and at peace. Instantly, a flash of memory came to mind. "Dear one, are you thinking about the time you were in the high desert when you encountered the fellow coming down the path?" Her question, of course, was on the mark. These two friends had known each for a very long time and were skilled at intuiting each other's thoughts. "Please share the story with us; it so appropriate for the moment." Smiling agreeably in response to the invitation, the story was shared with the group and their wonderful visiting teacher.

"This happened a few years ago when I was visiting a favorite trail in the southwest high desert area. The trails there are lovely and somewhat isolated so it is rare to encounter another person on an outing. But this fine day was unusual." Smiling and gesturing quotation marks around the word unusual, the storyteller continued. "At the time, I was deeply engaged in my spiritual journey. While trekking up, down, and about the rocky landscape, my heart ached with many questions. You know the ones to which I'm referring. The ones that keep you up at night! Who am I? Why am I here? What is my purpose? And so on! Needless to say, my thoughts were within, and at the same time, I was completely cognizant of the beauty surrounding me. 360 degrees of absolutely stunning views! Mother Earth truly is a remarkable life being. Incomparable beauty! How could one not be entranced and susceptible to an encounter during such an openhearted experience?" The narrator of the story paused as if reliving the exact moment. "Although this may not seem like a profound experience, it was one of those moments of synchronicity transpiring precisely at the right time to validate a particular concern currently commanding your attention.

So, there I was hiking up the trail, deeply engaged with the moment, when I saw a tall, rather sophisticated looking gentleman bounding down the trail. Even though the terrain offered physical challenges, his pace, both vigorous and confident, indicated he was familiar with the trail. As we neared each other, I greeted him first and was taken by surprise with his most interesting response.

'You're the new one,' he spoke assertively. Having encountered only one other person since my arrival several days earlier, I assumed information regarding a newcomer traveled fast in the small community where I was staying. I acknowledged his supposition was true, and then, he forthrightly inquired, 'What path do you follow?'

Admittedly, I initially thought the fellow was referring to the nature trails before it dawned on me that he was actually asking about my spiritual quest. Upon realizing his intention, I replied in a similarly straightforward manner, 'I believe in the concept of Oneness.'

Well, in a most gentlemanly manner, he looked down upon me and softly stated, 'Difficult path to follow, but one worthy of the pursuit.' And with that said, he continued on down the trail. Perhaps, nothing more needed to be said.

At the time, I presumed he was a messenger sent into my life to affirm my then-current aspirations. His quick entry into and exit from my life was unusual and noteworthy, and his message certainly soothed my many questions at the time.

And now, hearing that we have a choice to open our hearts to live life from the perspective of joyful optimism, I once again assume an honored teacher has come into my life, our lives, with a message of extreme importance."

Our guest sat peacefully with the gentle smile we all had come to love. *"The message is indeed one of importance. Far too many have forgotten that the gift of joy resides within everyone. Joy is naturally within us. We are birthed with this grace, and the seed always remains within us. So sad is it that humankind has not fully nurtured this seed. True, there are joyous individuals on the planet and there are others who frequent joy in various settings for a variety of reasons. But it seems only a few embrace life consistently from a joyous perspective.*

*Once again, we speak about the process inhibiting humankind's openheartedness. When we are driven by the joyful essence within, our hearts are open to others. We are filled with curiosity and we naturally greet newcomers with optimism and joy rather than with suspicion and distrust.*

*A passage from*
***The Book of Joy: The Invitation***
*(Chapter Four)*

> *"Imagine the pleasure of spreading joy everywhere you go to everyone you see. Picture that scenario in your mind's eye just for a moment and feel what transpires throughout your entire body as a result of your creative visualization. Stay with that image please, and pay particular attention to the influence it has upon your heart. Is it full when you witness yourself sharing your joy with another? Likewise, how do you feel when receiving a wonderful gift of joy from someone else? Visualizing these possibilities from within demonstrates the powerful impact joy has. By simply imaging the exchange of joy from self to another or vice versa, your consciousness awakens to the experience and you respond as if the event really transpired before you. Mind, body, and soul are activated.*
>
> *Take an additional moment, if you will, for another adventure in imagination. Allow your mind to fantasize about the joyful energy within you igniting your spirits and increasing your sense of wellness, happiness…and JOY. Imagine this energy welling up within you to the point that you feel compelled to share it with everyone…people (family, friends, strangers, everyone), animals, trees, etc. And just picture your joy spreading from one to another to another to another, each time magnifying in intensity as it reaches out further and further across the seas to other continents. Be with that glorious scene just for a moment and feel the reality of it. Fill your entire essence with the heartfelt beauty of such connection, and sigh a relief, knowing that it is possible, because it is! Is that not a joyful thought?"*

*"Would it not be an admiral endeavor to pursue a purposeful life driven by joyful intentions and maintained by an enduring belief in hopefulness? Would you, my dear friends, like to pursue this lifestyle for yourselves, and then mentor others to claim this healthy way of being for themselves? We speak of commitment, my friends. Commitment to self and commitment to others! Ponder this please. You are being invited to a new way of being."*

*A passage from*
***The Book of Joy: The Invitation***
*(Chapter Four)*

> *"Dear Reader, joyful intentions increase and expand the energy of joy and each and every being in existence is capable of such intentions. This is not a fantasy. While the earlier exercise in visual imagery demonstrates how the mind is capable of fantasizing, the ability to purposefully and intentionally do so is no fantasy. It is an actuality."*

Pat initiated conversation first. "Excuse me. I would like to say something if the rest of you are ready to proceed." Her friends, in various states of contemplation welcomed the opportunity for discussion about this new opportunity for change. "Well, I am intrigued by this new possibility and I really want to give it a try, but I must fess up to my limitations. Maintaining a joyful state of being is not something I'm accustomed to and it will demand a great deal of concentrated effort on my part. And quite frankly, I'm not sure this can be done alone. Honestly, I don't even know when I'm being pessimistic and/or joyless. These are traits of long standing and simply are a part of me. I will need assistance to achieve this task. I want to try, but please understand this will be difficult for me."

"You're not alone in this, Pat," declared her husband. "But I think you were really brave to speak out. I'm proud of you." Her friends rallied around with admissions of similar concerns. Pat was relieved, but bewildered.

"You're telling me I'm not the only one with this issue!" Her innocent disbelief was obvious, and once again, her friends offered reassurances. Much was being revealed through these conversations from the heart as the relationships continued to deepen.

*"A courageous admission, my friend. I applaud you! And I am most grateful for your willingness to share these heartfelt concerns. Even though you are unaware of this, you speak a truth for many. As revealed by your friends of long standing, you are not alone. In actuality, you are indeed in extremely good company!*

*Here in this cozy environment created by the Circle of Eight, you gather with good intentions. With your hearts filled with curiosity, you seek ways of bettering yourselves with hopes of assisting others. Suffice it to say, dear friends, you are people of good will. I speak this truth aloud to make a point. Even good people such as yourselves suffer a common characteristic that is prevalent among the human species. Yes, my friends, just as the eight of you share similar limitations, so do the masses who reside upon this beautiful planet. The characteristic, of which we speak, entails a flaw in humankind's ability to identify and manage their disposition from one moment to the next. This is a persistent issue within your species, which fortunately is one that is correctable. Some individuals are already awakening to this problematic situation and are making significant strides to overcome the undesirable behavior. However, for a momentum of global transformation to be achieved, the masses must be informed. After all, one cannot take appropriate action if one is not aware of the problem."*

Frank's good manners were overtaken by an overwhelming need to understand what was being discussed. Patience could no longer be maintained as words began to stream from his mouth. "Well, what exactly is this flaw? What's the underlying cause of it and how do we go about fixing it? If it's correctable, let's get on top of this. Time's a-wastin!" His wife shared her husband's exasperation, and internally giggled at his reaction.

"Fine, Sir!" she declared boisterously. "The man needs an answer NOW!" Their amiable teacher laughed joyously…so much so that his companions joined in, including Frank who was laughing at himself.

"Sorry about that," he apologized. "But, could you just bottom line it for us!"

*"There is wisdom in your request, Mr. Sanderson!"* replied their guest. *"As you requested, I will strive to bottom line my intentions.*

*Point 1: Before humankind can alter their present way of being, they must become aware they are driven by distraction.*

*Point 2: In order to effect change one must be present in the moment! Only when one is living in the present moment is one able to recognize the flaw inhibiting his or her life process. When one actually pauses long enough to witness the power of distraction, then the possibility for change reaches a state of momentum. With momentum comes curiosity and with curiosity comes the will to change.*

*Point 3: Acknowledgement and acceptance of the deception of distraction will propel one forward to fully address the flaw that diminishes full engagement with life. Distraction, regardless of its source, disables humankind's ability to live in the present. When awareness of this problem is gained, one can easily overcome the negative influence of the flaw of distraction.*

*Point 4: To accomplish this task one must learn to manage the wayward mind by providing it with models of discipline. Combine this with practice, perseverance, and commitment and the deed will be done."*

Everyone gasped for air as if they had been holding their breaths during this rapid-fire lecture, which of course, was the case. "Goodness!" exclaimed Jan. "You certainly granted Frank's request."

"That was impressive," Frank acknowledged. "And perhaps, I should just say thank you and leave it at that, but I have a question." Their mentor responded with a nod. "Models of discipline! I assume you are speaking about various kinds of meditation."

*"Meditation indeed, and more!"* came a reply. *"Actually any form of activity that quiets the mind, freeing it from distraction, is a means to a fuller, more engaged lifestyle. This clears the negative energy created by a distracted mind and replaces it with energy of peace and serenity, thereby allowing the individual to truly be in charge of his or her present moment. Much more will be discussed about this, but for now, I wish to return to our sharing of stories. Are you ready to change course, Mr. Sanderson?"*

"Yes, I am. And I thank you for elaborating upon your story by sharing these finer points of information with us." Frank broke for an instant and then suggested the focus return to Pat since it was her courageous leadership that had taken them to this point in the discussion. "How about it, Pat?" asked Frank. "Are you ready to share your adventure with us?" Everyone watched Pat as she responded in typical fashion for this group. She closed her eyes, took a deep breath, and prepared herself for the opportunity. When she was ready, Pat opened her eyes and faced her friends. Sitting more erect, her face revealed determination and when she spoke, resolve was evident. "Quite frankly, I am blown away by our conversation." Facing her mentor, she said, "When you challenged us to proceed with joyful optimism as our guide, I almost choked. Even though I don't perceive myself as a pessimistic person, the truth is, I've struggled with this for a long time. It comes and goes, but when it hits…it isn't any fun." Her friends looked on with empathetic eyes. Pat felt their compassion and concern.

"Having revealed my nonsensical ways, I think all of you will be particularly surprised and pleased by my experience into the silence." Pat's introduction piqued her friends' curiosity. She was pleased to see they were interested in hearing her story, just as she had been in hearing theirs.

"I think it is safe to say I was gone with the first deep breath." Shaking her head, as if in disagreement with herself, Pat countered, "No, let me correct that. It is more accurate to say, with the first deep breath, I was taken away. How this actually transpired remains a blurry image, but if I were to speak about it using the language of science fiction, I would say I had a time- warp experience. There was a massive swoosh of energy, which literally transported me from this setting to another. At times, I could see nothing other than the movement of bright, colorful energies. And at other times, I recall seeing galaxies, which were too beautiful to describe. I felt as if I had traveled throughout the universe in a blink of an eye." Pat took another deep breath before continuing. "Trust me, my friends, I know how crazy this sounds, but it truly is what I experienced. Upon my arrival to wherever my destination was, I found myself in a garden unlike any garden I've seen before. The arrival itself was amazing. One minute I wasn't there, and the next I was. There was no landing, no sudden jolt of impact, no floating down from above! I was simply there!

And the setting was spectacular! Vegetation of every size, shape, and color was bountiful. Plant life collided with one another in the most gracious way, and yet, every plant, every tree, every flowering bush had sufficient space to carry out its purpose. So, the best I can say is this. Imagine a forest so abundantly full it would be impossible for one more plant to sprout from the forest bed. That's how bounteous this setting was, and still, as you peered through the maze of plant life, each formation was individually seen. I was so entranced by the view that I actually felt implanted in the forest bed along side all the other life beings." Pat paused as she heard her own words and shook her head in affirmation. "Yes," she continued, "I said that correctly. The various plant species were life beings! I believe this is true here on Earth too, but for some reason, the truth was undeniable in that setting.

Before I even attempted to take my first step into the new location, the most delightful presence appeared from nowhere and invited me to accompany him (or her) on a tour through the garden. Needless to say, I accepted the invitation."

"Pat, were you comfortable with this presence? Did you have any misgivings about the encounter?" Even though Bill could see his wife was fine, he needed reassurance her experience was a positive one.

"I was completely at ease, Bill. Curious, of course, fascinated, actually! But I never felt insecure or concerned about the interaction. Accepting the gracious invitation felt as natural as coming here for one of our gatherings. Yes," she pronounced emphatically, "this is an important perspective for me to share. The connection with this being was instantaneous and it was as comfortable and intimate as our relationship with our esteemed teacher. The feelings were very similar, even though their appearances were quite different." Before anyone had a chance to ask the obvious question, Pat addressed the topic. "The presence was what I think is called a Light Being. He or she was aglow. While I could not ascertain any specific features of this being, I can attest to his or her beauty. My goodness! What a sight it was! This calm, gentle intelligence engulfed within a glowing mass of energy. It was truly spectacular! I felt as though I was in the company of an Angel. I did ask about that," Pat admitted. "But the presence denied the title and indicated that he/she was simply my companion."

Marilyn, intrigued by the Pat's interaction with the glowing Light Being asked, "Did you ask about the gender issue?"

"Yes, I did, and the response was so touching. 'I am what is needed!' was the reply. Isn't that lovely? I am what is needed!" Pat repeated the message lingering in the moment of the exchange.

"At times, I felt in the presence of a female and other times, the presence seemed remarkably male. But at the time it didn't matter. The time together just seemed to flow. He and she were wonderful companions and my experience was delightful. And what seems extremely relevant to our previous conversation is the reality that during my adventure, I experienced joy. Absolute joy! There were no doubts, no apprehensions, no concerns other than wanting to capture the moment." Turning towards their teacher, Pat affirmed, "I was definitely living in the moment and it was a joyous experience!"

*A passage from*
***The Book of Joy: The Invitation***
*(Chapter Four)*

> *"Our exercise in imagination demonstrates the ease with which we can positively affect our surroundings…and accentuate our potential. The point of this exercise is to inspire you to accept the extended invitation to participate in an act of generosity. Dear Reader, you can do this. I can do this. We can all do this. The energy lies within us, waiting to be accessed and utilized. What a waste it would be to ignore a gift of such remarkable influence."*

"My goodness!" declared Dee. "These stories, our individual experiences, are absolutely mind-blowing." Turning specifically towards Pat, she added, "Thank you! That was a spellbinding tale! Once again, I am fascinated by this storytelling process. In fact, it amazes me! As I listened to you Pat, I felt as if I was there experiencing every detail with you. Even though you did not describe the galaxies, I saw them in my mind's eye. And I felt the swoosh of energy you described as a time warp. Because you shared your adventure with us, my own experience has expanded. Can this really be happening? Can the telling of a story be so powerfully transformative?" Marilyn immediately interjected that she too had a similar reaction, and other members of the group also nodded in agreement.

"This is intended, isn't it?" Pat's question, directed toward their guest, opened the door for another teaching moment.

*"Do you feel as if you are growing? Do you feel you know more about the universe and your existence in the universe since you heard one another's stories?"* The rhetorical questions served their purpose. Each participant silently mulled over the personal ramifications of these exercises while also pondering the far-reaching potential it held for humankind.

"I cannot help but wonder about the impact this will have on our planet," mused Dee. "Perhaps, I've grown so old that the importance of storytelling has escaped me. My friends, we are participating in something extremely important here. Can you imagine how lives will change if this simple process takes off and spreads across the planet? The disposition of humankind truly may change. Just think about this."

"I'm very curious about the effect this will have upon the children of Earth," remarked Bill. "They are the ones with the greatest growth potential. I wish we had youngsters here with us now. It would be so interesting to see and hear their responses to our inner travels."

"I was having similar thoughts, Bill," responded Pat. "Wish the grandkids were with us!" Marilyn's fine mind, inspired by the introduction of children to the mix, was in strategizing mode.

"Friends, this adds another dimension to our To Do List! We have so-o-o much to do! We really are going to need help!" Marilyn's excitement about the potential outreach was invigorating and intimidating at the same time.

*"Indeed, my friends, there is much to do; however, before we are distracted by the details of our upcoming endeavors, may we continue being in the present?"* Subtle, yet germane, the teacher's comment refocused the group upon the matter before them. *"If my tracking of this evening's events is accurate, we have not yet completed sharing our stories."* Aiming his attention towards Bill, a broad smile exposed his intentions. *"Will you expand our horizons, my friend?"*

The invitation, though expected, still managed to bring on a bout of shyness for Bill. Determined to push through this inconvenience, he followed the lead of his companions. Taking several deep breaths, he reminded himself he was in the company of dear friends. *You can do this!* Whether this anonymous encouragement came from within or from Pat or from one or all of his friends, Bill didn't know or care. Regardless of its origin, the support felt good. And it served its purpose!

Emboldened by the unidentified reassurance, he began with a statement of empowerment. "Thank you! Even though shyness wanted to make an appearance just for old time's sake, the visit was brief, and I am both excited and ready to share my story. As with the rest of you, it began with a deep breath. Guess, I'm rather amazed at the power of a breath. It seems this simple, instinctive action has the capacity to transform one's world. It certainly did for me, and I hope my story will do the same for you as well.

Evidently, my adventure took a different spin than the rest of yours. When I inhaled the initial deep breath, I found myself in a state of complete darkness." Sensitive to his friends' reactions, Bill quickly elaborated. "Before I say anything else, let me reassure all of you the darkness was not foreboding in anyway. At no time did I feel fearful or ill at ease. That surprised me in the moment, as I think you are surprised now to hear me say this, but it's the truth. My experience simply unfolded without light, and in the darkness, I found a sense of quietude that was so profound, it is indescribable.

In the silence seemingly so empty, I heard a voice. In the darkness that seemed vast and never-ending, I felt a presence. And because of these experiences, I will never again be the same. I know now with absolute certainty we are not alone. Can I prove this? No, of course I cannot! I have no evidence to offer that will verify my experience. I simply know what was experienced was real. And I know it is my responsibility to share this experience with others, so they too will open their hearts to the possibilities that there is more. And there is! There is more than any of us ever imagined.

I don't know what else can be said. How does one describe the indescribable?" Bill's validating message which, of course, cannot be confirmed brought silence to the group. He was comfortable with the silence, as were his friends.

Those who observed from afar were impressed. The Circle of Eight demonstrated extreme trust. They listened. They heard. They accepted. No evidence was necessary to substantiate the friend's experience. He was the proof! He spoke the truth and his circle of friends believed him.

*A passage from*
***The Book of Joy: The Invitation***
*(Chapter Four)*

> *"The mind has an inquisitive attitude, does it not? Attend this please, when you have a moment, and allow the heart, your most valuable companion, to be your guide. With its ability to quiet the apprehensive and often fitful mind, the heart is an able leader. In your endeavors to discover the joyful energy within, your greatest benefit may be the relationship that develops between you and your incredible heart."*

"Bill, many questions are running through my head, and curiosity will not allow me to remain silent." Everett's approach brought a smile to his friend's face and a few chuckles from others in the room.

"Go for it, Everett! Bill can handle it! There's more to this story," Frank declared in a playful, almost childlike manner. "We just need to delve a litter deeper into his excursion."

"My thoughts exactly," responded Everett. "Can we try that, Bill?" Waiting for his friend to respond, Everett demonstrated gentle patience. He understood Bill's silence was not resistance, but an attempt to recall more of the interaction that transpired during his time in the dark, silent reality of his travels.

"Ask me some questions," invited Bill. "Perhaps, this will bring more memories to the surface. I have to admit this is disappointing, because I don't want to forget any of my experience." Once again the importance of these adventures became evident. Each participant had expressed similar concerns when sharing their stories.

Nodding his head in agreement, Everett began slowly, "Well, what most intrigues me about your encounter, Bill, is your clarity about hearing a voice and knowing a presence of some kind was with you. The confidence you exhibited when stating this was undeniable, and of course, such a demonstration of certainty leads me to believe there was an exchange between you and the voice. I presume a conversation transpired." Bill remained silent, wondering if his so-called clarity had escaped him, but he refused to give into his doubts and instead shared them aloud in hopes that doing so would generate additional recall. His admissions were brief and once expressed, he was ready to move forward.

"Thank you for allowing me to share my concerns, friends. I know it is suggested that expressing your doubts and/or fears aloud can diminish their power over you, so let's see if this notion is really true. Hopefully, these annoying misgivings can be laid to rest." Inhaling robustly, Bill prepared himself to delve more deeply as Frank had described it. The idea of delving deeply inspired a vision of standing on a very tall cliff looking downward into a peaceful pool of water. Of course, the vision was enhanced by a picturesque waterfall flowing noisily and peacefully down the cliff on the other side of the pool. It was a beautiful and somewhat ambitious image depicting an extremely long dive from atop the cliff to the distant pool below. His mind clearly exaggerated the distance and his courage. Fortunately, Bill was amused by the concoction of his mind rather than alarmed. Leaving the imagery behind, Bill began his quest.

"This is what I remember about my experience," he thoughtfully said. "An inexplicable sense of awareness regarding my place in the universe overwhelmed me. Somehow, I knew," Bill briefly paused before continuing. "Please forgive me, but this is very difficult to articulate. But somehow, in some way, I got it! I simply comprehended the reality that my experience here in this lifetime was not a mere coincidence, but was indeed a significant, intentional event, which was happening for a reason. Now the question is," Bill noted, more to himself than his companions, "how did I know this? Was the information provided to me via the voice? Or was it a download of knowledge from some unknown source, which in some unexplainable manner successfully managed to relocate and awaken into my own consciousness? Was it telepathic communication or did I actually have a conversation with the being whose presence was so obvious?" Bill closed his eyes. His wife knew he was trying to relive the experience. She closed her eyes in support of his efforts, and then, their friends did the same. Time passed as always is its way, and in its passing, an extraordinary event transpired.

"Wow!" exclaimed Marilyn. "I got it! Oh my goodness, Bill! What a lovely encounter!"

"Me too!" chimed in Dee. "Thank you, Bill. That was remarkable." Similar brief declarations quickly echoed throughout the room, followed by joyous laughter.

"My friends, do you understand what just happened? We've just experienced a simultaneous transfer of information. What Bill received earlier, we now have all received." A quick check-in revealed everyone had received the same information. "What I'm not certain about is the transmission process. Did we receive this information from Bill, as he attempted to retrieve his previous experience, or did we receive the information through the same source from which Bill originally received his message? And does it really matter? For curiosity's sake, I would love to know the specifics, but the truth is, we all just experienced a stunning example of a mutually shared intuitive moment." As I looked around my living room, gratitude filled my heart. Whether I would ever fully understood the physics underlying this event or not didn't seem to be the issue. The focus of this experience was the reality that it had transpired. Bill had experienced an inexplicable event, and because of his willingness to explore the experience more deeply, we also had the privilege of enhancing our personal experience of intuitive awareness. Somehow, in some way, we too encountered a transfer of knowledge expanding time and space from one location to another location, which enlightened the receivers of the information. It was indeed a mutually shared intuitive moment.

*A passage from*
***The Book of Joy: The Invitation***
*(Chapter Four)*

> *"Humankind is on the brink of profound change. The beginning of the new reality is already in progress, but many more participants are needed. Change is necessary."*

"Fine, Sir, can you add specifics to this mix?" Although Frank was content having had the experience, he knew specifics might solidify the event for himself, as well as his friends. "What I realize about myself is this. I am better able to remember these experiences if I have more than just esoteric information. Don't get me wrong, please! I trust what just happened here and if no additional information can be provided, I'm still going to be content. But I truly think we are able to understand more, and I wish you and your invisible entourage would trust us."

*"Your request is one of wisdom, Mr. Sanderson. The truth is, the eight of you just experienced a simultaneous transfer of information from a source located in another sector of the universe. The translocation of a thought from one point to another point is achieved by the manipulation of energy fields. This type of connection is a procedure that is considered basic in the field of existential communication. When you master this form of connection, you too will enjoy its simplicity. Do you need to know the specific energetic dynamics of this process to be able to achieve the ability?*

*As was just demonstrated, you do not. Those with scientific minds will pursue such answers and will delight in their discoveries, but in the meantime, neither you nor I require such explanations. And this is a blessing, since our work lies in other matters than scientific discovery. So let us be grateful for all who will attend those areas of discovery while we continue our own intended pursuits.*

*What may be of interest to you,"* their teacher continued, *"is the orchestration of what transpired. When our friend, Bill, closed his eyes and sought connection within, he initiated the process. Then, when the rest of you joined his efforts, you enhanced the receptive energy field in this location. While this was unnecessary for those who were transmitting the information, your efforts did indeed assist the transfer. You essentially made their efforts easier.*

*What is commonplace for them is not for the human species at this time. So when you participated in the process, the transference was easier because you were open to the possibility. With time, this form of communication will become as easy for you as it is for our companions."*

*A passage from*
***The Book of Joy: The Invitation***
*(Chapter Four)*

> *"You, Dear Reader, are the reason for hope. Remember the powerful energy residing within you and the uplifting influence it can yield. You have the ability to effect great change by simply sharing your joyful energy with all others that cross your path. When your joy combines with the joyful energies of other inhabitants of the planet, change will happen and when the energies of all involved achieve and maintain consistent vibrancy, success will be evident by an increase in wellness of the beloved planet Earth and all her inhabitants."*

"Can we presume if our hearts and our intentions are open to this type of communication, it will transpire more easily? And in return, our willingness to participate in this form of communication will accelerate our own skills as existential communicators?"

*"Indeed, Mr. Sanderson, you can presume this is true!"*

*A passage from*
***The Book of Joy: The Invitation***
*(Chapter Four)*

> *"An adage of relatively recent origins comes to mind that is worthy of review. You may remember it. 'If you want to change the world, change yourself!' These words of wisdom are certainly applicable to humankind today. It is time for each of us to review our manner of being and accept responsibility for what we find. As we do so, let us remember the energy burning within us enhances our ability to change, thereby enabling us to participate in the greater change that demands our attention. With awareness comes responsibility, and as we recognize the need for change, we must call ourselves to task. Through careful self-examination, each of us can truthfully and honestly review and assess our behaviors and the impact these behaviors have upon self and others. Then we can refine what we discover about ourselves so that our behavior is consistently a positive influence. We can do this, and if we are honest with ourselves, we know that we must do so."*

"I'm curious about this collective intuitive experience." Smiling in the direction of Everett, Bill admitted he also had many questions. "I think it's fair to say some of you have a lot more experience with this sort of thing than I do. Marilyn, you and your walking buddy here both seem to be familiar with intuitive moments or connections or whatever is the correct phraseology for this. And Dee, you fall in with this crew as well. Am I correct in my assumption about the three of you?" All smiled in agreement. "So tell me," Bill encouraged. "Have you ever experienced this type of thing before?" At first there was a pause and then the three designated speakers all spoke at once. Dee was encouraged to go first.

"You know, Bill, my immediate response to your question was no, and I think these two were about to say the same, but then I realized we have all had similar experiences numerous times before. Here," Dee elaborated, "in these gatherings we have collectively heard unspoken messages from our esteemed teacher and friend, and we have also collectively experienced messages from the unseen participants of our group. What we just experienced was a variation of this type of connection. Isn't that true?" she put the question to the group.

"You're right, Dee!" declared Marilyn whose enthusiasm was unmistakable.

"And I like how you phrased it. This was a variation of intuitive connection. Initially, my inclination would have been to say no, because this experience seemed different, but as you say, it is in the same category, but with a new twist.

"Marilyn, excuse me dear, but this old man needs details. Please tell me what you mean when you say this had a new twist."

"I'll be glad to, Frank, as best I can. Previously, I associated connection and communication with verbal interactions. This exchange was more experiential." Marilyn paused, giving her explanation more thought. "Well, this is complicated. Let me try again. For me, there was a sense of knowing or understanding what was being communicated. One moment I was unaware of the incoming information, and the next moment, I had it! I cannot say I specifically had a vision or heard a voice. That was indistinguishable; however, the moment awareness came into fruition, it felt as if I had experienced the information through all of my senses. Perhaps this is how an immediate downloading of information happens.

My friends, I'm not an expert in this field and certainly cannot speak with authority about our topic. All I know is this. During the experience we just shared, I was struck instantaneously by an awareness of information not known before." Marilyn turned towards Dee and me as if seeking validation for her version. Dee's twinkling eyes communicated her approval. Then she glanced in my direction and silently nudged me to go next.

"Goodness! Our conversations are so gratifying. Every time we come together, it seems we have an incredible experience that broadens who we are personally and collectively. I am so grateful for all of you, and for our beloved teacher, and for all our unseen guests who are assisting us." Tears welled up, as the energy of gratitude emanated throughout the room and beyond. *What more can I add?* The question thought but not spoken did not go unnoticed. One smile brightened a face, and then another, and then another. Frank began to giggle, and then, laughter spread about the room.

"Well, I guess it's reasonable to assume our communication skills are improving." Looking around the room, I saw a change in my friends. They were more than they were before. It was noticeable. "My friends, you are growing before my eyes! Look at one another, please! Can you see that we are changing? I am convinced if we could see our auras, they would be brighter and larger than before our meeting began. Although I cannot explain what I am about to say, this is what I see or sense, or perhaps both. I see men and women, my dearest friends, who are more confident, livelier, happier, more optimistic, more excited, more open to and actively engaged with life, and more joyful. We are changing, and it's for the better!" My observations elevated the group's mood, which was already high, and ignited a chorus of complimentary comments among the old friends. The consensus was unanimous; everyone recognized that changes were occurring. And everyone was pleased!"

*A passage from*
***The Book of Joy: The Invitation***
*(Chapter Four)*

> *"Change is necessary and it need not be a fearful act. Remember, Dear Reader, you are a carrier of the powerful energy of joy and this alone is a reason for hope. Within you is the real "you," you have always wanted to be...Seek within, and by all means, have hope! Have faith! Know with all that you are that change is possible and the necessary ability to alter humankind's present course lies within you.*
>
> *Your participation is needed. For the greater change to be achieved, all are needed. It is possible."*

Moments of intense communication alter the energy field and frequency levels within and about those who are participating in the interaction whether the participants recognize the occurrence of the changes or not. As the eight friends gathered, their energies merged and blended throughout the evening and as connection grew deeper among them, so too did the expansion of their awareness. This became evident when the discussion turned to gratitude, which is an energy, which plays a significant role in all healing processes. When one experiences a grateful moment, healing transpires within resulting in an expansion of wellness that facilitates the reception of increased awareness. And when one shares an experience of gratefulness with another, the potential for expansion increases. Most often one has no comprehension of the positive impact of such moments; however, in this particular situation, the eight friends were apprised of their influence.

*"My dear friends, being in your presence during this exceptional moment is a privilege and a joy. It is a privilege to witness your heartfelt, loving connections and even more so, it is a privilege to be embraced by your transformative energy. I am blessed and extremely grateful to be a part of this exchange. And my dear*

*friends, the experience makes me joyful. Not only do you share your love with one another and with me, but also, your influence reaches far beyond the boundaries of this setting. Heightened energy frequencies, founded in joyful goodness, have no limits. Do you comprehend this, Dear Ones? Please listen to my words with the ears of your heart. The energy of joy is a power source with unlimited potential.*

*What is experienced here in this room at this moment is felt in countless locations throughout the vast universe. Some, such as our unseen members at this gathering, are acutely aware of your present contributions and feel your combined energies similarly as do we in this moment, while others are also affected by your positive influx of healing energy without actually knowing the exchange of energy has occurred. The energy of joy is real, my friends, and this energy existing within each of you is a power source that you must become more acquainted with, for you are here to share this knowledge with everyone."*

Recognizing once again an important message had been delivered, the eight friends sat motionless while each processed the new information within the chambers of his or her mind.

*A passage from*
***The Book of Joy: The Invitation***
*(Chapter Five)*

*"At times, the mind is a marvel for which each of us must be grateful; however, the mind can be and often is quite a character. This too is a marvel to witness. In essence, the human mind is a remarkable asset and assistant to the human experience and just like the human it inhabits, it also requires attention, guidance, and leadership. Although most minds will disagree with the last comment, frequent observation will reveal the truth of this statement. Awareness and acceptance that the mind is in need of attention facilitates the reality that change is necessary, which hopefully will lead to a desire to effect change. Simply stated, by opening your heart to observing your mind, you are entering into a reality of new possibilities.*

*As you probably already recognize, The Book of Joy is written for a reason. There is purpose and intention underlying this endeavor. The purpose is to assist you in making acquaintance with a reality of possibility and the intention is to foster a relationship between you and this available reality. Although many remain unfamiliar with its existence, this reality does exist, has always existed, and always will exist. The reality of which we speak is the moment in which you exist at this point in time. Can you see it? Can you hear it? Are you able to feel the essence of this remarkably tangible moment that is called the present? Hopefully your answer is a resounding yes! However, if it is not, know that you are not alone. Simply accept, Dear Reader, that for the moment you are one of many who find living in the present challenging, which is indeed a bother, because living in the present is absolutely necessary to exist in the reality of possibility."*

"Goodness, my mind is on overload!" sighed Dee. "Honored Teacher, perhaps you overestimate the abilities of your students. I must admit, the idea of another task being added to our To Do List feels exhausting." Similar signs of fatigue were demonstrated as her friends shifted about in their chairs and uttered indistinguishable comments under their breaths.

*"My friends, let me assure you, my assessment of your remarkable skills is accurate and you will discover this for yourselves in the days to come, but the evening has grown long and it is time to bring our gathering to an end; however, before we do, I ask you to remember the moment of gratitude just recently experienced. Reach into the recesses of your heart and renew those thoughts and feelings of wholehearted gratefulness we shared. Embolden the sensations of connection just by choosing to do so. It was a beautiful moment shared then, and now again.*

*We traveled far this evening, and now I urge all of you to rest well this night. Do not allow other notions to distract you. Simply return to your homes and receive the gifts of a good night's sleep. I am most grateful to be a part of your sacred journey.*

*Namaste, my friends!"* And with that, the esteemed teacher faded from their vision. The friends remained still. So much had happened, and still, the evening didn't feel complete.

Finally, Marilyn stated what was on her mind. "Well, curiosity is still driving me, and I'm afraid the disobedient student within me still wants more information. May I ask another question before we go our separate ways?" Her friends readily agreed, and soon the attention was once again focused upon the organizer of this evening's gathering. "Dear friend, you were very quiet tonight, and it leaves me wondering what is going on inside of that incredible soul of yours? Can you give us a clue?" Marilyn's respect for her dear friend was evident. Her question, identified as one of curious nature, was actually founded in concern. Their friendship having survived the test of time resulted in many unusual quirks between the two of them, one of which was the ability to sense when something was amiss with the other. And throughout the evening, Marilyn had been troubled about her friend. Once the questions were posed, Dee quietly added to Marilyn's plea.

"I'm so grateful you brought this up, Marilyn. I've been wondering about our friend as well. Are you feeling all right, dear? Is there something the matter you might like to share with us?" With these questions posed, attention fell upon the one who had been responsible for bringing the family of friends back into close connection again.

"You're always so available and attentive to us," Frank added. "Let us do the same for you."

*A passage from*
***The Book of Joy: The Invitation***
*(Chapter Five)*

*"Open your heart to this experience. As you will soon discover, the heart loves to live in the moment and it will serve as an able guide. If, however, you possess a mind that prefers attending other matters rather than focusing upon the present moment, invite the mind to rest. Trust your heart to intervene and allow it to do what it does so exquisitely. Let your heart take the lead and progress will unfold rapidly.*

*Once again, you are being invited to participate in an act of generosity…one that will benefit others and one from which you will also benefit. By regaining the ability to live in the present, one is available to participate in generous deeds. Whether you are the giver or the receiver is irrelevant because everyone profits. Those who are the recipients illuminate for the givers another aspect of reality and those who are the givers remind the receivers that goodness and kindness still exist in their reality. How one participates in the cycle of generosity fluctuates throughout one's lifetime, yet each experience, regardless of the chosen role at any particular moment, is life changing; which brings us back to the topic at hand. Change is possible.*

*Let us pause just for a moment and remember one of the primary messages of The Book of Joy. Joy exists! Please bring this message of truth to the forefront of your mind, and more importantly, into the wellspring of your heart, for it is an essential component of everything*

> *you do and desire to do in this and every life experience in which you choose to engage. Joy does exist. Accept this truth please, and trust with humble gratitude that a reservoir of glowing, empowering energy resides within you, propelling you forward in all your preferred, chosen, and intended quests."*

"Oh my dear friends, you are all such a treasure to me. And I so appreciate your concern. More than anything I am just so grateful for each and every one of you. These friendships mean the world to me...you guys are my family! So thank you for checking on me. And I will try to figure out what is going on with me.

First let me say, I am okay! I am in no distress whatsoever. In all honesty, I don't really have words for what I'm feeling, which may be the reason why I've been so non-verbal this evening. I have been present, at least I think I have, but the stories shared this evening left me in a state of awe. I am mystified by what's going on. I'm humbled to be participating in what seems to be an extremely significant phenomenon, and I am grateful...and joyful! You know our teacher used this descriptor often tonight, and the idea of joy being an energy source makes sense to me. Numerous times during our storytelling experiences, I experienced joy in a way that was really new to me, and it's given me pause. It makes me wonder if I've ever really identified joy as a factor in my life before, and I don't know the answer to that yet. Perhaps, I have, but I'm not sure. It seems to be an essential ingredient in our wellness, and vitally important to our future well being too. We must come to understand the dynamics of this powerful energy if we are to assist in the changes that are undoubtedly coming. I'm excited! I'm onboard!" A look of shyness crossed the speaker's face. The exuberance just demonstrated waned, and then an extremely intimate admission was offered. "My friends, I feel called to do this work! It sounds crazy because I'm not even certain what the 'work' is, but I want to learn more about the energy of joy and I want to participate in bringing this important information to the world."

"You leave me breathless," declared Marilyn. "And I share the ache that's pulling at you. There's a reason we've all been brought together." Glancing about the room, her eyes embraced each friend. "Some day," she continued, "I hope a book is written about our shared experiences. Who would ever believe this tale of synchronicity?" Marilyn's question made her laugh, and then she concluded, "But it's a story that needs to be told!"

"Indeed, it does!" exclaimed Everett. "We're not the only ones having this remarkable experience." Pausing as if to collect his thoughts, Everett acknowledged his mind was racing with ideas. His thoughts included using the book to connect with others having similar experiences, as well as utilizing it as a teaching tool revealing the possibilities and challenges awaiting us. So many ideas, all of which needed to be addressed, and yet, the guidance of their teacher prevailed. "Rather than allowing all my thoughts to distract us, I want to remain focused on the topic of feeling called to do this work. I'm grateful both of you talked about this, because it helped me crystallize my own thoughts and feelings. The ache, as you referred to it, has been nagging at me since we began these meetings. I wanted answers!" He expressed demandingly. "And clarification and irrefutable proof that would validate my feelings. Unfortunately, a formal employment offer doesn't accompany a calling. At least I haven't received one yet!" Everett's humor opened the door for several more stories. Jan admitted she wanted an email confirming she had been called to assist The Island. And Pat imagined receiving a Certificate of Acceptance in the mail that she could hang on the wall. The truth was everyone wanted some type of validation that they were indeed being called to assist with this incredible project. They wanted to know 'it' was real.

Marilyn began to giggle, and I joined her. Then the room was filled with laughter. "Eight friends!" she interrupted the laughter. "Eight very good friends, all sitting in a circle wanting proof about his or her belief that he or she has been called to participate in a project intended to help humankind…what's ridiculous about this scenario?" asked Marilyn with an incredulous tone as she looked around the room. "Dear Ones, each person in this room has seven other trusted friends who also believe they were called to do this work. Folks, how much proof do we need? Every one of us has already offered support to our seven friends, and will continue to do so regarding these individual callings. And still, each of us wonders about our own right to believe we have been called to this task. My friends, this is nonsense!" With great flair, Marilyn shifted her position. Sitting rigidly erect and flaunting an air of sophistication, she declared, "I hereby announce to all present in this room I believe each of you has been called to a higher task. And likewise, I announce my acceptance that I too have been so called."

*A passage from*
***The Book of Joy: The Invitation***
*(Chapter Five)*

> *"Indeed, joy really does exist, as does the reality of possibility, and each gains vitality when the other is accepted and trusted. Acquaintance with the joyful energy within opens doors to more possibilities, and familiarity with the reality of possibility strengthens acceptance of and trust in the dynamic relationship between these two remarkable existences, which in turn allows one's own trust in and acceptance of these unbelievably believable existences to solidify. Through these wonderful experiential relationships, one begins to accept the reality that change is possible."*

"Marvelous! Your affirmation of our efforts inspires me!" responded Dee. Applause and similar comments circled the joy-filled room. Little did Marilyn know her playful ad lib would have such a significant influence, but it most certainly did!

"Well, perhaps our meeting has come to a close with yet another extremely important revelation. We all need support and reassurances about this journey we have undertaken. Marilyn's humorous gesture certainly demonstrated one of the reasons we've been brought together. Can you imagine what it would be like to pursue this path without one another's support? Whew, I can't! Once again, I am overwhelmed with a sense of gratitude for this evening's gathering, and I too want to state my belief in what is happening among us. We are being called, and I am so glad to be taking this journey with my dearest, most trusted friends." With that said, goodbyes and hugs were exchanged, as the group of friends escorted one another to the front door.

As my friends departed each to their respective homes, my heart felt full. *So blest am I!* My thoughts unspoken did not go unnoticed.

*"Indeed!"* came a familiar voice. *"All are blest! Thank you for making your home available for these gatherings. I am most grateful for your generous hospitality."* Nodding as if my companion could be seen, I replied.

"It is my pleasure. Feels like my house has been waiting a lifetime for this opportunity. It was a good gathering. Good night, my friend!" I said switching off the lights.

"Good night, dear house of mine. Once again, you have served well. I hope you enjoyed the company."

# ~ Chapter Three ~

*"Old Friend, we desire communication and connection. Are you available?"* The words easily heard and joyfully received were answered immediately.

*"I am always available, My Friends. May I assume you were pleased with the evening's activities?"* The one, who now was frequently referred to as the esteemed teacher, was confident his companions were as excited about the night's development as was he. His only reservation about his personal participation was how little was required of him as a teacher. His students, people of good character, were accepting with grace and enthusiasm the responsibility for becoming future leaders and teachers. Their willingness to engage with this project of unusual origins filled the teacher's heart with gratitude. Never had he imagined their response would be so overwhelmingly positive.

*"We too are astounded by their passionate response. Although our hope for their assistance was founded in our great trust in humankind, we are nonetheless overwhelmed by their earnest and rapid response."*

*"Indeed,"* replied the teacher. *"Their ability to address issues courageously is most reassuring. And then, stabilization transpires quickly, and they move onto the next topic. Yes, we have been most fortunate in awakening the callings within this group for they will indeed be of extreme assistance in transforming the energy of this populace in the days ahead. The plans made long ago are coming to fruition."*

*"It is of the future we wish to speak, Old Friend. Your role as teacher is changing and demands that you take charge as leader to this group. Although they already perceive you as such, you do not yet perceive yourself in this role. We come to apprise you of your calling, Old Friend. As one who has come to assist the masses of humankind, you must broaden your scope to include that of leader. Breathe into this! It is not a role which is new to you; however, even those who have lived many lives as a leader encounter the new experience with reservations. The time is upon you, Old Friend. Thus, many of your oldest and dearest Friends have come to this gathering to remind you of your truth and to offer support as you transform from your present role into your next role. We surround you now and hold the space for your transformation process."* Even though the able traveler had experienced such transformations countless times before, as was always the case in these humbling experiences, a moment of uneasiness filled his being. Inhaling fully, he aspired to live into the transition, and as he did, doubts filtered into his ethereal thoughts.

*"Will doubts be forever with us?"* he quietly asked his Companions.

*"They will be, as long as they are needed,"* came a response.

Chuckling, the esteemed teacher now experiencing the role of student, once again recognized another aspect in the universal process of evolutionary development. *"I suppose they are here for a reason,"* he mused. *"As long as doubts serve a purpose, they will continue to exist."*

*"And how do they serve you now, Dear Friend? How are they assisting you?"*

Accepting this moment as one of extreme importance, the student lived into the experience, carefully pondering the question. *"Actually, I believe the benefits of my doubts are numerous. Because they have surfaced at this particular point in time, I am able to receive wisdom and loving support from those who are my Friends of long standing. Therefore, I am fortified by the connection, and reassured that All Will Be Well! As a result of this tender moment, I feel enriched, enlivened, and healed. What a remarkable insight! Our doubts are actually opportunities for healing if we allow them to be. Oh, My Dear Friends, what a blessing this encounter is. I am most grateful."*

*"And do your doubts require answers?"* inquired a loving voice who spoke for many. The student heeded the question with the respect it deserved and realized the theme of his doubts was one that surfaced every time a new opportunity of service arose. The sensation of awareness washed over him. Instantly, the purpose of experiencing doubts was comprehended.

*"I presume, Dear Ones, it is necessary to visit our doubts on a regular basis so that we can remember who we really are. The theme of unworthiness seems to arise each time another opportunity to be of service presents itself. Can I do this? Am I good enough? Will I be able to serve to my fullest potential? Will I please the One whom I serve?*

*Goodness, My Dear Friends, the desire to be all that is intended wells up within us when we are called, does it not? Perhaps, these are ongoing, never-ending questions. Perhaps, not! Only time will tell.*

*To answer your question, Dear Friends, I am satisfied with the heartfelt connection existing between us in this moment and I am extremely grateful for your presence and loving support. I am what I am, My Friends. And with the help of All That Is, I am enough!"*

*"Your wisdom is your guide, Dear Friend, and we are here now, always, and forever. Please do not hesitate to call upon us. We are but a breath away!*

*In peace be!"*

# ~ CHAPTER FOUR ~

"Good morning, Master Sun! As always, it is an honor to be in your presence. Please excuse my reclined position, but today, I simply was unable to rise early enough to meet you on the trail. I apologize for my fatigue, but the days have been long. And profoundly meaningful! I am most grateful for your presence this morning, My Friend." Lounging in bed beyond my usual early morning rising seemed decadent, but also needed. *The days have been so full. I think a morning of quiet contemplation and assimilation is necessary.* Satisfied with my decision to enjoy the sunrise from the comfort of my bedroom, I marveled at the day's breaking light…a masterful display of ever changing beauty!

*"My good friend, you deserve a day of rest,"* declared an unseen voice. Agreeing by means of my inner voice, I refrained from initiating conversation. Although communication with the invisible ones was always welcome, I was enjoying my present circumstances.

*So much has been going on lately that a morning alone is refreshing.* Hearing those thoughts articulated in my mind, I felt overtaken by embarrassment. Remembering that my unseen companions were quite skilled in overhearing conversations from within, I feared my words might have been hurtful. "I trust my words were not taken negatively, my friends. The truth is I am embracing the morning, my life, just as it is in this present moment, and it is good!" I announced joyfully. "I am happy. And your presence, along with the blessing of the glorious sunrise, all contribute to my peaceful state of mind. There is much for which to be grateful."

*"We would delight in hearing more about your gratitudes, if you are inclined to share them,"* arrived the invitation through its curious means of transmission. Recognizing my list of gratitudes was growing, I assessed it was beneficial to share them with these Dear Companions.

"My friends, I will speak aloud, for it is easier for me to do so. I am extremely grateful for my life as it is presently unfolding. I am more aware than ever before, and this allows me to enjoy every day occurrences with much fuller appreciation. The sunrises, as you well know, have always been special to me, and now, it is even more so. Truthfully, I believe there have been moments of communication between the sun and myself. Perhaps this sounds ludicrous, but it feels real. There are times when my appreciation of the polychromatic performances is so deeply experienced that I believe the sun actually responds to my feelings and expressions of gratitude. I am convinced this is real. My digression about the sunrise is actually extremely relevant to how deeply involved I feel with most of my interactions nowadays.

I feel exquisitely alive! My heart is filled with love for my Dear Friends and for the new relationships being made because of the changes transpiring in our lives. My intuitive skills seem to be expanding, which is absolutely invigorating. And each morning, I wake up wondering what marvelous experiences will come my way. Life is very full right now, but not with busyness. Life is so deliciously rich because it is not filled with the distractions of busyness. How wonderful is that! Instead, life is full with a sense of purpose, meaningfulness, and heartfelt connections of such a magnitude that I am still reeling from these blessings. My attitude about the future is more uplifted, hopeful, and optimistic. I feel blest in every way, and I am most grateful."

*"You are in transition, Dear Friend, and you are growing beautifully. We too are grateful for what is transpiring within you and your friends, as well as the reestablishment of old relationships that span eons of time and countless realms within this never-ending existence. So good it is to be in the presence of all of you once again. For us, this is what those of your realm refer to as a dream come true. In truth, it is the result of well-made plans, which are now moving forward to aid the Earth and all her inhabitants. Together, our efforts will have greater outreach and our combined influence will affect change more rapidly. This pleases all who love the planet Earth and her children. Her health demands everyone's attention, and with your assistance, this will come to pass.*

*Because of your willingness to serve, you have assisted us in our efforts to restore the Earth to a state of renewed wellness. Words can never express our gratitude; however, we are aware of your expanding intuitive and empathic abilities. Thus, we know you will understand the gratitude residing within us."*

Silence engulfed the room as awareness was exchanged via a means referred to as existential communication. Without any utterance of sound made, the transmission of emotional gratitude filled my essence, creating a union of connection beyond description. What the Companions shared, I received. What they felt, I felt. And for a moment in time, I was one with those who remained unseen. The intimacy experienced during the interaction was unforgettable.

And once again, my life was enhanced and expanded by another unusual circumstance that at the same time challenged my sense of reality of the world. It seemed this new world I was entering brought new encounters with the unusual on a daily basis and what was once unusual was becoming less so with each new adventure. I reveled in the moment, enjoying another wave of gratitude. *I hope you can feel this, My Friends. Another round of gratitude especially for you and all!*

*"We did indeed! This is a wonderful means of connection, is it not? All senses activated and equally experienced by all participating in the shared union. A remarkable gift that naturally evolved over time."*

*A passage from*
***The Book of Joy: The Invitation***
*(Chapter Five)*

> *"Please take a moment, when it is possible, to ponder your possibilities. From our discussions, it seems there may be some new possibilities in your life that deserve consideration. For instance, right now, you may choose to capture the moment by making a decision on your behalf. You may, if you so desire, choose to live a life filled with joy. You may choose to fully and joyfully believe, trust, and accept that your life is abundant with possibilities because of the joyful energy within, which inspires and empowers you to embrace change.*
>
> *Indeed, Dear Reader, change is possible...and it begins with you. Great change is needed in the moments ahead. Will you accept the reality of this present moment and consider the invitation extended through The Book of Joy? You are needed. We are all needed. Will you, just for the moment, take the lead and accept the invitation to participate in an act of generosity? If you take the lead now, perhaps your actions will inspire another to do the same in the next moment, leading to another similar action and reaction in the next moment, and on, and on until enough momentum is reached for constancy, at which time the greater change will be achieved.*
>
> *Take a deep breath, give this invitation the heartfelt consideration it deserves and then make the decision that calls to you."*

"Exactly how does this work? What are the factors involved that actually facilitate the processes of intuition or telepathy or existential communication? And why are some individuals able to participate in these types of communication while others cannot? Please excuse my barrage of questions, but I would be very grateful to know the answers to this." In the distance, a familiar laugh was heard, and soon thereafter, the highly respected teacher and friend arrived in the sitting area of my bedroom.

*"I come without notice, my friend. May I remain in visible form for this important conversation?"* His question made me laugh since he was well known for materializing out of nowhere at any given time. I presumed his modesty was related to the time of day and the fact I was still in bed.

"Of course, you can stay if you are not offended by my baggy pajamas," I announced jumping out of bed. He responded by welcoming me into my favorite sacred space. Before entering the field, I bowed with respect, as always, and my guest did the same. "So, honored teacher, are you going to expound upon my question?"

*"Actually, I am here to discuss matters of the future, my friend, and in so doing, perhaps you will acquire more information about this simple means of communication that still remains mysterious to you."*

"Well, I must admit your intentions give me pause. Should I be afraid of this discussion regarding the future?" I was aware my energy had shifted and felt disappointed in myself. *Why would you be frightened about this? This kind, gentle fellow has done nothing to cause such a reaction.* "I'm sorry, my friend. I do not understand what just came over me, but for a moment, I was apprehensive about our upcoming discussion. I need not be afraid, do I?"

*"No, you do not! However, I believe you will gain clarity about your initial response during our conversation. Before we continue, may I say it is a pleasure to be in your company again."* What I saw in his loving eyes gave me reassurance. The tone of his voice and his look of sincerity quieted my earlier unrest, leaving me feeling at ease, and the love emanating from his essence embraced my own and filled me with a sense of peace never known before.

"I am grateful for your presence as well. And I sense you are here for a reason that is far more important than my impetuous need to understand all the puzzling and inexplicable means of communication operating in the universe. It is fair to say I do not have a scientific mind, and the chances that I could understand such a discussion are unlikely. So why are you here, dear friend?"

*A passage from*
***The Book of Joy: The Invitation***
*(Chapter Six)*

> *"As you continue reading The Book of Joy, please remember a joyous and wonderful truth about the existence in which you exist… anything is possible!"*

*"My friend, you are more than you allow yourself to believe. What you know and what you will continue to learn may surprise you, for as just said, you are more than you believe you are."*

"You talk in riddles, which are intriguing, but riddles nonetheless. So I ask again, why are you here?" Looking closely upon his face, many questions came to mind. Is this how he looked before he passed? Or has he continued to age in his present condition? How long ago did he pass? I wonder who he was before he became who he is now.

*"I am who I have always been. Indeed, my form has changed countless times before, but always, the I that I am, remains within me. This is true for all who come into existence. Once we are brought into existence, we remain a part of existence for all existence to come.*

*This is not new information, my friend. You are aware of this truth, and at times, you have memories, which provide you with the evidence you so desire to have. Trust yourself, my friend. You are more than you think you are. In essence, you are what was, what is, and what is yet to be. You are all this, and you are more. Because this is the truth of your remarkable reality, you are indeed more than you appear to be, and as such, it is time for you to know more about the future in which you are intended to serve. As you already know, you are here for a reason. You have served well, my friend, but more is coming and more will be expected of you in the near future."* Noticing the change in his student's vital signs, the teacher quickly came to a halt. *"Breathe, my friend! You are well, even though your anxiety level has soared. Please listen with the ears of your heart. All is well!"*

"Thank you for those words of reassurance. And I believe what you say is true. I do believe we are all well, and furthermore, I believe the future is inviting us to new realms of wellness that will include not only humans, but the Earth herself and all her other inhabitants. I honestly believe we are on the brink of great change…and we must all step forward and do our part for the greater good." A chuckle surfaced from the depths of my soul reminding me that my words did not sound as if they were my own. "Excuse me, my friend, but I am laughing at myself, because the words just spoken with such authority sound more like your words rather than mine."

*"Perhaps, my friend, these words are yours, mine, and others'. Regardless of their origins, these words speak a truth that must come forward so all the peoples of Earth are informed of what is coming. You are here for a reason, my friend, and it is time for you to accept the leadership role awaiting you. Much more do you already know about the future than you realize, but your awareness is merely associated with timing, and time is most assuredly on our side, dear one.*

*When you hear words coming forward from within you, do not be afraid, for the words are evidence of your reason for being. Indeed there will be times when you are surprised, and even in awe, but the truth is, the words resided within you for safe keeping until the precise moment in time when they were to be released to the one who came before you. You are not in charge of the timing of these moments of presentation, nor are you in awareness of the recipient until the words flow from your essence. However, the words, the messages, waiting within you, know exactly when they are to be released and to whom. This is your calling, my friend. You are here to assist in the deliverance of the Word. Worry not when, where, or how the situation arises, simply trust that you will be in the right place at the right time to deliver the words to the one who is intended to receive the message."*

"You do have a way about you," I whispered. A curious look crossed my guest's face. "The uneasiness, which rushed through me before when you mentioned the future, has totally dissipated. I feel at peace. And I am aware a delivery has just been received. You do good work, my friend! The message has been presented, heard, and understood. And I am very grateful to you. Thank you for reminding me of my calling." He nodded in his usual gentlemanly manner, began to speak, and then stopped himself. His eyes did not leave mine.

A rush of awareness inserted itself into my consciousness and left me certain in regards to what my friend was thinking. Grinning, I remarked, "Yes, your hesitation is founded in truth. Of course, I would like to know more about the leadership role you allude to, but I assume the information will come in time. Am I correct?" Returning my smile with one of his own, he nodded again. And then added.

*"No time like the present,"* he laughed. *"Are you ready to receive more of your message?"*

"Oh, why not!" I said humorously. "Tell me everything, Honored Messenger!" Our shared lightheartedness made the process joyful!

*A passage from*
***The Book of Joy: The Invitation***
*(Chapter Six)*

> *"Exactly what will reveal itself is yours to discover and how you proceed is yours to choose. And indeed, whether or not you continue is also yours to discern. However, as you enter into your discernment process, please remember these words of wisdom. During those moments when you are deeply settled and oblivious to the other matters that so frequently interrupt you, you are not alone. Even during those precious and joyous moments of peace of mind, you are lovingly, quietly, and delightfully accompanied."*

*"Everything may be more than we can achieve in one discussion, but it is my privilege to remind you of a wonderful truth about the existence in which you exist. Again, please accept this as a reminder of what you already know. When you hear words that are extremely familiar, it is because you already know the truth of the message being presented to you, and even though you may find the message repetitive, please accept that an underlying purpose exists for its being presented to you once again. Reject the tendency to discount or disregard a message of familiarity. If it is being delivered to you again, ponder why. Remember, there are no coincidences. Everything happens for a reason."*

Still remaining in my jovial mood, I quipped, "Do you really believe that coincidences never transpire? Please, my friend, surely there must be times when an incidence happens, and it is simply a coincidence. Surely, there must be a reason for the common coincidence!"

"*Indeed!*" My joyful guest retorted, "*There absolutely is a reason for, as you call it, the common coincidence. Ponder this, Dear One! When a so-called coincidence, common or uncommon, unfolds, ask why! Everything happens for a reason, even those incidences that many choose to refer to as coincidences!*" His manner was entertaining, and I could not resist enjoying his enthusiasm; however, his good spirits did not conceal the truth of his message. In his lighthearted way, this wonderful character from parts unknown had delivered another powerful message.

"That is a message worthy of a great deal of consideration. Looking back, I wonder how many times I've ignored opportunities by simply identifying an event as a coincidence. Goodness, this nugget of truth is too important to keep to myself. May I share it with others?"

*"Indeed, messages of truth are for the one and for the many. In this particular instance, you were given information important to your own development, and as you already recognize, this is information that will assist others as well. The purpose of the word is fulfilled when it reaches those for whom it is intended to serve. Sometimes, it is intended for the one, and other times, it is intended for the masses.*

My thoughts, taking me to places I did not want to go, caused me to think about changing the topic. Assuming this notion was no coincidence, I broached a topic that created a great deal of discomfort for me. "Your presence has been a remarkable gift! My friends and I have learned so much from you; our lives have changed because of the time you have shared with us. You have become part of our family. We are so grateful for everything you have done for us." My words faded into a whisper. I didn't want to continue, but knew it was necessary, "I fear you will not be here much longer. Am I correct? Will you be leaving us soon?"

*His eyes never veered from mine. "Your intuition is keen, my friend. Selfishly, this subject is one I would rather not broach, because I have thoroughly enjoyed my time with you and your beloved friends. Such goodness resides within all of you. It has been most gratifying to be in your presence. This has been a memorable experience. Nonetheless, we must address the reality of my departure.*

*As stated earlier, it is my privilege to bring you information about the truth of your existence, and then, our conversation briefly and intentionally guided us to other matters of importance. That was no coincidence, my friend. It was intended and necessary for you to be reminded about the repetitive nature of significant messages. They cannot be ignored because you have heard the messages before, nor can they be dismissed just because your mind announces it already knows about a particular message. If a message is repeated, even to the point of annoyance, it is happening for a reason. It is not a coincidence! And it is not an error!*

*This takes us to the message you are intended to receive today regarding a truth about existence. My friend, you are never alone! Please do not take this message lightly, for its meaning, as you well know, reaches far beyond the limited scope of your own planet. Unfortunately, even those such as yourself, who understand the meaning of this message, fail at times to remember its significance. Because of this, it is essential you hold this truth close to your heart at all times, and never forget its importance. You are not alone! Regardless of your location or your circumstances, you are never alone. This message is for YOU, and it is for all you encounter.*

*So, my dear friend, when you ponder my departure, please remember today's important message. You are never alone. I am always available to you and your friends, and although our time together will be less frequent, I am but a breath away."* My heart sank briefly before his words took hold.

"I will remember!" My voice was less than a whisper, but I knew my friend heard my response. "And I will share this with my friends immediately, so we can remind each other of this truth, when our memories fade." A moment of contemplation passed before I could continue. "It's odd!" I said peering deeply into his eyes. "As you well know, this is a familiar message, for it has been repeated countless times before; and yet, awareness of its reality slips away so easily. Why are humans inclined to forget such a vitally important piece of information? It doesn't make sense!"

*"No, it doesn't make sense, but it is what it is! Take comfort in knowing you are not unique in this particular behavior. For reasons yet to be fully comprehended, this tendency seems to be problematic throughout the human species. To remedy this puzzling situation, frequent reminders are strategically set in motion to keep you apprised of the remarkable truth about your existence. Hopefully, these interventions serve their purpose. Never were you intended to live without awareness of your fellow beings. You are never alone! Isn't that a reason for rejoicing?"*

"Yes, it is! And honestly," I interjected, "our lives have profoundly changed since you and your companions entered into our circle of friends. I suppose you have always been here with us, but having validation of your presence changes one's perspective about oneself and about one's place in the universe. The truth is, my friend, the eight of us have been very fortunate. We've all led meaningful lives, and we've always had one another to turn to for support. We've been blest! But your presence brought us an entirely new energy…a new way of perceiving life! And we are so grateful! We have renewed meaning and purpose in our lives…we have a reason for being more extensive than we thought before! Knowing that you and others similar to you are here with us changes how we are in the world. There is so much more to learn…to do! We are eager to participate. It is comforting to know we are not alone!" Feeling inept at expressing my gratitude, I paused to face the reality of what was transpiring. I knew the inevitable was coming.

"It has been a joy working with you. You will be missed, my friend."

*"My heart is also filled with joy. Such a good time we have shared!"* he remarked. *"And, there will be more delightful times to enjoy as well. Please remember this! We are not finished with our work here, my friend. Much remains*

*to be done, and our collaborative endeavors will continue. I look forward to more joyful productivity!"* His smile dispelled my inclination to experience sadness; there was no need for such reflection. His presence was eternal, and that was a joyous reality to remember.

*A passage from*
***The Book of Joy: The Invitation***
*(Chapter Seven)*

> *"Joy exists! Assuming we can continue from this conceptual foundation, then how do we proceed? Many aspects are wise to explore including what brings joy into your present life situation, as well as understanding the impediments that restrict you from experiencing joy or which diminish your experience of the joy that is about you. As you can see, exploring the reality of joy necessarily demands you to reach inward and discover more about yourself. Just as when existence learned to ponder its existence, so too must you learn to appreciate the process of contemplating your present existence; i.e., you must face and address your present way of being within your current circumstances."*

Tears moistened the corners of my eyes as I imagined his absence. Even though I believed in his eternal presence and understood he would still be available, a loss was keenly felt. I laughed aloud as a thought fleeted through my mind. "My friend," I declared, "It seems I've grown accustomed to your comings and goings, and I will miss your impromptu visits. And I must confess, I will miss your materialized form. My heart aches, because I so desire to embrace you before you leave."

*"The desire is mutual and I am presently enjoying the moment, as if it were really possible."* His eyes closed briefly, as did mine, and the hug was internally experienced. *"You are a wonderful hugger, my friend, and I will remember this fond embrace for all times to come."*

A smile replaced my tears. "That was the most remarkable experience I've ever had! What a gift! I don't know how you managed that, but your embrace was physically felt, and it will never be forgotten." The room fell silent, as I became lost to my thoughts and emotions.

*A passage from*

***The Book of Joy: The Invitation***

*(Chapter Seven)*

> *"Pause for a moment, if needed, and recognize as did existence so very long ago, that the art of pondering can be a most amiable and interesting companion. In other words, Dear Reader, to fully understand Self and one's relationship with joy requires time, commitment, and a desire to know more...more about Self, more about joy, and more about the relationship existing between Self and joy. How better to learn more about these engaging topics than to actively pursue more information about each one."*

"Curious it is to hold joy and loss both at the same time," I noted. "Joy makes loss more bearable and loss is less depleting when in the company of joy. Because the memories of our recent experiences together are so presently fixed in my mind, I am able to face your departure with less anxiety and heartache. Another important lesson! Even in times of struggle, one must not lose one's sense of joy. It is always there, residing within, waiting to bring clarity and hopefulness back into our lives. You are a gift, my friend! And will continue to be every time thoughts of you and our interactions come to the forefront of my mind. My heart is full!"

*"As is mine!"* he replied. *"It has been a privilege to work with you again, dear friend. Always, I am grateful when we have the opportunity to serve on missions of mutual interest."*

"I suspect we've done this many times before," My statement came with a raised eyebrow and a look that indicated certainty, but also wanted validation.

*"Many times is an accurate assumption!"* came his quiet reassurance.

"It is time for you to leave, my friend. I trust you will return to say goodbye to everyone."

*"Indeed, I will. And yes,"* he continued, *"it is time for me to evaporate!"* His boyish grin lightened the occasion of his departure. Rolling my eyes at his comment, I was taken by surprise, when he added, *"My friend, I ask permission to take my leave of thee."*

Prepared, but not ready to say goodbye, I did that which was necessary. Inhaling deeply and with palms joined before my face, I bowed to my esteemed teacher and friend, and quietly whispered, "Namaste, Dear Friend!" The gesture was returned and maintained as he faded into nothingness. Another deep breath was necessary, as I attempted to adjust to the absence of his visible presence. Trusting my friend was still there made it easier.

*A passage from*
***The Book of Joy: The Invitation***
*(Chapter Seven)*

> *"And now you must continue. Your present participation in discovering the truth about joy and the powerful life-changing effects it has is one way of being part of the solution to global unwellness. You are needed. We are all needed. Please continue."*

# ~ Chapter Five ~

*"Old Friend, we desire conversation with you. May we approach?"*

*"Indeed!"* came the reply from the intermediary serving both those of Earth and those beyond the awareness of those of Earth. *"I hope my interaction with the dear friend met with your approval."*

*"Impressive! This one understands much and is in a position to be extremely influential, as is everyone in this group of friends. Your time with these good people was exemplary. Are you satisfied with the progress made?"*

*"Yes, I am. They are highly motivated individuals, who are cognizant of a sense of calling being defined within each of them. Rarely are they of low mood, but when one wanes, another is readily available to take the lead. Each is creative in his or her own way and their ability to share and grow from heartfelt conversations is truly remarkable. Invariably, their discussions are both noteworthy and inspirational. They are also of fine character, demonstrating amiable natures and compassionate ways. We are extremely fortunate all of them responded to their callings. I believe they are prepared to take on their known and yet-to-be remembered commitments."*

*"Agreed! You will, of course, be monitoring their progress and assisting when needed. We too will maintain careful observation of their daily activities. We are most hopeful Old Friend. This group shows great potential. Energy such has theirs can alter the course of humankind. We are indeed hopeful. Please continue your exiting process. You have served well!"*

*A passage from*

***The Book of Joy: The Invitation***

*(Chapter Eight)*

> *"Factors involved in the creation, continuance, and/or dissolution of your experience with happiness, whether these influences are external or internal, play a vital role in your ability to access the energy of joy residing within you. Realizing that present, past and other factors may enhance or diminish one's possibility of accessing joy emphasizes the need for greater understanding of your circumstances. Joy exists. If you presently reside in conscious awareness of the joy*

*within and about you, sing praises. If you do not, hold fast to the truth that exists for everyone in existence.*

*Joy does exist! Joy does exist! Joy does exist!*

*This simple truth is true for all in existence, including you. We must all must learn how to access our joyful existence now in this moment with intention, faith, and absolute certainty that it does exist. Joy does exist and it is intended for and available to everyone in existence."*

# ~ Chapter Six ~

"Good morning, Marilyn! Have I called too early?" Calling before 7 o'clock in the morning definitely challenged my rules of courtesy, as well as my concerns about being intrusive, but knowing Marilyn's passion for early morning walks minimized the risk of my impromptu call.

"Are you kidding?" she replied with the energy of someone who was up and about and ready to greet the day. "I admit to running late this morning, but the trail awaits us. Will you join me?" And with that invitation, we each headed out our respective front doors to join paths on the way to the eastern trailhead. Ten minutes later we were greeting each other on the corner of our intersecting streets.

"Okay, tell me everything!" Marilyn was not one who denied her impatience or squelched the curiosity bubbling within her. She playfully teased and joked with me. "This isn't about exercise! Something's happened! You wouldn't dare risk calling so early unless something had happened. So fess up! What new and amazing thing is unfolding now?" As we progressed through the neighborhood to the outskirts of town, I shared the events of the previous evening. Unfortunately, reliving the conversation from the night before made my emotions surface again. Needless to say, I wasn't at my best, and my friend felt the consequences of my own struggles with the latest news.

"He's leaving!" she uttered in disbelief. "Surely not! We've just begun! And we've come so far in such a short period of time." Witnessing the look of confusion on my friend's face, I hastened to comfort her, but her desperation needed its own voice. And then the questions came in rapid fire. "Have we disappointed him? Or his companions? Have they decided we're not up for this? Surely not!" she repeated again. "I really thought he was happy and pleased with our progress." A childlike expression crossed her face, one of sadness and disappointment that awakened similar feelings within me, none of which were ready for articulation. Silence engulfed us as we walked towards the hills and rising sun, each consumed by our own individual sense of loss. Grieving, a lonely affair with complicated emotional reactions, requires company, but too often seeks solitude instead.

I looked towards the horizon for solace. The glimmering showcase of colors peeking over the distant hills brought renewed hope. Once again, as always, Master Sun devotedly arrived without exception. And with its arrival, I knew the grieving would pass, the reality of the situation would be accepted, and life would continue. The Master Sun's presence illuminated the similarity between its presence and the presence of our esteemed teacher. Even on those cloudy mornings that masked its presence, you knew the sun was there. Likewise, we had learned from our encounters with our new friend that he too was always present. Whether he was visible or not, his energy would always be near and available to us if we called upon him. Indeed, the rising sun was announcing the arrival of another day and reassuring us life would most assuredly go on.

"We're going to be fine, Marilyn. Even though we will miss his presence, we must remember everything he so ably shared with us. He will be with us. We are not alone!" My words were not eloquent, but they spoke a truth my friend and I both needed to hear. Nodding in agreement, Marilyn quickly wiped away a few remaining tears still moistening her cheeks.

"I was so enjoying his company," she uttered. "His presence ignited a surge of energy within me that was exhilarating. I have felt so alive! And I don't want to lose this feeling! Or the momentum our group has developed! We really are establishing a foundation of work that has the potential for assisting many people. I'm not just imagining this, am I?" She looked to me for confirmation, which was readily given.

"No, you're not! And fortunately, our group is capable of moving forward without his daily encouragement. He's prepared us well! Marilyn, we are never going to forget his presence or his teachings. Even though his upcoming departure is a shock, perhaps it is necessary. Maybe, we need him to leave so we will actually take the next steps." Listening to my own words, I realized we really were ready to initiate the next phase of our work. Although difficult to admit, it was time for us to accept our own capabilities; it was time to proceed.

"You're right, of course!" responded my friend. "I know we must accept responsibility for the tasks that are calling us. We have a treasure trove of information to share, and we must do so. We cannot keep this wealth of knowledge to ourselves." A tone of resolve was reflected in Marilyn's voice. Her grieving had not overridden the sense of commitment residing strongly within, and still, the grieving process was evident. "I do not like goodbyes, my friend," she confided in a whispery manner. "Our gatherings have brought me such pleasure. Reuniting with our dear friends has magnified my outlook on life. Please understand, life was good before, but it is significantly better now." Slowing her pace, she turned to me and admitted, "I didn't realize how much I had missed everyone. Truthfully, I didn't even realize there was something missing. Life had become so busy that time didn't allow for the luxury of assessing how life really was. I was busy. And each day that followed was filled with more busyness, and I simply assumed all was well, which it was for the most part, but now, I am aware something definitely was absent." Laughing quietly, as if to herself, she added, "Perhaps, it was me-e-e!" Then poking me in the ribcage, she continued, "How can one be so highly functioning without actually being consciously present? I was competent and extremely capable of focusing on matters of busyness, and yet, I was not truly present in the moment. How are we able to manage that? How can we be so busily and effectively doing without being consciously present?" Without expecting an answer, Marilyn turned to me and grinned. "Needless to say, many books have been and are being written about this topic, so we don't have to come up with a definitive answer for this issue on our walk today."

"Perhaps tomorrow," I quipped. Joining arms, we giggled together for a few yards before we were stopped in our tracks by the beauty of the view. We had just reached the bend on the trail that provides an overlook of both the verdant dale and a spectacular sight of Master Sun rising over the most distant hill. "Well, this gives one an opportunity to just be, doesn't it?" Marilyn mumbled something that resembled agreement before we both fell silent.

As the two old friends embraced the view, they were fully engaged in the moment. Other matters didn't matter. All that existed was the present moment and the present was more than either could ever imagine, for as is known by all in existence, the present is the only time of relevance regardless of where one exists at any given time within the expansive greater existence.

Time passed, as is its way, and as it did, the two friends were unaware of its passing, for each was consciously present only to the present moment.

*A passage from*
***The Book of Joy: The Invitation***
*(Chapter Nine)*

*"Begin now by becoming an active observer of your mind's incredible ways of acting, reacting, and interacting and record what you discover. Accept this opportunity as a gift for you to practice learning more about your mind and your relationship with this remarkable part of you. What you glean from this activity can be honed, modified and improved upon for future observations, for this one, right now, in this moment, is just the beginning. In essence this is the introductory phase*

> *of a new relationship between you and your mind. Dear Reader, the time has come for you to meet your mind, and likewise, it is time for your beautiful mind to meet its equally exquisite host."*

*"What a remarkable view, my friends! May I please join you?"* The familiar voice merged with our present moment, and for an unknown period of time, the three of us existed as if time did not matter. We enjoyed the shared experience and no other matters interrupted our precious union. *"It is a privilege to be with you in this way,"* favored the gentle man who had so enriched the lives of these two friends. *"You have successfully released the concerns and distractions of your lives and are fully, consciously present in this moment. Is this not a glorious way of being? I am most grateful for this opportunity, for it gives me a chance to express my gratitude to both of you. Please listen with the ears of your heart so you can fully experience my sincerity. Your presence is vitally important to the peoples of this planet. You and your family of friends are all valuable members of a task force who are specifically here to assist in a mission of extreme significance. Both of you already know this, but in this moment, your clarity of understanding is such that it allows me to speak more thoroughly about our collaborative mission. Old Friends, hear me, please. The time is now.*

*Mother Earth is in great need and she requires assistance from those who are the cause of her difficulties. Humankind is responsible for her declining health, and because of their mistreatment of her, the peoples of Earth are also now in grave danger of the consequences of her deterioration. The truth is tragically simple. She cannot improve without their assistance, and they cannot survive without hers.*

*My friends, you are here to assist with this rapidly advancing dilemma, and I am so grateful for your presence and your willingness to participate on the Earth's behalf. You are not alone in this effort. Others around the globe are also initiating action; however, every participant's participation matters. Progress is being made, which is most encouraging, and at the same time, others are blatantly denying and refusing to participate in this effort intended to save not only the planet, but also to save all her inhabitants. The point bluntly stated is this. Every person on this beautiful planet is needed. The efforts made by some cannot be counteracted by others. A joint effort is necessary and anything less than this will lead to profound and unspeakable consequences. Suffice it to say, every effort made on her behalf is in the best interest of everyone residing upon her. As such, my friends, every action you and your friends take will be of extreme assistance not only to all those you personally touch, but also to countless numbers you will never meet or have the privilege of knowing in this life experience. By shifting the energy of the people of this planet, the Earth's energy will shift as well, and she will be restored to a state of complete wellness. This is not a fantasy; it is a reality! It can and must be done!*

*You are desperately needed my friends, and I am so grateful to have worked with you again. This was not our first time to aid one another, and it surely will not be the last, nonetheless; I am so pleased to have been in your presence once again. It was a healing time for all, particularly for me. Words fail, my friends!"*

His message, quietly and gently presented, was indeed experienced in its totality. Marilyn and I heard his words, felt the emotions encompassing his sincerity, and understood the significance of his pronouncement at the depth of our souls. Perhaps it is best said in this manner. The fullness of his message was delivered and comprehended. Such an experience was not new to me, but it was one which makes me wonder if this is the true meaning of listening with the heart. Being truly present allows one to fully engage with a communication and its communicator. Too frequently, I'm afraid, our physical ears hear what is said, but because our minds are otherwise occupied, we are unable fully to process what is heard. This is not an indication of a hearing impairment, but is instead the malfunction of a distracted mind. The mind that is focused elsewhere interferes with our ability to listen with the ears of our heart, thereby limiting the extent of heartfelt connection.

*A passage from*
***The Book of Joy: The Invitation***
*(Chapter Eleven)*

> *"The journey continues with an exercise specifically designed to assist you in regaining command over your unruly mind. As your mind reads the previous sentence, notice how it reacts to being described as unruly. A brief review of your favorite dictionary will reveal numerous synonyms of this descriptor including wild, disobedient, unmanageable, and uncontrollable. How is your mind reacting to these not so complimentary words of assessment, and as you examine your mind's perception of this, what about yours? How are you reacting to this less than favorable account of your beautiful mind?"*

*"My dear friends, I will miss our frequent visits, but as you both know, we will meet again. Our paths are not separate. We simply proceed from different*

*planes of existence. When you need my assistance, I will be available, and when you need heartfelt connection, please remember, I am always with you."*

Unable to contain her emotions, Marilyn interjected. "Must you go?" she pleaded. "There is still so much to do, and we need you. Can't you stay a while longer?" His loving gaze quieted her even though she had much more to say.

*"I am not going anywhere!"* he reassured her. *"Our visits will be less frequent, but my presence will still be in this location. Even though you will not be able to see me, I will be here! By refocusing my work, you and your friends will be able to focus more upon your own tasks, which are many. You will be attending your work while I'm attending mine, and we will be able to aid one another when needed.*

*Trust me, my friend. This change is for the good of all involved. The sense of separation and loss will quickly dissipate as our work intensifies and more advancement will occur as we address our specific purposes. All is well, dear friend. Have faith in you and your friends! You are ready to proceed under your own guidance. Of this, I am most confident!"* Marilyn agreed with his assessment of their group. They were ready! And their list of tasks was long, so the obvious was staring her in the face.

"Oh, not to worry!" she declared demonstrating the confidence their teacher had professed. "You're absolutely right about us. We are sufficiently prepared to implement our plans and it is time for us to take action." Marilyn's words were concise, but more was brewing in her mind. Not knowing if she would have another opportunity to express her gratitude to this man, she felt compelled to take advantage of the moment.

"Honored Teacher, I will miss you. Although I have no clarity about previous encounters before this lifetime, it is apparent to me our relationship is of long-standing and intense connection." Softly, she added, "The bond of old still binds us. I am so grateful for this current connection. A simple thank you is not enough, but I don't know what else to say. Thank you, Dear Old Friend, for being my friend again! I trust you will be observing us from your location and keeping us informed as necessary." The friend of old nodded in agreement.

*"Rest assured, the bond does still bind us, and always shall. Friendship never dies; it merely transforms from one setting to another enjoying endless opportunities to express itself. I will indeed reach out to you and your friends if you are in need or if I am in need in accordance with the agreement made long ago."*

Witnessing the connection between Marilyn and her old friend took my breath away. The evidence of eternal existence was stunning; I marveled at our good fortune. *How blest we were to be participating in this remarkable project of interdimensional connection! How blest we were to be alive!*

*"Indeed!"* Our distinguished visitor once again demonstrated his exquisitely, refined listening skills by responding to my unspoken thoughts. *"We are all most fortunate to be alive. Regardless of our form, our location, or our standing along the evolutionary path of existence, we are all blessedly alive. Though it need not be said in this esteemed company, I will joyously exclaim this truth for the sheer beauty of its reality. Life is and always will be eternal!"*

*A passage from*
***The Book of Joy: The Invitation***
*(Chapter Twelve)*

> *"Joy does exist! Let us return to the topic of purpose with this not so subtle reminder...joy does exist! Our recent chapters have focused upon the characteristics of the mind as an introduction to its significant role in humankind's ability to enjoy the joy-filled energy that exists within. As earlier stated, joy does exist and has since its entrance into existence at a time when time did not exist in existence. Suffice it to say, the energy of joy has been around for a very long time."*

"My friend, shall we call another gathering so you can announce your departure to the others or will you apprise them individually? What is your preference?" My question lingered from the evening before. Before he could answer, I offered my own preference. "I believe a group meeting is necessary, but also understand each person will enjoy a private goodbye with you." Marilyn immediately agreed.

"Yes, the group needs an opportunity to process your departure. It will facilitate a faster recovery from the shock of your announcement." Recognizing we had shifted away from the extraordinary moment of connection back to the world of practicalities, I interrupted the process.

"May I bear witness to what is happening here? I completely altered the energy of our interaction by focusing our attention upon another matter of importance, but one that can wait. Let me facilitate for a moment, please. My friends, an extraordinary connection revealed itself between the two of you. Obviously, you have known each other for a very, very long time. May I ask how each of you are feeling about this now, in this present moment?" Marilyn turned to her old friend and he respectfully invited her to go first.

"How do I feel? Wow! There's a question!" In truth, Marilyn knew exactly how she was feeling but the internal struggle involving fear was warning her to be careful. *Don't talk about this out loud! You'll regret this!* The voice was oppressive, shaming, and one she hadn't heard in a long time. "Actually, I'm feeling happy! Maybe even joy! Obviously, I can't explain the intensity of connection because I have no memories to go along with these feelings, but I can honestly say I feel happy. And it's a wonderful feeling to experience.

Admittedly, there is a very old voice inside criticizing me for expressing my happiness. This voice seems to believe happiness is easily shattered and by sharing it aloud, you are putting yourself in jeopardy of losing the experience. Of course, the shaming voice dampers the moment anyway. But I choose not to believe the old voice, so I'm going to make new pathways here. I am blatantly announcing to both of you that I feel happiness…joyful. And I'm not going to allow old fears to diminish this wonderful sense of connection, which feels so preciously alive within me. I am happy!" she repeated again. Turning to her old friend, she gratefully expressed her appreciation for his presence in her present life. His smile expressed deep satisfaction.

*"Thank you, my dear friend! I am happy as well, and so very glad you are able to experience joy regarding this reunion. Your resistance to old habits is a wonderful sign of healing. I must admit it is easier for me on this plane of existence because I am fortunate to hold memories from previous experiences, which allows me to hold a more harmonious perspective of our earlier times together. It brings me great pleasure to see you in this present form recognizing the familiar while becoming acquainted with the new aspects of your present development. I am extremely happy and delighted for your growth…and for the privilege of being with you once again. This is a memorable moment! It is a blessing to be able to share our feelings about these very long-standing relationships. This is a rare occasion, my friends. Hopefully, in the future such encounters will become the norm rather than unusual events."* Turning toward me, our old friend expressed his gratitude for my facilitation of the conversation.

*"I am most grateful for your kindness. With able skill and efficiency, you refocused our attention upon the immediate concern. This conversation was necessary and healing for all of us."* Marilyn and I both acknowledged and agreed with his observations. If we had followed our human tendency to address the pragmatic aspect of upcoming events, we would have missed this

poignant moment. As it was, we experienced a special encounter and still had ample time to attend the reality of his departure.

*"Indeed, your assumption regarding another meeting is accurate. Reassurances about my departure must be given, as well as, additional information regarding the waning health of the planet and the tasks this crisis team has agreed to address. The meeting will be full. And of course, there will be time for farewells to be shared and appreciations to be expressed.*

*Another meeting is essential and we would be wise to pursue this with haste. I will leave you to organize the gathering. Shall we convene this evening?"* There was no need to speculate about other options. The group would, of course, respond to this initiative.

*A passage from*
***The Book of Joy: The Invitation***
*(Chapter Twelve)*

> *"It is time to pause and rest. Although it may be difficult to quiet the mind, please strive to do so. While the commentary presented is truthful and requires no aggrandizement, the mind may attempt to do so. Urge your mind to rest, please."*

Little more was said before the dimensional traveler disappeared from one plane of existence and presumably reappeared in another. The comings and goings of their friend had become so extraordinarily ordinary that jaws no longer dropped to the floor. Facial expressions actually remained rather nonplussed except for a casual grin of approval.

"Well, shall we continue our walk or head back?" Marilyn's question was not easily answered. Feeling compelled to immediately connect with their friends was a driving force for returning home; however, neither of them wanted to leave the trail. Knowing that phone service would be available at the next rise, they continued walking. As agreed, when they reached the highpoint, phone calls were made and the gathering was scheduled for 7:00 pm. With that task done, the walkers felt released to continue their morning ritual.

"Marilyn, do you mind if we walk in silence for a while?"

"You're reading my mind!" she responded. In agreement they proceeded each in the privacy of their respective minds. Quality alone time in the company of a dear friend!

*A passage from*
***The Book of Joy: The Invitation***
*(Chapter Thirteen)*

*"With full cooperation from your beautiful mind, shall we proceed with an exercise that will assist you in gathering information about your mind's truly amazing abilities to generate energy?*

*Let us begin the exercise by quieting the mind. Breathe deeply, gently, refreshingly, and simply allow your quieting process to continue. Proceed at your own pace, for this exercise is between you and your mind. No other during this exercise has access to your mind, but you and your mind; this experience is a private affair. Attend you and your mind with great care during this process.*

*As you drift deeper into a quiet state, observe your mind.*

*Is it quiet…*

*Is it pondering thoughts of its own persuasion…*

*Notice your mind's behavior.*

*Is it complementing your efforts of quieting the mind…*

*Is it creating exercises of its own design…*

*Notice your behavior…*

*Are you calm…relaxed…peaceful…at rest…*

*Are you agitated…restless…disconcerted…pensive…*

*Breathe deeply again…and as you do, flow quietly into the deep recesses of your mind and silently express gratitude for your existence. Listen to your grateful expression with the ears of your heart, and as you do, inhale another large deep breath and experience the gratitude you feel for your existence. Allow your gratitude to fill your body and your entire essence and revel in the moment. As your gratitude expands, let it merge with the joy-filled energy residing within you. Visualize your gratitude pulsating within you as it blends with the already existing energy of joy, and simply allow this union to reverberate throughout your entire being. Be with your gratitude. Be with your joy-filled energy. Be in oneness with the energy within. Simply be.*

*Notice your mind's behavior…*

*Is it quiet…*

> *Is it restless...and if it is, wish it well and notice where it wanders...*
>
> *Notice your behavior...*
>
> *Are you quiet...*
>
> *Are you restless...and if you are, smile gently within, and notice why...*
>
> *Continue your experience in the quiet as long as you desire; you are the leader of this exercise. Continue your silence or bring it to a close as you wish and then ponder this experience, if you will, and please journal about your process."*

When the pair reached the destination highpoint of their walk, they paused. The silence was broken by instantaneous reactions to the view. "Geez!!" Tears trickled down my cheeks. "I'm always taken aback by this view. "No matter how many times, I reach this point, my reaction is always the same. Surprise, delight, awe!"

"Amen!" exclaimed Marilyn in response. ""We are so fortunate to live here! We are so fortunate to be alive! Can you believe the life we are living?" she asked not really expecting an answer, but receiving one nonetheless.

"No, Marilyn, I can't! And yet, I think this is the way everyone is supposed to live." Turning away from the view, I faced my friend and peered deeply into her eyes, searching for some kind of explanation that would clarify our circumstances. "We both have so much to be grateful for...and still, that was true before our friendly visitor entered into our daily lives...but life is richer now, don't you agree? Have you thought about this? Since he joined us, we are more open to and aware of our surroundings, and we are more engaged and involved with life. No wonder life seems more exhilarating!"

*A passage from*

***The Book of Joy: The Invitation***

*(Chapter Thirteen)*

> *"Yes, Old Friend, the journey has begun...or continues... whatever your situation may be. Whether this is your initial voyage or one done a thousand times before, the greeting remains the same... Safe Journey!*

*Before moving forward, please review your experience of this exercise another time. Revisit your memory of the visualization as best you can, take another look at the notes you recorded about your experience, and as you do this, notice how you and your mind are presently reacting to this review process. Presumably, you gleaned valuable information about you and the workings of your mind during your participation in this act of generosity; however, observing your present reactions during this review process may prove as productive and beneficial as the exercise itself. In truth, your beautiful mind and you are always worth observing. Neither you nor your mind will ever cease to amaze you. Enjoy your sweet beauty!*

*You, Dear Reader, are a being of delightful creation, as is your mind. It is time that you get to know one another more intimately, don't you agree?"*

"The fact that our lives are so profoundly different now gives me pause," responded Marilyn. "Our recent experiences cause me to wonder not only about myself, but others as well. I think it is fair to say we, you and I, were content with our lives. But as you so appropriately said, our lives are now exhilarating. What does this say about us? Were our self-perceptions inaccurate before? Were we really content or were we so busy we didn't recognize our own discontentment? I'm a bit confused about all of this, and it makes me curious about humankind in general. Are we all so distracted by our lives that we aren't living the lives we are intended to live? Goodness! Could this be true?" Recent events had given us much to consider and Marilyn's articulation of her thoughts naturally steered each of us inward. Eventually, our conversation continued.

"Perhaps, this simply is all part of our developmental process," My statement came more from a place of optimistic wonderment than from certainty. "We do what we can do until we learn something new, and then we implement the new ideas and discover how much better life is with these new changes, which of course, causes us to wonder how we ever managed before the changes came about. Marilyn, our lives were good before all these exciting times came about. Let's not forget that or diminish ourselves for the place we were in at the time. In truth, looking back helps us to realize our far we've advanced, and that's exciting.

For reasons we are becoming more aware about, the eight of us came together again at just the right time, and in just the right places, to meet our new and unusual friend, who is probably an old friend to all of us in some other time and place. And this happened because we were all ready to take the next step! And we have! We've all moved forward inwardly, which has prepared us for advancing outward into the world. None of this is a coincidence, Marilyn. If we sat down and wrote our life stories, we'd be able to see everything that happened did so for a reason. Paths taken, choices made, people encountered, every aspect of our lives, whether positively or negatively perceived, all happened for a reason and enabled us to arrive at this particular place and time so we can take the next steps to live the lives we are intended to live. No coincidences! Puzzling, bewildering, magically, and naturally! Everything has happened for a reason.

I am so grateful we've walked this path together. You're a good friend, Marilyn! Thank you, for being in my life!"

"And you, my friend! I can't imagine having a lifetime without you being a part of it!"

*A passage from*
***The Book of Joy: The Invitation***
*(Chapter Fourteen)*

*"Dear Reader, your generous participation is deeply appreciated. Applause is definitely deserved, but unlikely to be forthcoming anytime soon, except from you. Please honor you now with a standing ovation. The heart smiles as this exuberant image flashes through the mind. Quite frankly, it is a lovely image to visualize and to think about and one the mind may choose to revisit countless numbers of times. One's mind can imagine you, Dear Reader, in various ways and in many different settings, and each time enjoy the new scenario with equal pleasure as the one before, until the wayward mind tires of the experience or refocuses upon another. As you and your mind become more acquainted, you may discover your mind delights in activities similar to this, and may in fact, spend extraordinary amounts of time in such reverie. Have you noticed your mind's predilection for such behavior?*

*Presumably, your answer to this question is yes, and if it is, simply know you are in very good company. The typical mind, which most possess, loves to create, and it is quite adept at doing so. As you become more familiar with your mind's exceptional skill sets, you will, with the help of your mind, discern which skills are most exquisitely fine tuned and efficient and which ones need attention for further refinement purposes. Through this intimate, intrapersonal relationship between you and your mind, great discoveries will be made. Working together for the betterment of the whole, you will ascertain much greater understanding about the magnificence of your mind and it will come to know your brilliance as well. Each has much to learn about the other and each has much to offer the other. Suffice it to say, Dear Reader, the relationship you establish with your mind will be noteworthy, and the benefits received, indescribable.*

*Turning our attention back to the topic of this book, perhaps you wonder about the book's title and question why it is called The Book of Joy when so much discussion is about the mind. Such a question is indeed appropriate and deserves an answer, which can be given quite succinctly. Joy is effectively crippled by the decelerating energy produced by the mind."*

"Welcome, my friends! Please come in and make yourselves comfortable." The fellowship of friends gathered promptly at 7 o'clock. No one had questioned the announcement of another meeting. They simply gathered because each in his or her own respective way knew the meeting was necessary. Dee recognized a pensive mood when she entered the house, but did not mention it. She accepted the underlying cause would quickly reveal itself.

No one dawdled! In fact, everyone moved directly into the living room, chose their preferred seating place, and was ready to engage within moments of entering the house. Marilyn sat with her eyes turned downward, wondering how the meeting would begin. Smiling and attempting to be graciously present, I also wondered how to begin the meeting. Not knowing when our guest would appear, I suggested a meditation as a means of initiating our gathering. Everyone was receptive to the idea and oriented accordingly for the journey into the silence. Selfishly not wanting to be the timekeeper, I set a timer for 20 minutes. In truth, this was an act of self-care because I needed time to quiet myself, which happened instantaneously.

*"They are in a peaceful state,"* remarked an observer from an unknown location.

*"Yes,"* replied another from the same unidentified setting. *"This is a most important gathering."*

*"Indeed!"* responded the initial speaker. *"Many reactions may be incurred, but we are prepared for this, and Our Friend is most capable of facilitating this emotional evening. We will stand alert and hold the space for healing and*

*transitional energies, as they discuss their futures. Our energies will be used to bolster their energies while they deal with these transitional issues; however, we must not allow our energies to influence or interfere with their reactions and responses to the news of Our Friend's departure. No reason is there to be concerned about their ability to manage this news. They will feel personal loss and grief, but each will be stronger for the experience. We have great admiration and hope for these fine people. They will transition well!"*

*"My Friends, I hear your words and request permission to join this conversation."* The familiar voice was immediately acknowledged and welcomed into the group discussion.

*"You are most welcome Old Friend. We speak gratefully and optimistically about this evening's gathering. You have served well, Old Friend."*

*"Thank you, My Friends, I am in agreement with your assessment of this evening's meeting. I believe it will go well, and I am indeed grateful for your assistance with the energetic releases and transmissions. They are, as you said, very fine people, and they will manage this transition and continue the good work already started. This has been a most agreeable assignment."*

*"Tonight will be emotional for you, as well, Dear Friend. You have known these earthbound friends for a very, very long time, and it will be difficult to experience less contact with them. We are available to you at all times."*

*"Yes, it will be difficult. I am grateful for your presence, My Friends. And now, I must take my leave and attend the meeting that awaits me."*

*"In peace be, Old Friend!"*

*"And to you, My Friends!"*

*A passage from*
***The Book of Joy: The Invitation***
*(Chapter Fifteen)*

> *"Understanding the mind's capabilities demands that your participation in these exercises is equal to, if not greater than, your mind's participation. A distinction between your mind and you exists; however, it will only be discovered if you are consciously present. Indeed, this means you cannot just show up, but you must actually be consciously present and actively involved throughout this upcoming exercise. With this in mind, your first act of participation will be to discern whether or not this is a good time for you to proceed with the*

> *exercise. If you feel ready now and are truly available to be present, then by all means continue. If, however, you simply cannot spare the time at this moment, then attend the other matters that are calling you; because quite truthfully, if you are not available to be consciously present, then your participation will be a waste of time. In an effort to distinguish between you and your mind before the exercise begins, can you, right now in this present moment, determine who is leading you? Are you acutely and decisively aware of responsibilities that demand your immediate attention or is your delightful mind, which really does not want to participate in another exercise, convincing you that other activities must be dealt with at this very moment?*
>
> *So, who is in charge? You or your mind? Be with this, Dear Reader, and discover who or what is really driving you. If you truly are not in the mood for another exploratory exercise, boldly declare it; there is no shame in wanting a break from the inward journey or any other journey for that matter. Perhaps you would rather play, do nothing, or some other activity of your choice. If that is the case, then please just honor yourself and follow your own preference. Whatever you choose is yours to discern, but please, if you will, be certain that your choice is yours rather than a mind's that has a mind of its own."*

Movement stirred among my circle of friends after the timer with its enchanting sound of a Tibetan bell brought an end to our meditation. I remained still wondering if our guest had joined us during the meditation. The serenity gained during the meditation quickly escaped me as I anticipated the farewells that were in store for everyone tonight. I longed for the silence of just a few minutes ago. Knowing and accepting with absolute certainty that the evening would evolve as intended, and also trusting everyone would be fine, did not abate my concerns about the situation. Trying to calm myself, I took several deep breaths, and eventually gained the composure to open my eyes and meet whatever was to be. Gratefully, my first sight was of our wonderful Friend. His gentle smile set me at ease.

*"Good evening, Dear Friends. So grateful am I to be in your presence."* Then, he clasped his hands in prayerful manner and bowed to the family of friends. *"I come with news, My Friends, and I ask each of you to listen with the ears of your heart, for my message is one of extreme importance."* For a moment, I felt as if my heart had stopped beating. Of course, it hadn't, but I had stopped breathing, which accounted for a brief moment of dizziness. My mind, a whirlwind of thoughts was disrupting my ability to be present.

*Calm yourself!* I yelled inside my head. *Surely, he isn't going to just blurt this out.* My mind was running away with itself, thinking the worst of this dear man who had demonstrated nothing but pure benevolence since entering our lives. His character simply would not let him act cruelly, but my mind anticipating the worst chose to leap into protection mode, as if my friends were incapable of taking care of themselves. My heartbeat, accelerating from the futility of my mind's own incredulous misdirection, reverberated in my ears. Finally, the voice of sanity reached through the complicated pathways of the nonsensical mind and stilled the chaos.

*"Be not afraid, Dear Friend. I will take the utmost care of your friends. Please trust me, and have faith in them as well!"* At last, I was breathing again. Sanity subdued the fearful mind and my heart rate returned to normal. Embarrassed by my internal outburst and worn out by my physiological upheaval, I was resistant to make eye contact with our guest. Fortunately, his will was more determined and insistent than my willful resistance, and I literally found my eyes staring into his. How this happened I do not know, because I have no recall of turning to face him; and yet, there he was, right before me looking deeply into my eyes and reassuring me that All Was Well and All Would Be Well. "*There is no cause for concern, My Friend"* Peace fell upon me and I found myself completely receptive to what was coming.

*A passage from*
***The Book of Joy: The Invitation***
*(Chapter Fifteen)*

> *"Although your mind may not initially appreciate the silent experience, eventually it will come to know it as a Dear Old Friend and long to be in its company. Likewise, as your mind and you realize how rich and expansive this way of being is, the benefits of peace of mind will be evident and keenly understood.*
>
> *With your participation, progress is being made and the act of generosity moves forward on its journey across Mother Earth. Peace of mind begins within and it is a generous act with unlimited potential. A joyful thought that brings a smile to mind!"*

As was the case since his arrival into their lives, the unusual gentleman who had become a beloved teacher and an accepted dear friend of old and present, was again greeted with great fondness and hospitality. The group having quickly adjusted to his unusual comings and goings always looked forward to the next opportunity to be in his presence, and since his attendance at their meetings had become customary, he was at this point expected to be present. Perceived as a teacher, as well as an active participant in the group, his arrival was anticipated with excitement. Though this was not spoken aloud, it was an internal reality experienced by every member of the group.

His presence unfailingly energized their meetings as he demonstrated the uncanny ability to broaden the horizon of the whole, while simultaneously reaching individuals in a manner that could only be described as enlightening. Tonight's meeting appeared to be no different than those held before. The family of friends had gathered and the beloved newcomer had arrived.

With the exception of Marilyn and the gathering's convener, the other group members anticipated the meeting would proceed in the usual manner.

*A passage from*
***The Book of Joy: The Invitation***
*(Chapter Sixteen)*

> *"So what do we pursue next…the mysterious and intriguing inference that we are not alone, the complex issues associated with loneliness, or shall we expand our awareness about this interesting, but perplexing, notion of an energy source founded in joy. All these topics warrant consideration in due time; however, exploring the last topic first will facilitate greater and fuller understanding of the others…"*

*"My dear friends, this evening is one of extreme significance; therefore, we must proceed with our conversation so we each have an opportunity to participate and to feel a sense of completion by the end of our meeting. If I may be so bold, it is my privilege and pleasure to apprise you that we are not alone this evening. As you all know, our meetings are often attended and observed by Friends from afar, and so too is the case this evening; however, this gathering is one that is attended by many more than the usual attendees. They gather on your behalf, for they have come to express gratitude for your dedicated participation and willingness to pursue greater understanding of the circumstances surrounding you.*

*My dear friends, we are all in great transition, and it is of transitions we must speak this evening. Our friends from near and distance places gather with us this evening because they wish to inform you of their continued support and assistance in the days ahead. These Beings of Old have long watched over humankind, and their commitment to the children of Earth remains their highest priority.*

As Dee listened to their Teacher, this gentle man who first came into her life some fifty years before, she knew where this conversation was headed. Her mind raced rapidly visiting despair, disbelief, sadness, and then back to the present moment, which she understood with clarity. The gamut of emotions colliding with one another in the backyard of her mind was not and could not be of service to her at this critical time. Of course, she would need time to do her own grieving, and she would do that, but not now. She had responsibilities! Both she and Frank would need to pull themselves together for the others. This was no time to allow the indulgences of the mind to lead them astray. As the elders of this group, they had to remain grounded. She sighed loudly enough for others to hear, but they were entranced with the discussion and not distracted by her breathy comment. Dee, hoping Frank was listening to her internal conversation, was relieved when she saw his right forefinger move several inches skyward, which was a private signal between them. He had heard her. *Thank goodness! We have work ahead of us, Dear!* And his finger reached for the sky again. As her mind quieted itself, Dee was able to return to the messages of their beloved Teacher.

*"Transitions, my dear friends, are transpiring at all levels of existence. You are not alone in your transitional period, but indeed, are functioning both singularly and collaboratively within interdimensional grand matrices in which incalculable transitions are materializing simultaneously. These are exciting times for some transitional participants, and also trying times for others. Unfortunately, the peoples of Earth are entering some extremely difficult times, which can be successfully managed with assistance. Many have gathered on behalf of the planet Earth and many more have been in preparation to assist with the Earth's transition long before any of recent times were even aware of the precarious and imminent predicaments transpiring upon and within this beautiful planet.*

*The time is now, my friends. We all must pursue our individual assignments for the good of Self, and for the good of All. This discussion is upon us now because it can no longer be delayed.*

*What is happening is happening, and for the sake of all involved, action must be taken.*

*In recent weeks, the eight of you have joined together to effectively create change within others. You have learned well, and your excitement and dedication are needed. Now you must move forward. The next steps must be taken, for the time is now."*

"You're asking us to step out…to move out of these comfortable meetings into the real world…and touch those who are ready to hear the messages we are to bring forward." Dee's impromptu summary brought a smile to the Teacher's face.

*"Yes, that is true! You have been amiable students…and a joy to work with… but it now time for you to move forward, to become the teachers to others who are also eager to learn more about their own situations so they too can become of service. You cannot remain in the sequestered comfort of these remarkable conversations from the heart. But you can take what you have learned and what you have recalled about yourself to others and create new opportunities for more conversations from the heart. It is time. Each of you knows this, and you also know it is time to take the next step."* His words were spoken with such confidence that it was impossible not to feel emboldened by his message. Each in their own way knew it was time to push forward. They needed to enact all the good ideas gained throughout their time in this precious learning cocoon. As enjoyable as the conversations were, they were impeding progress. A foundation of information, which had changed the life of each member of the group and had the potential for changing many other lives was at hand. It had to be shared! The Teacher's message was clear…take the next step! Emotions and thoughts struggled internally.

*A passage from*

***The Book of Joy: The Invitation***

*(Chapter Sixteen)*

> *"When speaking about the energy of joy, which must be done, let us approach the topic with joyful intentions. What better choice might be made? In actuality, many other choices could be pursued, but why? Why not choose to access the joyful energy of our discussion when embarking upon greater understanding about this life force existing within you? Of course, other options are available that will also lead to increased awareness; however, please pause for just a moment and peruse possible alternatives. Why choose to participate in a discussion about joy from a place of doubt, skepticism or preconceived ideas? If this is truly your point of reference, ask why, and then open your heart*

*to discovering all that can possibly be learned about the energy of joy from your present perspective. Whether you approach the study of joy from a hopeless viewpoint or one that is filled with optimism, the benefits gained from the research will be worth the effort. Remember please while reviewing and assessing various options, the goal is to expand your present experience and awareness of joy. Wherever you are in your present journey of life, you simply are where you are. Regardless of your present situation or past events that contributed to your maturational process, the journey of self-discovery, the inward journey, begins within.*

*Shall we continue now by welcoming a very long deep breath? Do so in the manner that most suits you. No other can dictate or determine your preference for entering into a quiet state; this discernment process is yours to command. Practice now. Try a technique that you have come to appreciate or attempt another that is of interest, and notice how your selection benefits you in the moment. Each time the breath is taken with intention a new opportunity arises.*

*Create a new opportunity now. Enter into your silent state as you breathe the breath of renewal that revitalizes your sense of wellness and stills the mind from unnecessary activity. Breathe deeply, follow your inner lead, and trust. Trust you to guide you within. Trust you to aid you during this time of self-care. Trust you to bring you inward to the Home of the heart, where you can dwell in quiet…at rest… in peace."*

"Well, dear friends, I think it is fair to say the energy of our group has shifted," declared Dee with a matter of fact attitude. Her blunt but calm manner tickled several members of the group.

"Oh really!" chuckled Marilyn as she resituated herself in the overstuffed chair. "Perhaps, everyone should take a deep breath and get in touch with themselves," she added.

"Please excuse Dee, everyone," Frank commented as he looked about the room. "I suspect she's already several steps ahead of the rest of us." Then pointing towards Marilyn and her walking companion, he went on to say, "Except for these two!" Frank looked as if he was going to say something else, but decided against it. But his insinuation caught the attention of his wife who immediately tuned into her two friends.

*So this is what I was feeling when we arrived,* she spoke silently. *Now, I understand the complexity of emotions that were palpable when we entered the house.* Dee, feeling relieved that she was not the only one aware of what was coming, smiled at her friends. The exchange was comforting for all involved.

To everyone's surprise, Everett, whose manner was typically reserved, took the lead. "By nature, I am one who prefers to observe a situation thoroughly before speaking out; however, tonight's conversation seems to beg for a different approach. If the gist of this discussion is what I think it is, then it is best to bring it out in the open now, so we can deal with the reality of it. Am I correct, fine Sir, in assuming that you are leaving us?" His question, blunt and precise, caused several gasps and exclamations of dismay. Frank, Dee, Marilyn, and the convener of the meeting were all surprised and relieved.

As each waited for a reaction from their venerable mentor, Marilyn silently prompted everyone to breathe, and as they did, they witnessed the elder gentleman close his eyes and inhale slowly and deeply. For a brief moment, he appeared to glow. Whether everyone in the room noticed his radiant state remains a mystery, for the curious phenomenon paled to the topic of the moment. When he opened his eyes, the love emanating from him engulfed the circle of friends. For those gifted with interdimensional sight, it was indeed a sight to behold; however, even those unable to appreciate the visual event were captivated by the magnificence of energetic transformation. What transpired simply happened. Naturally, without fanfare or technological wizardry, the transformation of energy depicting union, harmony, emergence, wholeness, and unity, all transpired in an instant. Each who participated in the transformation experienced it in his or her own unique way, and even without understanding the totality of the experience, each knew an event of extreme significance had transpired. While words would never do justice to the experience, the memory of what transpired would last forevermore.

"*My gratitude for our time together is everlasting, my friends! Such a gift it has been to be in your presence, to enjoy your company once again, and to see the spark of renewal ignite within each of you. It is as intended! Each of you had a specific desire, a preferred role to enact in this lifetime, and you are fulfilling that personal dream, that designated purpose. You are living your calling!*" His loving smile aroused another emanation of energy transference that was again inexplicable, yet eternally memorable. Eyes glistened with the release of cleansing tears and hearts were open to indefinable capacities. "*You are more than you appear to be, my dear friends, and within each of you is the capacity for great change. Do not forget this truth. You are here for a reason! Separately, each of you is outstanding. Together, your potential is unlimited. For reasons that will become increasingly evident to you, the eight of you came into this space at this time for a reason. Work together. Assist one another, as you assist others, and the work will be joyous and influential. The time is now, dear friends! You must continue!"* Silence overtook the eventful moment for an unknown amount of time, or perhaps, it is better said that time without time overtook the silent moment. Whatever your preferred viewpoint, suffice it to say, the time when time no longer matters engulfed the moment allowing each participant, regardless of their present location, to fully experience the splendor of the transitional event.

Whether the time was brief or lengthy, one cannot say. It simply was what it was until time once again became a factor of relevance.

"I assume," clarified Everett, " your response affirms you are about to depart our company."

*"Yes, my friends, because of your rapid advancement, my time here is quickly coming to a close. You are ready to proceed on your own, and because you have each other, my presence is no longer needed."*

"That's not true," exclaimed Jan. "Your presence is needed! Your guidance is invaluable!" Wanting to say more, but feeling as if she were about to burst into tears, Jan stopped herself. Her words, brief, but to the point, accurately articulated what her friends were also feeling. There teacher's response surprised everyone.

*"I will miss you too,"* he softly announced. *"Our time together has been immensely enjoyable for me. I have missed all of you. And having this time together was like old times. We have shared many good times and experienced difficult ones as well, but whatever the circumstances were, our preference was to experience the good times and the bad times together. And this we have done throughout the ages. It has been my privilege in this experience to be the keeper of our shared memories. I am sorry you cannot remember all of our memories, but I promise you they are good memories, fond memories, which will return to you when you enjoy your next life transitional experience. The memories are never lost, my friends, but sometimes they are purposefully forgotten for the sake of the current life experience. Please hear my words, dear friends. We have known each other longer than any of us would care to admit, and we will continue to be friends from this moment on for all times to come. I promise you this is another truth, which can be taken for granted. One need not worry about this truth, for it is, has always been, and will always be. Such is the truth about relationships in the Greater Existence of existence."* As he confidently spoke this truth for his friends, he reminded himself of their need to grieve his departure. Although he didn't want any of them to suffer this transition, he knew conversation was necessary.

*"Dear Ones, the truth about tonight's meeting is now out in the open. Shall we open this reality for discussion?"*

"Well, I'm deeply saddened by this," acknowledged Pat. "In all honesty, I can't say your announcement surprises me, but geez, it is hard to accept anyway. Your presence has been such a blessing to all of us, and the idea that we can no longer access you leaves me aghast!" Her voice cracking a bit caused Pat to pause, but she was not finished. "Am I right about not being able to access you? Will we ever have contact with you again, or is this the end for this lifetime?" Her questions raised the anxiety level for everyone in the group, who were equally unnerved by the idea of being separated from this remarkable teacher. Before he could answer, Jan voiced her concerns.

"Pat, thank you for asking those questions. I too am concerned about being cut off from this incredible source of wisdom. Is this really true? Will we not be allowed to connect with you? I understand you will not be participating in our meetings on a regular basis, but will we be able to access you if we really need you?" Jan wondered if she would be able to discern whether or not she really needed his guidance from her preference of simply wanting his input. Obviously, he could not be ever-present for them, but it seemed ridiculous to lose such a valuable resource. As her mind began to think about the situation from every possible direction, she realized her better judgment was being stripped away from her. She laughed aloud and then noted, "Please excuse me everyone, I'm going to need some time to adjust to this new development." Everett placed his arm around her, which seemed to give her tears permission to flow. "Oh goodness, please forgive me, but I'm just not ready for this!" Pat confirmed she was in a similar place, which was comforting and challenging at the same time. While Pat attempted to compose herself, Marilyn spoke up.

"Well, my reaction was very similar when I heard about our friend's upcoming departure early this morning. At first, I couldn't believe it! I was in shock! And then my mind started doing what it does so well. It took charge. In an effort to still the chaos, it created more chaos by inventing questions, countless questions that propelled me into feeling defensive and responsible for what was happening, and then, my spirits plummeted. Please don't get me wrong. I am extremely grateful for my beautiful mind; however, in this situation, my mind's willfulness was not helpful. In actuality, the questions were a distraction from the real issue. What I needed was time to grieve. Instead, my mind went off in numerous directions proposing ridiculous explanations for what was happening, none of which was founded in truth. I just needed to be with the sadness of the moment. I needed to cry, to pout…to express my despair and sense of desperation. I needed to be with my feelings." Recalling the events of the day, Marilyn doubted if she had offered any words that were useful to her friends, before realizing there was another thought she wanted to share.

"It's been a long day! Lots of ups and downs, which I imagine all of you will experience as well, but what seemed to be most helpful throughout the day were my reflections about my appreciations of the last few weeks. I am so grateful for every moment we've shared, and for all the experiences our Teacher provided us. When I focus upon the blessings of this precious time together, then the thought of his leaving is less painful. These thoughts have quieted my anxiety and helped me to regain some sense of balance again. Don't get me wrong, I'm still a bit wobbly about this, but I'm leaning into the idea now. I know we are all going to get through this, but in the meantime we need to be gentle with ourselves and each other."

"Marilyn, this is very useful advice," responded Jan. "Thank you! Now, I know what to anticipate in the upcoming hours and days." Pat nodded in agreement and the fellows gazing at the floor seemed to be grasping the importance of Marilyn's reflections as well.

"Isn't it interesting how the mind works?" mused Dee. "I'm curious, Marilyn, about your mind's inclination to infer that you were somehow responsible for our friend's decision to leave. I had a similar reaction, but firmly squelched it, thank goodness. For whatever reason, I was able to recognize the insinuation as a distraction and was able to immediately negate the idea. Again, I say thank goodness for that moment of clarity. How about the rest of you? Did your minds turn down that slippery path?"

"Oh gosh, yes!" Pat blurted out. "I immediately assumed we had disappointed our teacher and/or his companions. I was concerned that we, in general, and me, specifically, were not good enough; i.e., our participation in the mission was no longer wanted. Ugh!" she moaned loudly. "What a dreadful notion! I don't even want to think about it, and besides," Pat spoke assertively, "it's an absurd thought! We were participating thoroughly and progressing well. The idea was, and is ludicrous. Why does the mind instigate such nonsense?" The discussion quickly brought to light the advantages of being cognizant of the mind's antics. Their teacher and observers were extremely pleased with the direction of the conversation. Without assistance, the group had focused upon a primary issue for themselves, as well as everyone they would soon encounter.

"Good question!" inserted Frank. "I openly admit my mind can be a rascal at times. It's why I love working with wood. It takes me away from my mind to a place that's indescribable, but definitely more hospitable than my mind. I don't understand why it works in this perplexing manner, but I do know it's our responsibility to be aware of it; because the truth is, the mind can really mislead us at times, and we have to be alert to this possibility. I have no doubts that my mind would have taken me down a similar path as yours Pat, but Dee's determined mind led me in another direction. Because she so adamantly declared that we must stand firm in our present roles, my insecurities didn't take hold. I am grateful she had such a strong sense of clarity about the situation and was able to convey the information to me." Before Frank ended, he decided his male companions needed some encouragement. "Everett, Bill can I impose upon you two to share your experiences and perspectives about the mind's role in this particular situation?"

"That's easy!" replied Everett. "My experience was very similar to what has already been described. I was flooded with self-doubt and then quickly moved into blaming myself for what was happening. Even though I really didn't know what was happening, I was certain it was my fault. This conversation is illuminating for me. I had no idea how problematic this was until hearing everyone's stories. Is this common behavior?" Before anyone could reply, Everett began answering is own question. "Obviously, we are not unique exceptions. So," his thoughts turned over in his mind, "if this kind of behavior is common place, our species is in trouble. Frank, you are absolutely right, we have to be vigilantly alert to what our minds are up to. We have to be present, observant, and willing to take action, as Dee undoubtedly did without anyone's notice other than her husband's. Yes," he repeated, "we definitely have to be attentive to the functioning of our minds." As Frank listened to his friend, he felt uplifted by Everett's grasp of the situation and his resolve to take action. Jan, too, was impressed with her husband's response and voiced her desire to assist others in detecting the misguidance of their respective minds.

"Good idea, Jan!" praised Dee. "I think we should also be alert to these slippery moments here in the group. The more we tune in to one another, the more vigilant we will be in regards to our own internal operations. Good training, don't you think?" The other members of the group confirmed Dee's suggestion before Bill took his turn at the topic of the mind.

"Well, I'm on board!" he proclaimed. "My story is almost identical to what has already been shared. The good news, as I see it, is that we have a strong motivation for addressing this squirrelly nonsense of the mind. Our mission of outreach demands that we pursue more knowledge regarding the operations of the mind, not only for ourselves, but also for all those individuals with whom we soon will be connecting. Like you Everett, I find this discussion extremely noteworthy. In fact, I think it may be life changing. It's amazing that one discussion, which in essence has been rather brief, can be so profoundly insightful. My ability to concentrate is going to change because of this conversation...and so will my ability to meditate.

As often is the case in these meetings, our present conversation is happening for a reason. This is no coincidence," he asserted confidently. "It is prudent for us to learn more about the workings of the mind so we can understand how it interferes with our endeavors both personally and interactively. The timeliness of this discussion cannot be ignored; it is unbelievably believable." Chuckling with the wonder of it all, Bill noted, "Obviously, we are being reminded of the tomfoolery of the mind now, because we will soon be initiating our outreach programs. And before we begin those projects, we must each gain greater clarity about this phenomenon, so we can share our discoveries with those we encounter. Hopefully, our experiences will facilitate and foster keener awareness and rapid growth among the folks with whom we are privileged to work. Greater understanding of the mind's capabilities, both positive and negative, can improve one's own developmental process." Turning towards our guest, who was attentively observing our interactions, Bill stated, "I am really sad to hear about your departure, but I also understand the necessity of it for everyone's sake." Before continuing, Bill had to slow his emotions. "It occurs to me I may not have another chance to say thank you, so I want to do so now. It isn't easy for me to speak about such matters, but I need to do this, both for me and also for you. Your presence in my life has changed me. I'm a better person because of you, and I really want you to know this. Obviously, I don't remember our previous encounters, but for some reason, I know it's important that you hear these words. I'm a better person because of you, and I'm very grateful." Tears moistened Bill's eyes and several overflowed creating a barely noticeable stream down his right cheek.

The elder gentleman sat silently listening to every word, as if they were life's greatest gift. With great emotion, he acknowledged Bill's gift. *"Your intuition serves you well, my friend. I do indeed need to hear these words, and I am so pleased my presence has been of service this time. My heart is full; it no longer aches. Thank you for healing my deepest wound."* The tenderness of their exchange touched all who were present igniting a wave of energy that spread throughout all existence. In a moment of extreme heartfelt connection, the energy of joy emerged and changed the course of the future.

*A passage from*

***The Book of Joy: The Invitation***

*(Chapter Seventeen)*

*"Now that you are ready Dear Reader, visualize an incident that ignites the joyful energy within you. Remember, the energy of joy already exists and through this exercise, you will intentionally practice arousing and activating your inner energy source to elevated heights. This may be a visualization of a previously enjoyed experience or an incident of your own imagination; the choice is yours. Spend time either creating a joyful scenario or reliving the one already experienced and when you have captured the chosen image in your mind's eye, revel in the present, as you experientially embrace this joy-filled moment.*

- *Breathe deeply and envision your joyful incident…*
- *Allowing the image to stir the energy cells within you…*
- *Imagine each cell combusting with joy, radiating this enlivening and healing energy throughout your entire body and essence…*
- *And experience the "overwhelm of joy" flowing within you…through you… and all about you.*
- *Be with the experience…*
- *Imagine every cell within your shell ablaze with your joyful energy and simply be with that exhilarating experience…*
- *Allow all your senses to participate in the joyful experience and simply be present for this moment…*
- *Be with the experience of joy…Live it…*
- *Become exquisitely familiar with the presence of joy…and remember…*
- *Remember every facet of this joyful energy and also remember that you recreated it with intentions…*
- *Remember everything you experienced and accept with joyful gratitude the gift you just gave to yourself… "*

The group, deeply moved by the interaction between Bill and the revered teacher, honored the moment in silence. No one knew how long it would take for the two old friends to recover, but it didn't matter, because their recovery served everyone. Regardless of one's location or level of understanding of the experience of transformation, the healing nature of the event incurred affected every particle of existence throughout all existence. Time passed in its orderly timeless way while all in existence benefitted from a singular healing experience originating in a remote setting in an equally remote galaxy existing among countless other galaxies in an ongoing, never-ending existence that uniquely and exquisitely exists as one existence.

*"Old Friend, are you able to continue?"* the unvoiced question gently came from a distance unimaginable to those currently abiding along side the unusual visitor who had recently regained the status of a dear friend among his earthbound friends.

*"I am well, My Friends. My greatest wish has been fulfilled. The healing between us has transpired and we are free from the burden of the past. I am eternally grateful."*

*"Your contributions are noteworthy Old Friend, and we are joyful for the deliverance of this long awaited healing process. Once again the agony of the past is released and the burdensome energy can be restored to new vitality. Your patience has served you well Old Friend, and also your Beloved Friend. We are honored to bear witness to this remarkable event."*

*"I am most grateful for all who stood ready for this moment of transition. Gratitude abounds, My Friends."*

Wrapping her arm around her husband's, Pat whispered, "Bill, are you okay?" He turned and their eyes met and Pat knew everything was fine. She had never seen Bill so relaxed in all the years they had known each other. He was changed! Although Pat didn't really understand what this meant, she was eager to get to know this new person who was her husband of numerous decades.

Bill, taking the initiative, invited his friend and mentor to lead the conversation. "My friend, you have allowed us to lead this discussion for quite some time. Perhaps, it is your turn to address your heart's concern. The elder gentleman looked younger than before. A weight, not really recognized as such before, seemed to have lifted from his shoulders.

*"My heart is singing, my friends. I am so grateful!"* he laughed joyfully and joked about his repetitive declaration of gratitude. *"If one must repeat themselves, let the intention be directed upon the gift of blessings. There are so many reasons for us to be grateful, but too often we are distracted by matters that diminish our awareness of the blessings transpiring around us. But this is not the situation for us now! Now, in this moment, our awareness is high and we are all in alignment with the energies of gratitude and joy.*

*Before moving to another topic, I wish to check in with all of you. Does anyone need to address any particular concern?"*

Jan reluctantly raised her hand. "Forgive me, but I still need clarity about your leaving. Will we have the opportunity to connect with you if it is necessary?" Jan felt as if she was being an impertinent child, but her question was not received as such.

*"Your question does not offend, my friend, but may I beg your patience? Before we move into that topic, I would like to know if anyone else needs time to discuss my departure."* Jan understood and jokingly acknowledged she could feign patience. Frank Sanderson observing their interaction experienced relief. He needed to speak his piece before this fellow disappeared again. Fifty years ago, he was too young and brash to say thank you; he wasn't going to miss the chance this time.

"I need to have the floor, if that's all right with everyone," he announced more boldly than he felt. His request, needless to say, was received graciously. Shifting in his chair, Frank realized it was easier to think about saying thank you than it was to actually do it. *What is it about those two little words,* he wondered. From the corner of his left eye, he saw Dee's forefinger move upward toward the sky and knew it was her way of nudging him forward. Whether he actually heard her words or if he just imagined them was debatable, but regardless, Frank knew what she would be saying about now. *You can do it, Frank. Just go for it!* The thought of her encouraging words was as effective as the real thing, so he followed the advice his wife had offered untold numbers of times over the years.

"I'm not happy about your leaving," he began, "but I know you've got your reasons for doing this. And I trust you're making the right decision. Like everyone else here, I'm concerned about having further connection with you; however, in a recent conversation, not so long ago, you assured Dee and me that you would be available to us if we needed you. I'm going to assume this commitment still stands." Frank peered deeply into his friend's eyes for confirmation and received what he needed to know. "Thank you for that," he sighed in relief. "And thank you for everything you've done for us. For watching over us fifty years ago, and for bringing us back to life in the last few weeks. We're feeling confident again and optimistic about being of assistance to our friends and to the mission we're all embarking upon. We want to participate and we will…that's a promise." The elder friend, listening attentively to Frank's words, heard the vow of commitment and sighed with relief. Showing his appreciation with a simple, singular nod appeared to indicate an old agreement coming into fruition.

"I hope you will also continue to be available to these younger folks," Frank added. "They're going to be around a lot longer than Dee and me, and there may be times when they need you." This comment created a rumble from the group, but Frank refused to be distracted. "I trust you have already taken this into consideration and appropriate plans for managing all situations have been made." In response to this comment, their venerable guest smiled and confirmed Frank's presumptuous notion with another singular nod. Frank nodded back and concluded, "Then there's nothing more for me to say but thank you once again. You will be missed, my friend, but we look forward to seeing you again some day."

*A passage from*
***The Book of Joy: The Invitation***
*(Chapter Seventeen)*

*"As you proceed with this next exercise regarding the energy of loneliness, remember please, you are not alone. Remember all the other readers in their chosen settings that are also participating in this exercise…you are not alone. Shall we begin?*

*Take a long, delightful deep breath, Dear Reader. Do this in a manner that is particularly satisfying and right for you. How another participates in this natural process is of no matter at this time; all that matters is your preference, your style, and your manner of achieving this natural, life-giving breath.*

- *Breathe at a pace that is comfortable for you and ride your breath into the innermost being of your existence and rest…*
- *Simply rest…*

- *Quiet the mind as you sink deeper and deeper into your sacred space…*
- *Rest, Dear Reader, as long as you desire, before continuing with this process….*
- *Simply rest…*

*When you are ready, revisit a moment when you encountered loneliness. Relive your chosen experience or live the one you presently imagine and witness where the energy of loneliness resides within you.*

- *Be with the feelings of loneliness briefly as you discover more about this powerful emotional energy and the way if affects your present state of being…*
- *Recall how you felt as you completed the previous exercise…*
- *Notice how you feel now as you are exposed to the energy of loneliness…*
- *Breathe deeply into your own wellness as you courageously explore this aspect of your humanness…*
- *Feel the effects of this experience, but remember you are a carrier of the energy of joy, which you can access at any time, any place at your discretion…*
- *Remember what has transpired, remember every aspect of the effects of loneliness on your presence, and remember you are an energy of joy waiting to happen…*
- *Do so now, Dear Reader. Take a very long deep breath expelling the residue of loneliness from your being while expressing gratitude for what was learned…*
- *Release the energy associated with loneliness now, and replace it with the energy of joy that resides within you, patiently awaiting your invitation to come forward…*
- *Take another wonderful long, extended deep breath and welcome your joyful energy back…*
- *Remember the experience of loneliness, but now without influence, as your accelerated energy of joy fills every space within and about you, revitalizing you once again to a state of peaceful resonance and joyful tenor…*
- *Continue your joyful restoration until you feel complete with the exercise.*

*Dear Reader, now is the time to journal. By now you know the routine well. Record all aspects of your experiences during both exercises, detailing what techniques went well for you and which ones need improvement.*

*Diligently review your experience with your joyful energy. What did you learn about its power, its influence, its resilience, as well as your ability to command this energy? Notice everything, no matter how small or seemingly inconsequential, and please record your findings, because nothing in this self-discovery process is unimportant. Learning how this remarkable energy interacts within you and your surroundings is critically significant not only to your own wellbeing but to others' as well. Please recognize and accept the importance of understanding the energy of joy for it is truly a transformative energy."*

"Perhaps," Dee reluctantly voiced, "it would be wise if I participated in this moment of farewells." Dee's discomfort was a surprise to her friends; in fact, it didn't occur to any of them that she would be holding back. Marilyn quickly encouraged her to share her thoughts. "Well, when the focus of tonight's discussion became obvious to me, I immediately tried to escape the situation by quote-quote courageously moving into a role of caretaker, as if," she smirked, "any of you need me to play that role. On one level, my intentions were good, but on another level, the truth is now slapping me in the face. I was indeed trying to avoid saying goodbye. But I don't want to do that!" she announced firmly. Turning to face the man, who had rescued her from the forest half a century before, Dee melted. "You deserve more than that, my friend…so much more! I wish I were privy to the background information about our relationship. I suspect we've had some grand old times…and some doozies as well. But the past doesn't need to be known to appreciate this present life experience with you." Hesitating for a moment, Dee appeared to be reaching into her library files for a particular word or idea when the absent data suddenly came to the surface of her mind. "Ah, yes," she mumbled. "I remember now. On several occasions, when you have spoken about a special time or an exceptional experience, you referred to the incident as a 'Memorable Moment,' and each time you did this, I was overwhelmed by the power of your cherished memories. The energetic change was physically noticeable and I literally felt as if we were empathically joined with one another. So, this brings me to what I need to say to you, my friend. The time we spent together in this current lifetime has been a memorable moment and I'm absolutely certain this is a memory that will never be forgotten. Thank you, my dear friend, for everything you have done for us."

*"I promise you, my friend, the memories of our time together will never be forgotten. And many more memories will we enjoy in the future."*

"I feel certain about that as well," affirmed Dee, who then swiftly redirected the conversation to another. "And you, dear one? What do you have to say this evening? I suspect the two of you have already expressed your goodbyes," she announced confidently, and then quickly followed with a nudge for me to express whatever was still lingering about in the confines of my heart. Naturally, my inclination was to deny what she already surmised as true. Of course, there was still more heartache welling up inside of me, which needed witnessing by my family of friends.

"Oh, Dee! You know me so well!" Caught off guard, my mind wandered about trying to discern what needed to be said. There was no reason to repeat all the goodbyes exchanged the night before, and yet, something still felt incomplete. *What is it?* I thought. *What more needs to be said.* And then the truth rang loudly in the ears of my heart. *Oh my, gosh! Do I dare say this aloud!* My heart, racing in response to the idea, adamantly refused to accept the possibility of such an articulation, while my shyness wholeheartedly agreed with the swift decision carried out by the heart.

"Perhaps, you may want to rethink your decision, dear," interjected Dee, who evidently was tuned into the same channel. "I don't want to push you into doing something, which doesn't feel right, but in this case, I'm afraid your mind may be interfering. Think about this dear. Would it really be wrong to express these heartfelt feelings at this time?" Dee's position stopped me in my tracks. The idea that my mind was manipulating my decision did not sit well with me. *Do I really want to capitulate to old rules and weaknesses? Was it really inappropriate to acknowledge my innermost thoughts about our friend's departure? Is my heart advising me not to do this, or is my mind activating old, painful tendencies towards shyness and creating fearful nonsense?* Not knowing who was in charge bothered me. I didn't like it! My reaction to this situation came suddenly and fearlessly. I would not be misled by my mind via fears, weaknesses, or any other old misunderstandings.

"Thank you, Dee! You were right, I was confused, but I'm thinking clearly now primarily because of what I've witnessed this evening. The level of vulnerability shared this evening is striking, and it is rare. And the courage demonstrated tonight deserves to be honored by similar behavior. I momentarily lost sight of this until Dee challenged me. My shyness reared its ancient head again, as did old trust issues, both of which cleverly enticed me to believe remaining silent was preferable. Nonsense! Absolute nonsense!

My dear friends, we are so fortunate to have one another. The idea that I would shy away from participating in this remarkable moment is unbelievable to me. Here I am among the most wonderful friends anyone could ever hope to have, and my silly mind is creating ridiculous reasons for restricting myself. I won't have it!" My announcement sounded so willful that it made me chuckle. "Please excuse me, but I really do feel feisty about this. So, I am going to open my heart, as have all of you this evening, and share what's welling up inside of me.

I am so grateful for all of you, and for this extraordinary experience we have shared together, and the truth is, I don't want it to end. When our friend here announced his intentions last night, I was devastated. The idea that he would leave us so soon was simply unacceptable. My feelings were very similar to the reactions already shared; however, while all of you so bravely shared your feelings, I felt another emotion arising within me that I didn't know how to manage or how to speak about it. And I still don't, but I'm going to stumble through it anyway.

The sense of joy I've experienced since our friend joined us has been life giving. I don't know what descriptors to use, but the truth is, life is better now. And as you all know, my life was good before, but it is remarkably better now. I'm not sure the concept of joy ever really registered for me before. In fact, I'm not even sure it was a concept ever considered. But joy is actually part of my life now, and I think it is becoming increasingly more present. And this has happened because of our connection with this wonderful fellow who blest our lives." Our teacher sat quietly as he listened to my ramblings. He was a gracious listener. As I struggled to find words that would adequately express my feelings, he gently interrupted my thoughts.

*"My friend, I promise the joy you presently attempt to describe will not be lost because of my departure. The essence of joy resides within each of you, and this is true for all beings in existence. Sometimes the embers of joy dim, and the beholder forgets what lies within, but the essence of this elemental particle of existence existing within all existence never ceases to exist. Always, it resides within; always, it is accessible, and this truth is truth for all, for all times to come.*

*Currently, my friend, you think I am the reason for your joyful existence, but this is a misunderstanding. Because of our work together, the joyful energy was ignited within you again. That is true for each of you. Our camaraderie, the sense of purpose we share, has sparked the energy of joy within all of us, and even after I am gone, it will continue to burn brightly because of our heartfelt connection.*

*This powerful and influential energy will serve you well and it will assist you in ways you are yet to discover.*

*My friend, it pleases me that you are aware of the presence of joy within and that you were able to discuss it with us, for this energy is one capable of great change. In the days to come, much more will you learn about the energy of joy!"*

*A passage from*
***The Book of Joy: The Invitation***
*(Chapter Seventeen)*

> *"Yes, Dear Reader, please grasp the significance of your intentions. By commanding your mind and participating in these guided exercises, your ability to focus your intentions facilitated the awakening, ignition, and magnification of your sacred joyful resource. Joy does exist and the viability of this eternally driven energy truly resides within, as does your ability to command your intentions and effect positive and transformational change. Joy does exist…be joyful about its presence and its possibilities."*

Their mentor's message was carefully digested. Some confusion lingered, some wanted more information, as usual; however, for the most part, the circle of friends found the discussion about the energy of joy reassuring.

"This is very helpful," stated Jan while mulling over their teacher's comments. "I was concerned our enthusiasm would wane after you left, but this makes sense to me. Your arrival energized all of us, and because of the work we've done together, we can and will help sustain one another."

"Yes, I like the sound of that," agreed Frank, "and truth be known, we still have our memories of your presence, my friend. And these memories will keep our energy burning for a long time." Frank's sentiments sparked similar comments about the room, as everyone slowly adjusted to the reality that their beloved teacher was in transition.

"What makes me joyful," Pat added to the mix, "is the fact that we are actually talking about joy. Maybe it's just me, but I don't remember having conversations about the topic of joy with anyone, other than the few times it's been discussed during our meetings." Her comment received similar admissions from her friends.

Marilyn proposed the idea that joy was a lost concept needing a revival.

"Your point is interesting," responded Dee. "One would think, or at least I've presumed, joy was more present in the world than it seems to be. We are not a group of people who live desperate lives, and yet, our acquaintanceship with joy seems to be rather limited. I find this fascinating. Don't you?" Dee's question did not settle well among the family of friends, as each individual became aware thath joy had not played an active role in their lives. Determined to understand this mystery, Dee turned to their mentor.

"Perhaps, before you leave, you might enlighten us about the apparent lack of joy in our histories. This seems very odd." Their friend was eager to pursue this discussion. His response was immediate.

*"Actually, my dear friends, joy is, and always has been present in existence; however, the human species has not attended this remarkable resource with similar vigor as have other existences. Neglect, unfortunately, can and has become habitual, resulting in a decline and even a loss of connection with this resource. Because it has become increasingly unused, many on this planet no longer retain any awareness of its existence. How sad this is, because within the dynamic properties of joy reside unlimited healing capabilities. Despite this tragic development of circumstances, joy continues to be an ever-present source of energy, which is always available, easily accessible, and immediately responsive.*

*Not only is every person able to access his or her own powerful resource for one's personal well being, but this reserve can also be utilized for the benefit of others. No one on this planet need suffer. The energy of joy can heal any and all unwellness existing upon the Earth including the ill health of the planet herself. All are intended to live in wellness and abundance, and the energy of joy can insure this potentiality.*

*My friends, the reality that people, such as you, are unaware of the truth about this powerful energy existing within you demonstrates the tragedy of what is transpiring on this planet. The precarious nature of your planet's health need not be happening. The starving millions need not be hungry. The sick, the dying, and the despairing need not live in these unintended ways. The energy within can easily address the tragedies unfolding around the planet, but unfortunately, only a very few understand the power existing within them. So unbelievable is this!"* Tears glistened in the corners of their friend's eyes. His message was not easy to present, nor was it easy to hear, but the truth had to be delivered.

*"Humankind is capable of completely rejuvenating the Island in the Sky. Her strength can be restored and her well being can be stabilized. This monumental task is feasible and can be accomplished now by accessing and utilizing the energy source residing within you. Likewise, the peoples of Earth are also capable of*

*restoring peace and wellness to all the inhabitants of this planet. The ability to effect these changes is within your means; but instead, humans argue among themselves about the reality of your planet's crisis situation. In the meantime, the vitality of this Beloved Life Being continues to diminish as her symptoms become increasingly more and more evident. The foolishness and arrogance of the human species will be their downfall. It is most regrettable that all the Earth's residents will be subjected to the disastrous consequences of humankind's neglect."*

*A passage from*
***The Book of Joy: The Invitation***
*(Chapter Eighteen)*

> *"Dear Reader, where do you fall on the continuum regarding eternal existence? Are you a believer, a skeptic, a non-believer, or are you totally disinterested in the topic? Regardless of your present position, please continue with an open heart and open mind. Because one's personal viewpoint about eternal existence is ultimately a private matter, The Book of Joy would not ordinarily intrude upon the boundaries of such a heartfelt discernment process; however, greater understanding about this basic and ever-existing reality is necessary; therefore the discussion must be addressed forthrightly and you are invited to participate in the controversial topic. Allow your overactive imagination to rally in anticipation and wonderment, as you consider engaging in this provocative discourse. While you ponder your position and attitude about eternal existence, strive to remember how you came to this present state of understanding. Give yourself ample time to review how your opinions and perspectives of eternal existence evolved, and as you reflect upon your own journey regarding this topic, also please allow your imagination to consider the journeys of other readers participating in The Book of Joy. Obviously, each of you will bring your own uniquely personal journey with eternal existence to the discussion and isn't that wonderful? Although there will be many viewpoints to be reviewed and considered, greater understanding can transpire from the exchange of ideas and personal histories, through which individual differences can be honored, respected, and hopefully held with compassionate acceptance. Out of the many differences, which have evolved over time through many varying circumstances,*

> *unity of hearts can arise. This is not wishful thinking, Dear Readers, it is a reality that can and must be created.*
>
> *As we continue our discussion, allow yourself to imagine your fellow readers. See you and them sitting comfortably, engaging in heartfelt conversation as you learn about each other's preferences. Imagine coming together with new friends and old friends found anew for the purpose of growth, evolutionary expansion, and the betterment of humankind. Please open your mind and your heart to this possibility, for someday it may come true. Indeed, it is extremely possible and even likely that some day soon you may encounter another reader of The Book of Joy and instantly recognize and know you have found a companion of the heart.*

"When you speak about the Earth's situation, I have a difficult time managing my mind. It does not want to hear these messages." Frank's admission aroused similar comments.

"Guess it isn't surprising," interjected Everett. "These are unpleasant topics. Absolutely necessary, but difficult."

"That's true," Bill agreed, "but if we were able to embrace this idea about the energy of joy, our attitude about these depressing topics would change. If I knew for certain I could make a difference with this energy that supposedly is inside of me, then I'd be feeling extremely optimistic."

"That's the rub, isn't it?" questioned Dee. "How do we accept this idea? And how do we learn how to use this energy?" All heads turned toward the esteemed teacher. "You are going to provide us with this information before you leave, aren't you?" His response came quickly and surprised the onlookers.

*"My friends, my greatest desire is to inform you of everything needed to fulfill your missions of purpose. It goes without saying it is an impossibility to provide for every upcoming event that will transpire in the days ahead; however, you are ready to move forward on your own. In reference to your questions regarding the validity of the energy of joy, I ask you to ponder this thought. Why would so much time be given to inform you of this incredible source of energy, if it were not the truth? Why would any race of beings waste so much time reminding you of this internal resource if the information were not considered vitally important to the survival of your species?"* The demeanor of their beloved teacher changed as he continued to deliver what was obviously a message of profound significance. Although no one in the moment revealed any visible signs of reaction regarding his change of appearance, it was an incident that would be fondly remembered during many discussions in the future. What they witnessed would be referred to as

the time when their beloved teacher and old friend illuminated their path of understanding regarding the truth about humankind's eternal energy of joy. In that never-to-be forgotten moment, their unusual friend achieved a most unusual feat, which was evidently for him a simple, natural phenomenon; but for his students, it was a memorable moment. They observed his presence emanating a glow of light that steadily maintained itself throughout the entire presentation of the message. Only when the message was delivered did the ethereal light dissipate.

*"What is,"* he declared, *"has always been, and will indeed forever be; however, your species has regrettably forgotten the truth about your eternal existence. You are, and have forever been, gifted with the ability to transform energy. This gift came into existence long before your species entered into existence, and has continued to exist throughout all existence. All are gifted with this magnificent and benevolent energy. It is, as it is, my friends, and the time has come for you and all your brothers and sisters to remember this truth about your existence."* And with that said, our friend returned to his usual appearance.

Dee was the first to respond. "My friend, you have stopped me in my tracks, and I am so grateful for your courage to speak the truth. Why would we doubt what you have shared with us? You have given us no reason to distrust you. We have a choice. We can choose to believe you or we can choose to listen to the nonsense of our minds and our fears and decide to continue living as if this energy doesn't exist. Or we can confront our natural human tendency to doubt and be suspicious and simply choose to believe what you shared with us.

I choose to believe!" she adamantly declared. "I believe we are indeed old friends and have shared countless other lives together before, just as you have said. I also believe what you have said about our planet's crisis. Quite frankly, it confirms what we already know and it challenges us as a species to accept the truth and address it.

And I believe what you have told us about the energy of joy. Thank goodness you and your kind are informing the people of Earth of this reality. Let's hope we all choose to access this energy and use it wisely. Thank you, Dear Friend, for helping us!"

*"I am deeply grateful for this opportunity to work with all of you once again. It has been an extreme privilege, and one that will never be forgotten. My friends, you are prepared to continue. And the plans, which you already strategized, are ready for the next step. You must gather together, renew your commitments, and implement these ideas, which can potentially change the energy of this planet.*

*Although the mind will continue to play tricks on you, remember, you are more than your mind. With commitment and perseverance, you can and will regain command over its unruliness and your beautiful mind will assist you in regaining your abilities to access and utilize the potent energy within.*

*My friends, our situation is complicated. Because I am as I am, my memories regarding the eternal essence of all existence remains acutely within me, thus speaking its truth is easy for me; however, your perspective is different. Because you have forgotten the reality of your eternal essence, it is not easy for you to simply accept its existence because of hearsay.*

*I regret these circumstances, and more importantly, I regret your circumstances. I am so sorry that humankind exists under this unfortunate misunderstanding. And I am so sorry the Life Being Earth is suffering because of this misunderstanding. These circumstances need not continue. What is transpiring is correctable! The Earth can be restored to perfect health, and peace upon Earth can be the way of tomorrow.*

*This transformation is possible, my dear friends. All that is required is your acceptance of the powerful energy existing within you. You have the means and the power to heal the Earth and to effectively save the lives of all her inhabitants. You are capable of this.*

*Although this may seem unbelievable, dear friends, this is your truth. Comprehending the enormity of this may require a moment of your time. Do so, please. Take this moment to breathe your reality in, but do so quickly for unfortunately, a moment is all you have, because the Life Being Earth can wait no longer. For millennia, she desperately reached out attempting to get someone's attention, but instead, her circumstances continued to be ignored and compounded by blatant acts of disrespect and disregard. She cannot continue without assistance. Her needs are too great and she is too weak to recover on her own.*

*The truth of her failing health is now known. And the truth of your healing capabilities is also now known. My friends, you possess the power to heal her. She looks to you for help. You are the answer to Earth's cry for assistance. You are the answer!"*

Silence engulfed the room as its occupants each escaped to a place of serenity. The words, "You are the answer!" resonated throughout every cell within their respective bodies and beyond. Indeed the word was given…and heard by all. No boundaries did these words know; they were one with all in existence. They exceeded time before time came into existence and reached beyond into the unknown areas of existence still coming into existence. The message, purposefully delivered to eight listeners, but which was intended for all listening ears to hear raced across time and space to every existence existing in existence.

*"You are the answer!"* came a whisper from out of nowhere.

"I am the answer?" responded a listener whose origins were unknown.

*"Yes,"* replied the reassuring whisperer.

The interaction noted in time transpired in countless settings throughout existence, informing one after another the truth about his or her existence. And because of this remarkable communication, existence became more than existence was before.

*A passage from*
***The Book of Joy: The Invitation***
*(Chapter Twenty-Four)*

*"Many of you already participate in awe-inspiring generous deeds and these acts are proof of the energy that can be generated by purposeful intentions. What is proposed is an expansion of the good deeds you already know how to do. With a broader scope, a focused intention, and massive participation, the Earth's present situation can be improved. Again, this is not a dream; it is a viable course of action that is immediately possible. Attending the Earth's health now is critically necessary and it only requires cooperation and united purposeful intentions.*

*Wonderful ideas for addressing the Earth's present decline are now gestating and being promoted across the planet, and these new creative plans are noteworthy and must indeed be pursued and implemented, but immediate action must be taken while these forthcoming plans are in their developmental phase. Comparatively speaking, a few will attend ideas that address global warming, declining resources, water purification, world hunger, and much, much more, but the numbers available to change the energy of the planet include every inhabitant upon the Earth…and this can be done immediately from your present locations."*

Returning from a place that enveloped me with quiet, yet expansive serenity, I opened my eyes and noticed our friend from parts unknown was visibly waning. Assuming this meant he would soon be leaving us, I invited my family of friends to return from their journeys. Thankfully, no one seemed disrupted by the call to return, and once they witnessed what was transpiring with our friend, they understood the reasoning behind my invitation.

"Dear Friend, it appears your time here is brief." He smiled and nodded. "Then may I ask if there is any remaining task you wish to address before leaving?" His answer came quickly.

*"Yes, the answer to your questions regarding accessing the energy of joy is simple, and I say this because it is true. Seek within and ask permission to use your power source for the purpose of healing the Earth. Rest assured, permission will be granted. Then, pronounce your intentions to transfer a particle of your energy of joy to the Earth. This is all that is required. I urge you to only offer one particle of your powerful energy at a time, because this energy is far more powerful than you can imagine. One particle is sufficient to create massive changes. Do this daily, please. Initially transfer the energy to your present location, but as you become more comfortable with this energy transfer, you can expand beyond your present surrounding. After one week of practice, I urge the eight of you to choose different locations to transmit your energy towards. In this way, the healing becomes more expansive. This is easily achieved. Simply focus your intentions upon the location to which you wish to send your energy and it shall be done. My friends, so easy this is to achieve, and with the help of millions, just imagine what can be done.*

*You are the answer! And I have faith in you, my friends. I am so grateful for this time together. Please know you are ready to proceed without my presence, but I will always be near, and if my presence is critical, I will always be available."* His reassuring words quieted the anxiety rising in anticipation of his leaving. Expressions of appreciation were quickly proclaimed before his image began to flicker. Knowing this was an indication he was about to depart, the nine old friends simultaneously bowed to one another and whispered, "Till we meet again!"

As their beloved friend and teacher faded into nothingness, his departing message was, *"Remember, my friends, you are the answer!"*

Silence prevailed and then Dee did what she does so well. She took action! "I assume we will be meeting tomorrow night, same time, same place. It's time we formalized our next step."

*A passage from*
***The Book of Joy: The Invitation***
*(Chapter Twenty-Eight)*

*"Dear Friends, the energy of joy that powers all life beings exists within each of us. We have the means to restore Earth's energy to a healthy, functioning state once again. Many may find this thought preposterous. Unfortunately, there is no time to convince the non-believers. Earth requires our help now and each who begins their purposeful journey to share a particle of their original Source Energy with the Earth will indeed be participating in an incredible act of generosity. No more than this is required. Daily doses of the Source Energy we were all gifted will bring Earth back to health.*

*Will you help? Will you focus your intentions at least once a day and send this Beloved Life Being a particle of your own Source Energy? This requires so little time and yet it is the medicine that can facilitate her recovery. Will you participate in an act of generosity?*

*Your participation can have transformative effects upon the planet. You alone can help, but she needs more. Urge others to participate in this Mission of Mercy as well. Share the truth with everyone. Through prayer, through focused intentions, everyone can raise her energy level. Singularly, we can effect change. En masse, we can restore her to wellness.*

*Share the truth truthfully. Invite others to gather with you, and in union, intentionally and purposefully send her the medicinal doses of energy that she so desperately needs.*

*Dear Friends, this is not a preposterous idea. It is an ability that we gained when each of us received the Gift of Source Energy. We possess the naturally ability to help the Earth just as we can one another. No words can ever express this truth in a manner that is easily digested. You must seek within to know, to understand, and to accept this reality.*

*Have faith, Dear Friends. Seek within and remember who you really are. The Earth has generously provided you with a home and a setting to evolve for millennia. She now participates in the ultimate act of generosity by providing you with an opportunity to discover your truth. Seek within, Dear Friend, and discover who you really are.*

*The Life Being called Earth who has served beyond her means now needs an act of generosity. Will you help? Will you join in the Mission of Mercy and return Earth's many kindnesses? Will you participate in an act of generosity?"*

The dear old friends went their separate ways, each knowing that much remained to be done. And tomorrow, the next step would be taken.

…More to come…

Printed in the United States
by Bookmasters

Printed in the United States
By Bookmasters